Bigger Than Us

Bigger Than Us

BESTSELLING AUTHOR
Debbie Burns

Published by JC & Burns Publishing, LLC

authordebbieburns.com/authordebbieburns@gmail.com

Library of Congress Control Number: 2025912849

Printed and bound in the United States of America.

ISBN: 979-8-9987262-0-0 (pbk)

ISBN: 979-8-9987262-1-7 (ebook)

PRAISE FOR DEBBIE BURNS

"Women's fiction that sizzles with themes of family unity and division, communities coming together and reforming in unexpected ways, and a small family buffeted by forces well beyond its control and ken [...] perfect beach reading."
— Midwest Book Review for *Bigger Than Us*

"*Bigger Than Us* is exactly what the title promises to be: a story of people coming together due to forces that are bigger than all of us. Love, family, struggle, forgiveness...Burns shines a light on all the parts of life that make it worth living. I couldn't put it down. I can't wait to see what else she does in the women's fiction space, because this is where her heart and humanity truly shine."
— Lucy Gilmore, bestselling author of *The Lonely Hearts Book Club*

"*Bigger Than Us* is the tender story of a young widow trying to hold everything together as her world falls apart. Burns' deft touch balances her characters' raw emotions with their compassion and wisdom, and will make the reader believe in the healing power of abiding love."

— Carol Coventry, award-winning author of *Counting on Love*

"An engrossing book, one I highly recommend. Enriched with many layers pertaining to love and loss, misunderstandings, second chances, life-changing surprises, friends, and family."
— Jennie Marts, USA TODAY bestselling author for *Bigger Than Us*

"Auspicious debut...This heartstring-tugger is certain to win fans who are yearning for a wholesome summertime read."
— Publishers Weekly, STARRED Review for *A New Leash on Love*

"A heartbreaking and beautiful story with charming characters that will touch your heart."
— Harlequin Junkie for *Summer by the River*

"Burns is sure to win over dog lovers and fans of Kristan Higgins and Jill Shalvis."
— Publishers Weekly for *Head Over Paws*

"An amazing book for anyone who loves pets, romance, true life situations, or all that combined. I couldn't put it down."
— Lori Foster, New York Times bestselling author for *Home is Where Your Bark Is*

ALSO BY DEBBIE BURNS

Summer by the River

Home is Where Your Bark Is

Rescue Me Series

A New Leash on Love

Sit, Stay, Love

My Forever Home

Love at First Bark

Head Over Paws

To Be Loved by You

You're My Home

For Ann, without an "e"
but a bosom friend nonetheless

"The truth will set you free. But not until it is finished with you."
- David Foster Wallace

CHAPTER 1

MADDIE

Her hands had been trembling since she'd gotten off the elevator, but now Maddie's arms and shoulders were growing stiff, and there was likely a robotic quality to her movements. She tried sucking in a calming breath, but her numb lips refused to form an *O*. It wasn't too late to back out. No one was forcing her to do this. She could find her mother-in-law in this crowd and tell her she'd changed her mind.

At least the whole thing would be over soon. In another hour and a half, guests would head home with their well-crafted memorial cards and memories of Landon, and it wouldn't matter one bit to any of them would come out of Maddie's mouth minutes from now: a few small white lies, or a big, bold one.

After Maddie herded her kids into the empty women's bathroom at the far corner of the open-air rooftop restaurant, the twins filed into separate stalls. It wouldn't do to have a potty emergency in the middle of their father's eulogy. In a year from now—who was she kidding, in a month from now—neither Hazel nor Benji would remember much about today, but that didn't mean they didn't need to experience it.

Maddie wondered what images might stick—the blown-up matte photos of their dad on easels throughout the rooftop patio; the front and center urn; vases of all sizes bursting with stark, white lilies; the dozens of flameless candles, wicks pulsing rhythmically; or the slideshow featuring everything Landon, from his newborn days to shortly before his death at thirty-two. For all she knew, maybe all her five-year-olds would remember was the shiny, gleaming Arch peeking up over the skyline in the distance.

After setting her phone on the marble vanity, Maddie shoved her hands under the warm water and avoided looking directly in front of her at the stranger in the fitted black dress with mom hips and thick, curly hair. At what point had her children become more familiar to her than her own reflection?

"It'd be easier if you'd written something down," she mumbled to no one but herself. The nineteen days since Landon's death had been enough time to come up with something, but crafting the right words had been like wading through quicksand. She'd never gotten past the first sentence.

So, here she was, about to wing her part of his eulogy in front of a sea of mostly strangers. No surprise, people had turned up in droves. Not only was Landon's death tragic and unexpected, but he was also a Baxter. At least one of the three Baxter restaurants had made all the important lists each year in St. Louis for the last twenty-five years running.

"Mommy," Hazel called from behind her closed stall door, "you forgot to show us where you used to make cakes."

Maddie withdrew her hands from the stream of water, and the motion-sensored flow stopped as quickly as it had begun. "I didn't forget, but the kitchen is downstairs on the first floor. They're going to talk about daddy soon. We'll go down afterwards."

Benji had left his stall door wide open, and the pressed trousers Maddie had to bribe him into wearing today were in a mound around his ankles, spilling over his new shoes onto the floor. The part of her that cared about open stall doors or her little boy's pants touching a public tile floor was muted by the bigger worries of the day, and she said nothing.

"What floor is this? Is a roof a floor?" At the back of Benji's head, his soft, blond curls were flattened from having been pressed against his booster seat on the ride over. He'd gotten Maddie's curls but his father's blond color, while with Hazel, it was the opposite—she had Maddie's chestnut color but none of the curl. When they were newborns, Maddie had hoped at least one of them would wind up with their father's sapphire blue eyes, but their baby blue hues had quickly melted into Maddie's hazel color.

Given how calm they were, it was doubtful they truly understood what was about to happen, no matter how many times she'd explained it to them. The therapist they'd meet for the first time tomorrow had emailed Maddie a mound of paperwork and several articles on helping children cope with loss. One of the things that had stood out was the importance of letting them feel whatever it was they were feeling, and right now, they were excited to be in this fancy restaurant that belonged to their father's family.

"The rooftop is the third floor, and yes, when you can walk around on it like this, it's called a floor. Did Uncle Noel bring you up in the elevator, or did you take the stairs?" Uncle Noel. That always sounded foreign on her tongue. Noel was—had been—Landon's best friend and had no relation to her babies. Not that it mattered to them. To the twins, Uncle Noel was a vanilla cupcake loaded with buttercream icing and extra sprinkles.

"We took the lelevator," Benji said just before Hazel's toilet flushed two stalls over.

"*Ele*-vator!" Hazel corrected over the whoosh.

Benji hiked up his pants. "That's what I said!"

Given how Benji could slip into meltdown mode when

corrected by his nine-minute-older sister, Maddie opted for distraction. "Once you two wash your hands, we need to find Nana so she knows where we're sitting." Maddie's mother was late for just about everything. Landon's wake was likely no exception.

The restaurant, an all-brick building located in historic Lafayette Square, had been closed today in preparation for this. Eleanor, Maddie's mother-in-law and the mastermind behind the restaurants' continued success, had transformed the popular rooftop dining space for this afternoon's memorial service. The tables and dining chairs had been hauled out and replaced with one hundred and fifty white padded folding chairs while high-top bistro tables dotted the outskirts. Even the unpredictable mid-March weather had bucked meteorologists' predictions and cooperated with Eleanor, giving her clear blue skies with the high reaching into the low sixties.

It was Eleanor who'd suggested holding Landon's Celebration of Life here at the Row House Eatery, and she'd proven to be a woman of vision even in her darkest hour.

At the sink, Benji moved the soap over his palms long enough to satisfy Maddie while Hazel worked the suds between her fingers, over her palms, and the backs of her hands and forearms with the vigor of a doctor going into surgery. There was an intensity to her expression that contradicted her smooth, youthful complexion, thick lashes, and full lips.

Maddie's jaw tightened in concern as she watched. Hazel's germ fixation had certainly peaked in the last three weeks. "I think you got it, honey."

Benji was hopping toward the door, feet smacking against the painted concrete, when it pushed open, and the approaching voices filled the small room. "It's so sad. He was *so* hot. I would've given my left nut for a night with that."

"Oh God, me, too! And did you see who's—"

Maddie's palms broke into a sweat as two pixie-thin, hardly out of high school girls rounded the corner and spotted the family inside. *Left nut?* Not quite. They both had long champagne-blond hair, ample makeup, and were wearing snug black dresses that reached to the mid-thigh and would've been more appropriate at a posh club than here. They were hostesses or servers in one of the Baxter restaurants, no doubt. They hovered in the doorway for a moment, unsure whether to come inside. Clearly they recognized Maddie and figured she'd overheard them.

She handed Hazel a paper towel, and the young women filed in silently, heading for the mirror to check their reflections rather than to the stalls.

At the door, Maddie turned back. "You aren't the only ones." Her tone was more sympathetic than she would've suspected given the adrenaline racing through her. "The thing is, whatever part of yourself you'd have given away to make it happen, before long, you'd have been wanting it back."

They stared at her, mouths falling open, as Maddie turned away. Closing her hands over the twins' backs, she herded them into the fray once more.

"Wanting *what* back, Mommy?" Hazel asked.

Maddie was attempting to come up with an answer that would be equally cryptic and satisfy her daughter's curiosity when she spotted a third girl. Her feet were planted mid-step, and her gaze was locked on Benji in a way that raised the fine hairs on the back of Maddie's neck and had her reaching for his hand. This girl hardly looked older than the other two, but she was wearing a baby in a sling carrier. At least, Maddie thought it was a baby. Half the sling carriers she encountered lately were for dogs, but the form snuggled deep inside this one had the form of a small human.

Maddie doubted this girl ran in the same circles as the two inside the bathroom. Her long hair was devoid of highlights and dishwater blond, and she was the kind of skinny most people didn't strive for. Her long black jeans were faded and worn thin at the knees in a way that spoke of hardship rather than fashion, and her black high-collar shirt was oversized enough that she nearly disappeared in it. Something about her expression had Maddie's mind flitting to those first weeks after the twins were born, when her rapidly changing hormones had the world feeling as sharp-edged and heavy as it did beautiful.

Their eyes met for the briefest of seconds before the girl's eyes widened, and she turned away, taking off in the opposite direction.

Maddie was staring after her when she heard Noel calling her name. The twins swarmed toward him like bees on a can of soda, and Maddie followed.

The uncharacteristic flush coloring Noel's complexion reminded her that it was go time even before he spoke. "Hey, it's almost four. If you're ready, I'll head to the front and ask everyone to take their seats."

Maddie's stomach dropped like she was standing atop a rollercoaster. *Tell him you changed your mind. It's not too late.* Instead, she felt herself nodding. "Have you seen my mom? Or Saanvi?" The first two rows were sectioned off for family and those who were speaking. In this sea of Landon's people, Maddie wanted her mom and her best friend up there next to her for comfort.

"I haven't seen Saanvi, but your mom's over there." Noel nodded toward the north side of the crowded rooftop where, in a crowd of mostly black and gray and a few subdued blues, her mom Charlotte stood out like a macaw in green foliage with her long, brushed out curls reminiscent of '80s Cher and a flowy chiffon dress that was a blend of orange, pink, and red. Any other day, Maddie would get a bit of satisfaction at how much displeasure her mom's appearance would cause Maddie's perfectionist of a mother-in-law. Just not today.

6

"Thanks." Letting out a breath, she locked hands with the twins and guided them through the sea of people.

"Hey, Maddie," Noel called after her. When she met his gaze a second time, his brows lifted just a touch. "You've got this."

She nodded and mumbled a "Thanks" even though his words stabbed at her heart.

"Mommy, why can't Uncle Noel sit with us?" Hazel whined as they made their way toward Charlotte.

When her mom spotted them, Maddie pointed toward their seats and motioned her over. "He's sitting by your Grandma Baxter and your aunts," she said. "We're sitting by Nana and Saanvi. You can see him when the talk about daddy is over."

Maddie's stomach somersaulted as Noel headed to the podium and announced that the service was about to begin. Landon's life was a program now, a set number of lines to be recited in front of others.

Behind Noel, the St. Louis skyline gleamed golden yellow in the late afternoon sun, and the hum of conversation fell as people began filling in the seats. There were many more people than chairs, so there'd be a small crowd standing at the back and sides. *You'd like it, Landon, the way you sold out the house today.*

As Charlotte, not unquietly, got comfortable in the seat to Maddie's left, Saanvi reappeared from wherever she'd been —Maddie's best guess was talking business with one of the restaurant staff. "Sorry. I went looking for you but got trapped," Saanvi whispered before taking a seat on the opposite side of Hazel.

With her mom and Saanvi close, Maddie experienced her first hint of calm since stepping off the elevator.

It was still impossible to believe Landon was gone. Unlike her mom, Maddie didn't believe in ghosts, but she wouldn't pretend she hadn't gotten goosebumps a handful of times at home upon realizing she was talking aloud to him and half-expecting an answer.

Maddie sensed her mom studying her and braced for something witty and esoteric even before Charlotte leaned in. "It'll be longer now." She said it like Maddie should know just what she was referring to. Maddie was about to shake her head when her mom added, "Enough that it'll take some getting used to."

Whatever this was, it wasn't the distraction Maddie needed right now, but curiosity got the best of her. "What're you talking about?"

"The space between chaos. The number of easy breaths between anxious ones."

Maddie's eyes stung instantly. She wanted to pretend she didn't understand and return to worrying about a speech she hadn't prepared for, but Charlotte's declaration got her mind tossing up memories like a pitching machine. A remote smashed to pieces against the living room wall when it was being too sluggish. A slamming door waking up babies in the early days when every minute of sleep mattered. An overdrawn checking account in exchange for the latest new "must have" tech toy of the season. A brand-new car pulling into the driveway when he'd just gone out to grab a few groceries before the coming snowstorm. A palm smacking onto a counter, accompanied by a terse, "What the hell, Maddie? How come you always ride me about everything?"

A helmet discarded on the driveway.

That one would haunt her forever.

The memories were still flooding in when Noel began the eulogy, the tips of his fingers curled loosely around the edge of the podium like he had all day and nowhere to go. Maybe the microphone amplified it, but his voice was as smooth as a late-night radio host, somehow reassuring her that it didn't matter that she had no idea what to say when it was her turn. She'd figure it out when she got up there.

Just like Landon would've.

"It doesn't matter how well you knew him," Noel was saying, the rays from the sun shining on hair that was so dark brown it was nearly black. "Even if you were only around him a single day, no doubt you saw it, too. In less than five minutes, he could change the energy in a room. With his jokes. With his demeanor." Noel looked toward the crowd standing in back, most of them people from the three Baxter restaurants. "I know Tori's coming up here later, and I don't want to steal her thunder, but if I heard it once, I heard a thousand times how whenever there was an irate customer or a stressed-out server, it was Landon who they'd send in to fix things."

A murmur of approval rippled across the rooftop, reverberating in Maddie's chest. Maddie's eyes were drawn to a portrait of Landon on an easel near the podium. Tall, broad-shouldered, and classically golden blond, Landon had turned heads wherever he went, and the girls in the bathroom were no exception. While Noel was no stereotypical sidekick, Maddie had little doubt that when the two of them had been together, people would've noticed Landon first. Most of them, anyway.

"As for me, we met in fifth grade. Maybe he didn't save my life, but he certainly made it brighter at a time when it was full of nothing but gray." Noel's fingertips seemed to flex around the edges of the podium as he collected himself, and Maddie guessed which story he was about to share. She'd heard it from him personally and knew it wouldn't be easy to tell here. Noel's dad spent six months in the ICU after being hit by a bus at a crosswalk. At the time, his doctors said he'd likely never walk again. His distraught mom sold the house and moved Noel's family in with her parents, and Noel became the new kid in school. "Landon and I made a fort in the woods," he was saying when Maddie tuned back in. "We drifted apart a bit after college, but whenever I'd think about that fort and the part of him I got to know in there, I knew he'd always be the best friend I've ever had."

Another murmur rolled over the crowd, this one softer, making Maddie wonder how many people had known that side of her husband. Benji burrowed against her, rolling a die-cast metal four-wheeler that must've been in his pocket across both his lap and hers while Hazel sat rigidly on his opposite side, her hand locked in Saanvi's. As Charlotte liked to say, sweet Hazel had come out of the womb an older and wiser soul than most.

Concentrating on the rest of Noel's speech proved impossible as Maddie's mind raced with conflicting images of beauty and pain. After he was finished, she waited through Eric Clapton's *Tears in Heaven* before it was her turn to head up there. When she stood, tears began spilling down Hazel's cheeks. Maddie paused to press a kiss on the top of her head.

"Mommy, how long will you be up there?" Benji called loudly enough for everyone in the first several rows to hear.

"Not long, Benji."

The short declaration somehow loosened her tight throat. She had children to care for and a husband to mourn in her own, complicated way. She gave herself permission to say her piece—whatever it might be—and be done with it.

An aluminum stage had been rented for today, and the commercial gray carpet covering it seemed to grab at her heels like Velcro as she headed to the podium. Remembering where Noel's hands had been, Maddie placed hers in the same spot, hoping for a hint of warmth to remind her someone else had already made it through this, but it had already faded.

From up here, Maddie's westward view toward the late afternoon sun made it easier not to home in on the details of all the people waiting for her to say something worthy of the Landon they'd come here to mourn.

"Some of you know this," she began, "but I used to be

the pastry chef here. That's how Landon and I met." She waited for the soft murmur passing over the audience to end. "I think I'd worked here a good three months before Landon and I exchanged more than a handful of words, but Noel's right. My husband could light up a room like no one I've ever seen." A memory flashed of the first time those remarkable blue eyes had sucked the air right out of her lungs. "I'd made it a habit of avoiding people like that. I guess my world felt safer that way. But one day, when I was so sad it was hard to breathe, he noticed." She hadn't planned on saying this, but something stark and real about standing in front of this sea of strangers had the words tumbling out of her. "That day, I met the person Noel got to know in that fort in the woods, and I thought maybe, maybe…" She couldn't say that truth here. She couldn't go there. "Wow. I knew this was going to be hard."

Maddie took a shaky breath and focused on the four people in the first row she held dearer to her heart than any others. "My mom's always saying that life is an 'in breath' and an 'out breath.' One is pleasure, and the other pain, and they're inextricable." She huffed softly. "Silly how I figured that since the person saying this was my mom, those words might not apply to me." She swallowed hard. "The day before Landon died…" *I told him I wanted a divorce.*

This wasn't a confessional. It was a service to honor the beautiful parts of the complicated man her husband had been.

"The day before he died, I was away most of the afternoon." *Meeting with a lawyer.* "When I came home, I couldn't get in the front door because a chair was blocking it. The world's best builder of the blanket forts had created a mothership in our living room and foyer while playing with our kids." A look of recognition lit Hazel's tear-stained face. Benji had scooted into Maddie's empty seat and was curled against Charlotte, his head in her lap. Feeling their loss,

Maddie swiped at the tears rolling down her cheeks. "He used every blanket and sheet and hair tie in the house. They played in there all night and ate pizza under a roof of blankets, and the kids slept in sleeping bags on the floor even though it was a school night."

And for one night, I put aside a hundred grievances and joined in fully. We laughed and made love in a quiet corner after our babies were conked out for the night, and it wasn't until the next morning that I was reminded why I wanted a divorce.

Suddenly, it seemed as if the small stage had begun swaying. Maddie closed one hand around the microphone again to steady herself. "If there's one prayer of thanks I say in all this, it's that my children were old enough to play with their father like they did that day."

Aside from a few coughs and sniffles, it was impossibly quiet. Even the traffic sounds rising from the city streets below seemed to have silenced. Toward the back, the infant who'd begun fussing settled down. "Hazel and Benji, your father gave you so many gifts. I know how much you miss him, but those beautiful memories he gave you, you'll always have them."

She wanted to say more, but she found herself reliving the next morning in the living room—telling Landon that, if he was going to use every blanket and sheet in the house, he needed to help put them away, and him throwing up his hands because he was late for work and spouting off that she could be the biggest buzzkill he'd ever met.

Of course, it wasn't really about the blankets—it was a million moments leading up to it that had built up until they swallowed her whole. He wasn't thinking how, their entire marriage, it had been her cleaning up his messes, both the literal and figurative ones, and him running to the next thing.

That day, it was forecast to be unseasonably warm for late February, and he planned to duck out of work to go biking on the trails out in West County. With the tension between them mounting, he read something in her look she didn't realize was there and fired back with something rude and designed to hurt. In the wake of this, she admitted to going to the lawyer. *"We're at the breaking point, Landon. It's divorce or therapy. I can't keep swimming upstream anymore—I won't."*

That beautiful face he'd gotten from his mother's side of the family could twist so abruptly into a cutting expression. "Have at it then," was all he said before storming off without breakfast or saying goodbye to the kids.

Later, when she was loading the kids into the car to get them to school, she spotted his helmet at the side of the driveway in the brown winter grass. No doubt, he'd driven away with it still on the roof. It wasn't the first time he'd either lost or left something behind that way. She'd paused to snap a picture of it and texted it to him. She'd been in a hurry to drop off the twins on time and hadn't written anything with it, just sent the picture. He hadn't enabled read receipts on his phone, but she believed he'd opened it before getting out to the trail and had realized he was helmetless, but he never replied.

If she'd known it would be the last text that passed between them, she'd have told him she loved him, no matter how complicated of a love it was.

But there was no sharing any of this with anyone here. Instead, she made it through another few more lines about him being a great dad, thanked everyone for being here, and headed back to her seat. She made it through another two songs, several Bible verses, and the next three speeches while holding her babies close and rubbing their backs as they listened and wriggled and cried.

An hour later, while Benji and Hazel were eating toasted ravioli—the only thing served after the eulogy that they didn't turn their noses up at—Maddie's mother-in-law found her in the crowd. Eleanor's shoulders seemed to have visibly drawn in this month. Even so, she still had a commanding air about her, the kind that made Maddie feel like a recruit standing in formation, waiting for inspection.

For a split second, Maddie wondered if Eleanor might be about to tell her she'd done a fine job up there, but then she noticed Eleanor's outstretched hand. Maddie spotted her own cell phone lying there, face up.

"One of the staff gave it to me." There was something in Eleanor's look radiating past the layers of grief lining her complexion, something sharp and accusing enough to make Maddie's neck and shoulders tighten. "She thought it was mine."

Maddie's phone case had been a gift from Landon last Christmas and was personalized with a print image of him and the twins. It had been taken at Eleanor's in her library one morning while Maddie had been at work, so it wasn't surprising that the phone had been turned in to Eleanor rather than her.

"Thanks. I've been leaving this behind everywhere lately." Maddie pressed the button a touch guiltily to light up the home screen. A missed call and voicemail notification filled the screen, the name Bromac Law Firm, LLC standing out like a neon sign.

Locking eyes with Eleanor, Maddie offered nothing but a "Thanks."

A few small, white lies, or a big, bold one. As excruciating as this "out breath" was sure to be, it was better this way. Ever since the third grade when she'd gotten in trouble for her over-active imagination, Maddie had done her best to tell the truth.

CHAPTER 2

JORDAN

The young boy hanging on the bathroom door had touched Jordan unexpectedly. Those blond curls and that little-boy antsiness. Most adults forgot what it was like to be that age. Forgot how necessary it was to work out the crawlies that inevitably set in whenever they shouldn't. But Jordan hadn't.

Sitting still in class when the teacher was talking had been torture, and Jordan's imagination running rampant hadn't helped. The crawlies had been the worst whenever her mom had dragged her to church. That hard bench had been a torture device that inevitably got her mom should-ing on her the whole way home. "Did you see those big girls three pews up? You should try to be more like them. Good girls from the start, they are." Jordan also hadn't forgotten the flicks on the forehead from her dad whenever they stood in line at the grocery store and all those colorful candies at arm's reach proved too tempting not to touch. Every single time. At least, until he got locked up.

She'd braced herself for seeing Landon's family in person, but Jordan hadn't expected the rush of fondness at the sight of him—of the boy. Benji. Maybe he and his sister had lost

15

their dad, but Benji had something she was never going to be able to give Liam—privilege. Yet all it took for the resentment she'd been harboring to flee was one glance at those curls and that squirminess.

Then Maddie had stepped out of the bathroom and for no reason in the world offered her a small smile. A smile that promised nothing, yet, at the same time, offered to help pull Jordan up from the abyss she was sinking back into. Sharp tears had stung her eyes, and the only thing she'd been able to do was walk away.

Maybe the world was full of people who weren't so different from one another when you got past the window dressing.

Jordan hadn't even been certain she was coming today until she was cramming a bottle, a few of Liam's size 1 diapers, and a Ziplock bag of wipes into her backpack, and using money she didn't have to spare on a ride service to get here. It wasn't like anyone had reached out to invite her. She'd found out about Landon's death on Facebook.

Snug in his sling, Liam was proving to be his typical infant self this afternoon. So long as she was uncomfortable —in this case, standing and swaying despite her feet smarting from being crammed into her roommate's black boots—he was dozing away just fine. Anytime she sat down to relieve her aching back and feet, those fusses would start right up, and people would begin shooting looks in her direction.

So, Jordan got up from the comfy white chairs and stood in the far back as the eulogy started, doing her best to pay attention despite the piercing pain in her toes. She recognized a dozen or so staff from when she'd worked here at the Row House Eatery even though it had been nearly a year since she'd left. Hardly any of them so much as nodded her way, but Jordan expected as much. She hadn't fit in then, so she shouldn't expect to now.

Of course, she recognized Eleanor and Charles Baxter,

but she doubted they'd remember her if she went up after the service and expressed her condolences—and there was no chance of her doing that anyway. Eleanor frightened her like nobody's business just by being Eleanor. Still, they both looked small and frail today, shouldering their son's death as they were.

When it came down to it, Jordan didn't really know why she was here. Nothing anybody said this afternoon was going to give her comfort, but she still wanted to listen. If for nothing else, when he was old enough, Liam might be pleased to know he'd been here.

She gave herself points for thinking like an adult when it occurred to her to head over to the nearest black-clothed high-top table with its vase of serene lilies to take a prayer card and funeral program for Liam to have later. With him in one arm, all she could do was fold them into her back pocket. Just before walking away, she grabbed another pair and rolled them up so they fit in her front pocket. The chances of at least one of the sets not getting lost or washed in the laundry were decidedly better than taking only one.

When it came to the speeches, no one was saying anything Jordan didn't already know. Landon was the light people danced around. No one could replace him. She wondered what they'd all think if she walked up to the platform, took the microphone, and began telling her own Landon story. Certainly, in some other universe, she was entitled to do so.

Just not in this one.

She hadn't loved Landon, not any more than one can love the sun while hiding out in the shade. But beyond any doubt, she was still here on this earth—toes screaming for relief, the cool wind stinging her cheeks where tears had slipped down earlier, and the warm weight of a sleeping Liam resting against her chest—because of him.

She remembered the look that flashed across Landon's

face that night he'd caught her in the empty galley prep kitchen where she wasn't supposed to be, appraising the sous chef's knives. If she was going to slit her wrists, there was going to be a damn good boning knife involved. She'd snuck over there after coming in from the back parking lot where she'd been smoking back-to-back cigarettes during her ten-minute break while contemplating how tempting it was to check out completely and not coming up with any real reason not to. The second Landon spotted her, somehow, he'd sensed what she was thinking and made it his mission to change her mind.

If she said all that, though, she'd have to admit to an even bigger truth that had been nagging at her for a couple months now. "The thing is, I'm here, but most days I'm not sure I'm any better off than I was before." She didn't realize she'd said it aloud until the couple standing to her right looked her way uncomfortably.

Ignoring them, she patted Liam's tiny butt through the sling. Doing so gave her a bit of comfort. Lifting the sling fabric a few inches, she dipped her head and brushed her lips against his smooth forehead. He stirred but didn't wake, tucking his tiny fist more snugly underneath his chin. "Time to go home, little Liam. This is all you're gonna get of your dad today."

CHAPTER 3

MADDIE

"How many days in a row can I wish away before I'm officially wishing away my life?" Maddie sat sideways at the kitchen table, knees tucked into her chest as she skimmed the five-page questionnaire for the twins' therapy appointment this morning. She'd been stabbing away at one section at a time for the last few days, and she was finally done.

"When the days are filled with everything you've been dealing with, my guess is as many as you need." Saanvi was at the counter using the seven-hundred-dollar, barista-quality espresso machine Landon had bought last year on a whim after insisting that everyone had one nowadays. Given the way Saanvi was drumming her fingers on the counter as she waited for the water to heat, she was likely rethinking her decision to sleep in until six thirty and shower rather than hit the road at the ungodly hour of four o'clock as originally planned. Stilling her fingers, she glanced over at Maddie. "Which is it that has you more worried, the twins' therapy appointment or this impending lunch with your mother-in-law?"

A half smile pulled at the corner of Maddie's mouth.

"You know Eleanor. Which one would have *you* more worried?"

Saanvi snickered. "Yeah, good point."

Setting the questionnaire aside, Maddie massaged her thumbs into her temples. "I know she's going to bring up the call from the lawyer. There's *no way* she'll let that go. But right now, I'm more worried about the twins having a good first appointment. I don't even know if I wrote down the right stuff."

"If you ask me, there's no *right* way to do grief watch."

Maddie didn't know if it was an official term, but grief watch was what she'd coined her observations over the last several days. Benji's falling apart before bed last night. His short fuse and temper tantrums, his wetting the bed again, and twice not acting as if he understood Landon wouldn't be coming home. With Hazel, there was the occasional reverting to baby talk, heightened germ fears, and the intense scrubbing she'd been doing of her hands. "What if I'm being overly-paranoid, and it results in this stranger putting a label on one of my kids that sticks?"

Saanvi frowned. "If she does, then she's not the therapist for you." She lowered her voice even though, by a minor miracle, the twins were sleeping past seven. "Maybe Hazel has some OCD tendencies. It doesn't mean they're going to stick."

Maddie blinked at hearing the term OCD applied to her daughter. "No, it definitely doesn't."

"Sorry if that hurt your feelings. I've just noticed the way she's been about germs this week—changing her clothes when she walks in the door, the hand washing, not wanting to touch door handles. The way she is about her food."

Maddie let out a long breath. "I see it, too. But saying it aloud makes it so much more real. We're just in the crux of things, you know."

"Yeah, I'm sure it won't last." Saanvi's "we can do this" voice was additional proof of how serious this was.

"She wasn't this bad before Landon's accident, and I didn't notice it at all before they started preschool. Maybe I need to pull her out."

"Pull her out of preschool?" Saanvi repeated. She didn't need to say anything else for Maddie to know her opinion on the subject.

"It's just that everybody's so focused on germs these days. When we were kids, there was *bar soap* in my preschool. All those grubby little hands sharing the same bar. In the twins' pre-K class, nearly the entire first week was devoted to not spreading germs, like they're prepping four and five-year-olds for pre-op."

"That can't be helping, I'm sure. But pulling her out..."

Maddie sighed. "You're right. I know. Holing up and locking out the world isn't the right thing to do, either."

Saanvi headed over and pulled the nearest chair even closer before sitting down. "Be easy on yourself, huh?" She locked a hand over Maddie's knee. "Being a mom today has got to be one of the most challenging things anyone can do —which is why I have zero interest in ever doing it."

Maddie gave her a look. "Not to sound like my mom, but sometimes the hardest things are the best things."

"I'm glad you're seeing her wisdom. I get that she's your mom and all, but she's amazing. I always thought so, but getting to talk to her more these last couple weeks proved it."

"She is. For sure, but you've never lived with her. Nowadays, I have the vocabulary and understanding to realize it's probably a heavy dose of untreated ADHD, but she was all over the place when I was in my formative years."

Saanvi's murmur was thick enough to slice bread. "I'm sure the lack of predictability was challenging to live through, but to someone whose parents may well be the most pragmatic couple in the city, it sounds like that could have had its merits, too."

"Now that you say it, I've been blaming my mom's spontaneity on me not spotting Landon's warning signs, but honestly had I grown up in a stricter environment, I probably would've run right into his arms just the same."

"Either way, it sounds like you two were written in the stars."

Maddie huffed. "Landon and I were the product of poor timing and circumstance that mercifully led to two of the most beautiful souls on the planet, and the rest needs to be put to bed."

"Hmm. On that one, I'll continue to be on your mom's side. Astrology, baby. That's where it's at."

Maddie rolled her eyes. "I love you anyway, Saanvi Bear."

"And I, you, Maddie Bear," Saanvi said, tossing back the shared moniker they'd coined one night when they were drunken roommates pondering the meaning of life. "I only wish we'd met sooner. Back when we were kids."

"Same, but we couldn't have, given how we didn't move in the same circles. Your family's loaded. I doubt my mom ever made over thirty grand a year before I left home."

"Maybe it doesn't seem like it, but growing up in a moderately wealthy household comes with its own pressures, you know. Pressure to perform perfectly in school and choose a medical career like my parents and my brothers. To carve out a life in St. Louis because here is where everyone else is." Saanvi flattened a hand over her stomach. "To not eat red meat. Like cheeseburgers aren't God's little promise that everything's going to be okay. And I turned out pretty fine, didn't I?" Saanvi blinked her thick lashes. "With that mention in *Chicago Food Magazine* last fall and all."

"I think your rebellion has worked out for you just fine."

"And you yours," Saanvi added. "Despite the lack of predictability that came with being raised so untraditionally by such a free-spirited mom. You turned out all right, too, didn't you? I'm saying all this because, as scary as it is, odds are, those beautiful babies are going to turn out just fine, too."

Maddie folded forward and rested her head against her knees for a beat or two. "Unless..." she said as she sat up.

"Unless what?"

"Unless nature proves stronger than nurture, and they take after their father."

"If we're going to talk science, the whole nature/nurture debate is all over the place. And remember, he makes up only half of their DNA. You make up the other half, and you're one of the most stable people I've ever met."

Maddie bit back a retort about how half of her DNA was a wild card. Her mom had met her biological father down in New Orleans on a spur-of-the-moment trip to Mardi Gras when she was nineteen. They'd had one wild night together that led to Maddie joining the world nine months later, but all Charlotte knew about him was his first name, that he'd been studying law in New York, and that they'd shared one remarkable night of connection.

In pastry school, Maddie and Saanvi had created a hundred different fantasies about him over bottles of wine and whatever dish of the week they were perfecting. Saanvi had always found Maddie's unknown paternity incredibly exciting. She'd done her best to get Maddie to take a DNA test in hopes of finding him, but that wasn't something Maddie was ready for.

"Promise me one thing, will you?" Saanvi said as she got up and headed back to the espresso machine. "Two things, actually."

"You're using the tone that says I'm not going to love this."

"Best friends are supposed to be honest, aren't they?"

Maddie groaned. "I'm all yours for the shooting."

After a dramatic pause, Saanvi uttered one word. "Noel."

Maddie's spine stiffened even as she did her best to appear that the name didn't send adrenaline shooting through her veins. "What about him?"

"Look, I'm not a big Noel fan, either, but I've seen him with the kids these last couple of weeks. He's good with them in a way I can't be, even if I didn't live three hundred miles away."

"He won't be around much, either. Not for long."

"He'll be here more than I can be, and he holds the coveted godparent title thanks to Landon's blood-brother insistence and all that," Saanvi said with a wave of the hand as she headed back to the espresso machine. "What I'm saying is, yeah, you have a grudge, and I get it. So would I if he'd ghosted me like that. But don't let it get in the way of him doing his part now. After all, he signed up for this when he agreed to be their godfather." She held up a hand as if she knew just what Maddie was thinking. "Says the one who turned down an offer to be their godmother, I know, but you really weren't thinking of how little rapport I have with kids when you asked me. My point is, for the next few years, you're going to need all the help you can get."

Saanvi began foaming her milk before Maddie could answer, forcing her to sit with her thoughts. Did it show? The grudge? Whenever Noel was traveling for long stretches, she congratulated herself for being over the whole thing. Then, when he came around again, the hurt slammed in all over again. Of course, she'd gone and married his best friend, negating any right to have any of these thoughts ever.

Once Saanvi had created a thick foam, she added, "The way I see it is maybe him showing up now is the universe doing its thing. You thrived despite a lack of a father figure. And you could raise the twins just fine without one in their lives from here on out, I'm sure. But they have a godfather, and no matter how big of a douche he was six years ago, I still think he's a decent guy. If he wants to be a part of their lives, I say let him."

"And if they start to count on him, and he lets them down?"

"Life is a series of maybes, Maddie. You aren't going to know that answer until you get there. My gut says he won't, but if I'm wrong, I'll slap on a suit of armor and lance for you. Promise."

"If you're strapping on a suit of *armor*, then I think you mean joust." Maddie opted not to mention the fact that this didn't bode well for Saanvi's jousting skills.

"Yeah, joust." Saanvi poured the foamed milk atop her coffee and shrugged. "Ready for the second thing? It's easier."

"Yeah."

"I know I'm busy enough usually that I'm hardly keeping my head on straight these days, but if you really need me, I'm on my way. And if you don't, we're Facetiming once a week, at least. Promise?"

"Heck yeah. Something tells me I'll be needing all the Saanvi fixes I can get."

After Saanvi headed out, the twins were sitting at the kitchen table munching their breakfast of organic toaster pastries, red grapes, and wedges of Babybel cheese. Leo, their three-year-old silver Maine Coon cat, stalked the twins underneath the table and chairs, wanting dibs on their cheese. It didn't help matters that they purposely dropped food because they felt sorry for him.

Leo had figured out they were easy pickings and circled their legs as they ate, begging with his deep, throaty purr and half-meows. Whenever they were distracted, he'd hop onto the table and steal food straight off their plates even though it meant risking being sprayed by a water bottle if Maddie caught him in the act.

The whole thing was maddening, especially given that cats weren't supposed to crave human food like dogs. Landon had showed up with him one night after work back when the twins were toddlers and Leo was less than three months old. "If he doesn't grow on you, we'll find him a home. But I couldn't just leave him. He was hanging out under the dumpster behind the restaurant. He could've been hit by a car." Even though Leo was the most strikingly beautiful kitten Maddie had ever seen, she'd bought Landon's story that the exquisite creature had either been dumped or was feral-born.

Life was chaotic enough back then without adding a demanding kitten to the mix, but nevertheless Leo had stolen his way into all their hearts.

Months later, Maddie was moving a stack of paperwork to Landon's office that he'd left on the counter after cleaning out his glove box. She'd been in a hurry because the twins were having a playdate at the house, but she'd spotted the words Maine Coon at the top of a piece of paper sticking out from the middle of the stack. It turned out to be Leo's registration paperwork, and it was paperclipped to a bill of sale. Landon had paid twelve hundred dollars for a kitten he'd claimed to have found under the dumpster.

"I wasn't lying," he'd insisted when she'd confronted him, splaying his hands innocently, his charming smile both sheepish and beguiling before realizing how mad she was. "He snuck out of the breeder's car, and he was hanging out under the dumpster while I was checking out his littermate. He could've been hit and killed."

The ensuing argument had dragged on for days. Maddie couldn't remember any longer if he'd ever accepted fault, or if he'd stuck by his argument that Maddie was making a big deal out of nothing. Likely, they'd moved on to more pressing matters without any real resolution—par for the course throughout their five years together.

Finished loading the dishwasher, Maddie scooped Leo into her arms, nuzzling her face into his soft silver fur. At his last vet appointment, Leo had tipped the scales at twenty pounds. From his nose to the tip of his tail, he was a full three feet long, and Maine Coons kept growing until they were four or five years old.

A glance at the clock sent Maddie into high gear. "Hey, you two, finish up. It'll be time to leave soon."

Benji collapsed against his seat and crossed his arms. "I don't wanna go. I wanna stay here. I wanna wear my pajamas all day."

Reminding him that his favorite sweatpants and coziest long-sleeve t-shirt were clean did nothing to lessen Benji's look of dejected indignation. He was a homebody who loved his jammies. He hated anything scratchy against his skin, but even soft sweats and broken-in cotton shirts paled in comparison to the comfort and security of his PJs. When he was younger, it had been a battle to get him dressed. Come to think about it, it had been a battle to get him dressed for the last three weeks. *There you go. There's already something you forgot to record, and you've been dealing with it every day.*

Maddie had gone from life with her mom to life with Saanvi in pastry school to life with Landon and the twins in the aftermath of a condom fail less than a month into dating. After seven and a half months of more ups than downs, she'd married Landon believing that she'd rather have an imperfect marriage than raise a child—or, to her surprise, two of them —fatherless. And the sex had been good. There'd been that, too. She taken his impulsivity as bravery at first, and in a way, that had added to his sex appeal, at least until she'd begun living with the consequences of that impulsivity.

To give Landon the credit he was due, he'd been a great dad from day one. The way he'd cradled both their frail newborns at once, one in the crook of his arm and the other on his forearm, while he stopped their wailing with a deep, throaty lullaby of his own creation had melted Maddie's heart.

"Here's an idea," Maddie said. From opposite sides of the table, both her kids' hazel eyes locked on her like bookends. "If you get dressed quickly—which means no complaining and no stopping to play with toys—we'll take dad's car to the appointment. What do you say?"

This did the trick. With shouts of approval, they ran off toward the stairs, abandoning their plates and cups on the table. Landon's Audi was one of the most effective rainy day treats Maddie had up her sleeve, and they might as well put some more miles on it before she sold it, which she needed to do sooner than later. The bills weren't going to pay themselves.

As they raced up the steps, Benji once again skirting meltdown mode because Hazel had a head start, Maddie's phone beeped with a new text. It was from Eleanor, confirming Maddie's and the twins' ETA for lunch.

Remembering the accusing look on her mother-in-law's face yesterday, Maddie was tempted to cancel and put this lunch off another few days. But the fact remained, even if she could avoid her mother-in-law all week, it wouldn't erase what Eleanor had seen on Maddie's phone screen.

Best to get her questions over with.

Twenty minutes later, they were shuffling into the garage with Maddie congratulating herself for being several minutes ahead of schedule—never an easy task with twins. Most days, she'd have an easier go of herding cats.

When Maddie lingered by Benji's car door, he waved her away. "I got it myself." As much as the kids liked the car, it was considerably easier for them to buckle up in Maddie's SUV, a Volvo XC60, but they had enough time for him to give it a shot.

After tossing her purse across to the passenger seat, she sank into the driver's seat and shut the door. As she turned on the ignition, the automatic seat moved into its preset position for Landon. Swallowing hard, she used the side power button to move the seat forward another few inches. It was these unexpected things that got to her most.

The day after Landon died, Noel and another of Landon's buddies had driven out to the state park out in the county where Landon had had the accident. Noel had been fresh off a plane from Chile. His best friend had officially passed away while he was somewhere over Central America.

When he'd brought the car home, Noel had taken the empty bike rack off the car and placed it on an open spot in the middle shelf, not realizing it typically hung on the side wall. Maddie assumed the bike had made it to the police station, but she'd not received any calls about it. She hoped never to see it again.

In the center console, lid closed tight, was an empty bottle of Landon's favorite mango kombucha. She could picture him sitting in this seat, taking occasional swigs as he drove out to the bike trail. Even though they hadn't spoken that afternoon, she'd learned that he'd taken off work around two to head out there.

In the restaurant business, typically there was an afternoon lull between lunch and dinner rushes. Most days, Landon had come home for a few hours to play with the twins before going back to whichever restaurant needed him most as the dinner rush started up. Occasionally, he'd gone biking instead.

Maddie didn't want to drive with the empty drink beside her, so she got out and dropped it in the recycling bin. When she returned, Hazel had wedged herself between the console and seats and twisted toward the driver's seat, her face pressed against the headrest. Maddie attempted to shoo her back to her seat. "What're you doing, silly? Let's get buckled so we can get moving."

Hazel pulled away enough to look at Maddie. "The car smells like daddy." It came out sounding like both an assertion and a request for validation.

Heart constricting, Maddie leaned in to smell the headrest. Her eyes closed involuntarily as she got a faint whiff of Landon's bourbon cedar-scented body wash. "It does, doesn't it?" What would her babies give to hold their father one more time? What would she give, despite it all?

Behind them, Benji protested the confinement of a seatbelt he wasn't strong enough to unbuckle. "I wanna smell. I wanna smell."

Maddie opened the back passenger door and clicked his seatbelt unlocked. With Hazel still blocking the way, he attempted to wedge himself over the top for a sniff. On the way back to his seat, Benji paused to pick something up off the floor of the backseat. His hopeful look fell into one of disappointment. "Daddy had a sucker," he said, holding up a square blue plastic wrapper that was partially torn in half. "But he didn't bring us one."

The shock of her son holding an empty condom wrapper hit Maddie's system everywhere at once. She went numb and hot at the same time. The lack of a need for birth control had been the one advantage of her emergency partial hysterectomy in the aftermath of labor with the twins. "Let me have that, buddy. I'll throw it away."

Thankfully, Benji didn't fight her. He dropped it into her hand, and Maddie's stomach lurched to experience the feel of it against her skin. A part of her wanted to believe it had been there the whole time he'd owned the car. A car Landon had taken by the car wash weekly.

She walked over on shaky legs and dropped it in the trash can, shutting the lid tightly as if it might crawl back out on its own. *What the actual fuck, Landon?*

If the twins weren't watching, she'd fall apart or scream or even be tempted to smash the hood of his Audi into oblivion with the shovel hanging on the wall—resale value be damned. But they *were* watching, and right now they needed their only parent to keep it together in front of them.

"Get buckled, will you? We don't want to be late." Her jaw had grown so tight, the words sounded forced.

"Can we get suckers later?" Hazel asked, buckling herself into her booster seat a second time.

Maddie didn't think she'd be able to look at a sucker again as long as she lived. "I think it's more of an ice cream day."

The twins' cheers proved they had no complaints.

Maddie locked her hands around the steering wheel after slipping the car into Reverse. *This too? All the cuts and scrapes over the years, and I have to take this, too?*

Lest she ever forget again, this had been life with Landon in a nutshell—loving and mourning and hating within the span of a few minutes, one emotion flowing into another without warning. With the sensation of slippery plastic still lingering on her fingertips, it seemed impossible she could.

CHAPTER 4

Maddie parked in the empty circular driveway that belonged to her mother-in-law and turned off the ignition. It hadn't occurred to her until now that she should've cancelled in light of the condom find, but she'd been on autopilot ever since. Nothing good could come out of seeing Eleanor given Maddie's current state.

Despite feeling as if she were stuck upside down on a rollercoaster, Maddie took stock of the sprawling all-brick ranch with dormer windows and an elegant columned portico, such a stark contrast from the nondescript apartments and trailer homes she'd grown up in. Many of the newer homes around here were so grandiose, they overwhelmed the one to two acre lots they sat on. Not this one. The architect who'd designed it some fifty-odd years ago had considered the lay of the land.

One thing she'd grant her mother-in-law was that no one could say she didn't have good taste. Technically, the house was Charles's as much as it was Eleanor's, but no one thought of it that way.

In the backseat, Hazel unbuckled herself first, then Benji, and together they tugged on his door handle until Maddie clicked the unlock button. Sometimes it was like pulling teeth to get them here, but once here, the twins' favorite thing was to run circles around the dramatic three-tiered fountain in the center of the half-circle driveway. Benji got a head start which Hazel didn't complain about the way he would've. He ran with his arms out like airplane wings while she pretended to ride a galloping pony.

They'd dressed themselves today, and Maddie could already guess Eleanor's expression upon seeing them. Underneath their jackets, Benji was in his rattiest red sweatpants and a bright green t-shirt with a monster truck on the front, and Hazel was in purple leggings, calf-high horse-print socks, and a flowered dress that was a size 3T and passed more for a long shirt now than a dress. It needed to find its way to the donation pile, but it was such a favorite of Hazel's that Maddie had skipped past it during the last few closet cleanings.

The twins' unbridled happiness to move their bodies penetrated through Maddie's shock as she watched them. Aside from the first fifteen minutes of the appointment when she'd been in the room with the twins, helping to answer a handful of the therapist's additional questions, Maddie had sat in the empty waiting room, listening to the soft trickling of a tableside fountain, staring at one of the framed quotes on the wall. The bulk of their appointment had passed before she realized she'd been staring at a quote she'd not bothered to read. Once she had, she needed to read it a second time for it to sink in. *"No matter how long you've traveled in the wrong direction, you can always turn around."*

It was a good thing she was alone in the room because the simple absurdity of it made her laugh until she covered her face in her hands and her laughter turned into tears, then into sobs big enough to cramp her stomach. She was attempting to pull herself together when the waiting room door opened and a father walked in holding a timid-looking boy's hand. Maddie swiped several Kleenex from the far table then stepped into the hall to collect herself.

Her eyes were still as puffy as little bread rolls, and her cheeks were splotchy. Before falling apart like that, she'd been attempting to think through different scenarios that might not involve Landon cheating. Had he driven a friend anywhere that last week or two before the accident? Had he given one of the staff a ride home? If he had, he'd either not told her, or she couldn't remember. As far as she knew, the only person who'd been in his car had been Noel, but considering he'd driven the car home less than twenty-four hours after Landon had taken his final breath, the likelihood of it being his was minimal. And whether she wanted to admit it, the idea of Noel leaving a condom wrapper behind in the car had its own piercing sting.

As the twins circled Eleanor's driveway, Maddie called out to them. "Ready you two? Lunch is waiting."

Maddie rang the doorbell and suppressed a shiver at the chill breeze in the March air. She'd either left her jacket in the car or at the therapist's and was hoping it was the former.

The twins ran up next to her, panting but with smiles on their faces. The therapist had assured Maddie that today would be a light, getting-to-know-each-other meeting. The fact that Maddie had been the only one to walk out of the building puffy eyed assured her this had in fact been the case.

Eleanor answered the door in a light-colored pantsuit befitting a high-end brunch rather than a weekday lunch with her grandchildren. Maddie instinctively glanced at her own faded jeans and cozy green sweater that was pilling at the elbows and under her arms. At least it was a step up from the yoga pants and random sweatshirts she'd been wearing around the house lately.

"Thank you for coming." Eleanor did an obvious double-take at Maddie's swollen eyes before turning to her grandchildren.

At the last second, Hazel dove behind Maddie to hide, while Benji pushed through the door. "Grandma, can we play with our toys?"

"Say hello first, Benji," Maddie reminded him. Charles and Eleanor had baskets overflowing with toys tucked in the lower cabinets of the wall-to-ceiling built-in shelves in the library, full of novelties like a Pinocchio puppet from Italy and a porcelain tea set from the Netherlands that they'd been adding to since their first grandchild was born to Landon's sister eight years before the twins arrived. While the upscale food here was rarely anything the twins raved about, the toys and floor-to-ceiling movie screen in the basement theater made up for it.

The twins' hugs with Eleanor were as stiff and unnatural as always, especially Hazel's, something that struck Maddie as ironic. If either of her babies had the slightest bit of Eleanor in them, it was Hazel with her innate need for control.

Maddie caught a whiff of something enticing and savory even before Eleanor announced that Mario was in the kitchen, cooking. Mario had recently been promoted from sous chef to head chef at Baxter's, but he still came by here twice a week to prep lunches and dinners for Eleanor and Charles. For such successful restaurateurs, neither of them had cared to learn their way around a kitchen.

Hazel wrinkled her nose as they headed inside. "I don't like that smell."

"I can't see why you wouldn't. It's chicken marsala." Eleanor said it like everyone in the world enjoyed sauteed mushrooms and a marsala wine reduction. "But I figured that might be the case. Mario is making you two chicken tenders so that your mother and I don't have to watch you turn your noses up at a delicious meal."

Maddie's shoulders straightened reflexively. "I suspect what's delicious to adults and to five-year-olds are often two different things."

"Can we have macaroni and cheese, too?" Hazel had yet to budge an inch from the stoop.

It took Eleanor a second to respond. She didn't like to be negotiated with, but typically Hazel and Benji could do no wrong. "He'll be finishing up soon. How about mashed potatoes with no gravy to yuck it up, as you say? And there's strawberry shortcake for dessert if you do a good job with your lunch."

This worked. With a nod, Hazel dashed over to the library on the far side of the foyer and dropped to her knees next to her brother, who had three different cabinet doors open.

Eleanor gave Maddie a direct look. "Mark my words. That one will lead the debate team. But it runs in the family. Both my girls could negotiate with the best of them at her age." She smoothed the cropped hair that was already perfectly in place. "Not my Landon though. He never liked to make anyone unhappy. He was always so concerned about how people felt. I remember when he was no bigger than Benji, we passed a homeless man on the way to a doctor's appointment. He had a hard time falling asleep for the better part of a week thinking about how that man had no bed to sleep in."

Maddie shoved her hand into her pocket, the slick plastic from the condom wrapper still burning her fingertips the same as if she'd touched a hot stove earlier. "I could see that." As much as she might like to disagree, she believed every word of the story. Landon had hated seeing people in pain.

Maddie followed her mother-in-law through the dining room into the expansive kitchen where Mario had three different burners going at once. She'd met him a few times at Baxter parties and special events, but he'd been hired after she'd quit to stay home with the twins. "Need help with anything?"

While Eleanor likely hadn't used the stove to do anything

more than boil water in years, Maddie would happily step in and help, but Mario waved her off.

"No need. It won't be long now, Mrs. Baxter."

It took Maddie a second to realize he was addressing her, not her mother-in-law. Even though most people assumed she'd taken Landon's last name, she still did a double take anytime she heard that name spoken about her. In her book, "Mrs. Baxter" would always be Eleanor.

She was going to let it slide when Eleanor answered for her. "Maddie is a Trudeau. She didn't take Landon's last name."

At one point, Maddie had been considering hyphenating her last name to Landon's before the twins grew old enough to understand that their mother didn't share their last name. As the tension between her and Landon had risen, the idea had been less and less appealing.

Mario wiped a hand on the front of his apron before reaching for a handful of fresh thyme. "You're French then? Nice name."

"My mother's family is mostly French Canadian with a bit of Scandinavian mixed in."

He shrugged. "French genes. Latin genes. We're the ones who love to cook. Not the English."

"Those genes certainly didn't skip me," Maddie answered. "I'm at my happiest in a kitchen." If Mario had wondered why Maddie hadn't mentioned her father's heritage, he didn't comment.

Maddie glanced at Eleanor, but her expression was unreadable. She and Eleanor had never discussed Maddie's unknown paternity, but Landon had told his parents about it before he and Maddie were married. She could only imagine it had given Eleanor one more reason to disapprove of her, though Eleanor should understand Maddie's pain. Eleanor's parents had divorced when she was young, and she'd eventually cut off all contact with her alcoholic father.

When lunch was served, Mario was still finishing up meal prep for the weekend. Given that his cooking was as entertaining as being at a Japanese steak house, the twins twisted in their chairs to watch while they devoured their pan-fried tenders.

Happy to have company, Mario bantered with them, even getting the kids to eat a bite or two of broccoli by tossing small pieces in the air for them to catch.

Most of the time, meals at Eleanor's reminded Maddie of what it would be like to bring sugar-loaded toddlers to a garden party. Today, her mother-in-law hardly seemed to notice the way they were using their hands instead of utensils, the lack of linen napkins on their laps, or the bits of food falling onto the floor that her housekeeper would be cleaning up later.

Maddie wouldn't have believed it possible, but Eleanor seemed to take up so much less space than she had such a short time ago. *Grief has a way of condensing you*, Maddie's mom had said time and again over the years. Given how Charlotte had worked as a palliative care nurse the bulk of her career, she knew what she was talking about. A few years ago, she'd quit and struck out on her own as a death doula, something Maddie rarely shared with strangers because it invariably took the conversation an entirely different direction. *My mother, the death doula.*

Once Mario had headed off to the restaurant—leaving a pile of dirty dishes for Eleanor's housekeeper—and Maddie and Eleanor had finished a remarkable lunch of chicken marsala, mashed potatoes, and grilled fennel, Eleanor suggested the twins watch television while she talked with their mom.

Here it comes. Maddie figured it was fifty-fifty whether Eleanor would be tactful or accusatory when it came to asking about the missed call she'd spied on Maddie's phone yesterday. Whichever it was, on the heels of today's condom-wrapper find, this wasn't a conversation Maddie was eager to have.

She got the twins settled on separate couches in the hearth room, covering them with cozy sherpa blankets and turning on the gas fireplace. Helena, Eleanor's housekeeper, appeared from the back of the house to clean the kitchen now that the meal was finished, but Eleanor sent her on an errand instead, even though it wasn't like her to let a pile of dishes sit in the sink in exchange for an errand that could've been pushed off for later.

After Helena left, Eleanor stood at the counter, wiping a damp cloth over a few crumbs. "Would you like a cup of tea?"

"No, thank you." Sipping on tea was for casual talks, not this. Rather than return to the table next to the tall bay windows facing into the backyard, Maddie took a seat at one of the stools at the wide center island, her back to the hearth room, the familiar theme song to *Super Why!* in the background. "What is it you wanted to talk about?" Not only was Maddie not going to halt the conversation, but it seemed she was also going to start it.

Eleanor put the cloth in the sink but kept to the other side of the wide center island, facing her. "Finances." She folded the cloth into a trifold before laying it across the sink divider. "I suspect you've been giving a good deal of thought as to how you're going to support your children now that your primary source of income has disintegrated."

Maddie's jaw fell open. That was Eleanor for you, implying every bit as much as she was saying. Maddie was prepared to talk about her phone call to the lawyer, not the troubling state of her finances—something that consumed her thoughts during those sleepless hours before dawn. "Actually, given how it's only been three weeks since our world flipped upside down, not that much yet."

"Understandable, though I know from experience,

creditors don't give any grace for mourning, and given how my son didn't purchase another life insurance policy after cashing out the one his father and I transferred to him upon graduation, there is no boon coming your way."

Maddie attempted to lock down the defensiveness creeping in. Landon had spent the cash from that policy long before meeting her, and they'd talked about buying joint policies but had focused on other priorities those first few years as new parents. Then, after he was formally diagnosed with bipolar disorder, the premiums had gone up too much to handle without concessions in other areas, so they had decided to wait until after the twins finished preschool. Though Maddie had no doubt that other competing expenses would've arisen to delay it yet again. "No, there's no boon coming my way."

Eleanor eyed her silently, waiting for more.

"I can't see that this is your business, Eleanor, but I can make it another few months on what's in our joint checking. My pay rate and part-time hours at the grocery store aren't going to cut it for the long term—obviously. But I'm not going to dive into anything new right off the bat. The kids are dealing with momentous change already."

A pained look flashed over Eleanor's face. "That they are. Their father was a remarkable man."

Maddie caught herself fiddling with her wedding ring and stopped. She'd been wondering when the right time was to take it off. This morning on the way to the appointment, she'd nearly chucked it out the car window.

Eleanor's bony fingers flattened against the countertop like she was using it to support herself. "I have a proposal for you." She paused long enough to make it clear she wanted a response, but Maddie waited her out. "Landon's position within the family restaurants—it's yours if you want it."

Maddie blinked. Never in her wildest dreams would she have thought that Eleanor would make such an offer.

"You're…qualified for it," she added with the same tightness of tone of one about to swallow a bitter pill. "And Charles and I will provide you with enough of a salary increase that it should offset the additional childcare you'll need."

Maddie stopped fiddling with her ring and smoothed her hands along the top of her jeans. Her insides were a rioting mix of temptation and warning, like a hungry rabbit sniffing around a snare. Her money fears would be snuffed out with a solid six figure salary after taxes, but accepting the offer would mean more than long hours that clashed with the needs of her children. It would mean being under Eleanor's thumb. "I, uh, wow. I don't know what to say."

"If you accept, your lifestyle won't need to change. Your house. The twins' Montessori preschool. Any of it."

Maddie had never considered it this way before, but the big house, the prestigious location, the preschool—each one of them had been bones of contention in her marriage at one point or another, and it was more than his family's wealth at the core of the dissention. It was Eleanor.

Landon had been raised on excess; Maddie hadn't. Now, here she was being offered to keep everything status quo. All it would cost her would be stepping into a position she hadn't earned, even if she *was* qualified for it. "It's a gracious offer, Eleanor. Thank you, but I'll need to think about it. It's a big decision and not at all what I expected."

No, you don't need to think about it. This woman hates everything about you. You can't work for her. You absolutely can't.

Eleanor's eyes widened before she locked down her expression. Clearly, she'd expected Maddie to accept on the spot. "I hardly see what there is to think about. You've been making pennies on the dollar compared to Landon. You've been off-grid. You can't expect to walk into any other restaurant making anything close to what you'd be making with me."

Fire heated Maddie's veins. "I know what stepping away from my career will cost me, Eleanor. I knew it when I made the decision to be with my children full-time. And I recognize this opportunity for what it is." She bit her lip as she collected herself. "I'll need a few days to think about it. I take it you can wait that long."

Maddie didn't believe in auras the way her mom did but, at this response, Eleanor seemed to expand in size like the genie in *Aladdin*. "You won't win, you know. You don't have a chance! The restaurants are in a family trust that Charles and I have full control over until we pass away or deem otherwise."

Maddie shook her head. "Wait, what are you saying?"

"You're in contact with a lawyer. Clearly. Am I honestly to assume it has to do with anything aside from wanting control over Landon's share of the trust?"

Maddie stood up so fast her stool scraped against the wood loudly enough that in the adjoining room, Hazel lifted her head off the couch pillow. "Is it time to go, Mommy?"

"Almost. Just one more minute, baby." Turning back to Eleanor, Maddie leaned over the counter and dropped her voice. "That call from the lawyer is my business and my business alone, but I haven't given Landon's share of your family trust *one second* of thought in years. If you want the truth, before today, I've been more consumed with worry over what selling the house will do to the kids on the heels of losing their father than anything else—and yes, I do remember that we'd never have been able to afford our lovely house without that generous gift from you and Charles as a down payment."

Eleanor looked as if Maddie had slapped her. "Then what do you plan to do? Your income will hardly keep you above the poverty line, and you have young children to raise, children who deserve the world. Surely, you'll be sensible about this."

Sensible? Hadn't she been the sensible one her entire marriage? Her entire life? Anger rocked her with a clarity that had evaded her the last three weeks. "What do I plan to do? I'll tell you what I plan to do, Eleanor. I plan to *finally* start traveling in the right direction after traveling in the wrong one for way too long."

CHAPTER 5

ELEANOR

leanor's husband of forty-four years chewed with the rigor of a mountain goat, no matter what he ate. It was a wonder Charles hadn't worn his teeth to nubs the way he chewed. There'd been a time when Eleanor hardly noticed it, but in the quiet weeks after Landon's passing, her husband's chewing might as well have been in surround sound.

With frustration percolating inside her like carbonation in a glass of seltzer, she got up from the ten-person mahogany dining room table, leaving her plate all but untouched. She crossed to the floor-to-ceiling windows and stared into the yard below. Like the rest of the house, the backyard was meticulously manicured. From the inset planters dotting the stone patio, to the surrounding grass that hadn't yet woken up from its winter slumber, to the multitude of flower beds, not a single weed was allowed to poke its head. Their handsomely paid landscaping company saw to that. Unfortunately, the ground crew stopped their maintenance where the yard butted up to the strip of woods at the back edge of the property, claiming they weren't allowed to violate the rules of the common ground.

With an infinity pool designed by one of the most popular architects in the city, flower beds that had been spotlighted in the local paper on two occasions, and a patio that was envied by the governor and his wife, the irony didn't escape Eleanor as to how, whenever she looked out the rear-facing windows, her gaze was forever drawn to that wanting strip of woods with the scraggly trees, the unsightly vines, and the honeysuckle doing its darndest to spread into the yard every year. Whenever she complained about the woods, Charles rebuffed her with the comment that she should be thankful to have them blocking view of the Moberly's backyard. "No one needs any more opportunity to know what goes on over there than what they share on Facebook" was his typical comment.

Turning her back on the woods where her son had played in adolescence for hours on end—God only knew why—she brushed her finger over a tall blue and white porcelain vase on the side table near the window, sweeping for dust and having her finger come up with a soft line of it. She could hear Helena shuffling about in the kitchen, pretending to be busy. The woman had lasted longer than most other help they'd had over the years, but that didn't mean she was worth the money they paid her.

Eleanor shot an angry glance at her husband who, rather than noticing that she wasn't eating, was reading something on his phone as he devoured his dinner of sea bass, creamed potatoes, and garlic parmesan roasted asparagus. From here, his pudginess irritated her even more, as did the rosacea blotting his cheeks. The truth of the matter was, she had no desire to even be in the same room with him any longer. There was only one person she wanted to be in the room with —her son—and that was no longer possible.

Her frustration skyrocketed at the helplessness this stirred up, and Charles wasn't even going to acknowledge that she'd gotten up from the table. He knew how much this irritated her. But two could play that game. "I'm thinking about getting Gerald involved."

Charles looked up with a jerk as sudden as if the dusty vase had toppled over from her touch. Gerald was the family lawyer who'd done their bidding often enough over the last several decades. "Involved in what?"

"Maddie's going to turn down my offer. I could see it in her expression. That lawyer she called—I bet she wants one of the restaurants all to herself. She won't get it, but if she's wanting what I have, well, then I'd like to have a formal visitation agreement for our grandchildren."

Charles set down his fork and took a deep swallow of the sixty-dollar bottle of Pinot Grigio he'd chosen for tonight's dinner. "What would we need that for? Maddie's reasonable. Always has been. She came over today when you asked her, didn't she?"

"She won't be single for a full year. Mark my words. We'll see them less and less—have less and less influence on the people they grow up to be. That confounded girl! I swear, I never would've hired her."

Charles swept a chubby hand over his mouth, having felt the dab of cream that had collected in the corner. "You've made that point clear so many times I could never forget it, Eleanor, but I *did* hire her, and she married Landon, and now she's our daughter-in-law and a widow. As for turning down the offer, what did she say exactly?"

"That she needs time. That it's a big decision. But she was spiteful when she should've been grateful."

"If you remember, you tend to read more into Maddie's silences and facial expressions than I do. Maybe she does need time. Seems reasonable to me."

"Charles, why on earth would she want to work fulltime when she can sue her way into owning a third of a business that is in *no way* due her and then sit back and do nothing except find another man to provide for her?"

Charles winced. "Really Eleanor. You could cut her some slack."

What was wrong with him? Charles had been ridiculously enamored with Maddie right from the start. Eleanor would never let *her* restaurants fall into the hands of trailer trash who'd stumbled her way into becoming a decently regarded pastry chef and then slept her way right into this family. Damn Charles for hiring Maddie in the first place while she was away in Tremblant with a friend. It was Eleanor's job to hire anyone of any significance, not his.

No matter what Charles said, Eleanor knew exactly why her ungrateful daughter-in-law was in contact with a law firm. He'd never be able to convince her otherwise. But just because Maddie had married Landon, and he had been the majority heir to all three restaurants—Eleanor's self-absorbed daughters certainly hadn't shown any indication that they deserved equal ownership—didn't mean Maddie was entitled to them, either.

Landon had always been more Eleanor's son than Maddie's husband, hadn't he? He'd spent thirty-two years being her son, after all, and only five being Maddie's husband. And what a golden boy he'd been! What a light he'd radiated! So loving and giving. Why, she couldn't remember him having a single tantrum—quite unlike the other children in the playgroup she'd taken him to. But God forbid the day that one of those hooligans had stamped his foot on a butterfly that Landon had been admiring while it rested on the ground in front of them. You'd have thought he'd been witness to a murder, stricken as he was.

Her boy had had a kindness to him she'd never seen in another human.

A few times in recent years, Eleanor had been tempted to pass full ownership of one of the restaurants onto him, but she'd never done it, and this haunted her as much as it relieved her. Landon had deserved to know that his parents fully trusted his decisions, but had she done so, Maddie would own one of her restaurants.

Upon his death–*Didn't I tell him to sign a prenup?*–she'd become the majority heir to the Baxter family trust. But it wasn't too late to change this while Eleanor and Charles were calling the shots.

"She's clearly in contact with a lawyer of her own," she reminded her husband, "and when I asked her about it today, she wouldn't say why. So exactly how *much* slack should I cut her?"

Charles had scooped up a bite of creamed potatoes and paused with the fork halfway to his mouth. After a short debate, he returned it to his plate untouched. "There are a dozen reasons she could've been calling a lawyer—to create a will of her own, for one. If you'd only give it a few months for things to settle down. Forcing a visitation agreement on her would stir things up unnecessarily. Think of the relationship. Think about holidays and birthday parties."

"What relationship?" Her voice shook with the rage flowing through. "She's called me exactly once since Landon…" *Died.* Eleanor couldn't bring herself to say the word aloud. She returned to her seat at the table even though she didn't care for another bite. Perhaps it was ironic coming from a restauranter of her caliber, but if she could survive without another bite of food for the rest of her life, she'd do so.

She didn't know why she was egging her husband on so intently, other than the fact that she wanted to spur him into some sort of action. Their son had died—*died!*—and Charles was going to eat his way through it.

Despite her threat, Eleanor didn't want Gerald to draw up a formal visitation agreement or to take her daughter-in-law to court. She wanted to see her grandchildren; there was truth in that. But being with those wiggly children for more than an hour or two at a time gave her an insufferable headache.

What she wanted was for Charles to wake up and notice the depth of what they'd lost. Maddie, too. And if this was what it took, so be it.

"I won't ask for anything unreasonable," she said, hanging onto her fight because there was nothing else to hold onto. "What I'm looking for is consistency—one or two evenings a week and our choice of summer vacations. And...I want them to go to the school of our choosing." Charles turned a light shade of green at this last declaration. The man hated confrontation. But Eleanor was too angry to desist. "We'll pay the tuition, of course. But that mother of Maddie's— she's going to suck them in until they're wearing Birkenstocks and silly clothes and dancing under a full moon, I know it."

It wasn't until the words were out that Eleanor realized this was what had been bothering her the most. Without Landon in the picture, those children would be swept away in Charlotte's nonsense.

Rather than acknowledge her, Charles stared at his plate and fiddled with the placement of his water glass. She could tell by the set of his shoulders that he disagreed with everything she was saying. He'd gone to a mediocre public school and believed he'd turned out just fine. Perhaps he had, but only because of her effort and vision.

She gave him the space to respond but wasn't surprised when he didn't. He was angry enough that he'd lost interest in food—a rare occurrence. In a minute or two, he'd retreat to his study, and they wouldn't talk again until tomorrow evening at the earliest. That was how it always went when he disagreed with her. The important thing was that he wouldn't stop her. He never had, and he wasn't going to start now.

CHAPTER 6

MADDIE

I n the soft glow of the nightlight, Hazel's bedroom door pushed open a few inches, and Leo strolled inside, tail fluffed like a bottle brush. Maddie was curled in the twin bed next to Hazel and hoped Leo's intrusion wouldn't rouse her. Of the two of them, Hazel was the one who took forever to fall asleep, but her breathing had finally become slow and steady, so much so that Maddie was ready to sneak away. On the opposite side of the room, his mattress on the floor, Benji had drifted off a good ten minutes ago.

Getting there hadn't been easy, but prior to Landon's death in late February, Maddie had been ready to check off independent sleeping the same as she had nursing, potty-training, and sleeping through the night.

For the first four years of their lives, the twins had shared a room. While attempting to get Benji to sleep alone in his big-boy room, Maddie had spotted her first gray hair. She didn't think it was a coincidence.

Although Benji had been as excited as Hazel about the prospect of having his own room, going to sleep in it had been another matter entirely, but they'd finally gotten there. Before Landon died, anyway.

Three weeks ago, Maddie recognized a lost cause and dragged Benji's mattress to the far wall of Hazel's bedroom. Ever since, she'd been alternating nights as to whom she lay with first.

Having made his way across the room, Leo popped onto the bottom of Hazel's bed before Maddie could extract herself from underneath the sheets. He ambled up the side of her body like it was a tree limb and stretched out on top of her, his back legs hanging off one side, his throaty purr reverberating through Maddie's chest.

The poor cat was out of sorts. He'd been coming inside from the backyard where he was safely confined by their privacy fence just as seemingly dissatisfied as when he'd gone out. No doubt, he missed his playmate. While he got along with the twins just fine and was quick to cuddle with Maddie, Landon had been his person. It was Landon who'd taught him to play fetch with the catnip-filled play mice, and Landon who'd gotten on the floor to wrestle with him the way people do with dogs. But it wasn't Landon who'd made sure he was fed twice a day and had a clean litter box, that was for sure.

Landon.

Damn you to hell and back.

Given this morning's condom find, Maddie wanted to hold onto the anger and blame prickling her skin, but regardless of what had driven her into his arms, she'd loved him once. Not a clean, easy love that she could hang evidence of in her front window like a Valentine's display, but a complicated one to be stuck in a drawer alongside last year's tax to call upon if needed.

It was a bowl of lemons on the counter at Eleanor's earlier that had triggered the memory of that early, unstained love. Given the brush of nostalgia that swept across her along with it, it was starkly out of place with the chaos of late.

She lingered under the weight of Leo while soaking in the

rise and fall of her daughter's small chest next to her. Lately, when lying in here after the kids fell asleep, Maddie had been thinking back on her decisions, questioning what she'd been thinking, hooking up with Landon that first time. Or the second or the third, or all the other times too packed together to distinguish prior to her realizing their birth control had failed and she was six weeks pregnant. She'd even questioned whether some part of her *had* craved the Baxter family money with its promise of relative stability compared to the life she grew up in.

But the warmth that had swept over her earlier alongside the memory was a reminder that there'd been something real between them that first year or two, something as close to love as Maddie had ever gotten, even if acknowledging it made Landon's infidelity all the worse. Maybe it had always been complicated between them, but he'd made her laugh at a time when she was hurting and pretending not to be, and in the thick of their new romance, she'd felt beautiful.

Thinking back on that day with the lemons, she could almost feel herself standing at the stainless-steel counter under the bright lighting of the Row House kitchen, wearing her new chef coat, starched and unstained, the whisk in one hand, the shell of a freshly cracked egg in the other.

Her legs and back were accustomed to standing all day, and underneath her chef's coat, her stomach was flat and tight in a way it would never be again after giving birth to twins.

How many weeks had she been at the restaurant by then? Five? Six? Not much longer, surely. Landon had popped up out of nowhere, planting himself at the counter, facing her, and resting his hip against the edge. He'd been close enough that his forearm pressed against hers.

"So, you think you're hot stuff, Trudeau?"

When Maddie glanced up from her work, those deep blue eyes were hardly more than eighteen inches away. She blinked, cheeks heating. Was he betraying her confidence in front of an entire kitchen full of staff? Was he going to throw the stupidest and most impulsive thing she'd ever done in her face in front of a dozen people? Had she misjudged him that completely?

What had she been thinking, asking him to pass along a love letter to his best friend? It was a decision she'd regretted almost as soon as she'd done it—and even more so when it went unacknowledged.

Maddie was grappling with how to respond when she spotted the kindness in Landon's gaze that belied his words. He reached in front of her and pulled four eggs from the carton, one at a time. With his face inches from hers, Maddie stepped back, the unexpectedly pleasant scent of him lingering in her nostrils.

He wasn't her boss, per se. He was the son of her two bosses, one who was pleased with her, the other who seemed to despise her.

"Follow me," he said with a wink.

Maddie wiped her hands on a towel and trailed after him, passing several staff who'd stopped working to stare after them. Back here in the kitchen, most of the staff were heterosexual males and looked at Landon as nothing more than someone to be on guard around. It was the serving staff who adored him, and because of that natural charisma that outshone fresh car wax, he mostly worked up front with them, his charm bewitching customers and staff alike.

He headed toward the exit that led to the back parking lot where the staff sat and smoked on a worn bench equidistant between the waste bins and the big smoker. A prep cook named Miguel was sitting there alone, and his eyes widened at Landon's arrival. Maddie could relate to his surprise. Landon and his parents used the front doors of their restaurants, not the back.

Maddie was thankful for Miguel's company. She didn't

want Landon bringing up the letter, and the best way to keep him from doing that was to keep from being alone with him. She wanted all memory of that letter shoved away, never to reach the light of day again.

She didn't let people in easily, but she'd opened the door wide and let Landon's best friend storm in—after spending just shy of twelve hours with him. When she couldn't stand waiting the four weeks until Noel's return from Spain to know if he'd felt the same as she did, she'd passed along a letter through Landon, asking if he could get it to him before his flight. In retrospect, a text would've been more appropriate—might not have come across as baring her heart on her sleeve.

By the time Landon had called her, Maddie had already figured out Noel's answer. Her and Noel's shared night had meant more to her than it had to Noel. If not, he'd have responded. But he'd boarded a plane for Madrid, and Maddie hadn't heard from him since.

"Give him some time," Landon had advised when he'd called her after looking her number up in the payroll system two days after she'd passed along the letter. "Sometimes these things work themselves out."

That call had been four days ago now, and this was her first time alone with Landon since then. Looking him in the eye reminded her of what an idiot she'd been. Who wrote a love letter to someone they'd only met once? In her defense, it hadn't been a love letter, not really. She'd only written about how much the night had meant to her and retracted what she'd said as she and Noel were parting just after dawn about wanting to focus on her career more than a relationship. She'd also written something about experiencing a deeper connection with him than she'd been prepared for, which was why she'd shut down at the end of the night when he'd talked about seeing her again.

So not a love letter, per se. At least she could save a bit of face there.

Outside the restaurant, Maddie stopped a few feet from Landon, and he reached for her hand, depositing two of the eggs onto her palm. "Hold these."

It was about ten in the morning, and the sun had just crested over the roof, its warmth welcome in the chilly air.

"So, Trudeau thinks she's all that because she can break an egg and use a whisk at the same time."

Maddie shook her head. "I think everyone in the back of the house can do that."

"I can't," Miguel quipped from the bench before taking a drag of his cigarette.

"I bet every dollar I have that not a one of them in there can do it the way you do," Landon said. "It's like being at the beach, watching the waves. Right as they break, there's this moment when they're both advancing and receding at the same time. It's surreal. Graceful. You look like that when you're working, Trudeau."

Maddie shook her head, stunned by the compliment and wanting to downplay it at the same time. "And you dragged me and four raw eggs out here to tell me that why exactly?"

Landon splayed his feet and gave his broad shoulders a roll. He was six-foot-two, sun-kissed blond, and had deep baby blue eyes. Everywhere he went, no doubt, people looked at him.

"When I say toss, toss one at my right hand."

He began juggling the two eggs he'd kept, staring up in the high point of the arc rather than at his hands. Maddie was duly impressed and about to comment how his faith in her aim was unwarranted when he said, "Toss."

She tossed the egg in her right hand on reflex. To her surprise, he caught it and blended it seamlessly into the juggle, sending three eggs in a continuous x-shaped pattern.

Miguel whistled in appreciation.

"Toss," Landon said again.

Maddie braced for a splat as she tossed the fourth egg. She must've closed her eyes for a second or two because when she looked, he was in deep concentration, juggling the four eggs as they traveled too quickly to keep track of any individual one.

He'd become the wave advancing and receding at the same time, fluidity of motion too quick for the human eye to track. At first, Maddie held her breath. Surely, he'd slip up or break concentration, but around and around the eggs went in an arc too fast to track until she was confident he could do it as long as he wished.

"Catch."

And just like that an egg was headed her way. She wasn't proud of the squeal that escaped, but at least she caught it as he went back to juggling three eggs again.

"Catch."

Another egg flew seamlessly out of the arc, heading toward her, but Maddie still had the other egg in her right hand and wasn't about to attempt to catch the next one with her left. She had just enough time to duck sideways. The egg flew past, landing with a smack on the pavement five feet behind her while Landon stopped juggling the remaining two.

Miguel clapped as he stood up to head inside. "Impressive, Mr. Baxter."

"Landon, please. Always Landon."

Miguel nodded in consent as he headed inside, but Landon's gaze was on Maddie.

She was fighting back a smile and losing. "They don't teach that in pastry arts."

"No, that was the product of a lonely and isolated childhood." His smile was just wide enough to prevent her from asking if he was joking. He closed the distance between them and took Maddie's empty hand in his, placing one of the eggs in her palm. In the short time he'd been juggling it, it had lost some of its chill. "Your turn."

"Oh no. I'm not juggling eggs. Besides, just because I can cook with both hands doesn't mean I have good hand-eye coordination."

"Sure, you do."

Maddie shook her head. "I have three cheesecakes to get in the oven."

"You've got a couple minutes."

"I'm going to get egg all over my coat."

Landon raised an eyebrow, and Maddie found herself giving a little shrug of the shoulders.

They started with one. Miguel had left the back door ajar with a stopper, and for the moment, it was only the two of them and a few flies buzzing over by the big trash container, the smell of prime rib in the big smoker preventing her from catching Landon's scent again when he stepped close.

Within the first minute of instruction, the first egg had splatted at their feet, and within three minutes, a second one. Maddie's chef shoes could be wiped down more easily than his loafers, but he didn't seem to mind.

"Look, this was fun, but I gotta go."

"Come on. Give me another four minutes."

He wasn't her boss, not exactly, and the fact that it wasn't a question didn't raise her hackles. There was enough lightness in his gaze that it would be easy to refuse if she wanted to. Instead, she glanced at her watch. "Okay. Four minutes."

Landon dashed inside and came out with three bright yellow lemons held snuggly in his left hand. When he looked her way, he winked.

"Much smarter choice," she teased.

As he walked up, he took her by surprise, locking his empty hand around her wrist and adjusting both their bodies so that they were facing the same direction, her back to his front.

She started to step away, but he held her wrist. She craned her neck to look back at him and was half-surprised by the playfulness lingering in his eyes. "It's okay, Trudeau. I just want to help you get the rhythm, then I'll leave you to it."

Maddie stared at him for a moment, unyielding. Surely, he'd had enough HR training here to know better than this, hadn't he? He had full lips and a broad chin, and he towered over her by half a foot, at least.

If anyone walked outside, it would cement her reputation here as someone who was not only easy to get but also making a play for the boss—or the boss's son, any way. Even so, Maddie gave a nod of consent before facing forward as Landon stepped against her, dropping one lemon into a pocket of her coat, and placing the other two in one of her hands before cupping his hands underneath hers. Her breath stilled as she took in the feel of his warm skin against hers.

"Don't look down at your hands, just keep them in your field of view as you look at the spot where you want the lemons to travel."

Maddie nodded, but she was finding it hard to listen with his arms around hers and his body so close. Was he into sports? Did he jog? Did he spend two hours a day at the gym? She reminded herself that he wasn't her type—too outgoing, too often the center of attention. She didn't fall for people easily, but when she did, it was for the quieter, brooding types.

Like Noel.

She dropped the first lemon as soon as her thoughts flashed to Noel. As it rolled along the payment and underneath the trash dumpster, Landon slipped the third lemon from her pocket. "One of the good things about juggling, Trudeau, is that you gotta clear your head. Just keep it empty. Let this flow."

When four minutes had passed, Landon still had his arms around hers, and Maddie had stopped thinking about the time entirely.

A little over a week later, they had sex for the first time in Maddie's apartment while Saanvi was out with friends. Maddie was still catching her breath when Landon brought up Noel—brought up the letter. They were naked, their bodies entwined between Maddie's sheets, and Landon's words popped Maddie's bubble of okayness right then and there, reminding her that this thing with Landon was physical pleasure without the connection she'd experienced with Noel—or at least the connection she'd *thought* she'd experienced with Noel.

"What you don't know about Noel, Maddie…the letter you wrote…" It was the first time Landon had called her by her first name instead of her last, and the moment wasn't lost on her. "Whatever you do, don't go thinking it's you. His dad almost died when we were kids. His mom went to pieces, and she spent most of her time at the hospital and rehab facility for the better part of a year. My mom, she pretty much took Noel in. He was at our house all the time after that. Went everywhere with us."

"He told me about it, but Landon, really, I don't want to talk about it. Besides, I'm over it." It was the first lie Maddie told him and the biggest, too.

He reached for her hand and spread her fingers wide, tracing his thumb over her palm. "It's just…the shit our parents do to us without meaning to, it's hard to get past. Makes it near impossible to do the right thing sometimes. Especially when it matters most."

Maddie nodded and looked away. It was either cry and pretend she wasn't or lose herself in all-consuming sex, so she chose the latter, pulling back the sheet and climbing on top of him. "The only thing I care about right now is how many condoms you have in that wallet of yours, because I'm really hoping it's at least two."

The look that flashed over him, she could only describe it as one of sharp pain. For a second or two, she was certain he was going to get up and leave, like she'd broken a fragile trust between them she hadn't even realized had formed. But then his gaze dropped to her breasts, and he gave a little nod as his hands slid up her thighs. "If it's distraction you're looking for, I've got your back, Trudeau."

CHAPTER 7

Maddie was closing Hazel's bedroom door as she heard a soft knock at the front door. Peeking around the corner, she looked over the top of the landing rail to spy someone peering in through the sidelight windows. She jerked involuntarily before realizing it was her mother, smiling and waving like she was expected.

After setting Leo down, Maddie jogged down the steps, barefoot, and in lounge pants and one of her old t-shirts.

"Hey," she said, after unlocking the door and pulling it open. "Everything okay? It's late."

"Oh, please. It's eight-thirty." Charlotte gave a good-natured roll of the eyes. "When you were a kid, we'd just be sitting down to dinner." She glanced at Maddie. "I take it they're asleep?"

"Yeah, hopefully for the whole night. And for the record, our established routine works for us." Whether more nature or nature, Maddie didn't care to expound upon, but she couldn't imagine raising the twins with Charlotte's throw-caution-to-the-wind attitude.

After kicking off the hemp sandals she wore on all but the coldest months of the year, Charlotte headed inside with the confidence of someone who'd been invited over. She wore a colorful, flowy skirt and a buttercream yellow shirt and had a giant tumbler thermos in one hand. "Something told me you could use a cup of my nighttime blend."

As exasperating as her mom's fully embodied embracing of the supernatural could be, Maddie figured she was due some credit for her spot-on intuition. "What's in tonight's blend?" she asked, following her into the kitchen.

"Chamomile, lavender, and peppermint, and it's sweetened with a touch of licorice root." After plopping her oversized bag on the counter, Charlotte unscrewed the top of the tumbler and waved it in Maddie's direction for a sniff.

There was no denying the wave of calm that swept over her as she inhaled. "Mmm. Lovely."

Charlotte headed straight for the cabinet containing the mugs. "You ready to talk? Or do you need a bit?" Maddie was putting away the big pot she'd used to boil noodles earlier that had been air drying next to the sink. She paused to give her mom a look, but Charlotte waved it off. "I grew you in my belly for nine months and nursed you for eighteen. I know when something's upsetting you."

"I'm almost thirty-two. That was more than three decades ago."

"You can stand there and tell me nothing's wrong, but your energy's off, and after my reading tonight, well, let's just leave it at I knew you needed me."

Her tarot reading, no doubt.

In truth, Maddie had picked up the phone a dozen times this afternoon and had even hammered out a few texts but had changed her mind each time. She hadn't been ready to put any of the day's events into words, neither to her mom nor Saanvi. But now that her mom was standing here, there was no getting past it. "We took Landon's car to the appointment this morning. Benji found a condom wrapper on the floor in the backseat." With her throat threatening to lock up, she added, "He thought it was from a sucker."

Charlotte set the two mugs she'd chosen onto the counter. "Oh, Maddie. I'm sorry."

Because Maddie didn't want to acknowledge the tears stinging her lids that came with this confession, she shrugged and attempted to blink them away unseen. "I keep trying to remember if he'd given anyone from work a ride the last few weeks before the accident."

"And you can't?"

Maddie went back to drying the last of the dishes, and a bit overzealously at that. "Just Noel when he brought it home from the parking lot of the trail where Landon had been biking."

Charlotte poured the tea and handed Maddie a steaming mug of it. "Between the two of them, it wouldn't have been Noel's. I'm certain of that."

"What makes you so sure?"

"Timing. And character."

Maddie held up a hand. "If we're going to have this conversation, can we stick to verifiable facts please?"

After pursing her lips for a moment, Charlotte said, "Why don't you ask him then?"

"*Noel?* The last thing I'm going to do is ask him about this." Maddie headed for the living room with both hands cupped around her mug, soaking in the warmth a few seconds before setting it on the side table. She curled into one of the two armchairs and draped a chunky knit blanket over herself, craving all the cozy she could get in hopes it might numb the ache inside her.

When the twins' toys and books weren't overtaking it, the living room was Maddie's go-to spot to wind down. Before all this chaos had hit, one of her favorite parts of the day had been curling up in one of the oversized armchairs and reading under lamplight, a candle burning nearby. With its expansive wood floors, abundant windows, and rough-hewn wood ceiling beams, the living room and its classic Tudor-style were right out of a magazine.

"Why the *last* thing, if I might ask?" Rather than taking up the second chair, Charlotte sank onto the rug in the middle of the floor not far from where Leo was sprawled out and twitching his tail at their visitor.

"You know why, and I don't want to talk about it, Mom. Not right now. Not with all this going on."

After setting her mug on the coffee table, Charlotte swept aside a few stray toy planes and stretched out alongside Leo. She pulled her flowy skirt up to her knees and began to flex her feet back and forth, making Maddie wonder about her day. Given Charlotte's line of work, Maddie's mom had pretty much seen it all, but some days were weightier than others. After those days, she spent a lot of time on the floor stretching and working the tension out of her limbs. And smudging herself with sage—there was a lot of that, too. Captivated by her movements, Leo belly-crawled closer to bat at her feet. "Noel hurt you, Maddie. As deeply as Landon ever did, I suspect. But have you considered that it wasn't intentional?"

"You mean like maybe he just forgot I existed?"

Charlotte's reply was a single raised eyebrow.

"Listen, I can't talk about this tonight. Noel and his feelings and secret motivations aren't a priority for me. They haven't been for a long time."

Charlotte opened her mouth but bit her words back, then released an exaggerated exhale that made it clear that holding her peace instead of speaking it was exorbitantly taxing. "Okay."

Maddie recognized a win when she saw it. "Thank you."

"You're welcome." Charlotte lifted a brow. "And I suppose I don't need to remind you that this most recent injustice of Landon's is his shame, not yours."

"I know. At least in my head I do." Maddie locked her hands around her mug and blew before taking a sip.

"Landon's life path, it was both intense and cut short. He made his share of mistakes, even before this. But it was his life, and they were his mistakes."

"His mistakes in *our* marriage," Maddie interrupted.

Her mom continued as if she hadn't even spoken. "Once you've had a full night's sleep to sit with this, please remind me to remind you that no one can add stones to your bowl of light but you."

Maddie groaned loudly enough to draw Leo's attention. "Mom, can we just not? Not tomorrow, not tonight."

Charlotte leaned back to grasp her mug and took a sip. "As long as you accept that it's up to you whether you carry the weight of this moving forward."

Rather than answer, Maddie buried her face in her hands. How many times had she heard her mom comment that if only she had a dollar for every person in her caseload who said they just weren't ready for what they were being handed? When Maddie looked up, Leo had crawled into Charlotte's lap and was belly up, savoring a petting.

Maddie took a sip of steaming tea before returning it to the coaster and curling deeper into the blanket. "I called my OB/GYN. They're squeezing me this coming Monday. I want every STD test they offer."

"Do you need me to watch the twins? If everything goes as anticipated, I have a light caseload the next several days."

"Thanks, but it's while they're at school. They go back in the morning, remember? Knock on wood, that'll go smoothly. They've only been off for three weeks, but it seems longer. A lot longer."

"I trust going back will be just what they need." Charlotte was returning her mug to the coffee table when Maddie's phone, which had been abandoned there before she headed upstairs with the twins, buzzed with a new text.

Charlotte picked it up and stretched as far as possible without dumping Leo off her lap to pass it to her. "Noel." A small word said simply but with the perfectly understated inflection Charlotte had mastered, the same as stating that his ears must have been ringing.

Maddie stared at the screen a second before opening the text.

HEY, JUST CHECKING IN. HOW ARE THINGS? H & B HAVE A GOOD APPOINTMENT?

Ever since he'd flown in from Chile, he'd been texting or calling regularly. Maddie didn't know how long he intended to stay in St. Louis now that Landon's Celebration of Life was over, but she figured he'd be letting her know any day now that he'd be heading out soon.

She answered his text rather than putting it off for later.

THERAPIST SEEMS GREAT. KIDS WARMED TO HER RIGHT OFF THE BAT.

AWESOME, HOW ABOUT YOU, NEED ANYTHING?

ALL GOOD HERE. THX. CHARLOTTE'S HERE AND BROUGHT TEA. 😊

TELL HER HELLO. I'LL CHECK IN TOMORROW. SLEEP WELL.

The 'sleep well' stabbed at Maddie's heart.

You too.

When Maddie set her phone on the side table, her mom was watching her intently. "Mom, you promised. Not tonight. Besides, there's something else. Something way more pressing."

"I can hardly imagine what that might be."

"Eleanor offered me Landon's job."

Charlotte's eyebrows arched. "Of course she did."

"It's working for Eleanor, but it's a plush salary." Maddie waved a hand around the room. "Obviously."

"Obviously." Charlotte's tone had gone remarkably flat.

"Landon didn't have a life insurance policy, Mom. Our savings are nothing to write home about, and I have to support my kids somehow. Add to that I left work five years ago. The odds of me making anything close to what I was making then at anywhere else are nil."

"There's your work at the bakery. That should count for something."

"I work fifteen hours a week in a supermarket piping what amounts to powdered sugar and food coloring onto tasteless cakes and cupcakes. It won't count for anything."

"So, you're going to take the job then?" Charlotte didn't bother to hide her look of disappointment.

Maddie let out a long breath. All day she'd been telling herself that she was giving the offer honest consideration, but the "no" that rose up in her throat carried zero hesitation. The truth of it was that there was only one answer she could give Eleanor. "It would be nice not to have to sell the house right now, but I can't—I won't—work for her. I never would've gone to work for her in the first place. It'd be different if I was only working for Charles. Besides, the job would keep me away from the kids when they're most available in the years to come—in the evenings and much of the weekends."

"But you haven't given her an answer yet?"

"I told her I wanted to think about it. I guess I wanted to make sure I wasn't just being reactive, but I think I knew before I even started the car. Finding that condom helped, no doubt, but in the end, it's mostly about Eleanor. Landon hardly ever let her get under his skin. I wouldn't be that lucky. Besides, if I'm going back to work full time, I want to like what I do. I want to manage a kitchen and work as a pastry chef. Landon managed the front of the house—working with servers and customers," she added for the benefit of her mom, who didn't know restaurant lingo.

"Amen to liking what you do. It can't be underestimated what it does for the soul." Charlotte wriggled her fingers at Leo, enticing him to bat at them. "And you meant that about selling the house? You're ready to let it go?"

"It'd be nice to stay here a while longer for the twins' sakes. I can only bet their memories of Landon will fade faster if we leave, but I don't need a wealth advisor to tell me it'll be financial suicide to stick it out here for any longer than we have to."

"Emotional suicide would be more my concern given some of what Landon handed you."

Maddie couldn't disagree. "I figure if I can get it listed quickly, I can get a jump on the spring market." She dragged her fingers through her hair, making a mess of her curls. "In the midst of all of this, guess what my thoughts keep going back to?"

"I hope it's how your boat will rock so much less when you've gotten a bit more distance from Landon's stormy seas. Elsewhere the ocean really is quite calm."

"How his phone backed up automatically online,"

Maddie continued without comment. "I'm gonna try to figure out his password and go through whatever's there."

Charlotte blinked abruptly. "If he didn't share the contents of his phone with you in life, I'm certain he wouldn't want you to see them now that he's gone."

"Maybe so, but he *is* gone, and I want to know if he cheated."

Charlotte stared at her a beat or two in silence. "I suspect if you're honest with yourself, you'll find you already know."

Since it was better than releasing a fresh wave of tears, Maddie tossed back the cozy blanket and got up to pace the room. She suddenly had enough pent-up energy to win a shot-put competition. "There's this thing called proof that's quite helpful to most of us."

"Landon had his chance on this earth, Maddie. His ugly truth isn't going to give you the freedom you're craving. It's like you've been in a holding pen, waiting for someone to let you out, when all you've had to do is unlatch the gate."

Unlatch the gate. How was unlatching a gate going to pay the bills and put groceries on the table, or keep her from spending too much time away from the twins when they still needed her so much? "Do you have a suggestion, or are you sticking with homily tonight? Because honestly, I don't have the energy tonight, Mom."

"I do, actually."

Maddie paused in place, eyes on her mom.

"Move in with me. I knew there was a reason I bought a house that was three times bigger than I needed when I bought the place last year." Before Maddie could protest, Charlotte held up a finger. "Don't say no so fast. You'd have your space. You and the twins could have the bedrooms on the middle floor. I'd move up to the top floor."

Maddie began pacing again. It wasn't that she hadn't thought about moving in with her mom—she had. She'd even made a mental checklist of pros and cons, and she'd come out about even every time. "You mean you'll move up to the floor you were about to rent out but are holding off on until you can fix the leaky roof? You'll move to *that* floor?" The first time it rained, Charlotte would be prodding her in the middle of the night and telling her to move over, and before Maddie knew it, they'd be sharing a bed again just like they had all Maddie's life until she was a few weeks shy of fifteen and had chosen the couch instead of co-sleeping with her mom any longer.

"It's hardly leaking," Charlotte said with a shrug.

After searching for the better part of a year for something with just the right energy, Charlotte had bought her very first home a year ago, and Maddie had been immensely proud of her. Charlotte had dropped out of high school and left home at seventeen. She'd put herself through nursing school while raising a toddler and working odd jobs to make ends meet. While Charlotte could be a touch exasperating, Maddie still loved her ferociously.

The house Charlotte had finally landed on was built in the early 1900s in the sought-after Shaw neighborhood of St. Louis City, three blocks from the Missouri Botanical Garden and populated with two- and three-story brick homes shaded by towering trees whose roots pushed up the sidewalk in spots, but she'd gotten the house for a steal for a reason. It needed savings-draining repairs like tuck-pointing, plaster repair, and electrical work—all things Charlotte didn't have the money to fix.

The truth of it was that there'd be enough space for the four of them without Charlotte relocating to the top floor so long as Hazel and Benji went back to sharing a room.

Maddie's biggest hesitation was that by moving in with her mom, she'd be trading one impulsive, fly-by-the-seat-of-their-pants roommate for a different one. While Charlotte and Landon were two very different personalities, Charlotte did things like drive halfway across the country for a rare gem show when she hardly had the extra funds to get there, let alone buy new crystals to add to her collection, or she'd switch from being vegan one month and throwing out refined sugar because it was made using bone char before staunchly adhering to a high-protein diet the next. Unsurprisingly, that latter one hadn't lasted long, and she was back to being a vegan again.

And she'd be testing Maddie's boundaries. Constantly. Best not to forget that.

Maddie stopped pacing again. She'd also be a warm, loving body in the house should Maddie run out of eggs and need to run to the grocery store ten minutes before bathtime or a second pair of arms for the twins to run to for support when they were running in circles and smacked foreheads. And countless other things, too. Added to that, Maddie's rent money could help Charlotte knock off some of the essential home repair items she'd have a hard time getting to otherwise. While it might not be a win-win to boast about, it would be a win-win all the same. Besides, after life with Landon, Maddie would be going in a bit more versed in maintaining healthy boundaries—theoretically, at least. "Have you thought about what you'd want for rent?"

Charlotte shrugged like money didn't matter even though most months she drained her bank account to next to nothing to get the bills paid. "We could work that out later."

"I'd want to work it out beforehand. Budgeting works for me, Mom."

"Of course, but this isn't about me profiting off my daughter. It's me giving you the space to get back on your feet."

"It'd be temporary. Six months. A year, maybe."

"It can be as long as you need...or as short. And you know as well as I do, the kids love it there."

Charlotte's words triggered a memory of Hazel and Benji seeing the house for the first time. The street had been crowded with parked cars, and Maddie had parked half a block down while Charlotte had walked down to meet them. On the walk to the house, Hazel had tripped but Benji had kept going and dashed up the porch steps of the correct red brick house in a sea of them that looked the same.

"How'd you know this was the right one?" Maddie had asked when they caught up.

"'Cuz this one feels like home," Benji had replied, tugging on the big wooden door.

Tiny goosebumps popped up along Maddie's arms at the memory. *Dear God, you're getting to be just like Charlotte, reading into things that have no meaning.*

She knew exactly the sort of thing her mom would say if she reminded her of it, which was why Maddie didn't say a word. Even so, she longed to know if her mom remembered it.

On the floor, Charlotte was silent, waiting for a response.

"I appreciate it," Maddie said once she'd collected herself. "I really do. But I'd like a day or two to think about it. It's a lot to process, you know, everything hitting at once."

Charlotte nodded. "Of course. Take your time. Be certain. I wouldn't want to see you stepping out of that pen any other way."

CHAPTER 8

I t might be pushing it to get the twins to bed on time, but Maddie ambitiously committed to straightening and decluttering her and Landon's master bedroom closet before bath time. Benji was planted on his bedroom floor, narrating an imaginary battle using every plane, train, ATV, car, LEGO figurine, and Storm Trooper he owned, while Hazel was stretched out on Maddie's bed, a nest of picture books surrounding her. Leo was sprawled on the bed alongside her, batting at her feet while she swung them in the air. The floppy-from-wear golden horns on the fuzzy unicorn slippers had his full attention. The cat needed a good ten minutes of rough housing and fetch, but everything fell on Maddie's shoulders now, and it was ten minutes she didn't have. Not with a house to get on the market.

In a whirlwind week, she'd officially turned down Eleanor's offer and had taken steps to get her house listed and get a jump on the spring market. After interviewing three realtors, Maddie had settled on the one who hadn't eyed the twins like they were noise-making miscreants while going through those lengthy sales presentations.

The kitchen calendar showed a daunting handful of days

until the house went live, and it first needed to be professionally photographed, thus inspiring Maddie's frenzied cleaning spree. It'd be easier if she wasn't back at Walter's Food Mart while the twins were in pre-K, but she needed to keep in good standing there until she found something better —another thing that would have to wait until after the move. Lord knew, she missed Landon stepping through the front door most afternoons during his slow time between lunch and dinner, calling out for his little minions, Leo included. Most days, he'd only hung around for an hour or so, but it had been time Maddie had to herself that she didn't have now.

While pulling a stack of Landon's sweaters from the top shelf for the donation pile, she unearthed a pill bottle and sent it free falling. After setting the sweaters on the floor, she picked it up. It was a prescription labeled sildenafil in a bottle with Landon's name and about half full. Maddie knew Landon's prescriptions by heart; she'd picked them up from the drugstore every month. This wasn't one of them.

Bottle in hand, she headed for the bedroom and sank onto the edge of the bed after sliding one of Hazel's books out of the way. She reached for her phone on the nightstand, tension knotting in her muscles. Ignoring a text from Noel, she pulled up the internet and typed in the name of the drug. Held her breath as the search results pulled up.

Viagra.

Maddie stared at the phone as if doing so long enough might link sildenafil to something else entirely. On a second glance at the bottle, the small print directions confirmed her search results.

Landon had hidden a half-full bottle of generic Viagra in their closet.

Wouldn't he have told her if he'd needed it? Wouldn't she have known?

Like you knew about the condom wrapper?

In the wake of a clean report at her OB/GYN and not being able to get into Landon's iCloud backup, Maddie had left the mystery of the ownership of the condom simmering on the backburner to focus on the house.

"Mommy, what does this page say?" Hazel pointed to her book without looking up.

Numbly, Maddie leaned over to see. It was a Halloween book that was open to a page with a skeleton hanging in a tree in a field of pumpkins. Underneath it, two little kids were pulling a wagon across the field.

Of course she's looking at books with skeletons in them now. Of course she is. It was late March. She would've needed to dig the book out from the back of the closet.

What made Maddie think she could do any of this right? She was stretched too thin. Getting the house ready for market. Helping the kids through their grief. Earning a living and providing for them. Handling whatever the hell it was Landon had been doing. Or who.

She cleared her overly dry throat. "It says that the wind makes the skeleton look and sound like it's dancing." The energy she'd had earlier was draining as fast as a bag of melting ice with a hole in it. "Hazie, you remember that's just a pretend skeleton in the story, don't you? People like to read about skeletons and jack-o'-lanterns when it's Halloween the same way they do about elves and reindeer around Christmas."

"I know. I just don't remember what it says. Will you read it to me?"

Maddie bit her lip to keep from spouting off an instant no. "Can you wait three minutes? I need to check something first."

"Okay, three minutes."

Maddie squeezed her daughter's shoulder before heading into the study where Landon's autopsy report was tucked under a pile of mail that grew taller every day. She'd requested it when trying to make sense of Landon's death, hoping somehow it might answer some the questions swirling in her head.

With hands shaking so wildly it was a challenge to separate the pages, Maddie fumbled past the clinical history and a breakdown of the findings upon examination of Landon's organs, body cavities, and cranium that made her stomach curdle. Stopping at the toxicology panel, she skimmed through the daunting and half gibberish text. Sildenafil wasn't on the list of positive substances—so, he wasn't hard while biking, go figure. But something else stood out that hadn't the one and only time she'd first glanced at the report: traces of cocaine and cannabinoids.

She'd known about Landon's occasional pot smoking. He'd kept an emergency stash in the garage for nights when he couldn't calm his racing mind. The cocaine use was another thing. She'd caught him using it twice in their first couple years of marriage, and the fallout had upended their world enough that each time he'd sworn it was his last. The later instance led to his agreeing to see a doctor about his mood swings—the first of a string of appointments that resulted in his bipolar diagnosis and him starting medication. After trying a few different prescriptions that had adverse side effects, Landon found that lamotrigine worked well for him.

Maddie scanned the list of substances again. Lamotrigine —the prescription she picked up from the pharmacy without fail each month—didn't show up anywhere. Abandoning the report, she hightailed it through her bedroom into the master bath.

"This feels like more than three minutes," Hazel said without looking up.

"Almost done, promise."

The master bathroom had separate sinks, medicine cabinets, and mirrors. Maddie hardly touched Landon's side unless it was while running a sponge over the granite countertop. She'd trusted him to take his medicine. How many times in that first year had he praised it for helping him stay grounded?

Sifting through his medicine cabinet, she found a partially full bottle of it on the top shelf. Her stomach flipped to spy the fill date on the bottle: September 17th. He'd died on February 23rd. Sinking to her knees, she rummaged through the cabinet below the sink, her stomach curdling to find a handful of unopened prescription bags shoved behind new and partially used bottles of mouthwash, shaving creams, and deodorants. They were so poorly hidden it was almost as if he'd been hoping she'd find them. Had he been?

Tears flooded her eyes. "Screw you, Landon. Screw you for all of this." How could she both hate him so much and be rocked with such deep sorrow at the same time?

She squatted there, frozen in indecision, until Hazel called her again. Finally, she headed on shaky legs to her bed. Down the hall, through the open doors, Benji was making *vrooming* sounds as his toys clanked together.

She read Hazel the book without processing a single word. The next hour was a blur as she oversaw bath time and tucked them into bed. As soon as they were dozing, she grabbed her phone and headed downstairs. The first thing she did was open a bottle of wine, a California red blend that would go down easily.

She'd never been much of a drinker but had become even less so in the throes of motherhood. Tonight though, she drank a full glass without setting it down once, wincing from the bitter aftertaste. Leaning over the counter, the granite cool against her elbows, she squeezed her thumb and forefinger tightly against her temple and forehead.

A thousand unspoken declarations raced through her. She needed to talk to someone about this, or she'd lose it. She pulled up Saanvi's number and held her breath as it rang a handful of times before Saanvi's voicemail message came on.

"You can't seriously expect this chocolatier to pick up when there're so many delicious things to make, can you?"

Her voicemail was full and couldn't take any messages, but Saanvi would call back when she spotted the missed call. She always did. But when would that be? Maddie needed her right now.

She considered calling her mother, but she wasn't ready to cry.

She scrolled through recent calls with her left hand as she poured a second glass of wine with her right. She didn't bother pretending it was an accident when she clicked on Noel's number. Odds were he wasn't going to answer anyway, not at a quarter to nine on a Friday night.

"Hey Maddie, how goes it?" He answered by the third ring, the sound of his voice as comforting as it was painful.

She set the bottle on the counter and closed her eyes. Leo had followed her downstairs and was rubbing against her legs and purring.

What was she doing calling Noel? She'd poured out her heart once, and it hadn't been enough.

"Maddie, you there?"

It was too humiliating, admitting that it turned out she'd not been enough for Landon, either. She moved the phone away from her ear, and her thumb hovered over the End button.

"Hey, I'll try calling you back."

"I can hear you." It was out before she could pull it back. She put the phone on speaker in hopes that not having it against her ear would feel less intimate.

"Oh." This wasn't awkward at all—*not*. "How are things?"

"Things are fine. It's just... Did you know he'd stopped taking lamotrigine?"

A few seconds passed before he answered. "No. How do you know?"

"His autopsy report. It wasn't listed in the toxicology

panel. And I found several months' worth shoved under his bathroom cabinet."

"Sheesh. I'm sorry, Maddie. Though that explains a few things, maybe."

"You think?" It was a poor attempt at humor, and the words came out sounding hollow. Maddie's thoughts flashed to the abandoned bike helmet. So many other things, too. *How* had she not put it together sooner? The truth was this was around the time she'd started checking out of her marriage.

She could hear snippets of laughter in the background. She wondered what Noel was out doing tonight. Who he was doing it with. Her stomach pitched from the thought or the rapid influx of wine. Or both.

"There's something else." She was emboldened by the soft buzz from the wine coursing through her. "Traces of cocaine showed up. I guess he wasn't high when he died, but it was in his system. And that's not all." With her throat locking up, she took another swallow of wine. She could hear the hint of a buzz in her words. "I think he was having an affair."

She'd not told Noel about the condom. What was the benefit of telling him this?

Silence again. "Why do you say that?"

"I found a bottle of Viagra in the closet. As far as I know, he had no reason to use it other than to abuse it recreationally." She closed her eyes and shook her head. Hadn't that been humiliating enough? But if anyone knew the truth, Noel might, so she plunged ahead. "And I found a condom wrapper in the backseat of his car. If you remember, I had a partial hysterectomy when the twins were born."

If you remember. Landon's first call after the c-section when the bleeding wouldn't stop had been to Noel. That kind of panicked call couldn't be easy to forget.

"Oh, Maddie. I'm sorry. I wish to hell you weren't dealing with this."

There was more laughter in the background and the tinkling of a bell, then footsteps. Was he leaving a bar? It grew quiet enough that she could hear his light breathing as he walked. "Are you alone?" Concern lined his tone. "I'm guessing the twins are asleep."

"They're asleep, yeah."

"Want me to come over and sit with you?"

"No!" She shook her head. "Definitely no."

A silence fell that suggested he'd stopped moving. "What about your mom then?"

"I'm fine."

"Everybody needs somebody sometime, Maddie."

Her skin seemed to be lined with thorns, only they pointed inward instead of outward. A dozen retorts burned her throat, wanting to work their way out, but in the back of her mind, a quiet voice reminded her that Landon's infidelity wasn't Noel's fault.

"You just found out your husband might've been cheating on you," he added. "With all you're already dealing with, my bet is this is that time."

The last reserves of her energy drained at the sincerity in his tone. She stepped back a foot the as if he was right in front of her.

Dissatisfied with the lack of attention he was getting from rubbing against her legs, Leo popped up onto the counter, nearly knocking over the bottle of wine before Maddie grabbed it midfall. Hoisting him into her arms, she replanted him on the floor with a stern "No, Leo!" before answering Noel. "Thank you, but what I need more than anything right now is a good night's sleep."

"Okay. And I bet you do," he said, after a pause. "Maddie, trust me on this, it wasn't you. It was *never* you. You and the twins brought out the best in him. It just wasn't enough. Whatever Landon was up to, it was his failing, not yours."

His tone was gentle, but Noels words were making a large cut even deeper. "Tell me the truth. Did you know?" It was out before she considered the consequences of knowing the answer, considered how badly it would hurt if his reply was anything but an emphatic no.

As soon as the words left her lips, she knew his answer. Landon had been terrible at keeping secrets, and Noel had been his oldest friend.

The knife set in as silence slammed against her ear. The connection was quiet enough to hear a gentle breeze sweeping over Noel's receiver. "Actually, that's answer enough."

She hung up and dropped the phone on the counter like it was as hot as lava. Sinking to the floor, she doubled over, tears racking her body. Leo pressed in, nuzzling his way through her hair to lick her ear.

On the counter, the phone began to hum with a new call, and then a second one when the first one wasn't answered.

Maddie's tears turned into full body sobs, and she pulled Leo close, his thick, fluffy fur and big body serving as a pillow until he'd had enough and slipped out from the embrace. He hopped onto her back and began grooming himself, and something about it turned her tears into soft laughter. She dried her cheeks and rested her head against the tile floor, the cool seeping in through the skin of her cheek, temple, and palms, calming her as the buzz began to wane.

Leo used the opportunity to make himself comfortable, stretching out the length of her spine, his deep thrumming purr resonating through her body.

On the counter, her phone buzzed with a third call, then a text. After a few minutes, she pushed up slowly until Leo hopped to the floor.

Finishing off the bottle might take away the pain that the tears hadn't shed, but that would come with a price, too.

She'd wake up with a mother of hangovers and have a monster of a time making it through the day tomorrow.

No, the right thing to do was to lose herself in a giant pile of blankets, and if she was very lucky, the world would fall away.

Sweeping Leo off the floor, she draped him over her shoulder, dumped out the rest of the wine in her glass, and filled it with water. "If you want to sleep on Landon's pillow again tonight, I won't shoo you off, Leo, promise. It's time we start claiming some space for ourselves."

She headed upstairs, leaving her phone on the counter even as it began vibrating one more time.

CHAPTER 9

NOEL

After killing the ignition, Noel stared at the stately tutor-style house, and an itch blossomed over his skin, tempting him to slip his Jeep into Reverse and head out before Maddie noticed. God help him, all the effort he'd put in, the distance he'd imposed, and he still loved her.

Last night, he'd been quick to take off from the bar downtown where he'd been hanging out with an old friend, but by the time he'd gotten here, hoping she might be more willing to answer his knock than his return calls, the house had been entirely dark. It hadn't been his place to wake her up and beg for forgiveness for not knowing where the imperfect boundaries of his loyalty lay, either.

Now that she'd had the chance to sleep on it, he was back for another shot, but showing up here loaded down with doughnuts and hot coffees at eight thirty in the morning was kicking every lingering doubt into overdrive. Landon might as well be sitting in his empty passenger seat, giving him a look that conveyed, *So you think you can just pick up where I left off?*

"Not even close," Noel answered the ghost of his best

friend. As much as he wished otherwise, he could no longer envision a scenario where he and Maddie ended up together. Had it ever been in the cards, that time had come and gone. "I'm here to help mop up another one of your messes."

He'd have texted Maddie that he was coming, but after last night, she'd have only shot him down. She wasn't a pro at asking for help even when she wasn't furious with him. Remembering the two small humans inside the house whom he loved and who needed him roused his courage to get out and ring the bell.

Box of doughnuts in one hand and coffees in the other, he headed up the walkway. Clearing his throat, Noel rang the bell with the pointer knuckle of the hand holding the two-cup coffee carrier. Through the side glass windows, he spotted the twins playing on the living room floor at the same time they spotted him.

"Uncle Noel! Uncle Noel!"

Despite his reservations, Noel's heart lightened to spy their unencumbered joy. He heard Maddie in the distance calling for them to wait, but they were already on their feet and running for the door. As soon as it cracked open, the house alarm began its countdown. Ignoring it, Hazel and Benji ushered him in, bursting with exclamations of delight.

"Are these for us?" Hazel asked as Benji attempted to peek under the lid. They still had bedheads and were in pajamas. Benji's curls were flattened on the right side of his head while a handful of Hazel's fine strands were standing on end from electricity.

"You made it through your first full week back to school, didn't you?" The excitement on their faces brought a laugh to his throat. "Doughnuts and first weeks back to school go together. At least they did when your dad and I were young."

"Mommy's making popovers!" Hazel said, jumping in place. "Popovers *and* doughnuts can be me and Benji's first week of school thing!"

Benji collapsed dramatically to the floor with a solid enough thump that Noel winced.

Just then, Maddie stepped around the corner from the kitchen, heading for the alarm keypad. When the beeping stopped, Noel braced himself to be ushered right out the door, but all she said was "Hey" as she kept her gaze trained on the kids. She swept her long, tight curls into a half knot like she was worried about her own case of bed head.

"Morning." While planning this early morning intrusion into her home, Noel hadn't thought about her still being in pajamas. "I'd have waited for a return call, but I found out yesterday afternoon that I'm heading out for another stint in Chile. Some problems on site and all. You keep saying you've got everything under control here, but getting a house listed isn't easy. I'd like to help while I can."

"Help with what?" Benji tugged on his sleeve after getting up from the floor.

"With anything your mom needs. Changing light bulbs, touching up paint, yardwork, whatever."

"Can't you play with us instead?"

"I'm hoping I can take turns doing both." As Hazel squeezed behind him and shut and locked the door, Noel raised the cardboard drink carrier in Maddie's direction as a peace offering. "I brought coffee, too. As for the doughnuts, I remember reading in the godparent instruction book that such sugar-laden home intrusions are the godparent's guilt-free rite of passage at such times."

A laugh escaped Maddie. It was short, but it was an honest-to-God laugh. Her smile lingered a few seconds, lighting up her eyes and sending a jolt straight through him. No, he'd never be over her.

The first time he'd laid eyes on her had been in front of the bathrooms at the Row House. She'd been coming out of hers and he'd been going into his, and they'd each stepped in the same direction, nearly colliding. She'd been all curls and slender curves with a smile that lit the room, but it was her warm laugh that had stayed with him long after he was back at the bar where he'd been waiting on Landon.

Noel had never wanted to meet anyone more. The black jeans, black shoes, and plain white Oxford identified her as a member of the kitchen staff. While he hadn't remembered her name, he'd assumed from that hair of hers she was the new hire Landon had told him about. Landon's mom had been at his dad something terrible for hiring the new pastry chef without her input, and somewhere in Landon's relaying of this to him, he'd mentioned the curly hair.

Maddie had taken off her chef coat and was sitting at an empty booth in the corner flipping through a three-ring binder and writing notes on a legal pad. His first thought was that he'd ask Landon to introduce them, but then Landon texted that he was stuck at one of the other restaurants due to a couple of staff not showing up for their shifts.

She'd not been sitting in that bar to socialize, and the right words had never come easily for him. But he'd wanted to meet her badly enough that he'd gotten over himself and gone over there. Given that she ended up marrying his best friend, the twelve hours that followed were etched into him the same as the various faded scars from childhood and were hours he hardly allowed himself to think about.

Probably it had to do with him invading her home like this, but memory of that night rose up like he'd brushed his fingers over the most familiar of those scars, and he might as well have been standing in the Row House bar again, talking to her for the first time.

She stopped writing and looked up just as he reached her, and words fled. This time, it was her eyes that had him speechless. Not so much the color—blue gray, he thought, but wasn't sure in this lighting—or the long lashes and sculpted brows. It was that looking into them made him feel like he was stepping inside to a warm fire after a long walk in the bitter cold.

When he just stood there like an idiot, she shook her head, laughing. "Well, I know you're not about to ask me where the bathroom is."

"No, I'm not," he said, his words an exhale of relief. "But given that you're all anyone around here's talking about lately, I'm considering skipping dinner and going straight for dessert. Only I want to see what you recommend."

She sat back against the booth. "I wouldn't advise skipping dinner unless you're part hobbit, and you've already had your first one. Otherwise, all that sugar will be a shock to the system, and you'll walk away unfairly judging my desserts."

"Oh, I wouldn't do that. And with hobbits, there's never a second dinner, just dinner, then supper, and breakfast and second breakfast—and let's not forget, the few in the middle of the day, too."

She laughed. "J.R.R. Tolkien fan, I take it?"

"I think I finished my second read through of the *Lord of the Rings* series before my thirteenth birthday."

"Nice. I'm sorry to say I saw the Peter Jackson movies before I read the series. I never made it past *The Hobbit*, and I'm usually a book-before-movie person."

"Yeah, me too, but you're forgiven. Those movies were good, but you can't do books like that real justice in a movie."

"Mm. I felt that way about the Harry Potter books."

"Then you know what I'm talking about."

Just then, one of the servers Noel sometimes talked basketball with arrived with a platter of house-made sweet potato chips and cilantro lime dip, and Maddie flipped her binder closed to make room on the table. Under the binder's clear plastic cover was a color photocopy of one of the best-looking cupcakes he'd ever seen.

"'Sup, Noel?" Conner said. "How you been, bro?"

"Can't complain, man. How about you?"

After a bit of conversation, Conner headed back to the kitchen, leaving Noel standing there, hands in his pockets. Maddie's smile had a touch of shyness to it for the first time as she motioned to the platter in front of her. "Well, it's not true dinner, but it'll count for something. Help yourself. Besides, I can't make a dessert recommendation without having some idea of your taste preferences."

Noel nodded to the empty booth opposite her. "May I?"

Her cheeks blushed pink. "Yeah, sure. So, I'm still getting to know everyone, but I take it you either work here or used to."

"Neither, actually, but my best friend practically lives here, so I'm here quite a bit." After a pause, he added, "Landon."

"Landon Baxter?"

"The one and only."

She paused dipping a chip into the dip and straightened in her seat. "You might as well be a food critic then."

"Would a food critic tell you wings and beer were his typical go-to Friday night choices? That or pizza."

She clicked her tongue. "Good thing it's Thursday."

He took a chip, noticing her hands for the first time. Her nails were unpainted but otherwise manicured, and there was a feminine strength in her hands and fingers that hinted of a confidence in the kitchen that could turn out a cupcake as elegant and mouthwatering as the one on the front of her bulging binder. "Mind if I ask something personal?"

"I guess that depends how personal."

He nodded to the binder and notebook. "I noticed your lack of use of a laptop."

"And you think I'm old school?"

"I was going to go with unique."

"As I was growing up, my mom was pretty much anti electronic devices, and I guess it stuck. I have a laptop now obviously, but all my best recipes are in there," she said with a nod toward the binder.

"That's cool. May I?" He motioned to it.

Maddie fanned her face. "I don't even know your name, and you might as well be asking to look through my underwear drawer."

He couldn't help but laugh. "Noel Ward, and I'm sorry. I shouldn't have asked. You've just piqued my curiosity."

"Noel Ward," she repeated, testing the sound of it on her lips, and it was something he wanted to remember forever. "And go ahead. For real, it isn't that personal. But don't judge me for the fingerprint smudges please."

"No judgement here. Trust me." He opened the binder and flipped through the pages. Some were printed, some were handwritten, and others were pulled from an old cookbook. Those pages were most worn.

"*Baking with Julia*," she said. "Do you remember the show?"

"I never watched it, but I heard about it. Julia Child, right?"

"Yeah, it goes hand in hand with the lack of electronics, but we didn't have cable or home internet, either. PBS came in clear and sharp though. I'm pretty certain it's only because of that show and the things I learned to bake from watching it that I survived adolescence. Eclairs, French loaves, pies, tarts—you name it. By the time I'd entered high school, I think I'd tried everything. My mom gave me the book for Christmas when I was eleven or twelve, and halfway through pastry school, the binding gave out. That was the impetus for this."

"And here you are, head pastry chef at one of St. Louis's top restaurants, and I'm getting a first-hand look at your secret recipes."

"Yeah, well, you have a look about you that says you can be trusted." When he looked up from the binder, the table separating them seemed to diminish into nothing. Those eyes —he'd almost swear he'd been looking into them his whole life.

"Is that so? Well, thank you for that. I promise not to let you down."

And that was it. In less than five minutes, she'd inadvertently laid claim to his heart in a way no one else had before—ever. The rest of the night went like that, like they were the oldest of friends but discovering one another for the first time.

"What's a godparent instruction book?" Hazel sidled up close to him, attempting to cut off Benji, and jolting Noel back into the present that was Maddie's kitchen from a life she'd shared with his best friend. "Can you read it to us?"

Benji snaked to Noel's other side. "Does it tell you how to put us to bed?"

It was easy to forget how literal little kids could be. "I was making a joke with your mom. If there is a godparent instruction book, I've not read it, but should I ever need to put you to bed, I'm trusting she'll tell me everything I need to know."

"Oh." Hazel sounded disappointed, like the idea of a godparent instruction book had promised to be as exciting as the arrival of the tooth fairy.

Claiming she needed a moment, Maddie jogged up the stairs. "And no doughnuts until the popovers are ready, you two," she warned over her shoulder. Noel breathed a sigh of relief. He wasn't about to get kicked out, thank God. He was counting on this chance to make it right with her before heading out of town again.

Benji locked both hands over his belly and gave Noel a pained look. "My stomach's so hungry it may not let me wait to eat one of my doughnuts."

Noel chuckled. "Oh yeah? Well, how about we keep that stomach of yours busy for a few minutes and set the table?"

Benji groaned, but Hazel raced into the kitchen. She climbed onto the countertop with ease and raised onto her knees. "I'm getting the plates. Do you want *Paw Patrol* or one of my unicorn plates, Uncle Noel? Or one of the heavy plates my mom likes?"

Following her, Noel set the box of doughnuts and coffee carrier on the far side of the counter. "Surprise me," he said even though his bet was on getting a unicorn plate to match Hazel's.

When Maddie returned, she'd changed into a thin hoodie and yoga pants that hugged her hips and thighs in a way that stirred Noel viscerally, reminding him why he'd accepted so many overseas jobs the last several years. While she'd never been out of his mind, out of sight had proven to be the less painful option.

He handed her the coffee he'd ordered for her—a latte— before jutting his thumb toward the oven. "Those smell great. Way better than doughnuts."

"Thanks." Maddie cautiously lifted off the lid. A sprinkle of lavender buds still floated atop the thick white foam. She took a whiff and closed her eyes. "That smell, I swear. Vanilla lavender lattes make me weak in the knees."

He gave a little nod as he folded the linen napkins he'd found and set them by the plates Hazel had doled out around the table. "I remember you saying they were your favorite."

She blinked a few times. Was she trying to remember when she'd said that—their one shared night together or some random time since? In this case, it had been at the twins' second birthday party. "Would you like yours reheated?" she asked, not going there. "Mine's plenty hot."

"Nah, I'm good." While Maddie was a latte fan, Noel had grown accustomed to drinking his coffee black. With as much traveling as he did, the only creamer he'd been able to count on came in packets, and he'd never been able to tolerate the stuff.

At the counter, Benji shoved a hand under the lid of the doughnuts before pulling it out and licking the tip of his finger. "My stomach's *so* hungry. I don't think it can wait any more."

Maddie pressed her lips together. Aside from the hint of dark circles under her eyes, she didn't look like a woman who'd so recently realized her husband was cheating—late husband, that was. Of course, he realized painfully, being married to Landon these last several years had probably given her an unusual resilience. "I'll tell you what. You two run up and get dressed, and by the time you come down—fully dressed—if the popovers aren't ready, you can start eating a doughnut."

Hazel seemed ready to negotiate this, but when her brother took off at a dash for the stairs, she changed her mind and ran after him.

In the silence that followed, Noel dragged a hand through his hair. Was this really the first time in six years he and Maddie were alone in a room together? It felt like it.

Maybe Maddie was thinking the same thing because she turned her back to him and pulled down four short glasses from one of the cabinets. "Milk or water?"

"Water's fine."

She nodded and headed for the fridge, pulling out a pitcher of chilled water and milk from a local dairy that delivered. "So, Chile again?"

"Yeah." Noel's employer was based in Cincinnati, and when he wasn't on a jobsite, he worked remotely. "I'm hoping not to be gone long. A few weeks, three at most. I meant it when I said I'd help you move. You don't need to spend money on movers. I'll rent a truck. I'm sure my buddies from school will help." A stricken look flashed across her face and vanished so fast, Noel wondered if he'd imagined it.

"If you're sure. That's a big commitment."

"I'm sure."

"Okay. But I won't hold you to it if it doesn't work out timing wise."

"I'll make sure it does."

Whether they talked about last night or not, they were one step closer to a conversation Noel would go to the ends of the earth to avoid having. He turned toward the window that faced the backyard and stared at the thick buds on the dogwood tree, his throat locking. When Maddie learned what he'd unwittingly been made privy to, it would undoubtedly hurt her, etching away at his efforts this last month to bridge the distance between them.

He'd made it a habit of texting her daily, even when finding things to say was like pulling teeth. He'd never exactly been gifted at conversation, but this was torture. Still, he needed her to know he'd be here for her. He didn't think it was his imagination that she'd opened up to him a bit, too. Before last night, anyway. Earlier in the week, she even initiated a series of texts, telling him about the decision to move to her mom's after turning down Eleanor's offer to take over Landon's position in the family restaurants. He didn't want to lose footing now.

"When do you leave?" she asked as she poured two glasses of water, leaving the other two for milk.

"Tomorrow, late afternoon. Till then, I'm yours."

She glanced up just long enough to overpour the second glass of water, and he headed for a towel. "That's soon."

"Yeah. Things on the site are going south."

"So south you'll go."

While Maddie's play on words was an attempt to bring a bit of levity to the conversation, Noel knew this was as good a time as any to address the elephant in the room. "About last night. I'm sorry."

She shook her head abruptly before reaching for the bottle of milk. "He was your best friend. I get it. I just don't want to talk about it."

"Maddie, you—"

She held up a hand. "With everything going on, I have just enough energy to make it through the day without focusing on whatever it was that Landon was doing. But if you really don't have anything better to do today, there are a few things I could use help with."

Noel watched her for a second or two before answering. "I'm here till you kick me out. Anything you need. As for the other stuff, if you change your mind, I'll be ready to talk. Last night…I could've done better. I'm sorry about that."

Clearing her throat, Maddie returned the bottle of milk to the fridge. "One of the preschool moms is having the twins over for a playdate this afternoon, but you helping to entertain them till then would be nice."

"Yeah, for sure, but Maddie, seriously, put me to work. I've got the twins, too."

Her shoulders relaxed as the conversation veered from talk of Landon. "There are a few things I haven't been able to get to. The gutter on the far side of the garage is clogged. I haven't wanted to get on a ladder without another adult here. And I picked up a drywall patch for a hole in Benji's drywall from some overly raucous play a couple months ago. I was going to try to fix it myself, but given how you're a pro at rehabbing…"

"Consider it done."

She paused long enough that Noel suspected what was coming next carried a different energy. "There's Landon's computer, too, if you've got time."

"Something with it giving you trouble?"

"It's his passwords. I've poked around a bit trying to find them and haven't had any luck. Considering how good you are with computers, maybe you'll figure out a way in that I haven't."

Oh, Maddie, I doubt you want me doing that. "That's often as much luck as it is skill, but passwords for what?"

"His personal checking account for one. If you can't get in, I'll make an appointment at his bank now that I've got his death certificate." Her cheeks flushing, she added, "I'd also like to get into the online backup from his phone."

It was Noel's turn to drop her gaze. This last month, he'd been tormented by how much to tell her—tormented by whether it was his place to do so—and that was *before* he knew about the Viagra and the condom wrapper in Landon's car pointing to a more recent infidelity than the one he'd unwittingly been made privy to.

Even so, if Maddie got access to the contents of her late husband's phone that was buried in the leaves somewhere on a bike trail forty-five minutes west of here, Noel suspected there'd be enough damning evidence there for her to figure things out for herself.

"I know I just said I don't want to talk about it today—and I don't—but not knowing what he was up to won't make it not have happened," she added into his silence like she could read his thoughts.

What Maddie didn't realize was that once some of these doors were opened, her world was going to be blown apart, and just because she was asking for his help didn't mean it was his right to tell her. Not feeling the way he did. Not when it would almost certainly help her fall *out* of love with Landon—or the memory of him, at least.

"I want to know what my husband was hiding, Noel."

Noel let out a long breath. "I get that. I'll see what I can do. How about I help with your projects and hang out with the kids this morning, then I'll hop on his computer when you take them to that playdate later?"

Maddie's cheeks instantly tinged pink, and he got it. Not having the kids in the house as a distraction would likely be a whole other level of awkward for her when she returned. She was saved from answering as Benji dashed down the stairs into the kitchen barefoot, in sweatpants, and wearing his t-shirt backwards.

"Finished!"

Noel chuckled. "Sometimes part way there is good enough, don't you think?"

Maddie herded Benji to the table, box of doughnuts in hand. "The struggle is real."

CHAPTER 10

s Noel headed upstairs, the hum of the garage door closing resounded through the main floor. With every step, the hopefulness that had filled his last several hours fell away to be replaced by dread, guilt, and regret. Leo was sticking with him, at least. The giant of a cat jaunted up the stairs, bottlebrush tail fluffed high.

The hair on Noel's arms stood on end as he stepped into Landon's home office. "Knock knock." Landon's essence was so thick in here, Noel half expected him to answer.

Books, framed photos, and trinkets filled the floor-to-ceiling custom bookshelf on one side of the room, a handful of which Noel remembered his buddy acquiring firsthand. A large hunk of bark with a scratching from a bear. A bobblehead hula dancer that had been gifted to the groomsmen at a bachelor party of a high school buddy a couple years ago. An unopened bottle of whiskey with a misprinted label that had become Landon's lucky bottle.

Noel spotted himself in one of the photos. He lifted the frame off the shelf, wiping away a thin layer of dust from the glass. Landon's radiant smile dug at a splinter lodged in his heart. It was taken nearly a decade ago while the two of them were mountain biking in Colorado before life had gotten so complicated.

"I always figured something was wrong with me, the way I couldn't loosen up like you." He shook his head, setting the picture back in place. "You tore down those slopes like there was no way anything might cause you to lose your balance, and that night you had damn near the whole crowd at the bar hanging on to your every word."

He crossed over to the desk and took a seat, the cool leather pressing against his thighs and back. A digital photo frame on one side of Landon's monitor kicked to life and began circling through images. Noel froze with his hand an inch above the mouse. The second photo was a close-up of Maddie. She was lying in bed in a patch of morning sun, a soft smile on her lips and an intimate glow in her gaze.

"I can't do this." The hair on the back of his neck pricked as if Landon were leaning over him impatiently, ready for him to get on with it and find what he was going to find.

Before entering the login Maddie had given him, Noel flipped the digital frame face down. Even though he didn't really believe in ghosts, talking to the one in here threatened to unleash the flood of things unspoken between them. "You should've been the one to tell her. It needed to come from you. But you went and died, and now all anyone can do is miss you."

Leo bounded onto the desk then walked along the thin strip between the keyboard and edge of the desk like a tightrope, stepping over Noel's wrists. He curled up in the space next to the face-down digital frame and stretched out one paw so that rested atop Noel's hand. "Is this moral support, or are you taunting me? You were his cat. I haven't forgotten."

With a deep, thrumming purr, Leo blinked at Noel.

After a couple minutes of searching, Noel found that most of Landon's files weren't password protected. If his buddy had kept a document for his logins and passwords, Noel wasn't locating it. But what he hadn't shared with Maddie earlier was that he'd already broken one of Landon's passwords this month—one to Landon's Instagram account. As much as he'd hated doing it, snooping into Landon's private messages had cemented Noel's biggest worry into reality.

"You never minded getting your fingers dirty with other people's messes, but when it came to your own, you checked out entirely."

On a hunch, Noel tried Landon's Instagram password. !HazBen20. As erratic as Landon's behavior had been at times, some things about him had been entirely predictable. Even so, Noel sucked in a surprised and slightly terrified breath as Landon's Cloud backup began to open. "Nobody puts exclamation points at the beginning of passwords," Landon told him awhile back. "They always stick them at the end."

Noel's body went rigid as it loaded. Gazing at the private moments his best friend had captured in his life with Maddie was anywhere but at the top of his to-do list. Despite the inner warning not to, Noel opened the folder containing Landon's three thousand plus photos. The most recent one was a playful close-up of Hazel, eyes wide, cheeks ruddy from the cold, and tongue curled, nearly touching the tip of her nose. It was dated the day before the accident.

After a steadying breath, Noel scrolled through a hundred or so photos. Most were of the kids and Maddie and tore at his insides to view. Various plated dinners taken at the Baxter restaurants, sunsets, selfies, and a random car accident filled the screen as did more artistic shots of buildings, leaves, bare branches, concrete stairs at a park, and a swing set.

Noel's index finger froze as he spotted an image of a baby. For close to a minute, he stared at it the way people stared at the accidents they passed on the highway, not really wanting to see but not able to look away.

The baby was Landon's, no question. Noel had never thought babies looked like much else but babies, but these photos left zero doubt of the shared DNA between the tiny, frail human and his late friend. It was there in the shape of the eyes and face. For the last few months, Noel had been clinging to the hope that the girl had been wrong about her paternity claim, and Maddie would never have to deal with this.

A glance at the date showed the pictures were taken six weeks ago when the baby was nearly two months old. They also showed that Landon had been inside the mother's home. He'd held the baby in his arms and had snapped half a dozen intimate close-ups while doing so. The baby's small hands were curled into fists, and he was looking at the camera—or at his father—with the wide-eyed wonder of a newborn.

Noel's stomach flipped unsteadily at the realization that he was viewing a moment of intimacy between a father and son that might've been the only one they had. The boy would grow up not knowing his dad and, depending on what Maddie did with these when she found out, he might never be privy to this short, shared moment in time.

Leo had stretched out onto his side and was staring at the monitor with what seemed like interest, still purring, still blinking contentedly. That was the thing about cats. You couldn't tell what they were thinking, which was why Noel had always been a dog person.

He got up and paced the room. She needed to know, no question. And whether or not he liked it, he would have to be the one to tell her—and he'd be found guilty by association no matter what he said. He might as well just get it over with. But wouldn't it be better to wait until he was back in St. Louis again in a couple weeks? She was dealing with so much already. If he told her now, he wouldn't even be here to help in the aftermath.

Yet if he waited, would she forgive him?

Noel was at an impasse. Words from his and Landon's final conversation—a phone call—burned his ears like it took place minutes rather than months ago. Landon had jumped right into the thick of what he wanted to share the way he did when he was unsettled and not thinking about the person on the receiving end. "I messed up. So bad. Now it's going to cost me for the next eighteen years."

Noel had been in Rio de Janeiro working with a contractor and had stepped out of a meeting to answer the call. "What do you mean eighteen years? What're you talking about?" Given how Maddie couldn't have any more kids, a child shouldn't have been what popped into his mind, but it was.

And he hadn't been wrong.

Landon had—by his own account—slept with one of the hostesses who'd been working for the Baxters and now she was pregnant. He'd claimed it had only happened once, and the sincerity in his tone had made Noel believe him. Given how the baby's mother hadn't even been twenty-one at the time, Noel couldn't imagine Landon getting into a long-term relationship with her.

While this would invariably drop another bomb on Maddie, it would still leave big holes as to what—or who— her husband had been doing in light of the Viagra and the condom wrapper find.

Noel's vision had gone white with fury. "What were you thinking?"

"I *wasn't* thinking. It's never until the adrenaline wears down that I start to reason."

Noel hadn't responded to that. It was a conversation for another time. Landon had cheated, and things were about to get mighty complicated. "The timing," Noel had asked, "does it work out?"

"I guess it's not impossible, but seriously, it could be anybody's kid."

"Not quite anybody's."

Landon had opted not to acknowledge the accusation in Noel's voice. "This chick—she says it's not about money, but she knows my parents are loaded."

"And?"

"If she keeps it, she's going to want support. More support than I can give her."

"Have you told Maddie?"

"No, and I'm not going to. Not until the mom decides what she's doing with the kid, and I get a paternity test."

"So, you're telling me this because you'd like moral support on not telling Maddie that you cheated on her until you know whether or not you *have* to tell her?"

There'd been an edge to Landon's next words. "I'm calling because this girl can't decide any longer if she should give up the kid to some couple she met last week. She's due in a few weeks, and she wants to know if I want dibs."

"*On the baby?*" The building where Noel had been working had a view of the towering Corcovado Mountain. As everything Landon unloaded sank in, Noel stood at a window staring at the statue of Christ the Redeemer at the mountain's peak, watching tourists far enough away they looked like ants trekking up the stone stairs toward the statue's base.

"Yeah, on the baby."

Dibs. On a human life. He'd understood the deeper reason Landon was calling then. There'd been a big age difference between Landon and his older sisters, big enough that most of his childhood memories were lonely ones. Landon had always wanted a big family, and Maddie couldn't have more kids. "What're you going to do?"

"I don't know what to do. If I tell Maddie I cheated, it's over. I'm sure of it. It hasn't been easy raising twins."

Noel's heavy silence likely made as strong a point as the words that followed. "Maybe it needs to be over."

The tension in Landon's reply was sharper than anything that had passed between them in years. "You'd like that, wouldn't you? Thanks for the help, buddy."

It was the last time they'd spoken, although they'd texted a handful of times in the weeks afterward. Noel had decided he owed it to Maddie to make it his business if Landon didn't fess up once the baby was born and the paternity was confirmed.

And then the unthinkable happened.

Those first days after Landon's death, Noel wanted to forget the phone call altogether, wanted to box up the memory and shove it away in a dark closet corner much like the letter from Maddie that had crushed him so deeply six years ago.

The hum of the garage door sent a burst of panicked adrenaline through him. He hurried to the computer, shut down the open apps, and signed out. Maddie wasn't supposed to be back yet. She had a grocery list and had intended to run by the store before coming here, but the wailing of small lungs reached Noel's ears even before the door to the house flung open.

He jogged down the steps as Hazel rushed in, crying louder than he'd ever heard her, her face beet red and tear stained and with something unrecognizable on her shirt and pants that Noel suspected he didn't want to look at too closely. "What happened?"

Maddie stepped into the doorway behind her, fatigue lining her features. "Stop here so we can get your clothes off, honey." To Noel she added, "She threw up on the way over, and she's not one to get carsick, either, which means either something she ate wasn't sitting well, or it's the stomach flu. I'm hoping for the first, obviously."

"I bet. Sorry, Hazel. Did you drop Benji off then?"

"No, just in case it's a stomach bug. He wasn't happy about it though. He cried himself to sleep on the way home."

"Oh yeah? Want me to carry him in?"

Maddie shook her head. "Better to let him sleep out there for twenty minutes or so. If he wakes up, he won't go back to sleep, and he could use a short nap. Want to throw one of the couch blankets over him while I get Hazel in the shower?"

Noel was on it. "Yeah, sure, and I can run by the store to grab whatever was on your list, too."

As they crossed paths, Maddie squeezed his arm in thanks. Considering it was the first time in over six years that she'd touched him aside from the single tight hug they'd exchanged after Landon died, it was ironic how fast the still-familiar ache she'd created in him revved to life. Why hadn't she understood back then how well they fit? It would've saved her all this heartache, saved her from marrying a man who couldn't really love her, not struggling as he'd been.

But if she had, Hazel and Benji wouldn't be here.

It was like his father had said after an accident with a city bus nearly took his life and left him partially handicapped: there was no use attempting to swim in water that had already slipped downstream.

"Noel?" she said just before he stepped into the garage. "I was thinking on the drive home that we hold off on any more sleuthing until after I've got this move finished. I still want to know, but nothing's going to change if I wait a few weeks."

"I think that makes sense." Hopefully she didn't spy the way his shoulders dropped in relief. So, it wasn't on him to decide after all. He could wait until he got back, and when he told her, he intended to stay at her side. No matter how strong she was, she was going to need him.

CHAPTER 11
MADDIE

O f all the things Maddie needed to be giving her attention to right now, it wasn't the somber-eyed giant of a dog on the other side of the chain-link fence in her mom's backyard. She and the kids only had a short time here today. Inside, there were closets and rooms to measure and drawers and cabinets to scope out. While the square footage of the house was essentially the same as hers, Maddie didn't want to take up any more of her mom's house than necessary. Whatever couldn't fit into their two rooms, kitchen, or her mom's mostly empty sunroom would either be put into storage, sold, or donated.

But no matter how limited their time was here today, Maddie was mesmerized by the dog anyway. Her money was on it being a girl, and while she didn't know much about the breed, she suspected the big-boned, white fluffball was a Great Pyrenees. The giant dog watched them while stretched out in a strip of mud that likely hadn't seen a blade of grass in a while. Every few minutes, she barked in their direction, a single baritone woof that reverberated through Maddie's chest. Considering the state of the dog's backyard—thin, winter grass with wide patches of mud—it was surprising there was any white on her at all.

"Are you sure she's not a little polar bear, Mommy?" Hazel was on her knees beside her, her small fingers wrapped around links in the fence and her forehead pressed against it. Benji had lost interest and wandered back to the mulched landscaping alongside the patio where a colony of faded ceramic garden gnomes had been left behind by the elderly couple who'd previously owned the home. He'd been calling his sister over to play with him, but the standoffish dog was holding Hazel's interest the same as Maddie's.

Fishing her phone from the pocket of her fleece jacket, Maddie typed in Great Pyrenees and pulled up an image of one that was cleaner but otherwise identical to the dog next door. "It looks like she's a Great Pyrenees, baby." She offered the phone out for Hazel to see. "It says they were originally bred to help farmers protect their sheep."

Hazel looked from the phone to the dog, and her mouth turned down in a frown. Given how Hazel's two favorite animals were unicorns and polar bears, Maddie didn't blame her for being disappointed. "I'm gonna go play with Benji before he gets all the good gnomes," she said and ran toward the house.

Maddie sank onto the backs of her heels, flattened her palm against the fence, and whistled softly. "Come here, girl. I can tell you want to."

The big dog pumped her bushy tail but didn't move. Still squatting, Maddie took in the row of houses sandwiched together on this side of the alley and across it. They were double- or triple-story red-brick Victorians built nearly a century and a half ago, but the rest of the homes seemed in better condition than her mom's and the one next door. The brick of these two houses needed a good deal of tuckpointing, and the dilapidated deck next door needed more than just repainting. Charlotte had outbid a handful of developers on her house, ones who intended to flip it for resale, just like they'd want to do whenever the house next door went on the market. Around here, the houses that were better maintained had a handful of families bidding on them as soon as the listing went live, while the ones that needed more work mostly went to rehabbers.

Given her minimal savings and the fact that, prior to closing day on the house, Charlotte's sole tool was a rusted screwdriver, she'd had no business buying this home. But logic rarely stopped her before, and she hadn't asked Maddie's opinion of the matter, either. Now, just about every direction Charlotte turned had a pricey repair waiting for her.

Things didn't look any better next door, either. Maddie wondered who lived there and how well they cared for this dog. If Charlotte had ever mentioned her, Maddie didn't remember, which meant the next-door neighbors couldn't be treating the dog that badly. Charlotte would be up in arms to see an animal mistreated, and *that* Maddie would remember.

Judging by the doghouse, oversized water and food bowls, and the worn path carved along the fence line, this one spent most or all her life out here. While the postage-stamp-sized yard wouldn't afford much mental stimulation, Maddie reassured herself that a big, thick-coated dog like this one was fine outside.

"Feeling caged in?" Maddie asked her. "I know the feeling. Next time I come, I'll bring you a chew toy."

She was about to head into the house when the dog clambered to her feet and stretched, first kicking out her back legs, then dipping into a downward dog and releasing a giant, disinterested yawn. She turned away from Maddie and headed for the opposite side of the fence to begin patrol duty, walking slowly along the side and around.

Maddie held her breath as the giant dog approached, sniffing the fence, and flicked her tail a single time. A black nose and amber eyes lined in liquid black liner stood out against her thick creamy-white fur.

"Hey, beautiful. Looks like we're going to be neighbors."

On the other side of the fence, the dog's mouth opened in an easy pant, and she wagged her tail again slightly.

Maddie flattened her hand against the fence. Intrigued, the dog shoved her cold, wet nose through one of the diamonds and sniffed Maddie's palm. This tickled enough that the hair on Maddie's arms rose. "I think I know your type, disappointed by life and pretending not to care when you really care a ton, don't you?"

After licking her palm through the fence, the big dog bit down on one of the links and tugged it with her teeth as if trying to take down the fence.

"Oh, sweet thing. Hang tight. Sometimes those confining walls break down when we aren't expecting it, and something better is on the other side."

Abruptly, the animal released her hold on the fence and barked. Following her gaze, Maddie spotted her mom stepping out the back screen door, a still-smoldering sage smudge stick in one hand and a single, long feather in the other. When Maddie and the kids had arrived today, Charlotte was ready with a ceremony of sorts—a formal smudging of what would be their new rooms. The sight of her mom barefoot and hopeful in her breezy linen skirt and chakra-patterned blouse, her hair looking like she'd been in a windstorm when in fact she'd done nothing more than brush out her long curls, had left Maddie wanting to tuck tail and head right back to the car.

Biting her tongue, Maddie had pulled the twins close to watch Charlotte waving a big feather back and forth to disperse wisps of the sage smoke into corners and closets until Benji started to cough from the thick, sweet, earthy scent. Using this as an excuse, Maddie escaped with them out here until Charlotte was finished "cleansing old energies" as she put it.

Even though Charlotte had already done a thorough smudging upon moving in, sometimes the best thing to do was to let Charlotte be Charlotte. Standing there now on the top step, Charlotte gave her a little nod. Maddie half-expected her to go full *Poltergeist* and say, "This house is clean," but thankfully, even her mom had limits.

"I see you've met the neighbor's dog."

When the dog resumed walking along the perimeter of her yard, Maddie headed toward the house where the twins had begun bantering over who got which gnome.

"I don't remember you talking about her before."

"That's because she arrived here the day after Landon died. These last several weeks haven't exactly been bereft of conversation topics."

Maddie glanced at the twins at the mention of their father, but they were too deep in the intense negotiation of five-year-olds dividing up toys to hear so much as a siren go off.

"Arms up," Charlotte said, stepping onto the brick patio.

"Mom, I don't need to be smudged."

"You've had enough loss recently to last a decade. Of course you do."

Begrudgingly, Maddie lifted her arms as Charlotte fanned the smoke from the smudge stick in her direction. Maddie would never admit to liking the smell almost as much as that of a roaring campfire, but she did. Something about it calmed her to the core.

"Turn around," Charlotte said after fanning Maddie from head to toe.

"How many neighbors do you think are staring out their windows?" she teased as she turned the other direction, her arms still outstretched.

"Why should you care?"

DEBBIE BURNS

"Because I'm going to live here."

"You're nearly thirty-two years old, not seven. They'll either like you for who you are, or they won't, and there's nothing you can do about it either way."

Maddie blew out a breath. "We were talking about the dog."

"Yes." Finished with Maddie, Charlotte moved toward the twins and fanned a bit of smoke in their direction. Benji protested while Hazel lifted her nose to sniff a line of wispy smoke. "The dog belongs to their son. He lost his apartment lease because of her—and the forty-pound pet weight limit—but now he's taken off to do a bit of soul-searching and has left her behind anyway. His parents took her in, but they don't want her inside, so here she is, my companion when I sit out here at night and look up at the stars."

Maddie frowned as she watched the dog patrol the small yard. "Poor thing."

"She could have it worse; she could've ended up in the pound."

"She's being taken care of though?"

"They give her food and water if that's what you're asking. Not a lot of attention. They're in their seventies, their health is failing, and they have a neurotic Chihuahua who'll hardly step outside long enough to use the bathroom."

Maddie shook her head, shoving away the thought nagging at her. "I can't take in a dog who weighs almost as much as me. My life's chaotic enough as it is."

"No one is asking you to, but it's always easier to feel compassion for someone else's plight while you all but ignore your own, isn't it? Universal nature, I'd say."

She gave her mom a sharp look. "I'm not *ignoring* my plight. I just said I couldn't take her in, didn't I?"

Charlotte shot her a look. "Maddie dear, I love you, but you really know how to get in your own way."

Maddie threw her hands up in mock exaggeration. "I haven't even moved in yet, and we're already arguing."

Charlotte laughed softly and headed up the half flight of stairs leading to the sunroom. "There isn't a thing in the world for us to argue about. We're having a conversation. A meaningful one." She waved Maddie inside after her. "I need to put this sage out. Come on in. I'll put some water in the kettle."

"Thanks, but I don't have time for tea. We really were just going to be in and out. The photographer's coming in the morning, and there's so much to do."

"How about I make you some to go then?"

After reminding Hazel and Benji to play nice and that the gnomes were to be kept outside, Maddie followed her mom inside.

"To answer your question," Charlotte said as she snuffed out the sage stick into a large abalone shell on the island, "you get in your own way with all these rules you hold yourself to."

"Did I actually ask that question?" Maddie teased. "'Cuz I don't think so, Mom."

Charlotte wasn't deterred. "No mother is perfect, but you're a fantastic one. You were a pretty great wife, too, not that he always deserved it—or even *often* deserved it. You were an A student and the head of your class in pastry arts. I don't have a single memory of you getting in trouble in school after first grade when you got called to see the principal for stealing that girl's notebook."

Maddie rolled her neck in a slow circle, attempting to unknot the tension from her shoulders. Through the screen door on the other side of the sunroom, she could hear the kids' voices rising, promising an argument would ensue and likely sooner than later. It was chilly enough that the exterior door should be shut, but Maddie left it open so that she'd hear whenever the eventual falling out happened. "And you're bringing this up today, why?"

"Because it's time to let yourself get *messy*, honey. Throw up your hands. Say you can't do this alone. Ask for help. Turn to the people you love and hold on tight."

You filled the messy role for the both of us, Mom. To keep from saying it aloud, Maddie picked up the notebook, tape measurer, and pen and trudged up the mahogany switchback staircase to the empty bedroom that would belong to the twins. She didn't like the memory poking at her—the one in which she'd been a fifth grader with acne and breast buds and fretting about an oral book report on *Tuck Everlasting* she'd be giving the next day until her mom encouraged her to put off writing so that they could drive out deep into the country for a meteor shower coinciding with a rare planetary alignment. They'd stretched out on the hood of the car, and Maddie had dozed off under the light of a full moon, her jacket rolled up for a pillow.

Had the car battery not died, had there not been the unfinished book report nagging at her, it would've been the perfect night.

Maddie had disliked the idea of staying home and presenting her report out of turn a day later because no one ever believed you were actually sick when you didn't show up on the day of a book report, but it had promised to be better than showing up after three hours' sleep with a crappy report.

Charlotte wasn't having it, though. The most she promised to do was take Maddie in an hour late so she could finish writing the report before dropping her off on the way to work. But then Charlotte checked, and the battery was dead again after their two-in-the-morning jump from a AAA technician with a hard stare whose shirt reached no further than his belly button and who'd scratched at his gut while he talked.

Maddie had had exactly ten minutes to get dressed and

gather her things before the bus came. It was a Pop-Tarts breakfast on the bus and a lunch spent in her new school of three months writing instead of eating and socializing. She painfully recalled standing in front of the class with her hair a mess and a stain on her shirt she'd not spotted in her rush getting dressed, and presenting a considerably less-than-polished report.

It was Maddie exhausted and with a headache, crying herself to sleep when she got home that afternoon and hoping to be in a new school by the start of the next school year. It was Charlotte when she got home at 8 p.m. from her own long day, not the least bit sorry for what Maddie had gone through.

"But you made it," she'd said. "Life happens. It interrupts the most structured and well-thought-out plans. In ten years, you won't remember a thing about that book, but you'll know you can rise to the occasion when life demands."

It was one of the few nights of childhood that Maddie could remember falling asleep with the hot blanket of anger smothering her. Maybe it was because she'd wanted to prove her mom wrong, she'd not forgotten a thing about *Tuck Everlasting*. Rising to the occasion when life demanded—well, maybe that wasn't something you knew you were doing while in the midst of doing it.

Walking to the window that faced the backyard, Maddie peered down at the kids. Benji was tucking one of the gnomes under his shirt, Hazel had her arms crossed, and both were glowering at one another.

Maddie closed her eyes and pulled in a slow breath. *Please God, let this be me rising to the occasion.*

Forcing herself into motion, she went to work measuring the two rooms and closets that they'd be using. The house was a good sixty years older than Maddie's. The floors, though scuffed, were original hardwood—maple, she thought, but wasn't certain. Even here on the second floor, the ceilings were at least nine feet, and a thin haze of sage smoke hung in the empty room.

Despite Charlotte's repeated offer to relocate upstairs to the third floor, Maddie and the kids didn't need to take up all three bedrooms on the second floor, especially not when the third floor needed considerable ceiling repair.

Charlotte could keep the master bedroom on this floor, and Hazel and Benji would go back to sharing a room. Maddie would give them the bigger of the two guest bedrooms, and Maddie would take the smaller.

As she finished measuring the second room, Charlotte appeared in the doorway, a mug of tea in each hand, neither of them travel mugs.

"How are the kids?" Maddie asked. "Did you check on them before you came up?"

"They've come to a temporary truce and are setting up their little gnome kingdoms."

"Smells good, but I still can't stay," Maddie said, taking one of the steaming mugs.

"It's a blend. Serenity. Mint, chamomile, lemon balm, red rose petals, and lavender. I figured you could use something calming."

"That I could, but you might stop with your poking. That might help, too."

That half-suppressed smile of hers again. "I could, or I could poke a bit more, and you could tell me what you're really afraid of."

"That's easy. Not being able to provide for Hazel and Benji."

"That's it? As deep as your fear goes? I was hardly able to provide for you when you were their age. Without the Supplemental Nutrition Assistance Program and charity, I can't imagine how we'd have gotten by, and you turned out pretty fine. I thought for sure your fears ran deeper than that."

"What do you want me to say? Clearly you have the answer, so just tell me because I'm not going to give you what you're looking for. How can I? I don't even know who I am anymore."

Charlotte's mug was halfway to her lips, but her eyebrows lifted, and her mouth opened a touch. "I think we may have just gotten there."

Maddie swallowed hard. "Doesn't every mother of twins lose herself a little bit?"

"I can't say, given how I've only known one."

Tears stung Maddie's eyes, and she turned away, heading to the window to look down at the yard again. Hazel was squatting, neither her butt nor her knees touching the mulch, while Benji was stretched flat on his stomach in the muck.

"What is it you want? For you, not them."

"For me?" A soft laugh slipped out. "I've been too tired to think about what I want for five years now, Mom. I don't see that changing anytime soon."

"Then one thing is for sure; it won't."

"My kids just lost their dad. They're my only focus right now. I need to know they're going to be okay."

"That's the thing about life, Maddie. We spend so much time wanting everything to be okay, we forget that when things aren't okay, well, *they're still okay.*"

Maddie wanted to blurt out that this made no sense, but her throat locked up. Her back still to her mom, she used a knuckle to swipe at a stray tear. That was the thing about Charlotte. Maddie could poo-poo her smudging and crystals and love of feng shui all day long, but her mom was a master at cutting right through the bullshit and getting to the heart of the matter. "She's so far away, I don't even know her anymore," she said when she found her voice.

"Who?"

"Me—the old me, I guess."

"She isn't gone, just snuffed out like that sage, waiting for the right time to get relit."

"It isn't that easy."

"Isn't it?"

Was it that easy? A part of her wanted to trust her mom, to believe that things would still be okay even when they weren't, but that seemed impossible. Or at the very least improbable. Maybe Maddie's practicality came from her father's side, since it was clearly not from her mom, but that thought didn't make any of this any easier.

"Mom…" Maddie shook her head. "I just can't today. There's so much to do, and I'm so tired."

"Would you like some help?"

"Aren't you headed to a client's house?"

"Soon. But I could come by afterward."

"If it's not too late."

"It shouldn't be." Charlotte joined Maddie at the window. When Benji put his mouth around the head of one of the ceramic gnomes, Maddie tapped the window loudly enough that he released it. In the other yard, the dog had given up pacing and settled back into her spot in the dirt. "You have every right to be tired," Charlotte said, wrapping an arm across Maddie's back. "Just don't forget who's waiting for you. Don't keep her in the dark so long you don't remember how to get back to her."

Because a single spoken word would have her breaking into tears, Maddie took a sip of tea and attempted to make a mental checklist of everything she had to do before the day was over. It was the only way she knew how to get by.

CHAPTER 12

When asking politely didn't work, Maddie tapped Benji on the knee to get him out of his sister's car seat. "Move, please. We've got to run."

The agent and photographer would be arriving shortly, and Maddie had lingered in the kitchen after the twins finished breakfast, attempting to make it spotless again. She should've picked up something on the go instead.

Hazel had stopped in the middle of the driveway to inspect something in the crack, in no more of a hurry than her brother. Unless they pulled out in the next two minutes, they'd miss the curbside drop-off window, and Maddie would have to park and walk them in like she'd had to do two other days in the last week.

"Benji, in your seat. Now, please."

"But Hazel's seat is better."

"They're the exact same, just different colors. Like you wanted, remember?"

In her pocket, Maddie's phone buzzed. After a second of debate, she answered. "Hey, Mom, I'm trying to get the kids to school. Can I call—"

"Hi sweetie. I've been thinking I'll paint your rooms

before you move in," Charlotte interjected before Maddie could finish. "And I'd love to coordinate the colors with your chakra work, or at least what I hope will be your chakra work."

"Mom, I don't have the bandwidth to think about chakra work right now. And I appreciate it, but you really don't have to go to that kind of trouble for us."

"It isn't trouble if it's something I want to do."

"Well, I can't remember the walls looking that bad, but maybe it's something we can do together after the house sells." She glanced over to find that Hazel had found a twig and was poking the dirt inside the crack in the driveway. Jogging over, Maddie tapped her and pointed to the car. "We gotta go," she mouthed quietly. She followed that up with a stern look cast in Benji's direction, her finger pointed toward his car seat. "Your seat. Now!"

Whether it was her tone or the look in her eye, Maddie wasn't sure, but both kids got moving. Meanwhile, her mom had kept talking, and Maddie had completely lost track. "Can we talk about this later? We're running late. I gotta run."

"Sure, honey, but how about you three come over for dinner tonight, and I'll show you what I'm thinking in terms of paint colors? I'm in the mood for vegan lasagna."

Maddie shut the back-passenger door and jogged around to the front. "I wouldn't mind not cooking, but let me know if you've got any ideas on how to sell that dinner to five-year-olds."

"I was a mother of a young one once. I know some battles aren't worth facing. I'll make them my famous grilled PB&Js; hardly anything's better than that."

"Mmm. I wouldn't mind one of those, either."

"I'll make you one, but I'll make a believer out of you with this lasagna. Just watch."

As she hung up, Maddie frowned at the memory of the

last time her mom had made ricotta cheese from tofu—of course, she'd had a bit more practice since. And a good marinara could mask quite a bit, which was something Charlotte had mastered long ago.

As Maddie backed out of the driveway, she took a second to appraise the house. In the last two weeks, the windows had been washed, the leaves had been raked, and the still-hibernating burning bushes had been trimmed into conformity. It was a smart-looking home. Not that she deserved much credit for this—the house had been jaw-dropping when they bought it three and a half years ago, and Maddie had done little more than reside here and keep it clean.

Ten minutes later, she pulled up to the twins' Montessori preschool with thirty seconds to spare, and all without exceeding the speed limit. Without needing to walk them in, Maddie had just enough time to swing by the coffee kiosk at the front of Walter's Food Mart before clocking in for her shift. *What do you know, this day is looking up.*

The vanilla lavender latte on the menu made her think of Noel, so she opted for a mocha instead, saying yes to the whip cream and chocolate shavings, because why not?

Since she was still thinking about him, she pulled up Noel's text from last night while waiting for her drink. He'd been checking in daily, but last night, the kids had gotten to bed late, and Maddie had fallen asleep on Hazel's bed while getting them to settle down and hadn't answered yet.

Their texts flowed more easily now. Maybe enough water had finally passed under the bridge that face-to-face conversation would soon, too. She decided to use the opportunity to text him back rather than wait.

We're chugging along, thanks. The house is basically ready. It goes live this weekend. The kids

ARE EXCITED TO STAY WITH CHARLOTTE. IT'S ALL ABOUT
THE GNOME COLLECTION IN HER BACKYARD.

She wasn't sure how much lag time there was internationally
and was surprised when her phone buzzed as she was putting
it away.

GOOD TO HEAR. HEY, I WANTED YOU TO KNOW I'M GOING
TO BE HERE A LITTLE LONGER THAN ANTICIPATED.
PROBABLY ANOTHER TWO WEEKS. I WON'T LET IT STRETCH
ANY LONGER THAN THAT. PROMISE.

Maddie's gaze lingered on that single last word. Promise.
Something about it was decidedly intimate, bringing up a
mix of pleasure and pain.

SOUNDS GOOD. WE REALLY ARE DOING FINE.

I BET, BUT I WANT TO HELP. HEY, I GOTTA RUN. I'LL
CHECK IN TOMORROW. HUG THE TWINS FOR ME, WILL YOU?

She texted that she would before putting her phone away.
Hug the twins for me, will you? Of course that's all this was.
Noel being the godfather he'd promised to be. She hated that
her heart seemed to wish otherwise. She'd not been enough
once. Why would she be now?

Mocha in hand, she headed to the bakery where a
mountainous pile of cupcakes and cakes awaited her. She
could design and decorate intricate, multilayered wedding

cakes and mouth-watering cupcakes, but her manager was a stickler about the consistency of their products across the different workers. Since no one else here was trained to handle anything more than basic piping and a few variations of iced flowers, balloons, and cursive handwriting, this was as far as she was allowed to branch out artistically as well.

Most of the time, she didn't mind. She came in, worked hours that fit her schedule, and left it all behind at the end of the day, though sometimes she felt bad when she had to turn down special customer requests that, if it were up to her, she could fulfill in a heartbeat.

The morning flew by thanks to a stack of special orders and a half-dozen walk-up requests. She took the time to snap a picture of a special-order cake that, at the buyer's request, was overloaded with both balloons and roses in pink, yellow, orange, purple, and blue and was far from something she was proud to have decorated. She sent a quick picture of it to Saanvi and asked if she wanted to trade jobs. Saanvi texted back a blog-worthy picture of a raspberry ganache tart that she was decorating and added "Hard pass" along with a kiss emoji. Rolling her eyes, Maddie sent a middle finger emoji back.

Not long before it was time to clock out, Maddie caught someone watching her, someone she recognized but couldn't place. It was a young mom—or a nanny perhaps—with an infant cradled against her chest. She was hanging out near the cookie display and casting less-than-subtle glances in Maddie's direction. The baby was awake, wide-eyed, and staring at the oversized cookie and donut cutouts hanging from the ceiling, his mouth in a big "o."

The fine hairs on the back of Maddie's neck and arms prickled in one of those walking-over-graves moments her mom was always talking about. She'd seen her before. She'd swear to it. But where?

The girl didn't have a cart, just an oversized bag and the

baby. No other customers were around, but Maddie noticed a pencil-thin young guy hovering at the end of the cereal aisle, making a determined face at the girl. Something about their behavior was off. Maddie tried to recall some of the bullet points on the 'How to Recognize and Deter Shoplifters' flier posted in the back room because nothing else made sense. "Cute baby," she said to break the silence.

"Thanks. It's his saving grace." The girl shifted the baby from one hip to the other. "My mom used to say that about me, but I never got it until recently. He's a handful. No, not a handful. He's like a whole silo full."

After waving off the guy at the end of the cereal aisle, the girl walked up to the counter, her steps slow but deliberate as if her worn flip flops were sticking to the floor.

Maddie slipped the cookie cake she'd just decorated into the display case before sliding the glass door shut. "Can I help you with anything?"

The girl gnawed her lip for a second or two. She had long, blond-brown hair that draped over her shoulders like a curtain, a pronounced nose, and dark eyes, gray maybe, or a blend of colors. The girl continued as if Maddie hadn't spoken. "He's not much for lying still, either."

Maddie was about to respond when the little guy dropped his gaze from the brightly colored hanging cutouts and looked straight at her. He had big, round cheeks, brilliant blue eyes, and sparse strands of golden blond hair. As their gazes met, he offered her a smile that pierced her heart. *That smile.* Something between excitement and alarm dumped into her system, enough to make her feel faint.

"He likes to look at things," the girl added. "And he likes to be held. Like all the time. It's the nights, though. I swear, he cries *all* night long."

"I remember those days," Maddie said because she needed to say something. "My kids are five now. It doesn't seem like it in the moment, but it gets easier."

"That's what I'm hoping."

This. Is. Weird. "So, would you like something from the case?"

More lip gnawing. The girl glanced over her shoulder. A mom and little girl had walked over to one of the displays and were arguing about why they did—or didn't—need cupcakes. "My landlord's not crazy about babies, but we already had a signed lease when Liam was born."

"Oh."

The emo-looking guy reappeared at the end of the cereal aisle and made no attempt to pretend he wasn't eavesdropping.

"So, I, uh, wanted to give you something," the girl said, a flush turning her cheeks bright pink. "To read. Later." She switched the baby to her opposite arm and shuffled through the oversized bag slung over her shoulder. After a bit of rummaging, she pulled out a dog-eared envelope.

"Me?" The single word had been an attempt to clarify whether the envelope was something along the lines of a bakery order or for her personally, but nothing else came out.

Wordlessly, the girl extended the envelope. Maddie didn't know what else to do but accept it.

"Thanks." The girl said it a little too loudly as the envelope exchanged hands. "I need to go. You can read it later. Actually, I'd prefer if you read it later."

As the girl rushed off, Maddie caught the expression of surprise the baby made when he realized they were moving again. Her breath locked in her throat. She wanted time to stand still so she could think. Her ears were buzzing wildly, reminding her of when Benji had been fascinated with trains, and she, Landon, and the twins had been a hundred or so feet from the tracks as a big diesel barreled past them.

Maddie headed to the privacy of the kitchen and leaned against a long, stainless-steel worktable. The envelope was one of the generic return ones that came included with bills.

Maddie could see through the clear address window to a curvy, girlish print on college-ruled paper. Who could wait to read something like this later? Not her.

With shaky hands, she pulled out the letter and opened it, her breath locking in her throat as she realized it was addressed to her.

Maddie,

So, there's no good way to say this. If there was, I'd have figured it out by now. I would've told you sooner, but it wasn't mine to say. At least, not until Landon died.

Maddie leaned more heavily on the worktable. *Oh fuck.*

I'm sorry. That's the first thing. The fact is Landon saved my life that night. It wasn't the first time I was suicidal, but it was the only time I was ready to do something about it.

Marriage bonds that weren't mine didn't seem any more real than those stories I hear about abused girls in far off countries. Somebody else's problem. Somebody else's loss. God knows I grew up with enough of my own.

But all that was over a year ago now. Like I said, I'm sorry.

Landon was working out how to tell you. At least, that's what he promised. But then he had the accident and lost his chance to make it right.

The truth is, now that it's on me, I see how hard it is. You've probably guessed by this point, but we created a baby that night. Not on purpose. ~~I haven't had regular periods in all my life.~~

I guess you don't need the details.

But the fact is Landon had another kid, and I think you need to know about it.

His name is William after my grandpa, the nicest man I ever met, but I call him Liam because I like it better. He's hard to take care of. I feel like I'm sinking some days. I don't know if it was like that for you. I didn't want to have kids, but I fell in love with him when they laid him on my stomach, a giant, consuming love like I've never felt before.

But that doesn't mean being his mom is easy. I know it's a long shot, but I could use someone in his life who's trustworthy. Once you think it over, I'm hoping you'll be willing to talk sometime. I understand if you can't.

Sorry again.
Jordan
314-555-5284

If Maddie wasn't leaning on the worktable so heavily, she'd be on the floor. With hands shaking so wildly it was almost impossible to read, she skimmed it again. Surely, she'd missed a punch line or something to indicate this was all a joke. Maybe Landon wasn't even dead. Maybe he was in on it.

No. Landon was dead, and the truth, immense and terrifying, crashed in with a force that felt strong enough to topple buildings. Her husband had brought another child into the world before dying. The proof was in the shape of that baby's face and in the brightness of his eyes.

The only thing she knew was that nothing, be it big or small or seemingly inconsequential, would ever be the same.

CHAPTER 13

Maddie navigated to the twins' preschool on autopilot. Even numb as she was, the mother in her registered the look on Benji's face as he and Hazel piled into the car. As was the case most days, he was wiped out from being immersed in a semi-structured classroom environment for three and a half hours. While Benji was quiet, Hazel was calling for Maddie's attention as Ms. Pam stood at the car door giving a quick car-side report.

When Ms. Pam shut the door, Hazel leaned between the seats to wave a construction paper heart in Maddie's face. "Mommy, do you really think Daddy can see things we make for him? Because I made this heart for him."

Maddie figured her odds of not screwing up a question like that right now were slim to none. Hazel had drawn a stick figure on the heart, which was nothing atypical aside from the fact that this one had little protrusions for ribs—her first-ever skeleton—and she'd written 'Daddy' next to it.

To answer, Maddie pulled from conversations she'd had with the twins' new therapist and their pediatrician advising against having them believe Landon was watching their every move from heaven. "Remember what we talked about? The truth is, no one knows what kind of experience our spirits have when they leave our bodies."

"I saw Daddy watching us sleep in Hazel's room," Benji said, his words fading into a yawn.

"No, you didn't." Hazel dropped the heart onto the front passenger seat before she slipped out of her backpack and buckled in.

"Did, too!"

"Did not!"

Maddie drove out of the pickup line with both hands locked around the steering wheel as tightly as if she were driving alongside the edge of a cliff. Numb, numb, she was so damn numb. Her ears rang like a grenade had gone off. Her mom's long-held belief popped into mind—that it took some people longer than others to leave their earthly bodies behind. Maybe Landon *had* been standing in Hazel's room, missing his children and regretting the mess he'd left in his wake.

Damn you anyway for making these messes and not sticking around to clean them up!

She needed her mom or Saanvi, and she needed them right now, but her mom had back-to-back clients today, and Saanvi was three hundred miles away.

"How'd you two like to watch a movie this afternoon?"

A spirited debate over which movie to watch lasted until they pulled into the driveway. The twins settled on an oldie, *The Iron Giant*. Maddie guessed the oversized giant satisfied Hazel's need to nurture all things and Benji's love for mechanical things, too.

"Can we have noodles for lunch?" Benji pressed his hand gently against Maddie's cheek as she unbuckled him. If he were limited to nothing but buttered noodles for a year, she was certain he wouldn't complain.

"Yeah, sure. If you eat some peppers and fruit." Her voice sounded thin and high and as far away as her thoughts. A child. No, a baby. A baby that had Landon's big blue eyes and no doubt was going to keep them. *My sweet Benji, you've got a half-brother who's going to look more like your dad than you do, and I thought you were a pretty close fit.*

"I don't want noodles." Hazel crossed her arms as she got out of the car. "I want grilled cheese."

Maddie gave her head a shake, attempting to rid herself of the image of the baby. "Nana's making you two grilled PB&Js tonight, so how about we hold off on grilled cheese until tomorrow? What about a turkey sandwich?"

"With cream cheese?"

"Yes, ma'am."

Hazel liked cheese—any form of it—the way Benji liked buttered noodles.

"'Kay."

As they stepped inside and Maddie turned off the alarm, Leo jumped down from the front windowsill where he'd been watching birds and rubbed against their legs before dropping to the floor. He wrapped his front paws around Benji's legs, bit into his shoe, and let himself be dragged across the floor. Benji pulled him along several feet before Leo let go and sprinted across the room.

After that, Benji hightailed it for the downstairs bathroom, shimmying out of his pants as he walked. Like clockwork, he did his business after preschool each day. How he held it through the morning, Maddie didn't have a clue, but he hated to poop anywhere but at the house.

In the kitchen, the gently boiling water was a salve for Maddie's raw nerves as was smoothing the cream cheese onto Hazel's favorite nutty multigrain bread. Even so, Maddie managed to spill a small handful of steaming noodles onto the floor when she was transferring them back to the pot after draining them in the colander.

When Leo heard them hit the floor, he made a beeline for

them. "Really, Leo, you're part dog," she said, holding him off with her foot.

Before she could scoop up the mess, he caught a noodle in his front teeth and dragged it across the floor like he was making a kill even though he had no interest in eating it.

Halfway through cleaning up the noodles, Maddie's composure finally crumbled. She sank onto her knees and curled forward on the floor, burying her face in her hands. Nausea rolled in slow circles around her belly.

"Mommy, are you sick?" Benji had stepped around the corner without her hearing him, and his words were pitched in panic.

Jerking upright, she forced a lightness into her words. "Just stretching my back. How about we eat lunch while we watch the movie?"

Benji stared at her a second too long before running off to claim his favorite spot on the couch. Would her kids ever be able to let go of the fear that came with losing a parent?

Willing herself into action, she finished making the twins' lunches. A part of her still seemed to be waiting for the punch line. Landon had slept with someone she'd be shocked to learn could legally buy alcohol. And he'd fathered a child.

The twins had a half-brother.

A younger sibling had been the one thing she could never give them, not without adopting one. But Landon had brought another life into this world without her. There was another human being on this planet that shared half her babies' DNA.

An image of the girl popped into her mind. Jordan. Rail-thin body, long legs, straight blond-brown hair. At first, there'd only been the shock over the baby. But something else was rising to the surface: ripe, hot anger, blended with a heavy dose of jealousy.

Maddie wanted to scream and throw things and stamp

her feet. Damn him, anyway. Damn him to the darkest depths of hell.

That baby had no connection to her. She'd tell the girl to stick her request where the sun didn't shine, and she'd do her best never to think about them again. What on earth had Jordan thought she'd do? Hear her sad story and sign up for babysitting shifts the way she signed up to make meals on meal trains? That girl slept with her husband. Maddie had zero reason to help her.

No reason except your kids have a half-brother.

As Hazel and Benji lost themselves in lunch and the movie, Maddie curled up on the adjacent loveseat and pulled a blanket over her, wishing she could check out completely as she processed this. The irony was so thick, it was bitter on her tongue as she realized that—in this moment, of all times—she wished Landon would step through that door. "I've got the kids," he'd say. "You do you, babe."

It must've weighed on him, knowing he'd have to tell her the truth eventually. Tell his family. Tell Eleanor. It was hard to believe he'd kept it to himself.

Maddie's eyes flicked open. Noel. Was this related to why he'd shut down on the phone when she asked him if he knew Landon had cheated? *Please God, don't let him know this and not have told me. Not Noel.*

Her skin flushed hot and cold at the same time. No. If he knew this, he'd have told her. Wouldn't he have?

Now that the thought was there, there was no escaping it. Tossing off the blanket, she got up and headed for the kitchen, out of sight of the twins. She pulled the letter from her back pocket, opened it, and took a picture. As shaky as her hands were, she needed to take three pictures before getting one with the words in focus. Then she pulled up Noel's number and sent it off without any explanation.

She rested her head in her hands on the counter, waiting. It took less than four minutes for her phone to ring. She picked up his call, holding it tightly against her ear. "Did you know?"

"Where are you?"

"My house. Did you?"

"Did she show up there?" His tone carried a poorly disguised alarm.

He knew, and he wasn't hiding it. Damn him! The sting of betrayal flooded her.

"She found me at work." After a pause, she added, "She knows where I work." Her voice cracked.

"Maddie, I… I'm so very sorry. Are you okay?"

"Would you be?"

He let out a breath. "I wanted to tell you. God, I wanted to tell you."

"But you didn't." She was too numb to cry but not too numb to feel the pain.

"I couldn't trust myself to know I wouldn't be telling you for personal gain."

"Bullshit." She moved the phone further from her ear in a childish hope it might hurt less if his voice wasn't right against it, but then it was impossible to hear over the TV. When the receiver was pressed against her ear again, she heard "love him less." Had the other words been 'maybe I wanted you to' or was she making that up? "Who else knows this?"

"I honestly don't know. I suspect only me. Now you. Landon and I weren't exactly on good terms after he told me." After a pause, he added, "He promised he'd tell you. I was giving him the space to do it. Then, well, he died, and I couldn't just unload that on you, too. I was debating whether to tell you before I left, but I didn't want you to have to deal with it alone."

Maddie closed her eyes. She could hear construction in the background on his end, a big machine like a bulldozer. It was a strange time to wonder what bulldozers looked like in the Chilean desert. "And this the most unkindest cut of all." It was out before she could pull it back. With a hundred wounds piercing her, it seemed impossible that the words Shakespeare gave Mark Antony could ever have felt more immediate.

"Maddie…"

"I need to go. I just needed to know if you knew."

"I'm so sorry. I'm gonna make this right. I promise you."

How was he going to make it right? Turn back time and not walk away? No one could make this right. Most especially him. She needed to hang up. This wasn't doing any good.

"Have you called your mom? Can she help out today?"

She hung up before he could say anything else. Landon had cheated. The twins had a half-brother. And Noel had known about it and not told her.

Even you, Noel. Even you.

CHAPTER 14

JORDAN

Liam had been fussing in Jordan's arms long enough that they'd turned to rubber and her back ached, but as luck would have it, he wasn't showing any sign of giving in to sleep. What if one day he cried forever and never stopped? Most moms made it seem so easy, but it wasn't. Not for her anyway.

Uncomfortable as she'd become in the last twenty minutes since starting to rock him, she dared not move. Even slight disturbances could keep him from falling asleep. The hand-me-down rocking chair was just askew enough to feel like she was sitting in a dryer set on tumble mode, but if Liam was going to settle down anywhere, it was here.

Their nine-hundred square-foot University City apartment wasn't ideal for raising a baby, especially given that she shared the space with her two best friends, Ethan and Ainsley. The place hadn't been anything to brag about since the last time it was remodeled in the early '90s, but it was cheap enough, and the AC window units did their job in summer, which was better than the last few places she'd stayed. Her and Liam's tiny bedroom had been Ethan's when they moved in last year. She and Ainsley had shared the larger master bedroom with a walk-in closet nearly as big as this entire room.

That was before she'd decided not to pawn Liam off to that couple she'd chosen from a pile of potential adopters. She'd been drawn to the couple because they were the opposite of her parents—they were older, well-established, apparently without addictions, and capable of providing a child with soccer cleats, a baseball mitt, or even swim lessons that could potentially save a life. Jordan wouldn't get within ten feet of a body of water after one of her classmates drowned while crawdad hunting in what amounted to a swollen creek.

Then she'd met them in person. They'd wanted him with a lip-licking desperation that reminded Jordan of her mother back when she'd just given up drinking. Of course, she could've gone back to the drawing board, but by then she'd convinced herself she could do this—pregnancy hormones jacking up her confidence, probably. Once she'd announced to Ethan and Ainsley that Liam was here to stay, she got transplanted back here, and Ethan moved into her and Ainsley's room. Thanks to Ethan's and Ainsley's general dislike of babies, they'd become nearly inseparable over the last few months. Considering Jordan had introduced them, it wasn't fair. They were her friends first. Now, they exchanged whispers and looks that made it clear she'd be out of here if she had anywhere else in the world to go.

The earthy scent of weed was wafting under the doorframe, stirring up a hunger in Jordan that food never did. Drawing in a deep inhale, she was smacked with the desire to be out there smoking with them like she used to, back before she'd become immersed in everything Liam. She'd struggled through nine impossibly long, darkly gray months with no cigarettes and no weed, never deciding which she craved more. Then, when she kept him, she struggled through another seven and a half weeks while nursing him before taking so much as a puff of weed. So far, she'd managed not to start smoking cigarettes again, but most days, that was by the skin of her teeth.

All of this was far more than her mother had done with her. Not that anyone was patting her on the back. Jordan's support group consisted of two currently less-than-enthusiastic friends.

For no explicable reason, Liam's fussing abruptly escalated to the point that she could no longer hear Ethan and Ainsley talking in the living room. Shifting him in her arms, Jordan rocked harder. Maybe Liam fussed so much because, had it been up to him, he would've wanted her to make a different decision in the hospital the day he was born. Instead of broken and stained hand-me-down everythings, he could've had designer baby clothes and grown up in a house considerably bigger than this entire four-unit apartment complex. Should she have let the adoption happen? The thought had her chest tightening uncomfortably.

"You'll thank me one day for not having a mom who smells like stale coffee and who's older than your grandma—I hope. Even if you don't get handed a college fund or the keys to a car on your sixteenth birthday." After rocking a bit more, she added, "And that man had shifty eyes. No one wants a father with shifty eyes. Your father had beautiful eyes. Clear and direct. They could see right through you."

Liam's fusses leveled off as he burrowed his head against her chest, fighting sleep like always. This little guy had come out infatuated with the world around him.

"Wanna know a secret?" She stared at the plain plaster walls of the darkened room lit only by a nightlight and the red light of a smoke detector. "Everything's going gray again. When they put you on my stomach and told me you were a boy and a healthy one at that, the colors came back so strong, I thought they'd never fade again. But the gray's taking over, the same as always."

Jordan's gray was a musty wool blanket clinging to the inside of her skin. It was with her tonight, making it hard to appreciate Liam's soft cheek pressing against the bare skin of her sternum, making the weight of him feel like a bag of sand rather than a warm, living bundle in her arms. Making raising him seem impossible.

I know I tell everyone I don't believe in anything but cosmic dust, but please God, please make that woman call me.

Jordan didn't know what she wanted from Maddie, not exactly. But Landon had believed in her, and Jordan had believed in Landon, pointless as that had proven to be. Before the night she got pregnant, she hadn't spoken a single word to him that didn't have to do with where people were getting seated or how long Row House's waitlist was. In the three and a half hours they'd spent together the night Liam was conceived, first at the bar, then driving around, and after a while, *not* driving around, they'd made a connection unlike any she'd had before or since.

He'd never been hers to think about, not really. But a day hadn't gone by after that night that she hadn't. It wasn't love; she wasn't delusional. He'd been over a decade older and had struggles of his own.

It was envy.

Somehow, Landon knew about the gray, experienced his own version of it even, but didn't let it consume him. With those remarkable eyes and that big, easy smile, Landon was the bright summer sun shining on a sandy beach and reflecting in the waves. Jordan might as well have been locked in the recesses of a cave looking out at a light she couldn't reach. Even the few minutes he'd spent inside her, that warmth hadn't been able to penetrate her gray.

With her biceps on fire, she shifted Liam more squarely against her chest. He protested instantly, probably fearing she'd had all she could take, and he was headed for the crib to cry it out again.

Wiped out as she was, he likely would've been headed there were Ethan and Ainsley not itching to complain about Liam's incessant crying again. There were times they tolerated him better than others. When they were chilling and riding a buzz wasn't one of them.

"What's got your goat, little bud? Do you feel the gray sneaking in, too? Is that why you don't want to be alone?"

When he settled down against the warmth and security of her chest again, he stopped fussing, and just like that, he was finally giving in to sleep. Afraid to jinx it, Jordan did her best to keep rocking exactly as she'd been, knowing the slightest disturbance might jar him awake and require her to start over again.

As glad as she'd been to give it up, a part of her missed nursing him, missed the connection, missed providing for him in a way no one else could. She'd hoped he'd sleep better when he went to formula. While it hardly seemed possible, he'd started crying even more.

She kept rocking Liam until his breathing was slow and even, having learned the hard way that he needed to be sound asleep before putting him down, an act that took the skill of a ninja. In the quiet, she heard the muffled conversation and laughter of her roommates, reminding her of all she was missing out on.

Finally, she stood up as carefully as possible and held her breath after transferring him to the crib. She stood frozen over him, leaving him tucked on his side with a rolled towel pressed against his back.

Please just give me a couple hours. Just a couple. You can do that, can't you? She wanted to sit with her friends and smoke the gray into oblivion. She wanted to forget how rent was due in less than a week and how the three shifts she'd needed to call in for the last month weren't helping her come up with her share.

When she stepped into the main room, Ainsley and

Ethan hardly stirred as she nestled in between their splayed-out bodies on the couch. "I hope you didn't smoke it all."

"We didn't. Any chance you'll run out for pizza?" Ainsley nudged her with a bare toe. "There's nothing here to eat."

Jordan was lighting a blunt when, from the back room, Liam's wails burst forth fresh and strong.

Ainsley closed her hands over her ears. "Christ on a stick."

"That kid cries all the time." Ethan was no less displeased. "It isn't natural for a kid to cry that much. Think he's got cancer or something?"

"It's colic, you asshole, not cancer." Jordan held her breath and waited, but Liam's cries were mounting fast. She'd duped him, he'd figured it out, and he was angry about it. How long would he cry? She didn't have the energy to go through the cycle again. He was safe. He could cry it out, neighbors and landlord be damned.

She took a drag on the blunt and fell back against the couch. What would she give not to hear his cries for an entire night? For the first time in months, not to have to give more of herself than she was capable of giving?

Ainsley gave her a nudge. "Go get him, will you? I seriously can't take that kid crying anymore, Jordan."

"What makes you think I can?" She closed her eyes and didn't budge, wanting to cling to the hint of a buzz that warred with the tension flowing through her veins in response to Liam's wails.

Please God, make that woman call me, because I can't do this anymore.

CHAPTER 15

NOEL

"Maddie, just pick up, will you?" Noel's plea was swallowed by the still desert night so immediately that a part of him wondered if the sound had left his lips or only resounded through his thoughts. As much as he wished otherwise, forty-five-hundred miles separated him from her, as did the job keeping him here in the Atacama Desert for another two weeks.

Having given her the better part of the day to cool off after his initial attempts at getting through failed, he dialed her number one more time. The twins would be asleep now. Maybe she'd have processed this momentous news enough to have some questions—questions he committed to answering to the best of his ability. When she didn't pick up, he shot off a text.

Hey, Maddie, I don't want to leave it like this. Call me back please. If not tonight, tomorrow. I'll tell you everything I know.

It was a fool's hope to think she'd call him back tonight, but she would eventually. No matter how angry she was with him for not telling her, she'd want to know what he knew. After today, he was committed to not holding anything back—ever again.

He'd boarded the plane from St. Louis intending to having the right words by the time he set foot in the city again, but now everything had been upended. Wheels had been set into motion, and he was too damn far away to do a single thing about it.

"Just ten minutes in a car," Landon had protested. There was no way the condom in the car had been there for a year unnoticed, not with that car wash membership he used religiously.

Two women then. More than that? It seemed Landon had been freefalling much faster than anyone had known. Cheating on Maddie. Going off his medicine without telling a soul. Getting a prescription for Viagra.

Noel took off into the darkness, too full of tension to care about the cold air that had set in after sunset. A couple of work buddies were waiting for him at the hotel bar, but he had no interest in heading back inside. He'd been too distracted to process half of what they were talking about tonight anyway.

In the on and off months he'd been here, Noel had traversed the barren lands around the hotel enough to trust his footing along the packed-dirt road that led into sheer blackness, his muted footsteps the only thing to break the silence of the impeccably still night. Even this near the hotel, his eyes adjusted to a darkness so intense, he couldn't have imagined it before coming here. There was no moon in sight, and the Milky Way was aglow like an ancient god had tossed a handful of stars and stardust across the sky. It was one of those remarkable nights that drew astronomers here from all parts of the planet.

The few times over the years he'd allowed himself the painful daydream of what life would be like if he and Maddie were together, he'd known instantly that this was one of the places he'd want her to see. With the sky awash with so many stars, here nothing and everything seemed to make sense at once.

Noel had been hired at LightSource, a private-sector clean-energy company, shortly before meeting Maddie for the first time. The idea of traveling to places like this had been even more enticing than the cushy salary he'd been offered. Here in the sunny Atacama, the use of solar power was a natural fit. Given the way things had played out, an unseen perk of all the travel his job came with was that being a world away helped dull any sort of jealous remorse of the family of four in St. Louis consisting of his best friend, the woman he loved, and his god kids.

As he got further from the hotel, a soft breeze carried the saline smell of an ocean, but the scent came from the salt flats a handful of miles away, not the ocean far to the west. Perhaps it was impossible to distinguish their scent from the brine, but Noel would almost swear he could detect the hundreds of flamingoes who fed on the shrimp that thrived in the saltwater flats.

Off to the east, the vast, unending blackness that was the Andes lined the horizon, stretching up into the sky and blocking out the eastern stars almost as high as the outer Milky Way. Nearby, he could just make out the silhouette of a cactus in the darkness, its domed shape hugging the ground. Something small, likely a lizard or rodent, scurried off as he passed by.

He stopped walking when the light from the hotel had been all but swallowed up, and it was only him and the desert, the cold air cradling his bare arms and filling his lungs.

The crestfallen look on Maddie's face last week when he

told her he was flying out had besieged him with an unexpected hope. He'd wanted to tell her he'd find a way to stay if she asked him to. He'd let the past stay in the past, and he'd love her every remaining day of his life. It would be so easy, considering he'd never stopped.

Would it be so easy though? Considering? The sardonic voice inside his head was Landon's, not his.

"Do me a favor and stay out of my head." He growled in exasperation. "Why am I not surprised that the Landon rollercoaster is every bit as wild in death as it was in life?"

The only answer was that of the desert silence too impossible to decipher. Like it or not, Landon still stood between Noel and Maddie. Even in death, his friend's presence was so big it hardly seemed possible that there might be room for anyone else.

Though it didn't mean Noel was giving up. Not yet.

CHAPTER 16

ELEANOR

There was no getting past it. Eleanor found the house in all its expansiveness to be as quiet as a tomb even when it wasn't the break of dawn. Charles's snoring trailed after her out of the open door of the master bedroom, punctuating the silence.

The soft shuffling sound created by her suede-bottomed cashmere slippers grated against her ears as she traversed the hand-scraped planks of dark oak in the master bedroom to the marble floor of the kitchen. At only sixty-seven, it was hard to accept that she'd become shuffle footed, but in the face of such unprecedented silence, it was impossible to deny that she had.

After filling a kettle with water and turning on the gas stove in hopes that a cup of tea would ease the chill in her bones, Eleanor flattened her hands on the smooth quartz countertop next to the stove and closed her eyes. "What you need is to get back to work." Even the sound of her voice had become soft and unimposing. Clicking her tongue, she opened her eyes.

At the restaurants, the continuous hum of conversation of satisfied diners, the mostly well-meaning jeers between the kitchen and serving staff, and the clanking, scraping, and sizzling in the kitchens would help numb the visceral ache so present in this silence. Charles had gone back to work only nine days after Landon's death. Nine days! She wouldn't forgive him for that for a long time.

It had been almost six weeks now, and she couldn't bring herself to do it, no matter how essential she was to the restaurants' success. God only knew what kind of mistakes Charles would be making without her constant guidance. That man could hardly find his way to the bathroom in the dark without nightlights to guide him.

She'd married Charles when she was twenty-three and Charles was twenty-eight. She hadn't planned on working at Baxter's for long; the serving job she'd taken on after college graduation had only been meant to sustain her until she landed a marketing job. But there he'd been, managing the restaurant, his family's only one at the time. He was steady and unassuming—and sitting on a gold mine when he didn't even know it. So many things Charles didn't know. Why, the two of them were married before he even seemed to realize it was happening.

And look what she'd done for him and his parents, convincing them to take out a loan for a desperately needed renovation and then implementing that genius marketing plan. In less than two years, the renovation had paid off. In five, when the girls were just two and three, she'd convinced Charles and his parents to open a new restaurant. Apart from Landon and herself, none of the Baxters were visionaries, not even her girls. Why, Charles and his parents hadn't even considered the valuable real estate they had in that flat roof of their centrally located, historic building in Lafayette Square. She'd seen it though, and for the last twenty years running, it had been the premier rooftop dining experience in St. Louis.

And she wasn't finished. Before Landon's accident had knocked her to her knees, she'd been thinking of trying her luck with a distillery even though she knew nothing about distilling. Distilleries were monopolizing all the industry talk these last few years.

All she needed to do was step back into the game.

Eleanor headed to the walk-in pantry that was the size of a small bedroom and meticulously organized to her liking by Eleanor's housekeeper. A selection of loose-leaf teas was kept in stainless steel canisters on the nearest wall of shelving. Eleanor chose a rooibos blend and headed for the stove, still ruminating on whether it was time to return to work.

It wasn't as if the staff wouldn't be sympathetic to her unbearable loss. Everyone had loved Landon. Such a light he'd been! What she wouldn't be able to tolerate would be seeing how they'd moved on. Just thinking of the banter and laughter that would undoubtedly recommence after they'd paid their respects had the burn of acid on Eleanor's tongue. How dare they move on! How dare they laugh and poke fun at coworkers again. How dare any of them!

Most of all, how dare Maddie?

Teacup in hand, Eleanor shut the cabinet door with a smack loud enough to cut into the silence.

Maddie had rubbed Eleanor wrong from the first moment she laid eyes upon her. It hadn't been like Charles to be as excited about someone as he'd been about Maddie, going on and on about how lucky they were to have hired someone with her talent and her fresh-out-of-school pay rate. In a few months' time, he'd wanted her managing the entire kitchen at Row House. Most certainly he'd been undone by that combination of ambition and talent blended with that fake wholesomeness so many people fell for thanks to those big hazel eyes and that too-big smile. And that hair—it warred with Eleanor's sense of order.

It was fate you were reacting to, some quiet voice whispered, and her shoulders sank at the undeniable truth in the words. Eleanor hmphed in the silent kitchen, the sound resonating in the open space. With thoughts like these, she was beginning to sound like Maddie's mother.

On the stove, the kettle began to hiss. Eleanor turned it off and scooped a teaspoon of rooibos blended with rosehips, lavender, and currants into the stainless-steel infuser of her well-used single serve ceramic teapot before pouring in the steaming water. Her mouth watered in anticipation of the blend's natural sweetness as if it might damper the emptiness inside her.

How ironic that her legacy would be in the restaurant business when she'd never much cared for food. She could appreciate a finely cooked meal, but even before Landon's accident, she'd rarely eaten solely for the pleasure of it.

As if on autopilot, her feet carried her to her office while the tea steeped. No doubt, she was craving some physical proof of Maddie's disingenuousness. She'd not thought about the letter in months, but it was proof enough that her ungrateful daughter-in-law hadn't loved her son. How could she have when she'd written to Noel declaring her love for him only a few short months before getting pregnant— intentionally pregnant, Eleanor was certain—thereby forcing a proposal from Landon?

Taking a seat at her century-old keyhole desk, she opened the side drawer and fished underneath an assortment of stationery and all-occasion cards until her fingertips brushed against a cool brass key. Using it, she fiddled with the top-drawer keyhole until the temperamental lock worked free. Carefully, she sifted through various cards and mementoes until she came upon the old anniversary card from Charles hidden at the bottom. Should prying eyes search this drawer, no one would bother to open it. Pragmatist that he was, Charles had never signed more than his name in any card he'd ever given.

After opening the card, Eleanor pulled free the smaller folded paper hidden inside. She'd already been no fan of

Row House Eatery's newest prodigy baker when she'd noticed an envelope drop out of her son's jacket pocket in the parking lot one afternoon as they were leaving in separate cars. Could that be six years ago now? Time flew. She'd pointed to it from inside her Infiniti, but Landon had mistaken the motion for a wave and driven off. She'd nearly driven away herself, but curiosity had gotten the best of her.

She'd gotten out and picked it up, staring at the name on the front, an unexpected tension knotting her spine. How odd that Landon would be carrying around a sealed envelope addressed to Noel in handwriting that wasn't his. In a handwriting that was decidedly feminine. That was when she'd remembered Charles making a comment the night before about how Maddie and Noel had been hitting it off in the bar after Maddie's shift, so much so they'd been the last two to leave who weren't on the clock. "Wouldn't it be something if they got together?" he'd said as he was dozing off.

Eleanor hadn't thought it would be something. Not even close. Noel was practically a son to her, as much time and money as she'd invested in him over the years, bringing him along on vacations and making sure he was always on Landon's teams those early years. Maddie simply wouldn't do for him. Not then, and not now.

Eleanor had brought the envelope home and sat with it here in this very room for the longest time before carefully working open the seal, leaving almost no evidence of her deceit. Reading it confirmed her suspicion—Maddie was all but throwing herself at Noel, telling him how she'd never met anyone like him and how, if he felt the same way, she'd be eagerly waiting for him when he returned from his trip to Spain in two months' time.

Concealing the anger burning inside her, Eleanor had called Landon to explain that she'd found the envelope and to ask why he'd been carrying it in his pocket. She hadn't, of course, admitted to reading it.

"That new pastry chef," he'd said, "it's hers. Seems she's got a thing for Noel and asked me to give it to him since I'm driving him to the airport tonight. Great that you found it. I tore my car apart looking for it. I'd feel like an ass not passing it along as promised."

When he said he'd swing by to pick it up on the way to get Noel, she said she'd leave it on a table in the entryway.

Her sweet, charitable son. It had never been in his nature to pick up on imperfections in others the way Eleanor did. He'd had no idea what a mistake that would've been for his friend.

How many times since had Eleanor wished she hadn't called him and ripped it to shreds instead? If she could turn back the clock, if she could go back to that moment here in this very chair six years ago, she'd most certainly do just that.

Her son might still be alive.

Instead of destroying it, she'd rewritten Maddie's letter on her own fine stationery and sealed it in the same envelope so Landon wouldn't know it had been opened. Most of the contents had been rewritten exactly as they'd been in Maddie's letter, so there'd be no question as to the author's identity. It was at the end of the letter that she'd made the changes, telling Noel in what she hoped was a similar cadence that they could never work in the long term, that he should feel no sense of obligation to wait for her, as she wouldn't be waiting for him.

He who plays with fire gets burnt.

Heat rising in her throat at these memories, Eleanor refolded the letter and slipped it back into Charles's anniversary card. After tucking it away just as it had been ever since, she locked the drawer and hid the key in the side drawer once more.

After passing it to Noel as promised, Landon had come

by here the next morning for an impromptu breakfast. As fate would have it, Noel had read the letter in front of him.

"The thing I don't get," Landon had said after a moment's hesitation, "is why Maddie said one thing to me but wrote Noel another." There was an accusation in his tone, but he couldn't voice it, couldn't outright accuse her of such treachery. Not his mother.

She'd been making him eggs and sausage and had her back turned to him. "Did you mention this to Noel?"

"No, I didn't. I wanted to talk to you first. The seal... You didn't open it, did you?"

She'd kept silent as she finished her son's breakfast, plated the eggs and sausages, and carried them over to the island where he was drinking a cup of coffee, heavy on the sugar as he liked it.

Back then, he hadn't wanted a career in the family business. An artist and visionary at heart like her, he'd wanted to create.

"Do you remember how much time Noel spent here the year his parents were in that terrible accident?" she'd finally said in answer. "You two were always out in that strip of woods in that fort you built. He was so lost then, so unable to pick himself up—like his mother, who couldn't get back up herself for so, so long."

"Of course, I remember." His tone, that tension...

"He was a good boy, like you, and like you, he's becoming a good man. I know a plotting woman when I see one, Landon. What I did for Noel, I'd have done for you."

The look of horrified disdain that settled over his face might well have been a blade piercing her heart. He'd dragged a hand over his mouth and shook his head, seeming as if he might get physically sick. "Christ, Mom. You didn't." He'd shoved away his plate and gotten up, not having touched a bite. "I can't deal with this. I can't deal with *you*."

He'd walked out, and they hadn't spoken for three weeks,

the longest three weeks of her life. Until now, at least. As she'd suspected would happen, he'd run out of money and needed her again after he'd had time to cool off. They'd met for lunch and made it through the strained beginning until it felt as if this mess wouldn't sit between them any longer.

What she hadn't anticipated was the compassion her sweet boy would feel for that contriving girl. What she hadn't anticipated was that small stones became boulders as they rolled downhill.

If it would bring her boy back, if she could have a do-over, she'd never have opened that letter; she'd let Maddie have Noel, and Maddie would've left her golden son alone.

But life didn't hand out do-overs.

Bracing herself with a shaky hand, Eleanor stood up and turned her back on the desk. There was nothing she could do about it now, and in the kitchen, there was tea waiting that was over-steeped and getting cold.

CHAPTER 17
MADDIE

With Leo on her heels, Maddie stepped out of the patio door of a house that no longer felt like hers. Given that it wasn't even live yet, and her agent had already fielded a dozen calls from potential buyers, it promised not to be for much longer.

Maddie headed to the far side of the wide stone patio, suspecting that her mom would be trailing after her any minute. Red-gold streaks lit up the western sky where the sun had sunk low enough that the privacy fence blocked it from view, and a few faint stars were beginning to shine high overhead.

Maddie had come to the realization that her only possibility of an impeccably clean and beautifully staged home would be if the kids weren't around to mess it up. This meant she and the kids would be staying at Charlotte's starting tomorrow until the house had a firm contract, then it would be back here to pack.

While Maddie stopped at the edge of the stone patio, Leo stalked into the grass, heading for the bird feeder underneath which he hunted for mice with the intensity of a cat who caught them often rather than one who—to Maddie's knowledge—had never come close to doing so. How would he take to the move? This was the only home he'd known. At her mom's, the backyard's waist-high chain-link fence would hardly keep him confined to the yard, which meant they'd need to confine him to the house until they could trust him not to leave the yard.

The patio door opened and shut as Charlotte stepped out to join her. Last night, Maddie had cancelled dinner at her mom's and ordered pizza for her and the twins instead, using the very real excuse of a migraine in the wake of yesterday's news. Her mom had made the vegan lasagna anyway and brought the leftovers here tonight. Maddie had surprised herself by going for seconds rather than finishing Benji's half-eaten grilled PB&J. While Charlotte admitted to the lasagna's taking the better part of two hours from start to finish, it had tasted a lot better than Maddie might've guessed.

"I pulled out the Legos and promise to help pick them up. I'm hoping they buy us a few minutes." Less than five minutes into dinner, Charlotte had realized something was off, but she must've sensed the enormity of what Maddie was dealing with because she hadn't pressed while the twins were in earshot. "I hoped by now that husband of yours would be done wreaking havoc in your world, but given how unpredictably he left his, maybe I shouldn't be surprised he isn't."

"How do you know this has anything to do with Landon?"

"I wouldn't mind being wrong, but let's not waste time arguing about trivialities. What has he has done now?"

"It's more like what he did a year or so ago. Or who, if you want to get technical." Maddie didn't give her mom's sharp inhale time to settle. "It looks like while I was still giving our marriage my best shot, Landon fathered another child."

"Oh, Maddie. Are you certain?"

"Pretty darn." She swept her mass of curls into one hand and attempted to grab onto the anger humming underneath the surface of her skin. It promised to be much easier to handle than the sorrow threatening to flood her system. "The baby's mother cornered me at work yesterday. She dropped off a letter. I guess she worked with Landon in one of the restaurants."

"As much as I believe in taking the mother's side until there's irrefutable proof to the contrary, we both know a letter isn't proof of paternity. Especially not in a family with as much money as the Baxters have."

"It might not be, but the baby in her arms was." Her chin was beginning to quiver, and her words carried a distinct nasal pitch, but damn it, she wasn't going to cry. After her phone call with Noel, she'd hammered through the rest of yesterday in shock, and most of today, too. The numb emptiness had been easier to handle than all this emotion bubbling under her surface like a pot of boiling water ready for a batch of pasta. "Honestly, I think I knew before she even put the letter in my hands. Landon's in there, all right. In the baby's eyes. In his expression. I had goosebumps and couldn't figure out why."

"Oh, honey, I'm sorry. What a mess that man was. An absolute mess! I blame Eleanor for most of it. Overprotective, narcissistic..."

"It's a boy, maybe three or four months." Damn this quivering chin of hers. It wasn't getting the message. Charlotte stepped forward to hug her, but Maddie warded her off. "I can't, Mom. Not right now. I'll..."

"You'll what? Fall apart? Like I said the other day, maybe you need to. Sometimes we *have* to fall apart so we can put ourselves back together again." Charlotte closed a hand over Maddie's shoulder. "The universe works like that, you know. It keeps breaking us until we learn whatever it is we need to learn."

Maddie huffed. "How do you explain Landon, then? What did he learn, Mom?"

"Not everyone is lucky enough to get to stand back up again when life knocks us down."

Even in the thick of this mess, Maddie wished Landon was still here, still alive, and not only for the sake of the twins. She'd divorce him, no question, but this would've been his wake-up call. Maybe he'd have gotten back on medicine, gotten into therapy, gotten a hold of the part of him that had been spinning out of control. "What do I do?"

"What do you want to do?"

"I keep thinking how the baby's mother wrote that it only happened once. I know I have zero reason to believe her, but he got that damned car cleaned every week. If she's telling the truth, it means there was someone else, too."

Charlotte took a breath before responding. "It might very well mean that. But what you're going to do about the baby and how you're going to find resolution in your late husband's lack of fidelity aren't the same thing. One thing they do have in common though is that neither of them requires you to rush to a resolution."

"I was okay after the hysterectomy, you know. I won't pretend it wasn't a blow not being able to have more kids, but being a mom to those two precious little humans...how could I ask for anything else?" Maddie swiped at the tears running down her face with the back of her hand. "But Landon wanted four or five kids. Three at the very least. He kept quiet about it when the twins were little. The last few years, he kept wanting to talk about our options, and I kept putting him off." A dry laugh erupted and grew until she doubled over, resting her hands on her knees.

"I don't quite see the humor in it, dear."

"Don't you? He was just so damned good at getting his way." When Maddie stood straight, her mom smoothed back her curls and dried her cheeks, and Maddie found her touch immeasurably comforting.

"Hazel and Benji have each other. You aren't obligated to bring that child into their world, but if you do, you have my full support. Whatever you need."

"A part of me wants to forget about it. But my children have a half-brother, and now that I know it, I can never *unknow* it."

Charlotte closed her eyes and gave a single nod. "Isn't that the oldest truth? Once a rock is carved by water, it's always carved, even after the water's diverted."

Her mom's words rang with too much truth to deny. When Maddie had looked into that baby's bright blue eyes, those goosebumps lighting her skin had been a bell tolling to warn of an earthquake that had already happened.

Forgetting about that baby's existence wasn't an option.

CHAPTER 18

Nerves threatening to get the best of her as she approached the coffee shop, Maddie focused on the thump of her purse smacking against her thigh to avoid hightailing it in the opposite direction. When she placed a call to Jordan yesterday morning, she'd been convinced that the longer she waited, the more likely she was never going to call at all. Now, it was painfully obvious that this meeting today was too much, too soon.

She didn't owe anyone this meeting. It could've been pushed off for months or years even. Yet she was here anyway. Of her own volition.

On the drive over, it occurred to her how she should've chosen a meeting spot where there'd be no chance of running into someone she knew, but she'd spouted off the first place that came to mind. Her stomach flipped at the thought of introducing Jordan and the baby to one of the twins' preschool moms—or worse, to a whole pack of them. Didn't they meet up here sometimes?

Oh, well. It was too late to do anything about that now. Jordan was either already here, Landon's child in tow, or about to be.

Spying the coffee shop ahead, Maddie scanned the dozen or so tables through the glass. Her legs turned to noodles when she spotted Jordan, impossibly long, straight hair and all. Of course, she was here early. There went Maddie's chance of arriving first and feeling like she was in control.

The baby was planted on top of the table, one chubby hand fisting a colorful rattle that he shook with enough effort that the entire upper half of his body swayed back and forth. Young as he was, he'd topple over if his mom wasn't supporting him.

Maddie swallowed hard. *Landon had sex with that girl. He brought that baby into the world without me.*

Door jangling as she stepped inside, Maddie weaved through the crowd of coffee connoisseurs. Jordan's eyes widened as big as saucers when they landed on her, leaving Maddie in no doubt of her similar discomfort.

With her attention on Maddie, Jordan got smacked in the brow by the baby's rattle as he swung in a new direction. "Ow, buddy." She rubbed her forehead with one hand as Maddie walked up. "Thanks for meeting me. I wasn't sure if you would."

Maddie started to pull out the chair directly across from Jordan but realized the baby would be blocking their view of one another, so she chose the chair catty corner to her instead.

"You're welcome." She left her jacket on but slung her purse across the back of the chair. Was that bile she was tasting? Landon had been the one to jump into the pool from the high dive while she'd dipped her toes in a few inches at a time. But there was no sense holding back now. "Look, before we get started, I want to be clear that if you're planning any heartfelt apologies, you can table them today. They wouldn't do anything but get my defenses up, and we have a lot to talk about."

When Jordan's big eyes widened again, Maddie suspected she'd cut her off just in time.

Jordan dug her top teeth into her bottom lip—the full lips that girls in their late teens and early twenties so easily boasted. "Yeah, okay. Sure."

Underneath the cover of the table, Maddie locked her hands over the top of her thighs. Still facing his mom, the baby let go of his toy mid-pump, and it clattered across the table as he emitted a series of owl-like hoots. "Thank you." That hair of Jordan's went all the way to her waist. Maddie suddenly found herself wondering if it had gotten in the way while she and her husband were going at it, and she needed to shove away an unwanted image of it sliding over Landon's bare chest.

"So, uh, is there something specific you want to start with then?" Jordan looked as if she'd been asked to sit in the time-out corner.

Maddie opened her mouth but paused. The truth of it was, as soon as she'd sat down, any discussion plans had vanished entirely.

The baby noticed she was behind him and twisted to look at her. He grinned, revealing still-toothless gums. With his giant blue eyes, plump cheeks, smooth skin, and wispy blond hair, he could be a Gerber baby stand-in. Or Landon's baby. He could also be that. No question.

Looking at him, Maddie found herself thinking how, unlike the twins, this baby wouldn't have any memories of his father: the maker of blanket forts, the creator of whimsical stories, the toy-car-ramp engineer. He'd never hear his dad's rumbling laugh or be tossed high into the air and caught with such easy confidence and assuredness.

The baby reached a slobbery fist in Maddie's direction and pumped his fingers as if wanting to connect, and a wave of nostalgia as sharp as a knife stabbed at her. Those early days with the twins had swept by so fast, she'd hardly been able to keep her head above water, much less savor them.

With Jordan awaiting a reply, Maddie opted for frankness. "I know what you said in your letter, but I want to start by making it clear that if you're coming to me in hope of financial assistance, you're barking up the wrong tree. I hardly have solid footing to stand on right now."

"If I was looking for a handout, I'd go to Eleanor. Only then I'd have Eleanor to deal with."

This familiarity with her mother-in-law stung until Maddie remembered that Jordan had worked for her, too. "She'll need to know though. Eventually. Given he's Landon's."

"Yeah, I figure." She let go of the baby with one hand again to sweep a curtain of hair over her shoulder. "Not that I'm looking forward to it. I mean, it'd be nice not to have to choose between diapers and rent money, but what I said in the letter was true. What I need can't be bought. I want someone in Liam's life I can trust. Eleanor wouldn't hurt him intentionally, I get that, but everybody knows narcissists are energy vampires—not something I want my kid to have much exposure to, you know? There's Charles, of course. He's okay, but he's pretty much Eleanor's puppet."

Maddie attempted to stifle a snort—lest Jordan think they could share such easy camaraderie—but it slipped out anyway. She hadn't noticed the other day, but those big hazel eyes of Jordan's seemed to weep from the depths of their irises with unspoken wounds. What kind of life had this kid been dealt? Not an easy one, most likely.

"Look," Jordan said, her shoulders sinking. "I get you may not give a flip, but I can't do this by myself. The whole time I was pregnant—after I made the decision to go through with the pregnancy—I was back and forth about whether to keep him or give him up. Most of the time, I was set on giving him up. And then he was born, and it hit me like a bolt of lightning that this kid is the most important thing I'll *ever* do." Jordan huffed. "I just didn't realize how badly I was going to suck at being a mom. Like seriously. Some days...I can't even." After a handful of seconds, she added, "If you want the truth, if I'd had a clue it'd be this hard, I don't think I'd have jumped in this pool."

Whatever Maddie had been expecting, it wasn't this straight-from-the-heart honesty. No wonder Jordan and Landon had found their way together, even if only for a night. Come to think of it, this girl and Charlotte would probably hit it off, too. "I remember the early days," Maddie said, her tone softer than it had been a few minutes ago. "I won't pretend they weren't the hardest thing I've gone through." She paused, steeling herself. "How old is he?"

Liam was pumping his fist in the direction of the brightly colored star-shaped rattle that had slid across the table as if doing so would command its return. Seeing that Jordan's attention was fully directed at her, Maddie passed it his direction, careful not to make physical contact. Grabbing it, the baby let out a bear-like grunt of satisfaction, his face brightening in unapologetic joy.

"He'll be four months on Tuesday." Jordan's gaze swept over her son. "People keep telling me it should be getting easier. I guess I can see what they're talking about. He cries less maybe, but he's awake more and less content. He's really needy."

"Babies are needy. I hate to break it to you, but toddlers are needy, too. Their needs just change. For a lot of people, it's easier. Not for all. What kind of help do you have?"

"I've got two roommates, but mostly they're just pissed that I ruined all the fun by having a baby. When they're not at work or asleep, they're stoned. Like I used to be. Babies aren't so fun when you just want to chill."

Maddie blinked, thinking of the baby in an apartment

full of secondhand smoke. "Do you have any family to step in?"

The dark circles lining Jordan's hazel eyes and general pallor to her complexion were telltale enough. Skim-milk thin—that descriptor of new-mother tiredness had stuck with Maddie over the years, and clearly, Jordan was living it.

"My brother's up in Minnesota, but my mom's not far. She's in De Soto, my hometown, but she's a pothead and an off-again, on-again alcoholic. I don't have much to do with her. And I haven't seen my dad in over a decade. Not since before he got locked up." Jordan said this as flatly as if she were discussing a temporary bump in her gas bill. "But there's this older woman in one of the apartments on the lower floor. She takes Liam for me two or three shifts a week so that I don't have to pay a babysitter. She doesn't even charge me. Without her, I'd be up a creek."

"Are you still at Baxter's?"

Jordan huffed. "I was at the Row House Eatery, not Baxter's, but no, I quit the day I realized I was pregnant. I guess I figured by doing so I'd never have to tell a soul. I'm at Schlafly now. The one in Maplewood."

Maddie nodded, taking all this in.

"The thing is, even if I had the money to stick him with a babysitter more often, it wouldn't do much for Liam in the long run. He's exhausting, but that doesn't mean I don't love him. And Landon said...he said you were the best mother in the world. He said no matter how tired you are, you find a way to put yourself aside to give the twins what they need." She huffed and shook her head. "Like that was supposed to make me feel better about my lack of natural parenting skills, you know?"

Landon said that about me?

"Of course, I'm not asking you to have that kind of presence with Liam," Jordan blurted into Maddie's silence. "I just keep hoping since you love your kids like that, you'll understand that even half-siblings can fill a space that other people can't. And they all three lost someone, so I—I just thought I should ask, that's all."

Maddie ran her hands over her thighs. "They did lose a father; you're right about that. A good one. But your son is too young to realize it right now. The twins—they're acutely aware of what they've lost. They're reeling in it. If I can help it, no one they care about will walk out of their lives again for a long time."

Jordan's brows lifted. "If I was going to run off, I'd have done it by now. I'm not going home or hightailing it after my brother. No way. I came up here from De Soto because, like my mom says, I'm book smart and decision stupid." She paused for a shrug. "I had a full-ride scholarship to SLU. I was majoring in Environmental Studies, but I dropped out at the beginning of junior year not long before I got pregnant because I had an unraveling of sorts. Right now, I have no clue what I want to do with my life. And I've got nowhere better to be, either. So, you can rest easy that if you make Liam a part of your kids' lives, I'm not taking him anywhere."

Maddie could see in Jordan's eyes that she meant it, but something this important needed repeating. "If they meet, *if* I introduce them, I need your assurance this would be for the long haul. Even if parenting or personality differences divide us as mothers, that wouldn't be a reason to sever a connection between them."

Jordan's lips parted for a second. "Yeah, for sure."

Maddie's heart walloped in her chest. This was happening. She was *letting* it happen.

While they were talking, the baby had twisted and was cooing and reaching for her. Maddie had been doing her best not to pay attention to him. She was here to make a momentous decision, not to turn into a puddle over a charismatic little baby. "So…how do you see this playing out exactly?"

"I, uh, well, I'm hoping you'll want time with him, include him in some things you do and all." Jordan scanned the coffeehouse perimeter as if in search of something. "I'm not big on schedules when I don't have to be, but I'm cool with something more structured if that's how you roll."

"After being married to Landon for five years, I can confidently attest to needing a bit of structure in the midst of chaos."

The smile that flitted across Jordan's face masked the sadness visible in those hazel depths for a moment. It was going to be harder than Maddie thought not to let her in. Not to let the baby in.

Jordan scanned the room again. "We can talk schedules if you want. Only, I need to pee, and I don't know where Ethan went. He's one of my roommates—the one from the grocery store the other day. I don't have a car, so he drove me here. Only he's, like, nowhere. Think you could watch Liam a minute? It's a bit disturbing how cool he is with strangers, so he won't scream or anything."

"You mean just sit here with him?" Why did it suddenly feel as if she'd forgotten everything from those early months with the twins? "Yeah, I guess."

Jordan reached into a backpack on the open chair next to her and pulled out a bright and sparkly cloth baby book. "The lady who babysits him gave me this." Jordan needed to lean far to the side so she could pass it without Liam seizing it from her. "There's a fake mirror on the last page. If he fusses, show it to him. He likes to look at himself. Apple and tree and all," she added, her mouth quirking into a smile.

Maddie coughed back a laugh.

"Oh, and just so you know, he doesn't need a ton of help sitting up like he used to, but sometimes he lunges for things and topples over, so I keep both hands on him just in case."

Jordan took off as soon as Maddie scooted her chair closer and had her hands around Liam's sides. "Looks like it's just you and me for a minute. Hopefully, you won't notice your mamma stepped away."

He was half turned toward her now, and his bright blue eyes lit with excitement at the sound of her voice. He clamped a drool-covered hand over the arm of her jacket and burst out with a loud, "Oohhh!"

She attempted to lock down the rush of whatever this was mounting inside her. His resemblance to his father was uncanny. It was like Landon was hiding in there, promising that this was exactly what was supposed to happen.

In what seemed like a clear attempt to express himself, Liam bunched the loose material of her jacket sleeve in his fist and emitted a satisfied grunt.

A smile slipped from her, small at first, then spreading as he smiled back, his grin wide and gummy and his tongue pink.

"You know what?" Maddie said, after letting the moment sink in. "Something tells me you're just what the twins have been missing."

Without warning, he lunged for the book resting by her elbow, but Maddie steadied him before he toppled sideways. Then he forgot about the book and grabbed her nose and her heart right along with it.

"Honestly, maybe me, too."

CHAPTER 19

Before all this, had Maddie read a synopsis of the recent events of her life on the back of a book cover, she'd probably have put the book right back on the shelf. Moved on to something a bit more believable—something that didn't include a midday phone call with the twins' new therapist to talk about how best to introduce them to their late father's illegitimate child.

But this was real, and for the first time in forever, she wasn't letting the dust settle before making a decision. The whole thing felt a bit like sky diving without an instruction book. *How was Landon so okay living like this?*

In truth, Maddie had read up on bipolar disorder enough to answer her own question. Landon's impulsiveness had most likely been a combination of genetics and brain chemistry and structure. She wasn't designed like him.

But that didn't mean she was making the wrong decision. Her children had a half-sibling. One they could have a relationship with. If she chose not to seize this opportunity for them, what would they think of her decision when they were older? After a mostly sleepless night ruminating on the subject, Maddie simply couldn't imagine a world in which

Hazel and Benji wouldn't want Liam to become part of their lives.

So here she was, in the thick of it.

Just five-years-old, the twins were too young to understand the intricate details of reproduction or grasp the cost of infidelity. Untreated bipolar disorder and uncontrolled impulsivity weren't topics they needed exposure to yet, either. They weren't too young, however, to understand that sometimes parents stayed together and sometimes they didn't.

Maddie had hung up from her conversation with the therapist with a plan to share the simplest version of the truth that they could grasp, one that included admitting the baby's relation to them. As Hazel and Benji grew older, they'd certainly ask more questions, and Maddie would do her best to muddle through a complicated truth in a way that neither crushed nor glorified their memories of their dad. After all, Landon had cheated on her, not them.

To tackle such a complicated topic, she'd decided to walk with them up to a pizza place three blocks from Charlotte's for an early dinner. Charlotte had two families in the throes of the imminent loss of a loved one this week, and there was no telling when she'd be home. While her mom had offered to be there as a support if Maddie waited until she was home, Maddie was glad it was just the three of them tonight.

Given how two of the walkers could get distracted by just about everything at their age, the walk had dragged on. But when they'd gotten here, she'd done her best to break it to them, and for the most part, they'd been tired enough to sit contentedly and listen. She'd since been giving them time to process it all before broaching the subject again.

Across the booth, the twins were atypically quiet. The St. Louis-style pizza Maddie had ordered was the kids' go-to pick: half-broccoli for Hazel, half-cheese for Benji. Hazel must've eaten her fill because she was arranging the slim edges of uneaten crusts on her plate into the shape of a star while Benji was still going strong on the cheese side.

Given the bombshell she'd dropped, Maddie was determined not to deflect the importance of it by hopping to another topic nor to force this one any more than necessary. However, not breaking the silence proved challenging. It helped to remind herself that over the last half-hour, her two favorite humans in the world had learned that their parents would not have stayed married if their father had lived and that, while his love for them would never have lessened, their dad had brought another child into the world shortly before he'd died, one who had a different mother.

One of the therapist's comments circled Maddie's thoughts. Any humiliation Landon might've had over his actions didn't have to become theirs. It didn't have to become Maddie's, either.

With a square of thin-crust pizza clamped in his mouth, Benji ducked underneath the booth. Maddie bit back a comment as to how the underside of booths was meant to be like the dark side of the moon—not visible to the human eye. Or touched by little fingers, either.

Benji could've gone around the side, but it would've required sliding past his sister. Besides, with kids, it was often as much about the journey as it was the destination. A handful of seconds later, he wormed his way onto her bench seat and snuggled against her. Maddie patted his side, savoring the comfort of connection likely as much as he was.

Hazel was the first to break the silence. "I wish daddy had a girl instead."

"Is he going to want to play with my toys?" With his mouth full, Benji's words were muffled. "I don't want him playing with my toys."

"Well, first, when people bring babies into the world, we don't get our pick of what they're going to look like, what their interests will be, or whether they'll be born boys or girls."

"What about twins? Do you get to pick that?" Hazel stopped her crust arranging and looked up, her gaze sharp and direct.

"Nope. Most babies come into the world alone, but sometimes little miracles happen like with you two, and two or three babies grow inside their moms at once."

"But what about my toys?" Benji's interests were more singular, it appeared.

"When we meet Liam, it won't be like the play dates we have with your friends. He's very young, and he isn't moving around yet. He hasn't even learned to sit up on his own. Even if he's interested in your toys, you'll have a say-so in what you offer him as long as it's safe for babies."

"Is he as little as Monica's baby sister?" Hazel asked, referring to a girl in their preschool.

"Maybe a little smaller."

"That baby can't do *anything*." Disappointment layered Benji's tone.

"For now, but babies grow quickly." And become little terrors of toddlers who are all about older kids' toys. Maddie figured it was best to save this tidbit for another time.

"How come we can't meet him tomorrow?" Hazel quipped.

"Yeah, can we meet him tomorrow? I wanna meet him tomorrow."

"Tomorrow doesn't work for us. After preschool, you're seeing Ms. Jenna. But you'll get to meet him next week."

Maddie let her fingers get lost in Benji's curls as he reached for another piece of pizza while still finishing the one in his other hand. It never failed to amaze Maddie how much food he could fit into his little belly when he was hungry and loved what he was eating.

Seeing that her brother was getting all the cuddles, Hazel

came around and slid onto the outside edge of Maddie's bench seat. "Where's the baby going to sleep?"

"We're only babysitting one or two evenings a week. If he needs a nap while he's with us, we'll find a spot that's quiet."

"Can it be in your room, not ours?" Benji mumbled after a large bite.

"Sure, it can." She tapped him gently on the head. "Remember, we don't talk with our mouths full. And I think you might need some water to wash all that down."

"Do we have to walk all the way home?" Hazel asked, stifling a yawn. "My feet are tired."

"It's only a little over three blocks. You'll make it."

"Daddy carried me on his shoulders when we came here with him that one time."

"He carried me, too," Benji added as he reached for his glass, a touch of defiance in his tone.

"He took turns carrying you both."

Hazel twisted in her seat to look up at Maddie. "Did he ever carry Liam on his shoulders?"

As much as she welcomed their questions, this one came as a bit of a punch in the gut. "Liam would've been too little for that when your dad passed away."

"Will Liam understand us when we talk to him?"

"Simple words, maybe. Not a string of them. Not yet."

Hazel burrowed deeper into her. "Then when he's bigger I need to remember to tell him that I hope he gets a daddy to carry him on his shoulders."

Benji looked up at Maddie with the most earnest of expressions. "If he gets a new daddy, will he still be our part-brother?"

Maddie ran her fingers through his curls. "It's called a half-brother, and no matter who he has for a father someday, that'll never change."

"What if we get a new daddy?" Hazel asked.

As if that will ever happen given this soap opera I'm living in. It was a knee-jerk reaction and pointless at that. Maddie had no interest in dating for a long time.

"If we get a new daddy, then Liam gets a new daddy, too," Benji shot back at his sister.

"It doesn't quite work like that, Benji. If—"

"Is Uncle Noel his uncle, too?" Hazel interrupted, sitting up straighter.

Was it a coincidence how Hazel's thoughts turned from a future father to Noel in a heartbeat? Maddie hoped so. It wouldn't do to have their hearts broken by him, too—accidentally or otherwise.

"Noel's your godfather, remember, not your uncle, even though you call him that. Being a godfather is something parents ask of their relatives and friends. But no, I don't think your father asked that of Noel when Liam was born."

Hazel cuddled closer. "Poor Liam. We're a lot luckier than him."

Maddie was searching for a response when Benji beat her to it. "He can play with some of my toys if he wants. Not my Darth Vader though. He's too scary for a baby."

"He can play with my toys, too. Just not my unicorns. Their horns could poke him."

Maddie never failed to be struck by their compassionate hearts. "You know what I think? I think Liam will get something a lot of kids never get the chance to experience. He's going to have the two of you to show him the ropes."

How many times over the years had the twins talked about wanting a baby sister or brother? Without understanding the intricacies of it, they understood Maddie couldn't have more children. That it wasn't in the cards for them.

Leave it to Landon to grant them this wish when the granting of it had seemed so unlikely.

CHAPTER 20

Spying a hint of lightening sky at the side of the old blinds in her new postage-stamp-size bedroom, Maddie guessed it was somewhere in the five o'clock hour—an acceptable time to call this broken night of sleep quits. As she extricated herself from her tangled sleeping bag, she promised herself she'd not only find time for a nap today, but she'd also be ordering an air mattress.

They were in the thick of it now—halfway through opening weekend. As much activity as there had been, the first offer was expected any day. At least, that was what her agent had promised last night.

For the last few days, Maddie's phone had been on Do Not Disturb, and she'd done her best to ignore it entirely. With the sale of the house, the baby, and moving in with her mom, she'd needed to claim some space for herself. With her kids and mom under the same roof, an easy place to start was distancing herself from everyone attempting to reach her via phone.

When she'd glanced at it before going to bed last night, there'd been a dozen missed calls and texts from Noel and Saanvi, but Maddie hadn't been in the space to talk to either of them yet –Noel, because she was too angry with him, and Saanvi, because Maddie simply didn't have the energy to explain all that happened this week.

She'd also ignored Eleanor's text alerting Maddie that she was ready to resume their talk about what to do with Landon's ashes. Eleanor had been insistent on interring them at a cemetery an hour south of the city alongside three generations of her family, but she was no longer sure that she could go against her son's wishes. Maddie couldn't help but find it apropos how even in death Landon still had a knack for getting his way.

Technically, what happened to Landon's ashes was Maddie's decision alone, but had Landon lived, the divorce would've separated her from the burden of this decision. She wanted—needed—Eleanor's consent regarding Landon's final resting place. It might not have been the healthiest of loves, but apart from the twins, that woman had been the one who'd loved him most in the world.

Free of her sleeping bag, Maddie remained on the floor for a few cycles of cat/cow pose to work some of the stiffness out of her back. The twins, weighing next to nothing as they did, had woken up yesterday as spritely as ever. They loved being here, even if it meant sleeping on the floor. Maddie hadn't realized how much they'd needed this distraction.

It had been warm enough yesterday that they'd played outside with the gnomes most of the afternoon. Last night, the sleep gods had proven gracious, and the kids had slept right through a storm that had blown through after midnight.

Not Maddie—she'd lain awake listening to the winds whipping against the house. Now that she'd be living next door to a dog who was outside in all weather, she'd be thinking about storms differently.

Around dinner time last night, she'd seen the dog's caregiver refill her bowl with kibble and give her fresh water.

He was an older man with thin shoulders and a stooped back who didn't look especially kind, but he didn't seem like an abusive owner, either. With the dog's basic needs being met, Maddie needed to accept that the dog wasn't hers to have any say-so in her care.

After a few more cat/cow poses and a downward dog pose that felt like heaven to her hips and back, Maddie headed for the hall bathroom. Leo came trotting in from who knew where and jumped into the empty tub, staring fixedly at the faucet in hopes she'd turn it on. At home, he was loath to drink out of the water dish she freshened for him religiously in case he got thirsty when she wasn't around to turn on the tub. He hadn't wasted any time picking up the routine here, either. Leo liked his water running, and he'd proven finicky enough to turn his nose up at the seventy-five-dollar cat fountain Santa had left under the tree.

"I see you're acclimating just fine," she said, scratching the top of his head after she turned on the faucet a trickle. Licking at the stream, he twitched his tail contentedly.

While Leo lingered in the tub, batting at the water after he finished drinking, Maddie relieved her full bladder, brushed her teeth, and splashed water on her face, ignoring her mess of curls for later. Over the tub, the brightening sky illuminated the stained-glass window, an original from 1918.

Because of the age of the roof, plumbing, and electricity, the house had cost her mom less than a quarter of the one Maddie was selling despite the similarities in size, but Maddie was gaining a newfound affinity for it given its many intact original features, tall ceilings, and expansive woodwork.

Maddie scooped Leo into her arms, his damp paws soaking through her t-shirt at her stomach and sending a shiver down her spine as she headed down the hall.

After descending the switchback staircase, Maddie walked over to the living room window that faced onto the street and deposited Leo on the waist-high windowsill. The sun hadn't crested the horizon yet, but the eastern sky was beginning to glow pink and yellow orange. A few small branches had fallen from the towering oak during the storm and were scattered about the lawn, leaving an easy chore to do with the kids this afternoon. "I bet that tree has just as many birds for you to watch as the one at the old house."

Suddenly Maddie's gaze was drawn toward the rocking chair on the far side of the portico, and she jumped backward, cursing under her breath. A man was lounging there, legs stretched out in front of him, a jacket draped over his chest, and his head leaning back at an awkward angle, exposing the soft flesh of his neck and Adam's apple.

Her first thought was that a drifter had come up to the porch to sleep off a bender. As she had another second to take him in, she realized it wasn't a stranger at all. It was Noel.

Seconds ticked by, and he didn't so much as move. The silver-blue light of early morning had an ethereal quality that gave him an unusual pallor. Her heart walloped against her chest. Was he hurt?

The thought jolted her into motion. She dashed for the door and unbolted it. As she pulled it open, the scraping of the tight wooden door against the frame pierced the quiet morning. Noel jerked awake, bolting to his feet as the jacket that had been covering him tumbled to the porch floor. For a moment they stood still, staring at one another. In the silence that hung between them, Noel dragged a hand through his hair and cleared his throat.

Maddie was still having a hard time believing what she was seeing. Noel was *here* when he was supposed to be in South America for another week or more.

When Leo made a break for the door, Maddie nudged him out of the way and stepped onto the porch, pulling the door mostly closed behind her. The chill air circled her like she'd stepped into a walk-in freezer, reminding her that she was wearing nothing more than an oversize T-shirt and underwear. She locked her arms over her chest and looked out across the lawn as if some explanation might be waiting there.

"You alright?" he asked, picking his jacket off the porch floor. By the looks of it, he hadn't shaved in a few days. A thick stubble lined his cheeks and chin, reminding Maddie how it was anything but easy to travel in and out of the Atacama Desert.

"You're the one sleeping on my mom's front porch in the middle of the night, and you're asking me if I'm okay."

"It's supposed to be good for you, isn't it? Sleeping outside."

Seeing his sheepish smile poked at the splinter of betrayal lodged inside her. He'd known about the baby—and the girl Landon had slept with—and not told her. Suddenly she was twenty-five again and waiting for a response to a love letter that never came, the weight of a hundred boulders crushing her.

She stepped back involuntarily, as if a bit of distance might ease the pain. She wanted to ask how he'd found her here but knew it was Charlotte who'd told him. It had to be.

From high in the tree in the center of the yard, a bird erupted into song, and a jogger heading down the sidewalk glanced over and nodded. Maddie's bare feet were stinging, and she was shivering. "I need to get dressed."

She headed inside without waiting for a response or extending an invitation to follow her, but she didn't close the door behind her, either. Heading upstairs, she ducked into her bedroom, closed the door, and leaned against it, collecting herself.

Noel's low voice floated up the stairs as he deterred Leo from another escape attempt. When the door closed, Maddie paused to listen, wondering if Noel had stayed outside or let himself in.

Footsteps traipsing across the wood floors below were

answer enough. She tugged on a light sweater and yoga pants, and before stepping from the room, she dug through her overnight bag for a hair tie. Her hands were shaking just enough that she couldn't pretend they weren't. Noel had come back. Even hurt as she was over his betrayal, she couldn't deny the relief sweeping over her.

As she headed down the stairs, she spied a pair of work boots, a suitcase, and a laptop bag by the door and a Carhartt jacket hung over the top of the bench seat. Noel was in the kitchen, looking out the side window. He was in jeans, socks, and a LightSource logoed polo shirt.

"I know I messed up," he said, turning to face her. "I should've told you. I was about to, but I didn't want you to have to face it alone, and when you said that bit about waiting to get into Landon's phone, it seem like waiting was the right thing. I swear I intended to tell you when I got back." In addition to the thick stubble on his cheeks and chin, there were dark circles lining his eyes.

"Landon was your best friend, but he was my husband. Even if you'd been here, I'd be going through this alone."

His eyes pressed closed for a second or two in response, and Maddie was surprised by the urge to step close and brush her fingers through his hair or press a light kiss against his cheek as if doing so might wash away his sorrow. She'd attempted to bury that part of her forever, but nearly six years later, she still cared enough that it hurt to see him in pain. "You look like you could use a cup of coffee."

Noel waved a hand in the direction of the counters as if he'd already been searching for a coffee pot that wasn't there. "It's borderline cruelty to joke about coffee to someone who just spent fourteen hours on desert roads to get to Santiago rather than wait around for a charter, then almost another twenty-four in planes and airports before landing in St. Louis at three in the morning."

Maddie stepped around him to fill the tea kettle with

fresh water. "Mom is a tea drinker to the core, but she has a pour-over glass coffee pot for such occasions, though I can't vouch for the freshness of the grounds."

"You won't hear any complaints from me no matter how stale they are."

He was still at the counter, facing her now, and he was close enough that her shoulder brushed his arm as she moved from the sink to the stove. She met his gaze after lighting the burner. "I guess the downside of working in one of the most isolated places on earth is how difficult it is to leave it."

"If there was a way I could've gotten here sooner, I would've." His words cut through her, and Maddie stood at the stove, collecting herself. When she refused to meet his gaze, he slipped a hand around hers, pulling gently until she faced him. "I haven't stopped thinking about this since you called. I'm sorry. For everything."

She shook her head, her insides roiling in a mix of anger and pain. "I can't do this. Not today."

"Whatever time you need, you can have it. But I don't want to lose you, Maddie. Not now. Not over this."

A laugh escaped that didn't quite cover the pain his words stirred inside her. "That makes perfect sense coming from someone who's so good at walking away."

He stepped in before Maddie could brace herself. His hands closed on either side of her temples, leaving her nowhere to look but at him. "There are a hundred things I'd do differently if I could, but life doesn't hand out do-overs. All I can do is make better choices moving forward. From this moment on."

After Landon's death, Noel had hugged her once and held on forever. Aside from that single time, Maddie couldn't remember them so much as brushing fingers or shoulders throughout the course of her marriage. Until now. His hands were still cold from waiting outside in the chill air, but the heat from his body radiated against her. The still-familiar scent of him filled her nostrils, and a part of her seemed to be dissolving as she stared into those chocolate-brown eyes. Maybe it was the earliness of the morning on top of a poor night's sleep or maybe it was his proximity, but time seemed to be melting in on itself. How was it possible that anything longer than a handful of seconds had passed since he'd held her this closely?

"One of them is not letting you go through this alone," he added into her silence. "Whatever you need, I'm here for you."

Hearing Noel voice his care broke something inside of her. Even so, Maddie surprised herself by leaning in to brush her lips against his. When he went still as stone, it was clear he was even more caught off guard by this than she was, but reason abandoned her. She closed one hand against his cheek and rested the other against his chest, opening her mouth to his. It was just her and him, one second tumbling into another as she savored the combination of strength and suppleness of his lips, the ridge of his jaw against her hand, and the shaved short whiskers against her palm.

Her pulse roared in her ears but not so loudly she couldn't hear the whisper of warning as to how badly it would hurt if she proved not to be enough for him a second time. Then he responded, his mouth opening against hers. His hands dropped to her hips, drawing her against him.

When neither of them pulled away, Noel's kiss intensified, his lips pressing against hers even as footsteps began to echo from the floor above them. Maddie pulled away, her breath caught in her throat. Within a few seconds, a toilet lid clanked open on the floor above, and the sound of Benji peeing floated down from the open bathroom door.

Reality began to descend like a set of Russian nesting dolls, one tucking snuggly inside another until there was almost certainly no room for the interior doll to breathe. As much as Maddie didn't want to think about it right now, there was a much longer list of reasons *not* to be kissing Noel than to be kissing him, and she wiped her mouth like she was wiping away evidence of a stolen bite of chocolate cake.

"Mommy?" Benji's voice was brushed with fear in the still-new surroundings.

"Downstairs in the kitchen," she called. The ever-present mother in her noted the lack of toilet flush or running water in the sink before Benji bounded down the stairs and into the kitchen, his silky blond curls a disheveled mess.

"Uncle Noel!" Barefoot and in helicopter-print pajamas, he tore across the short distance before Noel hoisted him up into a giant hug. "I thought you were in South Merica."

"*A*merica, and I was, buddy, but I just got home and couldn't wait to see you." If Noel was as disconcerted as she was, his tone didn't let on.

On the stove, the kettle began to hiss, and Maddie swirled the dial to Off, thankful to have the distraction of making coffee.

"How long do you get to stay this time?" Benji asked.

Noel lowered him to his feet and ruffled his fingers through his hair. "Actually, bud, I'm making some changes at work. I'm going to be around for quite a while."

Maddie froze with the glass coffee pot halfway down from one of the overhead cabinets. As if reading her thoughts, Noel glanced in her direction, but Maddie wasn't ready to meet his gaze. "Quite a while" and that kiss of theirs were two more things too momentous to wrap her head around this morning. If she kept this up, she'd run out of nesting dolls to hold all her unfinished business.

Having grown up under Charlotte's roof should've been hint enough that Maddie brace for the unexpected while living here. Even so, when she opened the door of the bathroom, a towel wrapped around hair still soaked from the shower, she shrieked to discover a waist-high Great Pyrenees staring her down.

The dog's baritone woof was like a clap of thunder as it boomed through the house.

"Hazel, Benji, where are you?" Maddie called as the dog gave her a thorough sniffing.

The house was quiet aside from the canine's gentle panting. Its tail swished back and forth, fanning the odor of wet dog in a cloud around them. The soft sounds of Hazel and Benji skirting an argument greeted Maddie's ears, and she guessed they were in the backyard even though she'd told them to stay inside until she finished showering. "Mom?" Maddie called.

Nothing. With the dog still blocking her way, a hopeful look in her warm brown eyes, Maddie patted the top of her head. She could feel the caked-in dirt against her palm. "Seems you took a mud bath last night, sweet girl. But more importantly, what're you doing in the house?"

Down the hall, her mom's bedroom door was still closed. It was strange knowing that Noel was in there napping. It was completely nuts that only an hour ago, Maddie's lips had been locked around his—and *she'd* been the one to initiate the kiss! Her blood stirred all over again in equal parts heat and embarrassment.

Before they'd had time to address it, Charlotte had awoken from the commotion in the kitchen, and Hazel hadn't been far behind, so there'd been no end to the distraction. When a giant yawn had escaped Noel as he was finishing off a cup of coffee, and Charlotte learned that he'd only had a handful of hours of sleep over the last few days, she'd insisted he take a nap while she threw together a welcome-home brunch.

With the Pyrenees still staring her down, Maddie

frowned. "You're a bit of a roadblock, big girl, a dirty one, at that. And I just showered."

Abruptly, the dog's fluffy ears perked, and she took off, descending the stairs with the unexpected grace of a tomcat. Towel still on her head, Maddie followed her.

The door leading to the backyard was wide open, and sure enough, Hazel and Benji were out in the landscaping playing with the gnomes. Bypassing the kids with nothing more than a quick sniff, the dog headed deeper into the yard. As Maddie paused in the doorway, she saw that last night's storm had blown down a massive branch of what was likely a century-old tree at the back of the yard. The falling branch had collapsed the fence separating the two backyards.

"Kids, where's Nana?"

Without glancing up from her play, Hazel pointed toward the neighbor's yard.

"Did you two realize the dog had gone inside? Let's hope she didn't give Leo a heart attack."

Maddie watched as the dog scaled the downed fence like it was a picnic blanket and headed into the neighboring yard to retrieve a large bone. With it in her mouth, she climbed over again and beelined for the patio. With a grunt, she stretched out not far from the kids and commenced gnawing on her bone.

"She likes it here, Mommy," Hazel said.

"Can she stay? *Please!*" Benji added.

"She belongs to the neighbors. I'm guessing Nana is telling them about the fence now."

"But the doggy likes it here better," Hazel said. "Even if she *is* pretty smelly."

Maddie was working out a response when the side gate opened and Charlotte stepped through, her cheeks flaming red. The dog stopped gnawing to let out a single woof in greeting.

Judging by the punch in her mom's step and the set of

her shoulders, Maddie guessed whatever just played out over there hadn't gone well. "Not their responsibility," she muttered under her breath.

Hazel jumped to her feet. "Do we get to keep her, Nana? Do we?"

"No, Hazel," Maddie interjected before her mom had time to reply.

Charlotte locked her gaze on the twins rather than Maddie. "I can't promise she'll get to stay indefinitely. But she's ours to care for while they attempt to reach their son."

Hazel brushed off a shred of mulch on her pajama top. "What's indefinitely?"

"Not having a set end point."

"Forever?"

"Yes, forever." Charlotte sank onto her heels in front of the dog and scratched behind her ears. "No more muddy yard for you, sweetie, though I do hope you don't mind baths. You're caked in mud."

"Can we stay here forever, too, Mommy?" He couldn't have been out here longer than ten or fifteen minutes, but as he stood, Benji proved he was nearly as dirty as the dog.

"Benji, your grandma was saying the opposite, that there's no promise as to how long the dog *can* stay." Charlotte had never been much for baby talk in any form.

A dog her size in the mix with everything that's already going on? Maddie rolled her shoulders to ease some of the tension creeping in. They'd only been here two nights, and already chaos was ensuing. Maddie's thoughts flitted back to her four different elementary schools and to a string of nights spent in cars when there'd been nowhere else to stay. Was life with Charlotte going to be no different than life with Landon aside from the fact that her mother hardly lost her temper?

No, Maddie reminded herself before fear could lock up her limbs. Whether it was age or effort, her mother had a stability to her now she hadn't had then. Life with her now wouldn't be like life before. Besides, Maddie would never let it get there. She had her own children to think of.

Hazel joined Charlotte in front of the big dog.

"Honey, be careful not to touch her bone. She might not want to share," Maddie warned even as the Pyrenees' tail thumped contentedly, and her ears remained relaxed. She was so dang *big*. Charlotte barely made ends meet most months. Maddie couldn't imagine what it would cost to feed a dog that size. "Mom…"

Charlotte looked over at her. "They were set to take her to the P-O-U-N-D today. They never agreed to keep her this long. Now with the fence down, they're washing their hands of her."

"So, you're stepping in? Just like that?"

Charlotte glanced up, a smile pulling at the corners of her mouth. "What about that honestly surprises you?"

Maddie tamped down an answering smile. The irony of the whole thing was that Maddie had been crazy about the dog ever since she first laid eyes on her. *She* should be the one arguing to make her a part of the family, not Charlotte. Her entire life she'd wanted a dog, and a big one, too. Charlotte was the one who'd never been much of an animal person, and Maddie's unstable living situation while growing up hadn't enabled them to bring a pet into the mix, anyway. "You aren't a dog person."

"*You* are. At least, you always wanted to be. Now's your chance."

"We have a cat, remember?"

"Who acts like a dog. They'll be fast friends."

Maddie looked over to find that the dog's gaze was fixed on her like she knew exactly what stakes were at hand. She thumped her tail but didn't whine, as if asserting that she wasn't one to beg. The truth was this argument was over before it started. And Maddie didn't mind. "Let's hope so."

CHAPTER 21

NOEL

The tip of a small finger poking Noel repeatedly in the cheek pulled him from the deepest of sleeps. He opened his eyes to the sound of shuffling, and memory flooded in as a rainbow-colored silk streamer wrapped around a bedpost came into focus. Charlotte's room. Charlotte's bed. He'd fallen asleep on top of the bedspread but must've gotten cold at one point because now it was half folded over him like a taco.

His gaze flitted toward a small head of curly blond hair where Benji was hiding at the side of the bed. "Hey, little buddy." His voice was thick from sleep.

Benji peeked over the top of the mattress. "I'm not supposed to wake you," he whispered. "But I've been waiting for you to play with me forever."

"Oh yeah? What time is it?"

"I don't know, but we ate pancakes without you. Can you get up now?"

Noel glanced at his watch. It was almost one-thirty, which meant he'd slept over six hours. Charlotte had promised to wake him in an hour. Guess he'd needed more shut eye than he'd realized. "For sure," he said, throwing off the half of the bedspread he'd been using as a cover and dragging a hand over his face.

His mouth had gone dry, but he could still taste Maddie's lips on his, and a wave of pleasure tinged with guilt rushed over him. Had someone told him he'd be sharing a kiss with Maddie hardly more than a minute after showing up here, he'd never have believed it. Just like he wouldn't have believed she'd be the one to initiate it.

As much as he hadn't wanted the moment to end, it was a good thing Benji had woken up when he did. The last thing Noel wanted was for her to have regrets, and right now, her life was in chaos.

Just then, the cracked bedroom door burst open, and one of the biggest dogs Noel had ever seen pushed into the room and trotted across the floor. Even though Benji wasn't fazed by its approach, Noel was quick to sweep him onto the bed next to him.

"Don't you love our dog, Uncle Noel? We gave her a bath, and now she smells like Thin Mints."

"When did you get a dog?"

"Just today. While you were sleeping."

The dog planted both front paws on top of the mattress —causing the bed to rock under the weight of her—and leaned in to give Noel a thorough sniffing. Noel caught a whiff of something minty and sweet rolling off her as Benji buried his face in her fur. In response, the dog—a Great Pyrenees, Noel guessed—swept a big, pink tongue straight across Benji's cheek.

Raising onto his elbow, Noel gave the dog a good scratching, and she thumped her tail contentedly, her warm breath basking his face. Noel couldn't imagine Maddie setting out to adopt a dog with everything she had going on right now, so there was likely more to this story than Benji was relaying. "Where'd you get her from?"

"The scary old people next door."

"Oh yeah?" Maybe they were just dog sitting. In any case, the dog seemed easygoing enough that Noel relaxed as Benji slid to the floor and pattered toward the door. "Come on, Uncle Noel, let's play."

Promising he'd be right behind him, Noel went to the bathroom and splashed water on his face. As he descended the switchback staircase a minute or two later, he found that the living room floor had been transformed into a play place for the twins, with two distinct camps of toys spread out like armies, only instead of the army men and Matchbox cars he'd played with as a kid, the camps consisted of fairies, various plastic animals and unicorns, trains, Disney figurines, ATVs, and helicopters. The kids were nowhere in sight, but Noel guessed whose camp was whose based on its composition of fairies and unicorns versus ATVs and helicopters. Even traveling as often as Noel did, he'd seen how both Maddie and Landon had done their best not to stereotype the twins by their genders, but early on Benji had been drawn to anything with wheels while with Hazel it had been anything with four legs.

The dog was standing in a clear spot on the floor staring out the front room window. Following her gaze, Noel spotted Charlotte walking with a man—a contractor, Noel guessed based on his attire—toward the street. Hearing the twins' voices coming from the backyard, Noel rounded the corner into view of the kitchen. Maddie was in there, her back to him, whisking something inside an oversize ceramic bowl. Her hair was swept into a knot, exposing her smooth neck and a few stray tendrils of curls, and without meaning to, Noel envisioned himself casually closing his hand over the back of her neck as he walked up before guilt rushed over him.

"Hey there," he said, forcing the image away. When Maddie jumped with the same vigor as if he'd popped out behind a corner and screamed, he apologized for scaring her.

"It's okay," she said, facing him, her smile just unnatural enough to assure him that she was indeed battling with her own doubts about that kiss. "I didn't hear you over the gnome war erupting outside. I don't know what I was thinking, saying they could each bring one inside. Before we know it, it'll look like Lord of the Gnomes in there."

He dragged a hand through his hair, debating whether to bring up the kiss while they had a moment to themselves but deciding to hold off. "Sorry I slept all day. Probably would've kept right on sleeping too if it wasn't for my visitor."

"Benji?" Maddie's gaze narrowed playfully. "He swore he only went up there to get his Buzz Lightyear."

Noel held out his hands, fingers splayed. "Trust me; I needed to get up. But what's the story with that polar bear in there?"

"A long one that ends with my mother taking her in unexpectedly—or maybe expectedly, her being Charlotte—" Before she could finish, the back door flew open, and the twins raced in. As she'd predicted, they hadn't limited their selections to one gnome each. Benji's arms were stretched around three chunky gnomes, and Hazel's, two.

"Hold up!" Maddie called, setting aside the mixing bowl as they tried to run through the kitchen. "What did I say about one each? Pick your favorite. The rest stay outside. And we're rinsing off your picks in the sink."

From the surprised look on Benji's face, it was obvious he'd forgotten the instructions. "But I need *all* these!"

"And the other two will be outside waiting for you later."

"Uncle Noel, can you pick one of mine to play with, too?"

Noel wasn't about to choose a favorite from the gnomes needing to be put away and disappoint the other twin. "You know what Benji, there's plenty of toys in the living room for me to play with."

The twins trudged back outside with looks of

disappointment but were quick to return with their choices: Benji's, a white-haired, bearded gnome with a red coat and a Santa-like quality, and Hazel's, a slimmer one with a gray coat and a giant mushroom in one arm.

Maddie gave the gnomes a quick rinse and dry, then kissed the tops of the twins' heads while handing them back. "You two getting hungry? I bet Noel is," she said, her gaze flicking toward him again. "My mom made you a plate earlier. It's in the fridge. Help yourself."

"When do we get the cupcakes? That's all I want." Hazel stood on her tiptoes to peer inside the mixing bowl. "That smells delicious."

"Why thank you, and no fingers in the bowl, especially not dirty ones," Maddie warned, stopping Benji's hand as he sidled up behind his sister. "It'll be another couple of hours if we're going to eat them with the dog's."

Hazel glanced up at Noel. "Mommy's making cupcakes for the doggie, too."

"Oh yeah?"

"To celebrate her being ours," she added.

"That's not quite how it evolved," Maddie said. "But this first batch is for the humans: Nutella swirl. The dog is going to get one with a sweet potato and carob base. And despite handling our canine newcomer like a champ, Leo will have to be happy with a spoonful of tuna on his kibble tonight. I have neither the time nor the ingredients to make cat treats today, too."

Noel headed for the fridge and spotted a prepared plate loaded with scrambled eggs, skillet potatoes, a link of sausage, and a heap of silver dollar pancakes.

As he pulled it out of the microwave a minute later, the front door jangled open. "You who, we have company," Charlotte called out.

Judging by the looks on their faces, the twins were as shocked as Maddie to spy both their grandmas stepping inside. For that matter, so was Noel. From what he knew, Eleanor and Charlotte had only been in the same vicinity a handful of times over the years and that likely been a handful too many—for both of them.

In every way, they were opposites. Charlotte's red and yellow African-print dress stood out like a beacon next to Eleanor's winter-white wool coat and pressed slacks as did the contrast in their hair—Charlotte's unruly chestnut curls compared to Eleanor's dark-blond crop of hair that had been styled into perfect submission. And those were the surface differences.

The dog woofed loudly enough at the newcomer that Eleanor, looking considerably frailer and thinner than she had mere months ago, immediately side-stepped behind the younger and larger Charlotte.

Leaving her gnome at the edge of her play army, Hazel buried her hands in the dog's thick fur while looking from one grandma to the other. "Mommy, what if you aren't making enough cupcakes?"

"We'll have plenty of cupcakes. How about bidding your grandmother hello, you two?"

When Charlotte moved aside, Eleanor clasped her designer purse in front of her like a blockade, her eyes locked on the dog as she directed her words toward Maddie. "After not hearing from you all week, I woke up this morning and texted your mother. She mentioned you were here."

Plate still in hand, Noel was standing close enough behind Maddie to hear the restrained breath she took before replying. "I did text."

"Once." Eleanor tore her gaze away from the dog, and her expression of disdain melted into wide-eyed shock to spy Noel. "Noel! I thought—I thought you were in Chile for another few weeks."

"I was supposed to be. I ended up leaving early." He

motioned toward his luggage next to the front door. "Just got in today actually."

Eleanor looked from him to his luggage and back again. "And here you are," she replied coolly.

Considering the kissing that had happened in this very room mere hours ago, Noel didn't have anything to counter with.

The two women filed into the kitchen silently, Charlotte leading the way. Maddie busied herself by pouring the batter from the mixing bowl into blue paper cups lining a muffin pan. Following her lead, Noel fished a fork out of the silverware drawer and began eating his very late breakfast. "Thanks for the food, Charlotte."

"Don't thank me until you've heard how I hope to put you to work. That contractor might as well have been smoking something if he thinks I'm going to pay that much money to upright a fallen fence. We can do it, you and I."

"Sure thing, Charlotte. Whatever you need, I'll give you a hand." Leaning against the counter, Noel used the side of the fork to wedge a bite of the sausage link in two. He could tell by its color that no animal had died in its creation—or even been involved, most likely. At least the eggs seemed real—Noel drew the line at plant-based eggs. Taking a bite of the sausage, he was surprised to find it wasn't half bad.

Eleanor's expression had gone positively sour, and Noel could only guess it was in response to the easy camaraderie between him and Charlotte. As the dog decided to make a trip through the kitchen to visit her water bowl, Eleanor backed against the wall. "I really don't like the look of him."

"He's a she," Charlotte said. "And she's friendly, just getting settled."

"How settled?"

"For always. That kind of settled." Charlotte's tone left no room for debate. "She belonged to the next-door neighbors, but our shared fence went down in last night's storm and, as things happen, we're keeping her."

A look of displeasure lengthened Eleanor's face, her makeup softening the wrinkles that had first begun to show upon Landon's death.

"If you'd put your hand out so she can smell you, I'm sure she'll be fine."

Begrudgingly, Eleanor let go of her purse with one hand and held it out, revealing two thick, gold, and glaringly oversized diamond rings on her index and ring fingers. "I've never known anyone to keep a dog this big indoors."

"Then the good news is you do now," Charlotte quipped as she leaned over Maddie's shoulder and took a big inhale. "Smells delicious."

Displeasure clinging to her like a blanket, Eleanor waited until the dog walked out of the kitchen and stretched across the living room floor in a patch of sun before speaking again. "It works out well that you're all together, unexpected as it is." That calculating look again, classic Eleanor. "Now I can tell you all at once."

"Sure thing. What's up?" Noel refused to kowtow to Eleanor or acknowledge the guilt surging through him. Did Maddie feel it, too? Was that why she was so focused on pouring the last of the batter into the remaining cups?

"Uncle Noel, aren't you coming in to play with me?" Benji called from the living room.

"He's going to play with me, too!" Hazel protested.

"I'll play with you both, but I need three minutes to talk to your mom and grandmas." He'd been taught that when Hazel was involved, it paid to be specific when it came to time.

"I hope it's a real three minutes, and not the ones that go on forever," Hazel said before turning back to her toys.

"It will be." Noel's smile lingered until he returned his attention to Eleanor. For four people gathered in one room, it grew uncomfortably quiet. Whatever had called her to show up uninvited on Charlotte's doorstep on a Saturday afternoon, Noel could only guess.

"There's more on my mind than this, but it's the most pressing thing in my thoughts, so we'll keep it to this and save the rest for another time." Eleanor paused, pinching her thumb and forefinger at either side of her Adam's apple. "I've been giving some thought to this thing you both insist my son wanted."

Maddie stopped scraping the side of the bowl and looked at her. "About Landon's ashes?"

"My parents, aunts, uncles, a handful of cousins... They're all buried in one place," Eleanor continued without directly answering Maddie's question. "I want him there. For my sake. Losing a son..." Her body visibly crumpled upon saying it, most likely tugging at more heartstrings than only Noel's. "I wouldn't wish it on anyone."

In the other room, the twins began bickering about who Noel would play with first. At least there was no threat of them overhearing this conversation.

"But my desires and my son's final wishes don't coincide," Eleanor continued. "A few years ago, when I reminded him that his father and I would be buried there, I suggested he consider it, too—when the time came. It sent him into a complete tailspin." She shook her head at a memory belonging only to her. "For the better part of a week, every time I saw him, he warned how I'd better not bury him there, as if...as if he knew..." She paused to collect herself. "He could be quite focused when he made up his mind to do something."

"That he could," Noel agreed.

"I keep reminding myself that the wishes of the living are more important than of those who've passed." Eleanor's hands were shaking, and her words were strained. Noel set down his plate and pulled out a bar stool for her, but she waved him off. "That son of mine, he's become the voice in my head—and sometimes in my dreams. He doesn't want me taking him to some unfamiliar graveyard any more than he wants to be stuck in an urn in my home. He never liked being confined, not a bit."

"For what it's worth, you're right, Eleanor." Noel squeezed her shoulder. "Not every thirty-two-year-old has a vision for the end of their life, but he did."

"This Colorado bit you broached earlier—he mentioned it to me that day, too." She let out a shaky breath. "But if I take him there, I'd be abandoning him in the middle of nowhere. He might as well be tossed out on the side of the road." With a shake of her head, she disappeared into the sunroom, collecting herself.

Maddie used the short pause in conversation to slip the cupcakes into the oven, and Noel choked down one of the small pancakes without syrup or butter.

"With Landon, it was as much about the journey as it was the destination," Maddie said when Eleanor returned to the kitchen.

"Meaning?"

Maddie wiped her hands on a towel pensively. Noel wondered if she questioned how much she owed Landon given everything she'd learned these last few weeks. He also wondered how differently this conversation might play out if Eleanor had already been made privy to the fact that her son had brought another child into the world. "Meaning wherever Landon's ashes are spread," Maddie said, "he'd want the experience to take us out of our comfort zones. A quick drive to a cemetery to visit a headstone crammed between people he never met or hadn't known since he was a kid isn't what he'd have wanted from us. He'd want the experience to be something we'd never forget, the twins especially. He'd want his ashes spread in a place that the twins would look forward to returning to, and he'd want it to be somewhere breathtaking. Awe inspiring."

After considering Maddie's words for a moment, Eleanor looked sharply at Noel. "This spot of his, you can vouch for it?"

"Yeah, I can. We spent a whole afternoon there, and Maddie's right. Landon always wanted to make a trip back there. He was happy that day, grounded and content in a way he typically wasn't, which I guess is why the spot stuck with him."

"In my line of work, I've found that there's a great benefit to the living when we honor our loved ones' wishes regarding their final resting place," Charlotte said, bringing Noel's attention to the fact that she'd been exceptionally quiet as this conversation played out. "It enables us to reach a different level of peace than if we go against them, and much sooner, too."

Eleanor looked from Charlotte to Noel to Maddie. "I have my reservations. Too many to relay today, but for my son's sake, I'll consent to this." She nodded more to herself than to any of them, and her frail frame seemed to deflate a bit more before she turned to Noel. "You'll see to the arrangements, won't you? You two shared a bond like brothers. You'll make sure we're doing it the way he'd have wanted?"

"Yeah, of course." Eleanor's words were a punch in the gut. And of course, this conversation was taking place here in the exact spot he'd been kissing Maddie this morning. He could almost feel Landon leaning over his shoulder, a smirk on his face as he whispered in his ear. *"Bet you didn't see this coming."*

Noel cleared his throat. "We'll have to wait for the snow to melt."

With a nod of consent, Eleanor closed a frail hand over

his arm. "You'll know when to take us. I trust you not to fail him. I always have."

CHAPTER 22

MADDIE

Fluffy tail whooshing, the big dog gave the neighboring backyard an inquisitive glance before turning to Maddie.

"It's gonna take a bit to sink in, I'm sure, but you're with us now. No more roaming in circles because you've nothing better to do." Maddie dipped a hand into the five-gallon bucket of soapy water and swished the water in circles, mixing the hot water from the kitchen sink with cold water from the exterior faucet, then did the same for the bucket of rinse water. "Two baths in two days. It's a lot but, given how you sprawled out in the biggest patch of mud out here as soon as my back was turned, we don't have a choice. You can't go back inside wearing a coat of mud."

After yesterday's trip to the pet store, they had enough brushes, treats, food, and basics to get started...and Maddie would have a few hundred extra dollars on her credit card statement this cycle. Maybe it was muddying the waters as to who was responsible for the dog's care, Maddie or her mom, but Maddie didn't care. Charlotte had already overspent this month, stocking the pantry and fridge with the kids' favorite foods and loading the bathroom with essential-oil-based soaps and shampoos and fluffy, organic towels.

Leash in one hand and hose in the other, Maddie sprayed with the attachment set to a gentle mist, taking care to acclimate the dog to the water. The Pyrenees turned to lap at the spray, tail wagging, eyes closed, and face getting soaked. "Clearly, you have an affinity for water." Given the age of her mom's plumbing and the amount of dog hair and mud that came off her yesterday, Maddie knew better than to wash her in the tub, but the sun was out, the sky was a brilliant clear blue, and it had warmed into the mid-sixties. The hose water was cool but not chilly against Maddie's skin, and probably even less cold for the dog.

Before heading out earlier to visit a client with a loved one soon to pass, Charlotte had commented how people so rarely expected loss on beautiful days like this. "As if death has ever waited for gray and cloudy days," she'd said, bringing Maddie's thoughts to a helmet discarded on a driveway on an uncharacteristically warm and blue-skied winter day.

Sometimes Maddie didn't give her mom enough credit, but Charlotte knew what she was talking about more often than she didn't.

As water washed away mud, the dog's fur glowed stark white against the grime. Next, Maddie washed her down with soapy water and a big sponge. When she was rinsing off the suds, a familiar Jeep pulled up in the alley behind the house. Parking wasn't allowed in the narrow alley, but Noel was probably just dropping off the supplies to repair the downed section of fence.

The Pyrenees pumped her tail, spraying water like a faucet, and the twins rushed over from the patio where they'd been playing underneath the wrought-iron patio table.

"Uncle Noel!" they pleaded. "Can you come play with us?"

"We're pretending we're baby bear cubs without our mommy or daddy," Hazel added. "I'm a polar bear cub, and Benji is a grizzly bear cub."

"Oh yeah? Sure, I'll play," he said as he stepped through the back gate. "But I promised your grandma I'd fix the fence today, too, so I'll have to watch the clock."

"Can we help?"

"Absolutely. Only, who's hungry? I planned on feeding five-year-olds, but hopefully I bought enough chicken nuggets and fries to satisfy hungry bear cubs, too. And their mom," he added with a wink in Maddie's direction. "Another bath, huh?"

While the kids jumped in excitement over the promise of a tastier lunch than they'd been expecting, Maddie wiped the back of her free hand over her brow. "You didn't need to bring food, but thanks. And it'll be easier when the grass thickens up some. I left her out here a little while ago, and she went right for the mud."

"And now you're wearing more of it than she is."

Glancing down at her arms, Maddie laughed. "I guess I am—and she's been being good, too. Can you imagine if she'd been fighting me?"

"Well, if you need to be hosed down next, I'll make it happen."

Maddie blinked at the hint of flirtation in his gaze. She was working out how to respond when the Pyrenees pushed forward to sniff the two bags of Chick-fil-A in Noel's hands. Then, lifting her head, she shook herself off, spraying droplets of water in all directions and sending the twins scampering even as they called for her to do it again.

Switching the bags to one hand, Noel swept his thumb along Maddie's cheek to wipe off whatever had collected there, soap or dirt. A mix of pleasure and pain tore through her at his touch, reminding her how she still needed to address yesterday's kiss. Where could they possibly go from here? They'd lost their chance years ago. She'd married his best friend, after all.

"I'm blocking the alley. I'd better leave this on the patio table and get the trunk unloaded."

Noel and Maddie noticed at the same second that Benji had pulled down his pants and was peeing on one of the spring hostas poking up through the mulch, his bare butt shining in full view of anyone looking out their windows.

"Benji!" Maddie said, choking back a laugh. "You can't just pee outside like that."

"But our doggie does."

Spotting what her brother was doing, Hazel shrieked. "Mommy, he's going to kill the baby plant!"

Benji's expression instantly contorted, promising he was on the verge of tears. "No, I'm not!"

At one point, there'd been a month-long battle to keep Benji from peeing in Leo's litterbox whenever Maddie wasn't looking. At least this was a step up from that.

Noel touched Maddie's arm. "May I?"

"One penis wielder to another, huh?" Although her reply was playful, Maddie didn't know if she was more moved by the offer or that Noel made sure to ask her permission first.

"You know it," he said as he herded the twins over to the patio.

Smiling, Maddie turned back to the dog. "How about we get the last of those suds off before they dry, big girl?"

She hosed down the sprouting hosta after finishing with the dog, then hosed off her own arms, legs, and bare feet. By the time the Pyrenees was towel-dried, Noel had finished unloading a Jeep full of galvanized fencing, several posts, a couple shovels, a post hole digger, and a toolbox and moved the Jeep around front.

They ate lunch on the back patio under the pleading gaze

of a dog who was table height. Against her better judgement, Maddie slipped her a waffle fry when she didn't think either of the twins were looking, but Hazel sat up straight in her chair.

"Mommy, how come you can feed Elsa, but we can't?"

"Not Elsa, *Olaf.*" Benji puffed up.

Hazel crossed her arms, her face contorting tight in determination. "We can't call her Olaf. She's a *girl!*"

Maddie sighed. This wasn't the first time today they'd been skirting DEFCON 3, just the first time this hour. "Until we agree on what to call her, let's do our best not to get too attached to *any* names, you two." Maddie was crossing her fingers the chosen name wouldn't be from a character in *Frozen*. If they took her to a dog park, it'd be utter pandemonium with all the similarly named canines.

"Hey, you two pretending to be bear cubs got me thinking," Noel said. "You know how you asked about polar bear names yesterday, Hazel? What about Ursa? It's short for Ursa Major, a constellation in the stars known as the Great Bear." He slipped his phone from his back pocket. "Want to see a picture?"

As soon as he said it, a resounding *yes* went through Maddie. The big dog even acted like a bear as she moved about the house, sniffing corners and crevices as she surveyed her new surroundings.

After glimpsing whatever image loaded on Noel's phone, Hazel's eyes went wide. "That's it, Mommy! Ursa!"

Rather than disagreeing with his sister simply out of habit, Benji began to chant. "Ursa, Ursa, Ursa!"

The Pyrenees woofed at Benji's antics and wagged her tail.

"Ursa. What do you think, girl?" Maddie scratched her between the ears. "I know Nana said she'll be happy with whatever name we come up with, but how about we sleep on it tonight and decide in the morning?"

"Our doggie can't go to sleep without a name!" Eyes going as wide as if Maddie had suggested the dog sleep outside in an ice storm, Hazel slipped underneath the arm of her chair, stalked over, and closed her hands onto the sides of the dog's jowls. "Urrrsaaahh. Do you like it?" When the Pyrenees licked her from chin to forehead, Hazel giggled rather than panic about germs— a giant win as far as Maddie was concerned. She didn't think it was her imagination that Hazel's germ fears were receding a bit.

Maddie nodded toward one of the sunroom windows where Leo was perched, staring their way unhappily, his ears flattened against his head. Not only had he dropped a rung on his coolness factor with a dog in the house as far as the twins were concerned, but he'd also been relegated to the indoors until he could be trusted not to jump over the fence. "If you remember, Leo is named after a constellation, too," Maddie added. "The lion."

Hazel zoomed over to the window and tapped on the glass, cooing at the disgruntled cat, while Benji slumped in his chair in a temporary food coma after inhaling nearly as many nuggets and fries as Noel.

Glancing at Noel, Maddie shrugged. "Ursa is a good name. Thanks."

He winked as he gathered the trash. "My pleasure." His using Chick-fil-A's signature thank you probably wasn't intended to send Maddie's thoughts careening toward a very different pleasure she'd experienced in his arms yesterday morning.

But what was he doing anyway? Noel didn't wink. Not at her. Not in the five years she'd been married to his best friend, at least. That would've been entirely inappropriate. It was as if the kiss has unleashed a plug holding back more floodwater than Maddie would've guessed.

Even if she had the nerve to bring this up now, this question would need to be addressed when the twins weren't around. Until then, there was a downed fence awaiting repair.

When the repair work began, Benji and Hazel started out strong, wrestling one another for turns to dig and use the fence cutters, but they petered out and wandered back to their den underneath the table.

This left Maddie to work alongside Noel alone. The dog was napping in a patch of sun, and the kids were behaving remarkably well, allowing Noel and his repair project to have Maddie's full attention.

Like Landon, Noel jogged, skied, and went mountain biking, but something about this type of manual labor was an entirely different type of masculine and unleashed a fresh flood of pheromones inside her. Maybe it was the muscles of his thighs visible under his jeans as he strained with the post hole digger or the ropey definition in his arms as he cut through the downed section of fence with the fence cutters. Or maybe it was the quiet, inexhaustible energy he had about him. He knew what he was doing and didn't let bumps in the road—or roots and rocks in the fence line—deter him.

Maddie surprised herself by smoothing away a smear of dirt along Noel's chin. "Now who's the one needing to be hosed down?"

He was mixing a bag of quick-set concrete in a bucket to set the new posts in but paused to meet her gaze. "You gonna be the one doing the hosing?"

Maddie held his gaze long enough to be certain he felt it, too, the electrical current between them. She stepped back, wiping her hands on the backs of her jeans. What a fool she would be to go down this path a second time. Noel caught her hand as she turned away. She looked back at him.

"Noel, I can't."

"I know. Not now. But I'm here. Know that I'm here."

The seconds ticked away. As they stared into one another's eyes, Maddie could feel the words on her tongue, heavy and dry like she'd gotten a mouthful of sand. *Why wasn't I enough?*

Her lips parted. If only gravity would pull them out, then the question she'd held in forever would be over and done with. What would he say in response? What *could* he say?

Never had Maddie been so aware of the complete futility of words to make any of this better—or to quell it, either.

CHAPTER 23

On Thursday afternoon, Charlotte's house might as well have had a tornado tear through it. From toys —how could they have accumulated so many in five years?—to over-packed boxes and stuffed-full reusable totes, messes were everywhere. A few solid offers on Maddie's house had come through Sunday evening. While Maddie was navigating her chosen one, she'd accepted Noel's offer to scrounge up a few buddies and move a small rental truck worth of furniture, boxes, and tubs over here.

For ease of packing, she'd planned on still living at the house after the contract was signed, but Leo and Ursa were here, and the kids were having honest-to-God fun again. It didn't seem right to upend them again. Instead, they'd stay at Charlotte's, and Maddie would pop over to pack in the evenings and in the free time she was promised by both her mom and Noel.

And thankfully there'd be no more roughing it on the floor for Hazel and Benji. With their familiar bedroom comforts around them now, the twins had had a better night's sleep last night.

As for Maddie, the posh master bedroom furniture she

and Landon had purchased two years ago wouldn't be making the move. Maybe Charlotte was rubbing off on her, but Maddie wasn't about to bring the lingering energy of her failed marriage into her new life. When the house closed, she'd celebrate with the purchase of a new bed for herself. In the meantime, she'd ordered a deluxe air mattress rather than rough it on the floor another night.

When it came to all the furniture that wouldn't be making the move, Saanvi intended to post it on Marketplace for her and coordinate sales as best she could from Chicago.

The buyers of Maddie's house had offered more than asking price and offered a quick turnaround as well. Closing was only a month away. The soon-to-be new owners had three kids, a cat, and a dog, and Maddie loved that the house that had sheltered the twins in their early childhood would continue to be bustling with the lives of little ones.

A glance at the clock showed that they had another two hours before the baby came, and Hazel and Benji were jittery with excitement. They'd been waiting for this moment for a solid week now, and the countdown had been nearly as hard for them as the Christmas one, but who could blame them? It wasn't every day one met a half-sibling.

As the first meltdown blended into a second minutes apart, Maddie gave up attempting to get the main floor back into some semblance of order before Jordan got here. It was time for a bit of distraction. "How about we head for the park before the baby gets here?"

Benji's face, still wet with tears, brightened then fell within the space of a second. "What if we're not here when he comes?" Sniffling, he dragged a hand under his nose.

"I promise that we'll be back in plenty of time."

They must've been more stir-crazy than she'd thought because they hardly even dawdled as they got into their shoes and jackets. As they got ready, Maddie found her mom in the sunroom flipping through a recipe book.

"Hey there. I'm taking the kids to the park. The clock seems to be moving in slow motion this afternoon. Want to walk down with us?"

Looking up from the recipe book, Charlotte raised an eyebrow. "Good idea, but I have a hankering for sushi."

"I thought you weren't eating fish."

Her mom's mouth puckered in distaste. "There won't be any fish in this sushi. But unfortunately we're fresh out of nori."

"There's a shocker."

"I'm putting together a shopping list," Charlotte said, ignoring Maddie's playful jab. "Need anything? When I'm finished with it, I'll head down and join you."

"Who's nori?" Hazel asked, popping around the corner as she shoved one foot into a shoe, then the other.

"Nori is a thing, not a person," Charlotte answered her. "Seaweed paper. You tried it once before, remember?"

Hazel stuck out her tongue and tucked her shoulders up. "Yuck. It was disgusting."

"You say that now, but I doubt you'll think so when you're older."

Maddie planted a hand on top of Hazel's head. "How about we bring Ursa with us? She could use a walk, and I bet Leo could use a nap without keeping one eye open." Truth be told, Maddie was more worried about leaving the two animals unattended in the house than her mom was. While Ursa hardly gave Leo a lick of attention, Leo seemed to be in a losing battle to be top dog—with an actual dog. "Mom, we'll meet you down there. No rush."

Maddie grabbed a handful of treats and bags and leashed the dog, and they headed out. So far, Ursa was proving to be mild mannered on walks, hardly even pressing against the leash. Maddie was thankful for this. She could imagine that, of the two of them, it wouldn't be her who'd win a tug-of-war contest.

"I get the motorcycle first," Benji called as the far edge of the park came into view. He needn't have, though. It was the bouncy horse on a spring coil that Hazel was most interested in.

With just over a block to go, the twins pleaded to run ahead, and Maddie let them. It was a safe enough opportunity for them to earn a bit of trust. The street wasn't well traveled, and no cars were coming in either direction.

They took off with the eagerness of a track team but stopped as instructed when they reached the end of the sidewalk, grabbing one another's hands and looking in both directions. The sight made Maddie proud and wistful at the same time. At one point, each day had seemed like a small eternity, but now they were flying by in a blur.

Ursa woofed, unhappy that her charges were running ahead. She pulled against the leash for the first time, leaving Maddie no choice but to pick up her pace.

A handful of other families were at the playground, and both the motorcycle and horse were in use. Hazel ran to one of the open swings while Benji skulked around, kicking at the mulch in frustration. Maddie held her breath, wondering if this would lead to meltdown number three in less than an hour. The poor guy simply wasn't having his best day.

She bit back an urge to call out, suggesting he try something else while he waited. Given his mood, the comment would likely draw attention to the waiting rather than any potential reward.

With Ursa along, Maddie stuck to the periphery of the playground. She was touched by the way the dog's watchful gaze stayed locked on either Hazel or Benji, and she seemed oblivious to other kids. How quickly she was bonding with them!

Maddie pulled out her phone and snapped a picture from behind, catching Ursa's profile from over her shoulder. The big dog was staring intently at Hazel, who was visible in the background in mid-swing, her feet pushed forward. It was one of those cloudy, gray days in early spring that didn't do much for people's moods but could turn out a good photograph. Ursa's furry white body filled most of the photo, but the bright yellow and red of the swing set and turquoise of Hazel's jacket added the perfect splash of color. Marking it as a favorite, she determined to get it printed and hang it on the fridge.

Looking up, Maddie saw that Benji was interacting with a tall, lanky girl waiting for the motorcycle, too, so Maddie used the opportunity to text the picture to Saanvi. Earlier in the week, she'd finally had the energy to give Saanvi the phone call she was due. They'd talked for three hours, and when they'd finally hung up, Maddie felt like a weight had been lifted. There was nothing quite like the reassuring presence of a best friend who had your back. As Maddie had known she would be, Saanvi was in her corner about the decision to bring the baby into their world.

Saanvi reacted to the photo with a heart emoji, and they were texting back and forth when Benji's tone caught Maddie's attention. Pocketing her phone, Maddie watched Benji's face redden and his hands ball into fists. "That's not true! And you're a *meany!*" he yelled before taking off across the park, away from the playground as fast as his little boy legs could carry him.

Ursa woofed and lunged forward with enough umph that Maddie was jerked onto her knees. In nothing short of a miracle, she managed to keep hold of the leash as she scrambled to her feet. Ursa dragged her along after Benji, cementing Maddie's fears that when the big dog really wanted something, she had considerably more pulling strength than Maddie had resistance.

Maddie yelled Hazel's name to get her attention, but her daughter was in her own world, lost in the rhythm of the swings. Thankfully, one of the parents noticed and yelled that they had eyes on her.

"Benji, stop your feet!" The command that had kept the twins safe at street crossings when they were younger either didn't work any longer, or Benji was too upset to hear her. Thankfully, a hundred or so yards from the playground, his legs must've grown tired. He ducked behind a giant tree whose base was wide enough to disappear behind.

Ursa didn't stop moving—or dragging Maddie along behind her—until she was upon him. He was curled in a ball, hands covering his head, a few tight, blond curls sticking out between his fingers. Ursa planted her front legs on either side of his feet and gingerly sniffed the top of his head, the picture of a satisfied guard dog who'd reconnected with her charge.

Maddie was pulling out her phone to call her mom when she spotted Charlotte in the distance headed toward the playground. "Thank goodness!" she muttered. Waving, she got her attention, then pointed toward the swings. Charlotte acknowledged her with a thumbs up.

After a thorough sniffing of Benji, Ursa pushed to the far edge of her leash. Staring off toward Hazel, she whined pleadingly, melting Maddie's heart all over again. What an incredible dog to have been wasting away walking circles in someone's backyard.

Maddie knelt next to Benji and rubbed his back. His thin frame shook with sobs, sending a few tears down Maddie's cheeks as well. This reaction wasn't the result of a random comment from some kid he'd just met. This was deep and raw and had likely been needing to come out for a while.

"There, there, bud," she whispered over and over until he was drained of tears. By then, Ursa had stopped whining and was wagging her tail. Maddie craned to see around the tree and spotted Hazel and her mom heading their way.

"Want to talk about it?"

Poor Benji. His face was red hot, and his eyes were already puffy. The poor kid wasn't going to have an ounce of energy left to get through the day. He dragged a hand over his nose and looked up at her. "That girl waiting to ride my motorcycle asked where my daddy was, and I said he's watching me from heaven. But that girl is stupid! She said heaven's not real."

"Oh sweetie." Maddie would circle back later on Benji's name calling. Right now he needed nothing but love and support.

"Mommy, can daddy still see me?" Benji's tone was raw and desperate and so much more grown up than his five-year-old self. "If he can, how come we can't see him?"

"Those are some tough questions, Benji. The truth is a lot of people spend a lot of time trying to answer them."

"What do you mean?"

"I guess it depends on who you ask. Like when you argue with your preschool friends about who's better, Chewbacca or Baby Yoda. Sometimes the best thing to do is to accept that what you believe is what's right for you."

"Do you believe in heaven?"

"I do, Benji. But that doesn't mean I don't have my own questions. Maybe it'll help some if you think of heaven as a state more than a place."

"Like St. Louis?"

"Not quite. St. Louis is a city in our state. I was thinking of something like water. Most of the time, the water around us is liquid. We can drink it, swim in it, pour it, or water the plants. Then, when it gets cold enough, it freezes."

"Like ice?"

"Yep. And when it gets really hot, it turns into steam. And when water turns to steam, we can't see it, but it's still there in the air, and we can even kind of feel it because of the moisture in the air. When I think of dying and going to heaven, I think of it like that. Your dad's spirit couldn't stay in his body anymore after his accident, but that doesn't mean it's not still a spirit."

"But you can't see spirits." That sweet, round face of his remained set in a look of fierce determination.

"No, you can't."

"Then how can you know it's real if you can't see it?"

"I know love is real, and we can't see that. I know your father loved you and your sister more than anything. Even when you were tired and cranky or fighting with each other, he loved you so, so much."

Maddie used the back of her hand to dry Benji's cheeks.

"Grandma Eleanor says that daddy's up in the sky, and he can see me. Only he doesn't have his body, so how does he see?"

Maddie could feel the tension still locking up his body as she rubbed her hand over his back. "Remember how we talked about having faith, and how that means having a belief in something you can't see or touch, like the water that's turned into vapor?"

"Like Santa?"

Ouch. Someday he's really going to hold this Santa thing over my head. "Pretty much, yeah." He'd just lost a father. She wasn't touching the Santa thing with a ten-foot pole this year. "The way I see it, faith is listening to what's in here..." She paused to tap his chest before moving to his forehead. "... over what's up here. And that's not always easy to do because our minds are full of words and images, and we learn that it's easier to listen to words than to listen the way we need to listen to understand what's in our heart."

Ursa stepped close again and began to lick the side of his face, drawing a smile from him. He threw his arms around her thick neck and buried his face in her fur. "Don't let her leave, Mommy, please."

"Ursa is here to stay, sweetie."

Charlotte and Hazel finished their walk over and joined

them. As if she'd heard every word—although she couldn't have—Hazel looked as if she needed a hug of her own. Maddie stood and lifted her onto her hip. Hazel wrapped her arms around Maddie's shoulders and burrowed her forehead against Maddie's neck. Close as the siblings were, they'd been feeding off one another's emotions since the day they were born, but who could expect anything less from two humans who'd come into this world together?

Letting go of the dog, Benji wiped his face, smearing dirt from his hands across his cheeks in the process.

"Life begets life, Benji." Charlotte knelt and closed a hand over his shoulder.

Maddie figured her mom's words would be so far over Benji's head that she'd lose him, but he looked up, giving her his full attention. "What's begets?"

"It's a very old word that no one uses much anymore." Charlotte's expression carried the calm assuredness that her career had given her—or perhaps she was so good at her career because whatever created that look had come first. "But it's a pretty word that means to bring or become. Life brings life. Life becomes more life." She looked from Benji to Hazel, who'd lifted her head off Maddie's shoulder and was paying attention as well. "My parents used to tell me to look to heaven for all the answers, and I remember how frustrating that was because you can't put your finger on heaven. My advice to you both is, rather than trying to get your head wrapped around *where* your father's soul is, it may be easier to think of all the pieces of him that he left in this world. Pieces that help make it a better place. There's you two, of course. All those stories of his, all that fun you had together, that's forever a part of you." She spread her hands in the direction of the trees around them. "It's your duty to share all that as you beget more life."

Hazel and Benji both looked up at the trees like they expected to see something miraculous.

"He gave the world more than just the two of you and Liam," Charlotte continued. "There's your mom and Uncle Noel and all his friends who are better for having known him. There're the restaurants where he worked and thousands of pictures he took that show the world from the unique way he saw it. And there's his ashes. When they're spread, they'll become part of the earth, and that will give life to flowers and plants, which feed the bees and butterflies."

Hazel's eyes brightened. "And the birds."

"Yes, and the birds."

Benji stayed quiet, working the fingers of one hand deep into Ursa's fur until the dog seemed to deem no one was moving anywhere quickly and laid down. Benji looked up at Maddie. His curls were a disheveled mess. He was red-faced and dirty, but something about him seemed lighter, washed clean. Using his jacket sleeve, he dragged it over his face.

Glancing over at the playground as he got up, he saw that while they'd been talking, it had emptied of two of the families, and both the horse and motorcycle rides were empty. He brightened instantly. "Hazel, our toys are open!"

Rather than running off as he typically would, he waited until his sister slid off Maddie's hip, then reached for her hand.

"Of course, honey. I'm fine. And I have my mom here if I need her."

Latching hands, they dashed off, neither one attempting to outpace the other as they traversed the still-patchy spring grass. Benji's behind was a mess from sitting on the damp ground, but Maddie would wash his pants when they got home.

Ursa lumbered to her feet again and glanced at Maddie expectantly. "Thanks for that. I should've asked you to explain it to them sooner."

Charlotte closed a hand over the back of Maddie's

shoulder as they headed across the park at a slow pace. "They weren't ready to hear it sooner."

"Well, it seems like it was exactly what Benji needed to hear now. Hazel, too."

Charlotte shrugged. "What can I say? Death comes easier with a bit of practice."

Maddie huffed at the truth in her mom's words.

"And Maddie…"

"Yeah?"

"As often as I've said how Landon wasn't right for you, all my readings lately…that baby… You know what I'm going to say. There are no coincidences. None this big, at least. You're right to trust your instincts. He's meant to be in their world. Just like Landon was meant to stray when he did. I'm proud of you for being brave enough to see it."

Not for the first time lately, Maddie found herself in full agreement with her mother. Maybe that, too, was a part of growing older.

CHAPTER 24

By the time they made it home, the twins had gone from wired to thoroughly spent. Charlotte headed to the grocery store, and Maddie helped Hazel get comfy on the couch with a handful of new-to-her books from this week's library trip while Benji sprawled out across the floor with a single toy ATV in hand.

In the time it took Maddie to fix a quick snack of cheese cubes, grapes, and almonds, Benji was fast asleep and drooling on the decorative rug in the middle of the hardwood floor, the picture of little-kid exhaustion. Hazel wasn't far behind him judging by the way she picked at her snacks and her eyelids drooped.

"The best laid plans," Maddie mumbled.

When the doorbell rang fifteen minutes ahead of schedule, Maddie's limbs locked up the same as if she'd made the ridiculous decision to go skydiving and was at the make it or break it point of either jumping—or being pushed—out the cargo door. What was she thinking? Her decision to welcome Landon's illegitimate child into her home carried the whiff of Charlotte's untamable nature rather than the thoughtful scent of control Maddie had worked so hard to embody.

Suddenly it hit her that perhaps if she weren't so focused on embodying the structured qualities that Landon and her mom had either lacked or been able to harness, she'd probably have a lot more fun along the way.

Ursa trotted over Benji toward the door, and he didn't so much as stir. Hazel's eyes grew wide in a last-minute panic before she lunged headfirst underneath a blanket and curled into a ball.

"It's all good, sweetie," Maddie assured her. "We've got this."

Ursa sniffed underneath the crack at the bottom of the door. After ushering her aside, Maddie opened it to spy Jordan standing on the far side of the front stoop, swinging the baby in an infant car seat carrier. She was dressed for her upcoming shift in serving attire, a Schlafly T-shirt and jeans. She wasn't wearing a stitch of makeup, and the dark circles underneath her eyes seemed even more pronounced than they'd been when they'd last met.

"I was freaking out that you'd call and cancel." Jordan's thin frame was swaying along with the carrier. "I swear, I didn't even want to peek at my phone."

It seemed they were skipping right past hello. "He's sleeping, I take it?"

"Yeah. He cried all morning. Like *all* morning. He's been a little less of a monster since his noon nap, then the car ride knocked him out again. He hasn't been out long, maybe ten minutes. With any luck, he'll stay zonked out a bit. Maybe then he won't be such a creeper for you."

Waving her in, Maddie reminded herself that Jordan's choice of vocabulary didn't make her less of a dedicated mother, not when the baby was too young to understand her. And a young, struggling mom needed some way to let off steam. Maybe that was Jordan's. "This is Ursa. She's new to the family, but she's been great with my kids. How she is around infants is anyone's guess, so I'll be cautious while she gets used to him. Leo—the cat in the window—is big but friendly and used to little ones."

"Beautiful animals, and love the names. I can talk astrology all day long. One of my best friends is a Leo. I'm a Scorpio, but my moon sign is Cancer, so there's that. You can't say you weren't forewarned."

Maddie nodded, wondering how long it would take her mom to learn she and Jordan shared a mutual interest in the subject. "So…" Maddie motioned toward the lump that was her daughter. "Let's see. Hazel's around here somewhere," she pretended. "Hazel, want to say hi or wait a bit?"

The blanket rustled without being pulled off. "Wait a bit."

"You can take your time, sweets." Maddie followed up with a disclaimer over how Benji had been jittery with excitement all day, though clearly, that energy had come and gone.

"It seems too much to ask that Liam will ever sleep like that." Jordan sidestepped around Benji's sleeping form before focusing on the lump underneath the blanket that was Hazel. "You and I speak the same language, Hazel. I'm twenty-one, and I still want to do that every time someone knocks on my door."

Twenty-one. Maddie had guessed right. *Really, Landon, why am I not more surprised you slept with a twenty-year-old?*

Hazel's only response was a slight wiggle of her body.

After giving Benji a sniff, Ursa spread out on the floor alongside him and thumped her tail. Leo hopped down from the window and walked over, tail erect, to sniff and rub against the carrier.

"Nice house," Jordan added. "Great vibe. Seems like a great place to raise kids."

"Thank you. It's my mom's." Maddie nodded toward the

tubs and boxes. "The twins and I are just getting settled." Somehow Jordan's easy camaraderie was at once off-putting and reassuring.

"So, where would you like him?" Jordan said, looking around. "If it were me, I'd leave him in his seat until he wakes up. He doesn't transfer well."

It struck Maddie that she was about to take on a several-hour babysitting shift of an infant—and a stranger at that. With luck, it'd be like riding a bike, and the important stuff would come back. "Uh, the couch, I guess. Next to that lumpy blanket." Thank goodness Liam wasn't mobile yet, and she didn't have to worry about him exploring in this mess of stuff needing to be unpacked.

"Sure thing. Oh, and just a heads up. He usually sleeps best in commotion. It's when it gets dark and quiet that he fights sleep the most."

As soon as the weight of the infant seat could be felt on the couch, Hazel lifted the blanket a handful of inches to peek at the baby, and Maddie turned her focus on the baby the way Hazel must be seeing him: those heart-melty plump cheeks, long eyelashes, and smooth skin.

"Aww," Hazel whispered. "He's so cute."

Maddie had a feeling she'd remember her daughter first laying eyes on her half-brother forever. Even Maddie longed to brush her fingertip over his soft skin and experience the locking of that perfect little hand around her finger. *Life begets life.*

"He's so little," Hazel said, still mostly hidden under the blanket. Without waking, the baby sucked in an uneven breath and jerked, both fists tensing for a second or two before he resumed his peaceful doze. "Do you think he's scared to be here?" Shaking out of the blanket, Hazel sat up and leaned closer without touching him.

"I don't think he realizes he's here yet," Maddie said, "so, no, I don't think so. He was probably dreaming just now."

"Sometimes I pretend to be asleep."

"I bet he's too little still to pretend." Jordan slipped into the narrow opening between the coffee table and the couch and sank onto her heels, sandwiching herself smack dab between Hazel and Liam. "It's nice to meet you, Hazel. You look a lot like your mom."

"Except my hair's straight. That's what everyone says. I wish I had curly hair, but Benji got it."

"And except for that, he looks like your dad, doesn't he?"

"He looks like Benji. My dad was a lot bigger."

Was. It came so naturally now. For all of them.

Maddie waited through a bit more small talk before going through a checklist of what she'd need for the baby, from diapers and formula to a change of clothes and an extra onesie, and then Jordan was heading for the door.

"Text if you have any questions, or if the little creeper's giving you too much trouble." Jordan tossed her hair over her shoulder. "Actually, I'm really hoping he doesn't. I'll take all the breaks I can get right now."

Maddie didn't know how to respond to this. "I know you're not sure when you'll be off tonight, but what time should I start getting him to sleep? I can put him down on my bed and stack pillows around him if need be."

"Yeah, so, I haven't managed to get him on a schedule yet, working evenings and all. When he gets cranky enough that nothing satisfies him, it's my clue he needs to check out from the world."

Maddie would be hard pressed to forget those early months with the twins. One of the handful of things that had helped her muddle through them was establishing a routine, but Jordan wasn't seeking advice right now, so Maddie kept quiet.

All too quickly, Jordan was stepping outside and shutting the door behind her...and leaving her stuffed-full backpack and baby behind with hardly a glance. She dashed for the passenger side of the idling clunker at the curb where a girl about Jordan's age was waiting behind the wheel, hitting a vape. *Please tell me she doesn't do that while Liam is in there.*

"When do you think he'll wake up?" Hazel asked, still hovering next to the baby but not attempting to touch him.

"I'm not sure, but did you hear that bit his mom said about letting him sleep as long as he needs so he won't be tired and cranky with us? I'm sure you want him to wake up, but it's best we let him sleep."

"Yeah."

If Ursa realized there was a living baby in the car seat on the couch, she wasn't acting like she cared an ounce. Eyelids growing heavy, the big dog let out a satisfied exhale and rested her head on the floor not far from Benji and began drifting off. Leo, on the other hand, jumped onto the back of the couch and stared down at the infant seat with his ears turned back in a look of dissatisfaction.

Maddie sat down on the opposite side of the couch from the baby and ran her fingers through her daughter's silky fine hair. Turning away from the baby, Hazel curled into her. "Liam's mom doesn't look like any moms I ever saw. She doesn't talk like them, neither. How come daddy wanted to marry her?"

Maddie took a few seconds to answer. "Well, if you remember, your dad and I were in the process of ending our marriage when he passed away. He never had the chance to talk to me about Jordan." On the other side of the couch, the baby let out a satisfied sigh in his sleep. "One thing I learned about your dad was he could really get excited about things, but he didn't always think them all the way through. Most of your friends have parents who are married, but some people have babies together but don't get married. I suspect that would've been the case with your dad and Jordan. They were two very different people."

"Who would've kept Liam then? Daddy or his mommy?"

"I suspect they'd have taken turns."

"Would you have gotten a turn?"

Maddie blinked at the unexpected question. "No, actually, if your dad was still alive, I wouldn't be a part of Liam's life the way I will be now." And right then she knew that, as terrifying as it was, she was thankful to have this opportunity with the little human on the other side of the couch. She was going to get to be a part of her children's shared world with their half-brother.

Hazel reached for Maddie's cheek, pressing her soft, small hand against it the way she'd done back when she was a toddler falling asleep and wanting connection. "I'd never want not to have you as a mommy."

Maddie pulled her close, savoring the feel of her daughter's small body pressed against her. A handful of feet away, Ursa and Benji were breathing off-sync in their dozes. Still on the back of the couch, Leo's ears had relaxed, and his tail had stopped flicking. The baby stirred in his sleep again, but his eyes stayed closed. His tiny, socked feet stretched outward, his toes coming to a point, and his hands curled into fists before lodging underneath his chin.

Perhaps because silence was such a rare commodity in her home during the daylight hours, Maddie was certain this was one of those moments she'd remember forever. "You know, Hazie, I'm willing to bet the biggest reason I was put on this earth was so I could be your and Benji's mom."

Hazel broke away from their embrace to lean toward the baby, closer than she'd gotten yet. She closed her eyes and inhaled.

"What are you doing? Smelling him?"

"Yeah," she said, sitting upright again. "He smells like daddy."

"Oh yeah? I'd have guessed he smells like a baby."

"I don't know how other babies smell, but Liam smells like daddy." Hazel cuddled into her again. "I think my little brother's going to be happy you get a turn with him, too."

Maddie brushed Hazel's hair back from her face. "As much as I wouldn't have wanted it to happen this way, I'm getting pretty excited to have a turn with him, too."

CHAPTER 25

NOEL

Noel wasn't proud of how he'd been feeling since walking through Charlotte's front door an hour and a half ago, but he knew the feeling for what it was. He was jealous. Of a four-month-old. He'd promised to support whatever decision Maddie made about bringing the baby into the twins' lives, and he'd meant it. Yet here he was, jealous anyway.

It had been nearly dinnertime when he'd arrived. He'd taken the day off and had spent it with his father, driving him to neighboring Illinois to visit a three-hundred-year-old fort that his military-history-buff dad had been wanting to visit forever. Knowing Maddie would have her hands full with the twins and a baby and unsure if Charlotte was working tonight, he'd called, offering to drop something off for dinner, but instead Maddie had invited him over. Charlotte was home and cooking. "So long as you're up for vegan sushi or plain buttered noodles with the twins," she'd added with a laugh.

When Noel had gotten here, Liam had been in as good a mood as could be expected of a four-month-old in a totally new environment. Over the last half hour, he'd grown clingy, and any little thing was setting him off. He was only content when Maddie was holding him, and he kept working one hand underneath the V-neck opening of her sweater to lock his tiny fingers around her bra strap as if he was prepared to be dragged away at any moment. The sight tugged at Noel's heartstrings but didn't do much to taper the jealousy circling in his veins.

It was a jealousy that promised his hope that he and Maddie might have a real chance together now had been unfounded. It wasn't just the kiss that had ignited it; it was the way Maddie had begun looking at him. Like there was no longer a million miles separating them.

Now, here was this baby of Landon's, popping into the picture with his all-consuming needs, claiming another piece of a woman who was already so taxed.

It wasn't the kid's fault. Nor his mother's. She was neither financially stable nor had a healthy support group to call on. Regardless of whether there was someone to be blamed, the baby's needs would most likely snowball—like his father's before him—soaking up Maddie's time and energy when she hardly had enough of either to spare.

After dinner, Noel had been relegated to kid duty while Charlotte cleaned up and Maddie paced in circles, introducing the overtired infant to one thing after another to keep him entertained. The twins had been excited to show him the baby, but they seemed to have adjusted to Liam's presence in their home with the lightning speed of five-year-olds. The baby was fun when he was fun. When he wasn't, he was their mom's responsibility.

As the kids cuddled on either side of Noel while he read them the pile of books they'd dropped on his lap, he realized what was really bothering him. It wasn't the baby; it was Landon. Even in death, he was finding a way to claim more of Maddie.

When the fourth book was finished, Maddie headed

upstairs with the baby to draw the twins a bath. The three of them followed while Charlotte headed outside with the dog for a late evening walk.

When Noel reached the landing, Maddie was seated on the edge of the tub, balancing Liam atop one thigh. For the moment, the little guy was neither crying nor fussing, but his eyes were red-rimmed, and he was sucking on his fingers discontentedly.

"I've been thinking about Eleanor and Charles," Maddie said when Noel leaned against the doorway as she tested the water with the inside of one wrist, her opposite arm supporting the baby.

"What about them?"

"That they need to know about him. They miss their son. It's only fair for them to know they have another grandchild."

"I agree with you. Is Jordan on board?"

"I don't know, but I'll talk to her. Hopefully, she'll come around. I can see that it would be terrifying. If she wants to be the one to tell them, I'll offer to go with her. If she prefers me to tell them instead, I will."

"Count me in, if that's the case." He glanced over at the twins. Rather than heading into the bathroom as Maddie had asked, they'd dropped to the floor and were pretending to be turtles from one of the books he'd just read.

"You okay?" Maddie asked.

"Yeah, you?" He turned toward her again.

Satisfied with the temperature, Maddie plugged the drain before standing up and shifting Liam in her arms. She stepped in closer than Noel would've anticipated, and he had nowhere to look but those impossibly rich hazel eyes of hers. "No, not really," she said. "My life is a soap opera, and there's a million things I should be focused on right now, but if you want the truth, there's only one thing I've been able to think about the last hour."

"What's that?" There was a fire in her expression he hadn't seen in a long time.

"I'm pretty sure this is the first time since you walked in tonight that you've made real eye contact with me. Why is that?"

This is Maddie. You owe her the truth. "If that's true, it wasn't intentional. I'm just seeing the reality of all this for you. Can you handle it right now? With all you're already taking on."

"*It* is a *him*, Hazel and Benji's half-brother. And to give you an honest answer, I suspect I'm not going to know what I can't handle until I get there." The baby clamped his hand on Maddie's face in what seemed to be an attempt to explore her mouth. She turned away, and his fist locked around a thick curl. "But if you want to know my Achilles heel, my guess is it'd be losing you over this."

If there was an antiserum for jealousy, Maddie had just delivered it. "You aren't losing me, Maddie. Not over this. Not over anything. It's just a bit of stupid jealousy, that's all."

"Of a baby?" Her eyebrows lifted almost playfully.

"No." He huffed. "Of his father."

"Landon was your best friend."

"And he was your husband. And even from the grave, he's making your life harder."

Her eyes searched his. "Is it the harder or the fuller part that's really bothering you?"

"When you put it that way, I'm pretty sure I sound like the world's biggest ass."

Maddie glanced down the hall at the twins before reaching out unexpectedly and brushing the tips of her fingers along the ridge of Noel's jaw. "What would you think if I told you that by the time Liam was conceived, my marriage was all but over? That this last year or so, I was hanging on for the sake of my kids."

That I love you. That I never stopped. That if what you say is true, I'll wait for you forever. Heck, I'll wait even if it isn't.

Only the words wouldn't come. Noel's gaze had shifted to the baby at the exact moment Liam had noticed him standing there, and his big blue eyes had widened. Something in his expression resembled his father so precisely that Noel would almost swear Landon was standing here in this close circle with them. "Maddie..."

She swallowed. "I know. Not the time or place."

Noel locked a hand around her hip, one finger curling around one of the belt loops of her jeans. "Maybe not today. But it will be. Someday."

As if steadying herself, she closed her free hand around his forearm. Her touch was as painful as it was comforting. "At the risk of sounding like my mom—the master of certainty without facts to back her up—I know this thing with the baby is the right thing to do. Call it a mother's intuition if you will. Liam *and* his mom need us, but it wasn't until this afternoon that I saw how we're going to be better for it, too. All of us." Without warning, Maddie offered over a heavily protesting Liam, leaving Noel no choice but to take him. "Including you."

"Hey, I'm not—."

Liam twisted in Noel's arms, reaching for Maddie and whining, but Maddie stepped back, smiling. "Some Band-Aids just need to be ripped off."

"How about I give the twins a bath instead? I'm not good with babies."

"Yet," she said, undeterred. "He needs sleep, but he's fighting it. I thought the bottle would knock him out, but it didn't, so we'll have to make do until Jordan gets here."

"What do you mean, make do?"

Maddie brushed her fingers over Noel's arm again. "He likes it when you talk to him. And when you're moving around. When he's on the verge of crying like this, I've been able to distract him with running water, so maybe try the kitchen faucet. He likes the twins' toys, too, but don't give him anything smaller than his fist because it'll go right to his mouth. And if nothing else works, find a mirror. He's a Baxter, after all, and easily distracted by his own reflection."

Noel chuckled despite his unease. "I guess I know where to find you."

Her answering smile reached her eyes. "Don't worry. If it gets to be more than you can handle, I'll hear it. And my mom will be back before long."

Noel was still coming to terms with the fact that he'd just been assigned infant duty when Maddie stepped around him to wrangle the twins into the bathroom.

Once she got them in and closed the door, the house got quiet. To keep Liam from lunging out of his arms in the direction of the bathroom as he whined for his preferred caregiver, Noel headed downstairs and circled the front room. He attempted to call the baby's attention to things like the remote, his keys, and the controller for Benji's battery-powered monster truck, but Liam whined and tugged at his ear while eyeing Noel uneasily.

"How about you give me a hint? Maddie's not an option right now, so what's going to do it for you?"

Noel had missed most of the twins' infancy. They'd been toddlers by the time he'd become involved in their lives, even sporadically as it had been back then. It had taken that long to handle seeing Maddie again. Under the circumstances, Noel didn't think he could be blamed.

Leo, who'd been staring out the window into the dark, turned toward him, eyes narrowing in a way that suggested he doubted the wisdom behind handing Noel such a big—and temperamental—responsibility. "You and me both, cat. You and me both."

At the sound of his voice, Liam stopped whining and gazed up at him, eyes widening and mouth falling open.

Those blue eyes were the exact same deep hue of his father's. A smile lit up the baby's face for the briefest of seconds—tugging at Noel's heartstrings—before his mouth opened in a big, toothless yawn.

"Guess you haven't been exposed to too many baritone voices, have you?" Noel's thoughts flashed back to the pictures he'd found of Liam in Landon's arms not long after he was born. "You won't remember it, but you got to meet your father before he died. Someday, when you're old enough to understand all this, you'll have pictures for posterity."

Liam brushed the tips of two fingers over Noel's lips like he wanted to explore where the sound was coming from. Noel was surprised by how much the baby's unsolicited touch moved him.

"Your dad... Just so we're clear, you couldn't have healed him. That's something he'd have needed to do himself. Had he lived though, you'd have been one more giant reason for him to get it together." The baby squeezed Noel's lower lip like he'd found a stress ball, and a smile broke across his face. There was so much of Landon in that expression that the hair on Noel's arms raised. "And here I thought Benji was a lot like him. Hazel, too, at times. But you, you're the whole package, aren't you?"

As if in answer, Liam emitted something that was between a babble and a grunt.

"Sorry, I don't speak baby." Liam's small hand moved to Noel's nose and gave it a squeeze.

After extracting Liam's hand, Noel circled the room again. "You're going to stir our lives up, only you're going to be so busy being yourself, you'll never notice. That's a gift he gave you, isn't it? You get to be so brilliantly alive you won't even notice the way everyone starts to orbit around you. You'll just keep doing your thing, and you'll grow to expect we'll always be here, held by your gravity."

Liam's sleepy eyes were transfixed by Noel's soft words,

and he watched Noel's lips move with keen attentiveness. Then, abruptly enough it took Noel by surprise, Liam let out another soft yawn and burrowed against his chest. Within seconds, it was clear he was finally giving in to sleep.

Noel stopped walking and swayed in place, listening to the twins and Maddie upstairs behind the closed bathroom door, feeling Liam's solid baby weight resting atop his forearm, and noticing the heat where their bodies pressed against one another. A soft, sucking sound slipped from Liam's closed lips for a few seconds before he grew silent once again.

"No need to worry, little bud. I'm betting we always will be."

CHAPTER 26

ELEANOR

Eleanor wanted time to stand still. She wanted Charles to stop shaking that foot of his in the air like it was a damn basketball. She wanted Noel to break free of whatever spell Maddie had over him and remember his connection and indebtedness to the Baxter family.

Mostly, she wanted Maddie to stick her words where the sun didn't shine. How dare she defile Landon's memory like this! And in Eleanor's own home, of all things.

It all circled back to money. Eleanor was certain of it. Of course her son would fall victim to such claims upon his death. How foolish of Maddie and Noel to be so gullible.

"I don't believe it, not a word," Eleanor spat, unable to keep silent under the weight of Maddie's accusations any longer. "The girl is lying. Clearly. Landon was a good man. He was raised Christian, baptized even. He wouldn't do that —have an extra-marital affair. I'm certain of it."

On the opposite couch facing her, Maddie pressed her eyes closed a second, clearly biting back a retort. It was Noel who spoke up. He turned from where he'd been standing at the window near the floor-to-ceiling shelves loaded with books, most of which Eleanor had never read. He walked closer, stopping at the edge of the couch. "I heard it straight from him, Eleanor. He confided in me about a month before he died. Before the baby was even born. I was in Brazil at the time."

Eleanor stood up so fast she nearly lost her balance. "And all this time, you never told me? How could you!" She could see the sting of her words in Noel's eyes. But how *could* he? Eleanor credited this failure to his parents, to a failure in Noel's upbringing. It had to be.

"It was always my intent to tell you, Eleanor. You and Maddie both. You've been dealing with a lot. We all have. Maddie especially."

"What's the woman's name?" Charles interrupted.

Maddie and Noel looked at each other. "Jordan," Noel said after Maddie nodded almost imperceptibly. "Jordan Hill. She was a hostess at the Row House for about six months. She left about a year ago now."

Eleanor watched her husband drag a hand slowly over his mouth, the skin of his plump cheeks glowing pink in its wake. "I remember her. Thin little thing. Kind of a tragic look about her."

It irritated Eleanor to no end that Charles could picture her, and she couldn't, but hostesses were a dime a dozen. It was the kitchen staff and servers who Eleanor concerned herself with. "Paternity tests can be faked. All she needed was a lock of Landon's hair to test him without his consent. We have no idea if he even agreed to it."

"Even if that were the case," Maddie interjected, "in a reputable paternity test, there's no faking a genetic relationship that doesn't exist."

If this terrible accusation Maddie and Noel were making was true, which Eleanor wasn't agreeing it was, there was only one reason Landon would've strayed, and most certainly everyone in the room knew it had to do with Maddie failing to please him. Yet, no one was mentioning it. The words were burning Eleanor's tongue, but somehow she found the grace to refrain. She couldn't always be the one pointing out the obvious.

"You've seen them then, the test results?"

Noel and Maddie looked at one another again, and Maddie shook her head.

How dare they team up against her son like this! "I haven't come across them while packing, and he never shared a copy with Jordan, but after he got the results, he no longer questioned the baby's paternity. He paid her share of rent and expenses while she was on maternity leave, too."

"How gullible you are! That doesn't mean a thing! Everyone in this room knows how soft-hearted my boy was. Who knows if he even took a test?"

Maddie, whose hands had been locked over her knees like she was trying to stop herself from pouncing out of her seat, abruptly began digging through her purse. "If you want to test him again, Eleanor, we can. There are still some of Landon's things that could give us the DNA we'd need, a toothbrush, a hairbrush, things like that. There're his ashes, too." Eleanor's stomach curdled at the thought of degrading her son's ashes in such a manner, but Maddie didn't leave her the space to respond. "But the twins DNA would suffice. Either of yours, too, for that matter. But this isn't about your money or the restaurants. It's about a little boy who on some level is going to be in the twins' lives. Mine, too. And Noel and I thought you'd want to know that you have another grandchild." She opened her phone and began scrolling through it.

"We do, Maddie. Thank you." Charles shook his head the way he did at a surprise ending in a movie.

Eleanor was about to sit back down when Maddie found what she was looking for. "Maybe it would help to see a picture of him? He looks a bit like the twins, but more than that, he looks like his father."

Eleanor glanced at Charles before remembering that he'd never been one to step to the rescue. "Babies are babies. They look like everyone and no one at the same time. If there's a resemblance you're looking for, you'll find it."

Maddie held the phone on her lap, not moving. "Would you like to see him?" she repeated.

Still poised to take a seat again, Eleanor stood there as one second lapsed into four or five. "Yes," she said, standing straight. "I would."

They met in the middle of the room. It was bright enough that Eleanor needed to take the phone and move it from the glare. She stared at the backlit image of a blue-eyed, wispy-haired infant, sheepishly grinning into the camera, one hand outstretched like he was reaching for it. She stared and stared, life draining and filling her all at once like a roar of seasons moving at light speed even as she reminded herself of the words that had just come from her own mouth, babies looked like babies. Finally, she passed the phone back to Maddie, motioning for her to show Charles.

She walked from the room on steadier legs than she'd have counted on, headed down the hall, and closed herself in her study. The item she was looking for was on the bookshelves. She headed toward it, her vision clouding, and sank with it into the chair behind the desk.

The cool metal frame stung her hand as she held it and, using the cuff of her sleeve, she wiped away the finest layer of dust. Before her eyes clouded over entirely, she took in the photo taken thirty-two years ago of a baby who looked uncannily like the one she'd just been staring at on Maddie's phone screen.

One life so cruelly cut short, another just beginning, and their paths never again crossing. Abandoning the picture on her lap, Eleanor folded forward as the first in a stream of heaving sobs raked through her, and the weight of the world pressed in.

CHAPTER 27

MADDIE

Maddie rubbed her eyes in the darkness as she woke from a deep sleep. They'd been at her mom's for three weeks now, and she hadn't been this disoriented in a while. Something had woken her up. She just wasn't sure what. Aside from the sound of Ursa's steady breathing from the floor, the house was quiet.

Rolling to the edge of the pillowtop air mattress, Maddie stepped around Ursa's sleeping form and padded out of the room to check on the twins, but they proved to be sound asleep. Hazel was in her bed, curled into a ball, while Benji had abandoned his and was nestled on his favorite blanket on the shag rug on the floor next to his sister's bed. Some nights, even being in the same room with his twin wasn't comfort enough. Perhaps he'd called out for Maddie but had fallen asleep there when she didn't respond. After a short debate on whether to poke the sleeping bear, she opted to cover him with a blanket rather than move him and let him wake up on his own.

She used the bathroom and headed back to bed. At two-thirty in the morning, there was every chance she'd be able to get back to sleep with ease. She was tucking herself under the covers when her phone buzzed from the crate serving as a makeshift nightstand.

When she flipped it over to view the screen, adrenaline dumped into her system. There was a slew of missed calls and texts from Jordan. *Please let the baby be okay.* Her hands shook as she clicked on the texts. Half were pleas to return her call, while the others were declarations of being at a breaking point.

Jordan's roommates were kicking her out.

The air mattress rocking underneath her as she sat up, Maddie tossed off the covers again. By now, Ursa was awake, tail thumping as she watched her. "It's okay, girl."

Maddie waited until she'd descended the stairs before tapping on Jordan's number, and she held the phone against her ear rather than put it on speaker. There was enough streetlight pouring through the windows that the living room was navigable in the dark, and Maddie refrained from turning on a light. The first sound emanating from the receiver was an exaggerated sniff. "Sorry to wake you." Jordan was the kind of nasal that only came with a deluge of tears or a bad cold. "I don't have anyone else to call."

"It's okay. Are you still at your apartment?"

"No. The fighting got so bad I took off."

"Where are you now?"

"Sitting outside. A couple blocks from my apartment."

Maddie could hear sirens in the distance. "Did you call the police?"

"Uh uh. Living here, you stop hearing the sirens after a bit." Jordan took a shaky breath. "They're my best friends, and they kicked me out. *They're all I have.*"

In the middle of the night...with a baby in the mix? What kind of friends did that? "Oh, Jordan, that's rough."

"Tell me about it."

"I suspect it doesn't seem like it right now, but it's gonna be okay."

"Nothing has been okay for a long time."

"Is Liam with you or in the apartment?"

"He's here. On my lap. I grabbed a blanket as I was walking out. He's actually pretty chill right now. Go figure. It's not like they said I needed to leave right this second, but I seriously can't take it anymore. I'm just so tired. Of everything." Jordan's voice pitched precariously the last several words before a burst of sobs erupted.

Once she'd calmed some, Maddie asked if she had a ride-hailing app on her phone.

"I did, but my phone's out of memory, so I deleted it."

"That's okay. I can schedule you a ride from my account if you send me your location. You can sleep here tonight."

Jordan sucked in a few uneven breaths as the baby began crying, too. Then she muttered something before hanging up that Maddie couldn't decipher over Liam's wails.

Maddie tapped her heel anxiously, gaze locked on her phone, as she willed a new text to come through. One with an address. "Come on, Jordan. As much as I don't love the idea of sleeping under the same roof as you, this is the right place for you to be tonight."

An excruciating two minutes later, the text came through. After entering the location into her ride app and finishing out the request, she held her breath as the Locating a Driver notification circled for several seconds before one was confirmed, and one who was only eight minutes away at that.

GOT YOU A RIDE. ONLY EIGHT MINUTES AWAY. HANG TIGHT. YOU SHOULD START GETTING TEXT NOTIFICATIONS.

Ursa followed her downstairs and headed straight for the back door. Maddie let her out even though whenever the dog went outside at night, she was inclined to hang out in the yard until someone herded her back inside. As Maddie headed into the kitchen, she heard footsteps on the stairs and was thankful when they turned out to belong to her mom and not one of the kids.

"Everything okay?" Charlotte asked when Maddie met up with her in the living room. Leo had followed her, and he dashed over to Maddie, rubbing against her and purring, probably hopeful this atypical night activity would result in an impromptu snack.

"Jordan's roommates kicked her out." Maddie scooped Leo into her arms and headed for the couch. "I told her she could come here tonight. I just got her an Uber." Dropping her phone next to her, Maddie sank onto the couch and hugged Leo against her chest, her belly tight with unease.

"Baby in tow, I hope?"

"Yeah." Maddie waited as her mom headed into the kitchen and returned with two glasses of water.

"Want to tell me where your thoughts are?" her mom asked.

In the last couple of weeks, they'd babysat for Liam four times, and Charlotte had been home three of them. "I think I'd rather not voice them."

Charlotte placed Maddie's glass on a coaster on the side table and headed for the opposite end of the couch. "If you're thinking how you were that baby once, and I was her, you aren't far off."

Maddie huffed. "I was more thinking about how she reminds me of Landon. In some ways."

"By how she walks in chaos, you mean?"

Maddie pointed a finger in her mother's direction but said nothing.

"As did I. For years. Many more of us do than you might expect."

Leo planted both paws on Maddie's chest and rubbed the side of his face along Maddie's chin, a deep purr thrumming in his chest. "Is it why I'm letting her in? Because it's a world I'm so comfortable in?"

Charlotte swept her unruly hair into one hand in contemplation. "We both know that depends on who you ask. We could talk about habits and conditioning, or we could talk about karma and destiny, but you're asking me, sweetie, and I find most comfort in the belief that we're here to grow our souls."

Closing her eyes, Maddie rested her forehead against Leo for a moment before he hopped off, meowing in the direction of the kitchen. "Meaning?"

"Meaning that our wounds, our brokenness—our *humanness*, for that matter—are where the light gets in, if you'll allow me to paraphrase Rumi. It's how we grow our souls."

Maddie collapsed against the couch. "Mom, none of this tells me if I'm doing the right thing by letting her come here. Letting her in in a deeper way."

"What do you think is the worst thing that could happen?"

"That all this could circle back and hurt my children."

"Funny how it's so much easier for us mothers to care about the well-being of our children than of ourselves."

"She promised she's not going anywhere, but how can she promise that when nothing about her life is stable?"

"She might not be going anywhere, but that isn't a promise she should make. Not at her age. Not in her position. And I know Hazel and Benji have had a rough time of it, but your job isn't to keep them from getting hurt. It's to teach them resilience, and you're doing a damn good job of it."

Maddie folded over and closed her face in her hands, resting there until she heard a scratch at the back door. There was a bit of progress. Ursa was ready to come back inside on her own and was letting her wishes be known.

As she was about to stand, Charlotte got up. "I'll let her in. And I'll make us a snack."

"Then I'll head to the basement for the porta crib."

"Good of Noel and his friends to have brought so much over, isn't it?"

Maddie agreed as she flipped on the basement light switch at the top of the landing and her eyes adjusted to the bright light. Last weekend, Noel had brought over a second truckload of furniture, boxes, and storage. A lot of it would stay in the basement until they had a place of their own, but it seemed the porta crib wouldn't be collecting dust down there. For now, at least.

Telling herself it had nothing to do with the fact that she'd been afraid of old, dark basements since she was a kid, she flipped on all three light switches as soon as she got down there. She made quick work of sorting through the boxes and tubs until she found the twins' old porta crib alongside a few other early childhood items she hadn't gotten around to selling. As she was gathering it in her arms, Leo sent a jolt of adrenaline straight through her by hopping up out of nowhere onto a nearby box, a deep purr rolling off him as if asserting that he had zero fear of old, dark basements.

By the time she hauled the porta crib up two flights of stairs to her bedroom—she'd sleep on the couch the rest of tonight—and got it set up with a few extra blankets and pillows, Maddie was awake enough that it might as well have been nearing three in the afternoon instead of three in the morning.

As she returned to the main floor, she spotted a pair of headlights pulling alongside the curb in front of the house. Ursa spotted them too and woofed, trotting to the front window for a look. Her long, fluffy tail stuck out straight behind her, but thankfully she didn't keep barking. The last thing they needed was to toss two five-year-olds into the mix right now.

Charlotte joined Maddie at the door as Jordan headed up the path to the porch. With the baby, a couple bags, and a blanket taxing her thin frame, an unexpected headwind could've toppled her.

"Sorry to wake you." Jordan sounded every bit as nasal in person as she had on the phone. Her eyes were as puffy as sandbags, too, and the sight of her compelled Maddie to place a hand on her shoulder as she stepped inside.

"I hope you don't have to work in the morning."

"I'll be okay." Maddie had to be at work at eight-thirty, and she needed to get the twins to school before that, but she'd power through with the help of a few cups of coffee. She couldn't call in, not with as much as she'd requested off lately.

"I don't know about Maddie, but I was already awake and struggling to get back to sleep," Charlotte said. "It happens in your fifties."

Ursa sniffed Jordan, then pressed her nose into the bottom of the blanket, smelling Liam as well. He was out like a light and curled against his mom's chest. "Will one of you take him? My arms and back are killing me."

Tamping back an instant 'yes,' Maddie glanced at her mom, who nodded. "I'm making tea and cinnamon toast. You go ahead."

Liam stirred as he was transferred but not enough to fully awaken. He burrowed into Maddie, letting out a soft sigh that made her weak in the knees.

Free of her son, Jordan collapsed on the couch, piling her bags close against her, reminding Maddie of a twelve-year-old who'd just been told she wasn't allowed to hang out with her friends.

"Hungry?" Charlotte asked.

"I don't get hungry, not really, but cinnamon toast sounds heavenly."

"It was my go-to comfort food when I was a kid. I'm not

as much of a sucker for sweets as I used to be, but this felt right for the occasion."

Jordan snorted. "'Occasion' is a weird word for a mom and baby invading your house at three in the morning."

"The more, the merrier, and I do mean that. Not only tonight."

Maddie shot her mom a look, but she'd already turned toward the kitchen. Maddie remained in the living room with Jordan but kept standing, swaying side to side.

"Your couch is comfy." Jordan rested her head against it. "Softer than my bed; that's for sure."

A dozen questions burned her tongue, but Maddie bit them back and hoped Jordan would come forward with more when she was ready. "You can have my bed tonight. It's an air mattress but comfortable enough that you forget you're on it until you have to roll off. I hauled the porta crib up there so that Liam will have a safe place to sleep, too."

"Thanks, but where will you sleep?"

Maddie was about to say the couch, but Charlotte intervened from the kitchen. "Maddie, my bed's big enough for two if I don't decide to stay up entirely. You sleep up there. I'm not meeting with any clients tomorrow until after lunch. I can nap in the morning."

"Thanks, but I don't mind the couch."

"Suit yourself, but I'm in the mood to stay up and do some readings."

"Readings?" Jordan asked, lifting her head off the couch.

"Tarot," Charlotte clarified.

"*Sweet.* I love doing tarot, but I'm not that good at it."

"There's no being good at tarot. There's only learning to read the cards—or listen to them, I should say."

"Well, I'd love to get better. I watch a lot of videos, but unless someone's there to walk me through them, I struggle with my own readings."

Of course, they're talking about tarot cards. It wasn't like

Jordan had just been kicked out of her apartment and had no place to live or anything.

"Get some sleep tonight, and tomorrow, I'll teach you."

"Yeah? Cool." Jordan's face rose and fell within the space of a few seconds, and she sniffed back fresh tears. "It's been my experience that people mostly aren't nice like you two."

Charlotte headed in with a tray filled with mismatched plates of cinnamon toast and mugs of steaming tea. She got all her dishes from thrift stores and hardly ever bought more than a few of any one pattern. "Chamomile. It's settling for the nerves."

Ursa had stretched out on the floor but lifted her head when Charlotte set the tray on the coffee table. Looking from the tray to Maddie, she thumped her tail hopefully. With the baby in her arms, Maddie dipped at the knees to swipe a half slice of toast off the table.

"I thought you were talking about the cereal," Jordan said, waving one of the saucers of toast under her nose even though she sounded nasal enough Maddie doubted she'd be able to appreciate the scent of melted butter and broiled-crisp cinnamon sugar blend on top. "But this is so much better."

Maddie took a bite, careful not to drop crumbs on Liam, who'd nestled his head between her left breast and shoulder and was sucking on his lower lip in his sleep. If Charlotte had used vegan butter, it was impossible to tell. For such a simple list of ingredients—white bread, butter, sugar, cinnamon, and perhaps a pinch of salt—it was perfection. And Charlotte was right—it was just what the moment called for.

"My mom..." Jordan continued. "It's a point of personal pride for her that she's never learned to cook. She's never brought home anything that couldn't be pulled out of a box or stripped from a wrapper and put in the oven or microwave —or served right from the package, of course. She's never wanted to be like her mom, cooking over a stove all day for a husband who'd slap her senseless if there was too much salt or not enough or whatever he found to complain about—I can't say for sure given how my grandpa died before I was born."

Charlotte had settled on the floor on the other side of the coffee table, her legs crossed and her posture straight enough to look like she was ready for yoga class. "Women should never have to experience that."

"Yeah, well, the not-so-funny thing is my dad was no better. He found his own list to complain about, and he hit just as hard."

Charlotte stayed quiet at this, though the compassion on her face was evident. Maddie found herself thinking how her own childhood spent without a father figure could've been far worse.

Nibbling on her toast, Jordan nodded toward Liam. "Thing is, I swore I wouldn't have kids because of that asshole, but in the end, it was my mom who about killed me, checking out like she did."

Jordan's gaze flicked to Maddie, right as Maddie pressed her cheek to Liam's head. Guilt rushed over her even though Jordan didn't seem to register the gesture of affection.

"She likes to claim her hands-off approach was intentional. To make resilient kids." Jordan set down her half-eaten slice of toast and yanked up her sleeve. "I wouldn't have most of these if it weren't for her."

Maddie braced herself for the thin scars running horizontally across Jordan's inner forearm even before spotting them.

"I'm not cutting anymore. I haven't for a couple years. I've been close a couple times the last few months. I keep floating in and out of this gray place and can't pick myself up, but I don't want to be a mother who cuts."

Liam stirred in his sleep, resting his other cheek against Maddie's sternum. "What support could you use, Jordan?" Earlier her thoughts had gone to what sort of help Eleanor and Charles might offer now that they were adjusting to the idea of having another grandchild, but this, this was something entirely different that Jordan was laying out before them.

A ghost of a smile flashed over Jordan's face at Maddie's question before she dabbed at her nose with her sleeve. "You want the truth? Or would you rather have an answer that doesn't scare the hell out of you?"

Maddie's heart thumped wildly in her chest. "The truth."

Jordan shot Maddie a direct glance. "I know it'll piss you off after what you made me promise, but I keep thinking about reaching out to the agency and asking if they'd call that couple back. See if they've found another kid yet."

Nausea dumped into Maddie's system, and her few bites of cinnamon toast knotted into a ball in her stomach. She opened her mouth and closed it again. No good would come from addressing this until Jordan had a solid night's sleep and had calmed down from what had played out tonight.

"You need a license to drive a car," Jordan continued into their silence. "So you don't hurt someone. But you don't need anything to have a kid. It's crazy, really. No one can hurt you like your mom." Maddie was searching for a reply when Jordan added, "I screamed at him last night. Like loud. His eyes got so big. I've never seen him afraid before. I didn't even know he could feel that yet."

Tears of compassion stung Maddie's eyes for both the baby and Jordan.

"If it helps, I used to have to lock myself in the bathroom," Charlotte said. "I'd stamp my feet or punch the air until I didn't have anything left. Other times, I just cried and cried until my eyes puffed up like tea bags."

Maddie blinked, picturing her twenty-year-old mother doing this, and all in one fell swoop, she realized she'd never given her mother enough credit for what she'd taken on, raising her alone like she had. Tears stung Maddie's eyes, but she blinked them away.

"The thing is, I wanted to shake him. It was one of those urges that makes you feel like you're standing on a beach and a tsunami is coming and there's nothing you can do to stop it."

"But you didn't," Maddie said. It was a plea as much as it was an assertion. Liam's small fist had locked around one of her curls, and Maddie suspected she was getting even more comfort from rubbing his back than he might be.

"No, I didn't. But what if one day I can't stop myself? When the world goes gray like this, I don't trust myself."

"Jordan, has anyone ever talked to you about postpartum depression?" Charlotte asked, her words as gentle as mist.

"Not exactly, but I've been on meds before. I hate the way I feel on them."

"Medication isn't the only option."

Jordan lifted a brow. "Light therapy? Talk therapy? Meditation? Getting out in nature? This isn't my first rodeo with depression. The first time I swallowed a bunch of pills I was twelve. Getting your stomach pumped triggers things."

Maddie swallowed hard. "You don't have to do this alone. You'll have help now. If you need more help than Mom and I can give you, there's Eleanor and Charles. Eleanor's coming around to this, and we can make sure any relationship with them is on your terms."

"I know that. Thank you." Jordan closed her eyes and rested her head against the couch. "The thing is, I'm not entirely convinced I should be doing it at all."

CHAPTER 28

Maddie might as well have sand in her eyes, dry as they were from lack of sleep. She was en route to pick up the twins from preschool when her mom texted, shooting off a series of texts back-to-back.

Since Maddie was driving and didn't currently have her infotainment system connected to the phone, she held off checking the texts until she reached the pickup line. However, when she pulled in at the back of the long winding line ten minutes later, her mind was elsewhere, and her thoughts were as sluggish as her progress.

She remembered them as she pulled out of the parking lot, two talkative twins in tow. Oh well, she was headed home anyway. Whatever her mom wanted could wait another ten minutes.

When Maddie left the house earlier, Jordan hadn't yet come out of Maddie's room. Her mom had still been wide awake when Maddie's phone alarm went off at seven twenty —the last possible minute to sleep to and still get ready for work, get the kids fed, and arrive at preschool on time—but Charlotte had headed upstairs to bed as Maddie herded the kids out the door.

It had been a little after six when Maddie fell back to sleep herself. She was bone-tired and as groggy as if she'd polished off a full bottle of wine last night. All morning, her thoughts had been focused on only one thing as she decorated cakes and cupcakes.

Jordan needed help.

She needed sleep, support, and stability. Maddie, Charlotte, and Eleanor could work together to ensure she got all that she needed.

She also needed a therapist, that was clear. Maybe the twins' therapist could recommend someone. Come to think of it, with Jordan being only twenty-one, maybe she could see Ms. Jenna, too, Maddie thought with a snort.

Jordan didn't have good healthcare, but there were services out there for single moms, especially ones who earned below the poverty level, and Maddie was determined to connect her with them.

This was just a bump in the road. Things were going to be okay. They had to be. For Liam and for Jordan. Maddie one hundred percent vested in this outcome.

Liam deserved it, and so did Jordan. If it was at all in Maddie's power to help them, that's exactly what she'd do.

Arriving home, Maddie glanced over at the house. Now that she was street parking consistently, getting the kids inside when they got home proved considerably more challenging than funneling them inside from the garage like she'd done at her house. There were spring flowers, abundant whirlybirds from the maple tree, chittering squirrels, rocks, and tall blades of grass calling their names at every step.

Maddie spotted both Ursa and Leo staring out the window as she headed up the path. Leo was perched on the windowsill, and Ursa was standing next to him, wagging her fluffy tail, eager to greet them. "Come on, kids. Let's get inside. We'll come out and play later."

Jordan and Liam were still sleeping when they left this

morning, but on the drive to preschool, Maddie had let the kids know that they'd spent the night and would be here today. As she stood at the door, digging through her purse for the key, she heard Jordan call from inside that the door was unlocked.

Maddie pushed it open and was hit with a blast of earthy incense even before spotting the hazy trail of smoke emanating from the incense stick on the coffee table. Jordan was wedged on the floor between the couch and coffee table, and Charlotte's tarot deck was spread in front of her.

"Your mom did a reading for me," Jordan said as Maddie lingered in the doorway, waiting for the twins, and blocking Leo from slipping outside.

"Oh yeah?" Considering that Maddie knew which reading her mom had done by the alignment of the four face up cards and how the Six of Swords was as much a positive sign as the Devil and Death cards were ominous ones, Maddie knew more about tarot readings than she'd own up to. There was the Fool in the last spot, too. Her mom would interpret that, along with the Six of Swords, as a silver lining in Jordan's future more than she'd focus on the chaos and drama promised by the other two cards.

"She's great, your mom."

"I don't always give her the credit she's due, but yeah, she is." Maddie glanced into the empty kitchen. "Where is she?"

"Upstairs. With the one human who dislikes me the most out of everyone on this planet."

"Oh, Jordan, it might feel like that somedays, but you're his everything."

Jordan's answering huff resonated in her nostrils. "Impossible."

"He's just teething or growing or who knows what causes them pain when they're so little."

Jordan's expression went from bewildered to amused in the space of a second. "I was talking about Noel, not Liam.

Liam's in the porta crib taking a nap. Knock on wood, a good long one."

"Noel's here?" Glancing at the street, Maddie spotted Noel's Jeep four or five cars down from hers. Noel had been here when she and the twins weren't. Why she found that unsettling, she wasn't ready to admit. And what were he and Charlotte doing upstairs?

"Your mom said she told you." Jordan's eyebrows knitted together. "Didn't she tell you?"

"Tell me what?"

Jordan swept her hair into her hand and smashed her lips together as Maddie lifted Leo into her arms to prevent a second escape attempt. Ursa, on the other hand, was content to wait for the kids at the door. "Maybe you could join them upstairs? I'd rather you hear it from her."

Maddie frowned. It was either fish her phone from her purse to read the texts or head up and find out in person. She turned toward her kids. "Hazel, Benji, inside. Now, please."

Jordan hopped to her feet. "I'll get them in."

With a nod, Maddie headed up the switchback staircase. The hair on the back of her neck stood on end at how quiet it was as she crested the landing. Liam's door—technically Maddie's door—was closed. The rest of the doors were open, but not a sound was coming from any of them. Then Maddie heard footsteps overhead.

Her mom and Noel were on the third floor? Glancing across the hall, Maddie saw that the door at the base of the narrow staircase leading upstairs was ajar. She knew what this meant even before hearing the distinctive crinkle of a tape measure blade above her. As she headed up the second flight of stairs, she wondered if she should feel more upset about it than she did.

Tape measure in hand, Noel glanced at Maddie as she stepped onto the hardwood floor, her footfalls resonating through the unfurnished space. "Hey." She didn't think it was her imagination that his smile was exceptionally hesitant today.

Technically an attic rather than a true third floor given its lack of a finished closet, the twelve-hundred-square-foot space had been converted into a playroom in the early 1990s. The floor was original hardwood, and the walls, covered with wainscotting, were a faded seafoam green. The angled ceiling had been cut away in spots underneath which Charlotte kept buckets to catch drips that seeped in during heavy rain.

When she first moved in, squirrels had been nesting between the ceiling and roof, but she'd had them trapped and relocated and had patched the roof to the point that it kept mammals at bay, just not water.

There were windows seats at the front and back sides of the room, and the back windows had a decent view of the Missouri Botanical Garden. Charlotte had brought them up here last Christmas to look out over the garden's holiday light display before heading there to see it firsthand.

"So, what's going on?"

Noel looked over at Charlotte. She was sitting on her heels in front of one of the rear window seats, going through the contents of a tub that must've been inside the cabinet door at the window seat's base.

"Maddie, come look at this. The family who lived here before must've left it. You played with most of these at one point or another."

Maddie headed over to a faded gray Rubbermaid tub that looked every bit as old as the contents inside. She fanned her nose at the stench of old plastic and mildew, but the toys seemed to be in decent condition. There were My Little Pony figurines, half a dozen Trolls in a variety of colors, an Etch-A-Sketch, a Care Bear that had likely been light blue once but was now a dingy gray, and some Masters of the Universe figurines.

"I wonder where they are now," Charlotte said, not

looking up at her. "The kids who played with these. If they have kids of their own. If they think back on this room and argue over what shade the walls were or wonder if the tree out front is still standing. If they have any idea how good they had it, to be raised here in this house. Not every house has such good energy about her."

Kneeling, Maddie picked up one of the My Little Pony figurines. It was pink with an orange mane and light pink tail and an image of a rainbow on its hip. "I think I had this exact one."

"You did."

"Mom, what are you doing up here?"

Charlotte met her gaze for the first time. "Didn't you get my text?"

"I didn't read it yet."

"Oh." Charlotte looked at Noel. "It's such a big space, going to waste, and we know two people in need of just that."

She'd known it was coming, ever since she heard the footsteps above her, but likely even before that—likely ever since her mom's comment last night about the more, the merrier. A string of arguments lined up inside her like toy soldiers, but Maddie was unable to voice a single one. Hadn't she just promised herself she'd do whatever she could to help?

But I meant pitching in extra baby-sitting shifts and chipping in to help Jordan cover rent in a place of her own.

But Maddie knew without her mom having to say it that Jordan needed more than that. She needed support and reliability—people she could count on. And maybe for a little bit, that was best done right here.

"You know, I've seen that exact look from your father. He didn't know quite what to make of me, all order and sense as he was."

"Mom, how can you say that when you only met him once?" If Maddie wasn't so tired, maybe the words wouldn't have slipped out so harshly, but Charlotte didn't seem to be offended.

"Sometimes it only takes one night to know everything there is about someone—everything important anyway."

Maddie's thoughts shot straight to Noel a split second before the tape measure retracted at high speed. He cleared his throat and crossed to the opposite side of the room, and Maddie sank onto her bottom, locking her hands around the My Little Pony doll to keep them from shaking.

Had there been a little less going on, maybe she would've addressed one of the mountains in the room, but there wasn't, and she didn't have the energy anyway.

"Jordan and the baby will have their own space up here. This house is so big," Charlotte said with a nod toward the tub of toys. "So ready for life. You said it yourself—that there were so many other houses I could've bought, but fate led me here. Led you here, too."

Maddie glanced over at Noel. He was watching her intently from the other side of the room. "And what are you going to do?" she asked, directing the question his way. "Put up a wall and move into the other side?" It was meant to be a joke, but it didn't come out sounding like one.

Something about the way he was staring at her promised he wasn't in a joking mood anyway. "Patch a few holes. Rough out a closet or two. Get some guys to help me repair the roof."

Maddie looked from Noel to her mom. Everyone here knew Charlotte didn't have a dollar to spare right now. "When my house sells, I can pay you."

"I don't want your money, Maddie."

Maddie tucked a lock of hair behind her ear. He'd fixed the fence, hauled over her furniture, and now this. But how much was he willing to give? And was now the time to ask about his career? He'd told her that he'd been debating taking his boss up on the offer to stay on at LightSource and work remotely on various projects until he was ready to travel again. Maddie felt guilty for not having asked him recently where that stood.

More than asking about money, she wanted to ask why he'd sign up for all this. For Landon's sake? For his god children?

For her?

"Then maybe you'll take my help. I'll be finished with the last of the packing soon, and I'll have plenty of time once the sale is final."

"If you're offering, I won't refuse."

Even though her mom turned toward the box of toys, Maddie caught sight of one of her eyebrows arching into a peak. Not for the first time, Maddie marveled at how much more could sometimes be expressed without the use of words.

CHAPTER 29

NOEL

While the upstairs smelled of freshly cut two-by-fours and the chalky scent of sectioned drywall, the scent of melted butter and pancakes greeted Noel more prominently with each descending step. The main floor of Charlotte's home was bustling with activity, and before he even had time to say hello, Hazel popped up from where she was playing to lock one of his legs in a hug and press her cheek against his outer thigh.

"Hey, Hazel." He gave her back a pat, noticing the slightness of her shoulder blades against his hand. "How was the birthday party?"

The baby and Jordan were on the floor, too, Jordan balancing Liam on her knee so he could watch the twins as he gummed a curved section of wooden train track, but Jordan had a far-off look about her that hinted that the kid could reach for a live snake, and she might not notice.

"We got to go inside a real live train as big as this house, and now all Benji wants to do is play with his trains again."

"Oh yeah?" This coupled with exhaustion likely explained why Benji had yet to even glance up from the train he was rolling on the floor, his head resting on the rug. Typically, he was as quick to greet Noel as his sister was. Not that Noel minded Benji's inattention. There was something rewarding about becoming an everyday occurrence in their household compared to the rainy day treat he'd been most of their lives.

"Mommy's making pancakes," Hazel added. "You have to tell her your favorite so she can make yours, too. Me and Benji like chocolate chip and banana best. Liam's too little still to eat pancakes."

"Chocolate chip and banana sounds good to me, though when it comes to pancakes, I'm not particular as long as they're smothered in butter and syrup." Technically, though, even if he had labored in their house most of the day, he hadn't yet been invited to stay for dinner.

He made his way into the kitchen, Hazel trailing after him.

Maddie glanced up from the stove. "Oh. Look at you. You're probably going to want to shower, aren't you? You can't be expected to eat like that."

Given the drywall dust that had transferred to Hazel's cheek and sparkly unicorn shirt, Noel took a closer look at the state of his arms, t-shirt, and cargo pants. They were covered in construction dust. "I intended to wash up in the sink, then hop in the shower at home, but maybe this does call for something more immersive. Up to you though. I won't stay long…assuming I'm invited."

"Of course you're invited," Charlotte called out from the sunroom. Around the corner as she was, he could hear but not see her. "And not just because you spent your whole day working here. You're always welcome, but don't wait for an invitation. I'm terrible at delivering them, and it doesn't seem as if my daughter is any better."

Maddie rolled her eyes playfully but whispered, "Don't let her know, but she might have a point." She'd been at work this morning, then taken the kids to a classmate's birthday party after preschool, so this was his first time seeing her today. She had checked in via text twice though, first asking how things were going, and later seeing if he needed her to pick up anything from Lowes that could fit in her SUV with two kids in tow. He'd turned her down but sent a few progress pics.

She'd returned his photos with a few of the twins playing at The National Museum of Transportation. It looked like they'd had a great time, even though he'd heard them from two floors up wailing as they'd come inside earlier. That was nearly an hour ago now and, from the looks of it, they'd recovered nicely.

"Seriously, though, you're welcome to stay as long as you'd like," Maddie added. "Do you have clothes to change into? I can throw those into the wash if you'd like."

"I don't have anything, or I'd take you up on that."

Maddie frowned. "Perhaps I can shake them out while you're in the shower? I don't have anything here of…"

Landon's. Even unspoken as it was, his best friend's name hung between them like a lead balloon. He and his buddy had worn each other's clothes dozens of times over the years, but Noel would walk around naked before wearing them here in this house.

"No worries about that. I've got your back," Charlotte said as she rounded the corner from the sunroom. "A few items are probably just your size, too."

Noel raised an eyebrow. Charlotte was wider in the hips and a bit shorter in the legs than him, but something with an elastic waist might have a chance of sufficing. Though never in his life had he worn a woman's clothes.

"In men's," she added dismissively. "And plenty of unisex options, too. Follow me, and we'll save the conversation for another time as to why men should be just as comfortable in women's clothes as women can be in men's."

When they reached the second floor, Charlotte sent him into the hall bathroom to get ready and returned a few minutes later with a maroon button-down Gingham shirt, a pair of thick corduroy pants, a worn-in belt, and a towel.

Noel took them but raised an eyebrow.

"The owner isn't dead and didn't sleep with the woman you love. Is there anything else you really need to know to put them on?"

Noel's jaw dropped open. Thank God the shower water was already running and offering a decent sound buffer because she hadn't lowered her voice one bit.

Charlotte closed a hand over his shoulder. "We so seldom trust the unfolding of the universe when it's unfolding for us," she added. "But my advice is to surrender and let this go where it goes. The both of you. Some happy endings are a longer time coming than others."

It was as close as the two of them had come to talking about what had played out between him and Maddie six years ago, though he'd figured she knew about it. Maddie and Charlotte were too close for Maddie not to have told her.

Right now though, Charlotte was the one doing the talking, and Noel was staring at her, words having abandoned him. He knew numbers and formulas. Knew theory that was so tested it had become grounded into law.

This was most certainly not his realm. But as he closed the door with nothing more than a nod, he thought about these last couple of weeks. Ever since Maddie had so unexpectedly kissed him, he'd been doing his best to tamp down the rising hope that maybe, just maybe, they'd get another chance.

Shutting the door, he stripped down and stepped into the tub, eyeing the pink and purple bottle of unicorn shampoo, the body wash shaped like a robot, and the bright, poofy loofas on the lower shelves. On the top shelf was a razor and adult shampoo, body wash, and conditioner.

A fresh wave of guilt slid in. Would he always feel like

this? A second-rate imposter who was sidling in like a vulture catching a meal of leftover scraps from a hawk's kill?

Closing his eyes, he stepped fully into the erratic stream of hot water and did his best to breathe through the feeling, trusting it to ease like it always did when he shoved it down far enough.

He glanced up at the shower head, which was partially encased in limescale and needed a soaking in vinegar to flow properly again. He could take care of this for them easily, but should he? It was different when Charlotte outright asked him to help with something. He'd been sixteen when his second cousin who flipped homes for a living hired him to help with that first rehab, and Noel had done them on the side through college, right up until the summer before his senior year when he took a summer internship at an engineering firm. He could do most of this stuff in his sleep.

As he washed his hair with Maddie's rosemary mint shampoo that he could pick out of a scent lineup, he was still attempting to bury the imposter feeling deep enough that it wouldn't bother him for the remainder of the night.

Yeah, have at it. That's physics for you. The deeper you bury it, the harder it'll pop back up.

Noel stayed with the thought as he rinsed off. Maybe that's what he'd been doing wrong all along. Maybe what he needed to do was stop trying to ignore the elephant in the room that was his best friend. *"You'd like that role just fine, wouldn't you, buddy? Still being the elephant in the room months after you've actually been in one."*

It felt like he'd hit on something new, though. Maybe he'd been trying so determinedly to *not* deal with this that he was just making it harder on everyone. Maybe what he needed to do was help honor the good and stop ignoring the bad. Admit to Maddie how, even though this was hard, he still wanted to be here, regardless of all the rough waters that had passed between them.

The longer he sat with the idea, the more right it seemed.

He shut off the faucet—which was leaking and likely needed a new O-ring—and dried off, the mirror over the sink too steamy to catch his own reflection. Even so, he suspected that if it wasn't steamed over, for the first time in months, he might not spy quite so heavy of a guilt weighing down the man in the mirror.

Landon had been here first. He was the father of all three of those kids downstairs. Nothing was going to change that. But it didn't mean there wasn't space here for Noel now, too.

CHAPTER 30

MADDIE

Maddie locked her lips together to suppress a laugh as Noel stepped into the dining room. Dressed in those clothes, he might as well be walking into a freshman history class—to teach it. There was still food to get on the table and two hungry kids teetering on the edge of becoming monsters, but she couldn't resist. "Stay right there."

Detecting her amusement, Noel raised an eyebrow.

She dashed off to the sunroom where her mom liked to read in the evenings. She was back within a minute, giggling to herself, her hands full with Charlotte's reading glasses, pipe, and a ten-volume set of Shakespeare—the most scholarly tome she could find in a quick scan of the books on the shelves.

Maddie maneuvered around the dining room table to where Noel was still standing behind a chair. She handed him the book, tucked the decorative pipe into his front pocket, and slipped the dark glasses onto his face. Her fingertips burned hot as they brushed his temples, and her breath locked in her throat to be so close to him, but the moment was too priceless not to do this.

"Moooommmy," Benji cried in mock five-year-old exasperation. "What are you doing to Uncle Noel?"

"I'm helping him to own the professor vibe he's sporting. My first thought was a history professor, but we're going with literature because of our limited library." Stepping back, she nodded. "There. You're ready to inspire. We need a photo, or Saanvi won't believe me."

She started to step away to grab her phone, but Jordan interjected that she'd take one. "You should be in it, too."

Heat zinged Maddie's cheeks. She and Noel had never had their picture taken together. She was debating whether to step away anyway when his hand closed over her lower back, and there might as well have been one of those giant magnets that move cars around at junkyards holding her to him. Heat from his body pricked all down her side while Jordan snapped a handful of pictures.

Maddie promised herself she absolutely would not stare at them later, zooming in to dissect what they looked like next to one another.

When Jordan gave a nod and sank into her seat to look at the pictures she'd taken, Noel whispered in Maddie's ear. "What I want to know is what your mom puts in this pipe."

As Maddie looked up and met his gaze—her mom's glasses magnifying those chocolate brown irises—the tug in her chest was a reminder of how nice it had been in his arms those few hours they'd had together a thousand lifetimes ago. "Uh, probably exactly what you're thinking."

Charlotte was at the far end of the table, the baby on her lap. "Watch it, you two, or I'll invite you to join me when the kids are down."

Jordan thunked a hand on the table. "Uh, hello, if you're handing out invitations, I'll take one."

"I'm fresh out, but we can certainly make that happen some night. I don't do it often, but when the occasion warrants, it can make for a nice evening."

"What can?" Hazel asked.

"Reading," Maddie interjected.

"Nana, you're always reading!"

"True," Charlotte said. "I do love to read."

Hazel switched topics. "Why are you taking pictures of Uncle Noel?"

"Because of his clothes," Maddie said, noticing how the Gingham shirt was a bit tight in the shoulders and a half inch too short in the arms while the taupe corduroys were a little baggy around the hips, but the belt was keeping them in place. "He's borrowing them because his are dirty from working in the attic."

Hazel's brows knitted together. "Whose clothes are those?"

"An old friend's," Charlotte said. "Someone I've lost touch with the last several years."

But she's held onto his clothes even through a move? Was there something Charlotte hadn't told her about her love life? Aside from a few items for posterity, Landon's clothes had been donated. Maddie had dropped them at a local shelter last week and doing so had felt like the first easy decision she'd made in a long time.

She'd grown up thinking about her mom as someone who wasn't interested in having a romantic partner. Charlotte had certainly joked enough times over the years how a good vibrator was as therapeutic as a trusted therapist—a comment that sent Maddie walking from the room holding her ears. As far as she was concerned, children never needed to envision their parents having sex—with or without a partner—but suddenly she was wondering about the owner of those clothes. What had happened to him...and what had he left wearing?

Perhaps it was good that the conversation took a turn as the baby lurched for the silverware in front of him, grasping onto the butterknife with a surprising dexterity. He wouldn't let go until Benji ran to get him one of his Thomas the Tank Engine friends, Toby, to play with. Perhaps because he'd seen Benji playing with it earlier, Liam was thoroughly enthralled by the train, and Charlotte extracted the knife easily. Train in hand, the first big smile in an hour lit his face.

"Have a seat, Professor," Maddie said, waving her hand toward the open chair in front of them. "I'll grab the pancakes out of the warming oven."

"If you don't need a hand?"

"I'm good. Everything else is already here. Thanks."

Once Hazel and Benji were served their special bear-shaped pancakes, they scooped out strawberries and bananas from ceramic bowls in the center of the table and went to work creating faces on them, something their father had done with them dozens of times before.

"How'd you like those pancake eyes outlined in chocolate syrup?" Maddie asked after she settled into the last open seat and popped the top off the chocolate syrup.

"I do, but Benji's pancake has only got one eye now," Hazel said matter-of-factly while Benji chomped the slice of banana that had served as his bear's left eye for less than a minute.

"True, but unless he wants to replace it, I can make his bear winking. What do you say, Benji?"

After studying his bear for a few seconds, Benji swiped one of the strawberry slices that were serving as its teeth then slid his plate over. "I want him to be missing a tooth, too."

With everyone watching, Maddie used the syrup and a toothpick to make a snaggle-toothed thick-lashed winking bear for Benji before nodding at Hazel's plate. "What about you, Hazel? Want your bear to have lashes?"

Shaking her head, Hazel lifted her banana slices off her pancake and left them cradled in one palm. "I don't want eyes on mine. When you're in heaven, you don't have eyes, and I want daddy to know I made my bear face for him."

Hazel turned her plate around for them to see. The chocolate chip and banana pancake consisted of two small pancakes for ears cooked into a bigger one and a precise line of strawberry slices turned up in a smile but nothing else. Given how Hazel seemed perfectly content with it, Maddie stole a glance at her mom, and Charlotte shrugged almost imperceptibly.

Jordan hmphed. "I like it."

"It's nice of you to decorate your pancake for your dad, Hazel," Noel said.

"I decorated mine for him, too!" Benji protested.

When Hazel turned on her brother, eyes narrowing, Maddie interjected that they could both be thinking of their dad and showing it in different ways. Mercifully, Hazel sank back against her seat, her shoulders relaxing, and peace prevailed a bit longer.

"I think about him a lot, too," Noel said. "At all sorts of times."

"Like what kind of times?"

"Uh, let's see. When I pass by somewhere we went together. When I hear mention of a movie we saw or a game we played together." He nodded at his pancakes. "When I eat something like this and remember how your dad and I took you two to breakfast just before your third birthday. Lots of times."

Something about the way he was saying it seemed like a weight had been lifted from him, and Maddie wondered what the cause might be.

After digesting this, Hazel nodded pensively and pushed her plate in Noel's direction. "Will you cut my pancakes, Uncle Noel?"

"Sure thing."

"Make sure they're the same size please."

Jordan's brows arched in amusement as she wedged off a bite of her loaded chocolate chip and pecan pancake with the side of her fork. Compared to how talkative she'd been the previous times Maddie had been around her, her quiet demeanor tonight stood out. More than once, Maddie had wanted to give her shoulder a squeeze.

Noel cut Hazel's pancake ears first, then the face into equal pie-shaped wedges. When he was finished, Hazel nodded approvingly and arranged the slices into four equal piles at the sides of her plate. She poured her own syrup in the center, keeping it out of reach of the pancake wedges.

Maddie glanced over at Benji's plate to find that he'd poured his own syrup while her attention was on Hazel and Noel. One side of Benji's plate was drenched in syrup, and he was dipping one of the rounded pancake ears into the syrup with his fingers.

"How about using your fork like a big boy?"

"But I like eating pancakes with my fingers."

Noel took a bite of his own pancake. "You know, when we were kids, your dad had a way of making everything fun, even the boring stuff."

"I bet," Charlotte muttered with just enough zing that the adults could pick up on it but not the twins.

"Like what?" the twins asked in unison while the baby thwacked his train against the side of the table.

Noel nodded toward Benji's syrupy mess. "For one thing, he'd draw pictures in syrup, too." Pausing, he drummed his fingers on the table. "Let's see. What stories haven't you heard? Did he ever tell you about the time we were on a road trip in college and hiking in the Grand Canyon in the dark under the light of a nearly full moon?"

"What's the Grand Canyon?" Hazel asked midchew.

"I guess you'd say it's the opposite of a mountain. Instead of rising upward, it's a mile-wide stretch of land that dips into the earth. It's like that because it's been carved out by a river over a very long time."

When the twins nodded, Noel went back to telling his

story, a story Maddie had heard for the first time while sitting as close to him as her daughter was now.

"You know how when you go for walks in the woods, a lot of times you're walking on a narrow trail? Well, it's that way at the Canyon, too, except the trail there has been cut into rock along the rim of the canyon wall, and it winds back and forth along it, taking you all the way down to the river if you want to go that far."

"Did you go to the river?" Hazel asked.

"We did." Noel smiled at something only he could see. "The hike was more than we bargained for. You see, it's almost eight miles from the top rim to the river, longer than it is from here to your old house, and it's hot down there, especially in the middle of summer. We had a few snacks and bottles of water, and we messed around in the river to cool off before starting to head back an hour or so before dark. By the time we'd reached the narrow trail winding along the canyon wall, we needed moonlight to navigate."

"What's navigate mean?" Benji asked.

Noel drummed his fingers again. Most certainly, his pancakes had gone cold. "It's how you figure out a way to get from one place to another." When this satisfied them, he went on. "We were both tired and very hungry, but it was incredible the way the moonlight shone over the canyon. Like it was an ocean almost. When we still had a couple miles left to reach the top, we heard something snorting on the trail in front of us."

The twins' eyes widened. "What was it?" they said at the same time.

"Well, it was dark, and it took a bit to figure that out. We stopped moving and listened. I was in front, and it took a few seconds for it to come into view." He lifted his arms wide apart. "It was a full-grown bighorn sheep, a big male, and I'm sure it weighed every bit of two hundred, maybe two hundred and twenty pounds, which is around what your dad weighed."

"That's big!"

"And the sheep wasn't happy to see us standing there, blocking the direction he wanted to head. For a few seconds, we all three just stood there. As much as I didn't want to get rammed with those big horns, I *really* didn't want to get thrown off the edge. Right about the time I decided the best thing for us to do was plaster ourselves against the canyon wall, Landon shoved past me, spreading his arms and hollering, and for a few seconds, the sheep was charging right at him."

"Oh, no!" Hazel covered her mouth. "Did daddy get hurt?"

Noel shook his head. "Nope. Once there were only five or ten feet between us, the sheep dashed up the steep canyon wall like Spider-Man and stood over us, snorting and huffing, and your dad and I hightailed it up the rest of the trail."

"Did you see what happened to him?" Jordan asked, her interest piqued for the first time all evening.

"Nope. We kept moving, and let me tell you, adrenaline carried us another full mile up before it wore off."

"Of course Landon would charge a bighorn sheep, of course he would." Charlotte said as Noel pulled up a picture of a bighorn sheep on his phone.

"Is that the one you saw?" Hazel asked in awe.

"I doubt it, but I can promise you that's just what he looked like."

Sitting across the table from him, listening to Noel tell her kids stories like this, Maddie found it easy to recall why she'd been so taken with him that first night. His voice was deep and rich like a thickened molasses that took a bit of effort to cajole from the bottle, and he was grounded and steady—contained within himself—in way that Landon had never been.

Given life with Charlotte, no wonder Maddie had fallen so hard—and no wonder why she'd retreated into herself so deeply when he hadn't answered her letter.

Almost like he could hear her thoughts, Noel looked her way. After a few seconds, Maddie dropped his gaze and took a drink of water. Given how she hadn't been enough for him once, it seemed like a fool's hope to think things could be different now.

But a fool's hope was better than none at all.

CHAPTER 31

Maddie wasn't normally one to make New Year's resolutions, but after a slew of arguments with Landon over the holidays, she'd tucked herself in a quiet corner on January 1st and written a page of them for the coming year. An appointment with a divorce lawyer had been at the top. Giving her notice at Walter's and securing rewarding work had been second. Saying a final goodbye to the father of her children hadn't been anywhere on it. *Obviously.* Nor had selling the house and moving in with her mom. Nor falling in love with Noel a second time or Liam a first one. But these were happening nonetheless. And here it was, only early May.

Had this cross-country trip to spread Landon's ashes in the company of her in-laws, Charlotte, Noel, and Landon's one-night stand and resulting child been predicted in the New Year's Day tarot reading her mom had forced her to sit through later that day, Maddie would've laughed so hard she'd have snorted.

Yet you did draw the Three of Swords, didn't you? Charlotte had audibly tsked at seeing that one, and Maddie had gotten up from the table to pour a glass of tea, reminding herself why she didn't do tarot anymore.

In any case, here she was, carrying a week's worth of packed bags to the front door just shy of four in the morning. Noel had texted as he was leaving his apartment and would be here any minute.

Was it crazy to drive a thousand miles with three kids ages five and under in one vehicle? Probably so. But now that Jordan was living with them, there was no leaving her out of this, especially not when she wanted to come along. Maddie wasn't willing to risk an unnecessary setback in Jordan's mental and emotional healing. Whether it was more credit to the additional support with Liam or Jordan's virtual therapy sessions, who knew, but Maddie didn't think it was her imagination that her mood seemed lighter.

And thankfully, the fully equipped Toyota Sienna Noel had rented for the occasion included an entertainment system to help the twins pass the long hours in the car. With any luck, the moving vehicle would lull Liam into catching up on missed sleep.

If there was a saving grace, it was that Eleanor and Charles were flying out and meeting them at the cabin. It was difficult to imagine a less pleasant experience than being confined to a vehicle with her never-to-be ex-mother-in-law for sixteen hours in each direction. Five days and four nights under the same roof would be plenty, now matter how roomy and luxurious it was.

After rolling the jam-packed cooler to the entryway, Maddie unlocked the front door before heading to the kitchen for the pot of tea that was nearly finished steeping. Her mom and Jordan were awake and moving about but hadn't come downstairs yet. Maddie was dividing the black tea and lemon blend between their stock of three thermal mugs when Ursa let out a baritone woof just before the front door swung open. "Knock knock."

"Morning," Maddie called over her shoulder, not bothering to lower her voice. Ten minutes ago, she'd opened the twins' door and had turned the hall light on, hoping they'd stir on their own before she needed to wake them. "You ready for this?"

Either Noel didn't need much sleep, or he'd gone to bed early. Nothing about his appearance screamed four in the morning like she was certain hers did. "Ready as I'll ever be. You?" Stopping on the other side of the island, he flattened his palms against the butcher block, his smile reaching his eyes.

Maddie would be the first to admit it was a weird space they were in—texting all the time and touching hands and exchanging long looks but nothing else. Like Lewis and Clark's expedition team, this territory they were charting wasn't anything anyone could've prepped them for. Rather than hacking away at the weight of all that lay between them and venturing into the unknown forest, they were hanging out in the canoe and avoiding it entirely. "Yeah, surprisingly. I guess I need to give Eleanor some credit. Now that we're doing this, I suspect it's just what the twins need."

"I bet it will be. How about you? Think it's what you need? For some closure, I mean."

There was something in his tone, something direct and challenging that caught her off guard. Was this Noel venturing into the forest? She'd opened the fridge door for the creamer and paused a beat or two longer than necessary before grabbing it.

More than once lately, she'd promised herself she'd bring up the letter. That she'd ask why she hadn't been enough then given how she'd almost swear she was now, assuming she could trust what she was seeing in his gaze. But the not knowing seemed as if it could carry less pain than the knowing, and she hadn't yet summoned the courage.

Creamer in hand, Maddie shut the fridge door. "Not in the same way they do."

Barely audible from two flights down, the baby started fussing. The ceiling overhead creaked, and Jordan could be heard thumping down the attic stairs. This was followed by the pattering of small feet. One of the twins was awake. Hazel, Maddie guessed by the sound.

Recognizing another missed opportunity to air some of the unspoken things between them, Maddie closed her hand over Noel's. "But it'd be nice to carve out some time in Colorado to talk about the things I do need. The things we might both need."

His brown eyes searched hers. "I was going to say that exact thing. We owe us that."

Breath hitching in her throat, she nodded. Us, not ourselves. Maybe Noel was as ready to step out of the canoe as she was.

———

Typically, Maddie had a hard time sleeping in cars, but after the twins and Liam conked out when the excitement settled, she dozed most of the way across Missouri. As she floated in and out of sleep, she picked up bits and pieces of the conversation between Jordan and Charlotte, who'd left talk of astrology behind to dive into numerology, and Maddie knew there'd be sightings of angel numbers the rest of the trip.

Given how they were seated on opposite ends of the Toyota Sienna XSE, with Charlotte in the front passenger seat and Jordan sandwiched between Benji and Hazel in the third row, the conversation was in stereo. Noel threw out the occasional question or two from the driver's seat. He'd seemed entertained but unconvinced by Charlotte's insistence that his tendency to be unerringly loyal and just a touch obstinate had more to do with the fact that he'd been born in early May in St. Louis in 1993 than it did either his upbringing or his genetics.

No doubt, the seating arrangements would switch several times over the long trip, but Maddie was enjoying the middle row bucket seat. The twins were within arm's reach behind her, and Liam was in the other bucket seat, comfortably tucked into his rear-facing car seat. Last but not least, Ursa was sprawled along the walkway between the middle row bucket seats. Thanks to the rented rooftop cargo carrier that was loaded with luggage, they'd had the space to bring her along.

Maddie felt a touch guilty leaving Leo behind, but a neighbor of Charlotte's promised to spend ample time with him at the house during his twice-a-day feedings. This would certainly be less stress on his system than bringing him along. Easygoing as he was, dogs tended to be better travelers than cats.

The other passenger—of sorts—on the trip was in the rear of the van, bubble wrapped for safety and tucked snuggly into a crate. Maddie had spotted Landon's urn while loading the bags, cooler, and suitcases. It made sense that Eleanor had given the urn to Noel rather than taking it on the plane, but it had been so long since Maddie had been around it, she'd nearly forgotten the way her limbs grew heavier around it. This was only one of the reasons she'd let Eleanor keep it after the Celebration of Life. She hadn't wanted the twins fixating on their father's remains while they were debating what to do with them.

Charlotte and Jordan circled back to astrology talk as Maddie was drifting back to sleep. Charlotte was using Landon as an example of someone who embodied the most classical Aries qualities she'd ever met, and Maddie couldn't disagree. Impulsive. Confident. Competitive. Passionate. Creative.

As Maddie's doze deepened, she slipped into a dream in

which she was walking through a pine forest during a voracious snowstorm, her feet sinking deep into powdery snow. She rounded a corner and found herself at the edge of a vast, frozen lake. Without knowing why, she dropped to the ground at the lake's shore, knees disappearing into a sea of white, and began brushing the powdery snow off the lake's surface to reach the smooth layer of ice covering it. The fresh falling snow made a mockery of her work, so she worked harder to clear it. Somewhere in earshot, Hazel and Benji were playing, and their laughter rang in her ears. Her mother and Noel were with them, just out of sight. Even though she couldn't see him, Maddie knew the baby was there, too.

Maddie brushed away snow ceaselessly only to find the glassy-slick surface of the frozen lake covered again after each sweep. Finally, a strong hand stopped her mid-sweep. She looked up to find Landon kneeling in front of her on the ice in a spot that was somehow void of snow.

There he was, radiating light as he had on his best days, but seemingly calmer and more grounded than he'd been in life. His impossibly blue eyes cut her to the quick, and tears slipped unchecked down her cheeks. Why hadn't she known he was leaving? She could've thanked him for the good parts, could've forgiven him for the rough ones.

She jerked awake sometime later, tears streaming down her cheeks, the dream clinging to her like a sticky web. She swiped at her wet cheeks, the words "It's bigger than us" fading as they met conscious thought.

Wiping her cheeks dry with her sleeve, she stared out the window. She was still processing the dream when Benji woke up and declared he needed to pee. It was seven-thirty in the morning, and he'd held it so long, the panic in his tone made it clear he wouldn't be able to wait for the next gas station. Noel made quick work of pulling to the far edge of I-70's shoulder. After maneuvering around Ursa, Benji stood at the edge of the open door and peed onto the gravel.

"I want to try that," Hazel muttered with a yawn from the third row. The van coming to a stop had woken both her and Liam. In his rear-facing seat, Liam spotted his half-sister leaning forward in her seat, and his little face exploded into the brilliant smile he'd gotten from his father.

"Can you wait a bit?" Maddie stopped Benji for a squirt of hand sanitizer before he clambered over Ursa again. "That kind of thing isn't as easy with girl parts. Besides, I need to pee, too, and I bet Ursa could use a stretch of her legs." Her tears had left her quite nasal, and she'd hoped no one noticed. When Hazel grumbled that she wished she had a penis, Maddie figured the attention wasn't on her anyway.

Charlotte twisted in her seat to gaze back at her grandchildren. "If you had a penis, you'd never be able to grow a baby in your belly. One might say it's a tradeoff, a lifetime of standing up while peeing, and the possibility to grow a human inside you, but I myself am quite thankful to have had a fertile womb and the vagina that goes with it."

Benji puffed out his stomach as he fastened his seat belt. "I want to grow a baby in my belly, but not enough to not have my penis."

A round of chuckles circled the car, making Liam burst into laughter of his own. It wasn't the first time Maddie had heard him laugh, but it was the first time she'd heard him laugh in response to other laughter. He was in rare form, grinning ear to ear as he grabbed his toes and babbled. Maddie spotted the little bumps on his upper and lower gums where teeth would soon emerge. Feeling the urge to lean over and tickle his belly, she reminded herself that his mother was also within arm's reach.

Just then, she spotted Noel studying her in the rearview mirror, and something in his gaze caught her breath in her throat. Turning away, she looked out the window. How crazy of a hope was it to hold on to—their making it long term given all this?

It's bigger than us. Had they been Landon's words or hers? And what had they meant? Even if she figured it out, what was she supposed to do about it? Maddie, Noel, and Jordan —Landon had drawn each of them in, whether for one night or nearly a lifetime, it didn't matter. He'd left a mark on each of them all the same. Then there were Hazel, Benji, and Liam. Maybe they hadn't sprung from his womb, but they each carried parts of him and always would.

She recalled one of Landon's go-to arguments when attempting to get her to forgo logic and entertain his unfettered idealism. *"One plus one doesn't always equal two."*

She stared out the window as they passed expansive fields glowing in the early morning light. Pops of light green sprung from the earth in long rows as far as she could see.

Maybe this time one plus one equaled three.

CHAPTER 32

JORDAN

Jordan adjusted Ursa's leash as she gazed around at the chalky-looking towers rising above the barren Kansas grasslands. After nine impossibly long hours of driving broken up by a handful of shorter stops, they'd needed something different. This something different included a detour off the highway on rutty, unpaved roads that led them somewhere smack dab in BFE in grasslands that stretched out forever. Jordan bet someone could go missing out here and never be found. "I've heard of the badlands before. I always thought it would be fun to come here."

"I bet you're thinking of the ones in South Dakota. They're the ones most people talk about." Noel's tone was gentle enough that Jordan wasn't put off the way she'd been her first few times around him. She'd thought, in his restrained silence, that he was judging her. Now she realized he was just dealing with his own shit.

How different would her life be if she'd grown up with parents who had his patience rather than ones who'd flown off the handle at the slightest wrong twitch of a finger? "Not too many people from out of the area know this is here."

Hazel looked up after smashing a pebble-sized piece of packed dirt between her fingers and letting the dust crumble to the ground. "Then how come you do?"

"Because I took a handful of archeology classes in college. A long time ago, millions of years in fact, this area used to be part of a big inland sea. There have been some archeological digs around here. Some pretty cool fossils have been found, too."

Benji popped up from checking out something in the grass to lock his small hand in Noel's. "Dinosaur fossils?"

Witnessing this easy display of trust triggered a stab of jealousy in Jordan. It wasn't like she had a thing for Noel. Or Maddie for that matter. But being around them reminded her how dysfunctional her childhood had been. She couldn't imagine her five-year-old self taking her father's hand like that—even before he was locked up—or trusting him enough to want to. But as her mother was fond of saying, "You get what you get, and you don't throw a fit."

"A few pterosaurs," Noel said, giving Benji's hand a squeeze. "And sharks, sea turtles, and lots of different fish."

As Benji and Hazel marveled at this, Ursa stopped to sniff the ground, bringing Jordan to a halt as well. It was the middle of the afternoon and the kind of warm temperature that cradled her skin like a hug, but Jordan bet in mid-summer this area would be sweltering. Ursa would be miserable then. Even now with her thick coat, she was panting.

The hope of this side trip had been to wear the kids out so they could squeeze in another couple hours of driving before calling it quits for the day. They were supposed to be hiking, but Hazel and Benji kept dropping to their knees to play in the dry earth, and grasshoppers were probably outpacing them.

They were cute enough kids, but like all kids, they were

high maintenance enough that nine hours confined in the van with them was wearing on her. Jordan wished for a moment she was back in her old apartment, sandwiched between Ethan and Ainsley, riding a buzz and listening to Pink Floyd, Ainsley's favorite band. Maybe that life wouldn't get her anything that different than the one she'd grown up knowing, but it was so much a part of her, the urge for a toke was carved into her the same as the scars running across her left arm and thigh.

Ethan and Ainsley kicking her out had about killed her. What kind of life was it when you couldn't even count on your best friends? A shitty one, for certain.

She'd asked to walk Ursa as they'd gotten out of the van just so she didn't have to carry Liam—not that he'd minded. A minute or two ago, he'd practically lunged out of Charlotte's arms trying to get to Maddie while Maddie had pretended not to notice. Jordan didn't blame her. Maddie was dealing with her own shit, too. It couldn't be easy, falling in love with your late-husband's bastard baby.

Jordan had figured Maddie and Noel would've hooked up by now, but after staying with Maddie the last few weeks, she had her doubts. They would eventually, Jordan was certain, and not just because of the way they looked at one other.

She hadn't come out with it yet, worried as she was about pissing Maddie off, but she and Landon had grown to be unlikely friends the last month of her pregnancy. And the thing about being friends with Landon, well, he wasn't the kind of guy who could keep secrets. They slipped out like water through a sieve. Some were darker than others, and most were layered in the ugly black tar of shame. Jordan blamed Eleanor for him never getting his shit together, selfish old fart that she was, but honestly, Charles could've stepped up to the plate a time or two, too. He was the opposite of Jordan's father the way he feared power rather than abused it.

But all that mattered now was that one of the secrets

Landon had shared would change things. Maybe everything. Jordan was terrified of getting shuffled aside in the aftermath —well, not so much her, but Liam. She needed Maddie to love her baby boy. Jordan loved her son enough to know this other woman's love was the best gift she could give him right now.

Even knowing this, it irked her how comfortable he was with Maddie now. Hadn't Jordan been the one to grow him in her belly, keep him when she could've given him up, nurse him, and spend countless sleepless nights rocking his unhappy ass? And he couldn't care less.

She shook her head abruptly, like doing so might bring an end to her dark thoughts. She was growing into her mom. Soon she'd start spouting off "After all the shit I've done for you" every time he whined.

Her new therapist had told her that underneath the gray, underneath the anger, was a sadness that needed to be shed rather than stuffed down into the darkest corners of herself. Physical abuse. Emotional abuse. Neglect. "This stuff takes a toll, but you can come back from it. Bit by bit. Piece by piece."

Jordan had already read enough blogs and watched enough videos on her phone to know it was the weight of all those ugly seeds from childhood still inside her, weighing her down—a karmic sludge that prevented her from experiencing happiness the way some people could. Her belly was curdled from the weight of it. But knowing a thing and actually doing it weren't one and the same. An old doctor had told her this feeling inside her had nothing to do with karma and everything to do with her depression, but Jordan figured some things made more sense when you didn't have a medical degree distorting your beliefs.

She caught Charlotte eyeing her intently and pretended to study the towering sandstone formations rising out of the flat earth. That woman knew things. She'd understand about the seeds if Jordan told her. What would Jordan have given to have grown up with a mother like *her*?

Finished sniffing, Ursa pulled forward again, wanting to explore more of the dusty trail leading deeper into the towering sandstone hoodoos.

"You good, Jordan?" Charlotte asked.

Jordan swept her hair back from her face and nodded. "Yeah, just need to stretch my legs." Unsure if she wanted to hurl, scream, or cry more, she gathered Ursa's leash in both hands. "Come on, girl, let's run."

She took off down the trail abruptly, tugging Ursa along for the first few steps before the giant dog burst into a gentle lope of her own. Jordan's flip flops came off in the first fifty feet, but she kept running, the earth beneath her alternately soft and inviting and cruelly piercing. She ran until she'd left everyone far behind and her lungs burned like fire.

Feet scraped raw, she finally collapsed onto the sandy earth, her hands sinking into the same bits of earth and rock that the twins had been appreciating, earth as old as time itself. Tears were streaming down her face, and she hadn't even known she'd shed them.

Ursa stood over her protectively, panting and wagging her tail. Turning toward the others, the loyal dog woofed several times. The twins were running toward them and had made it halfway, thinking it was a game.

They were good kids, really good kids. When they neared, Jordan had an urge to take them in her arms and hug them tight enough to ease the ache running through her blood. As life would have it, when they reached her, rather than running into her arms, they collapsed onto the ground a few feet away, breathing hard and squirming with laughter as Ursa doused them in licks.

A part of Jordan wanted to crawl under a rock and sulk, to wallow in the belief that love was never going to leap into her arms, but after a beat or two, she found herself following

Ursa's lead. She crawled over and tickled their bellies as wilder laughter erupted from them both.

Still breathless herself, a smile broke across Jordan's face. The twins' laughter proved contagious. It was surprisingly easy actually, the way it began spilling out of her as well.

CHAPTER 33

NOEL

Noel was plenty ready to get out of the van, and he wasn't the only one. It had been a good but long two days getting here. They'd made better time yesterday, covering nearly two thirds of the total distance. This morning, they'd gotten a later start than anticipated, and nothing since had been seamless. While the hope had been to arrive this afternoon, it would be nearly 8 p.m. when they pulled in.

The baby had done great the first day, sleeping most of the trip. Today, he'd hollered and screamed enough to outlast everyone's patience. The first few hours, they'd progressed at a snail's pace, stopping at various lookouts, trailheads, and the occasional parking lot to get Liam's mind off his anger at being strapped in again and to take some of the screaming-baby tension out of the air. At one point, Liam had finally conked out and slept through a few hours' stretch. Even the twins had hardly breathed a word for most of that time in fear of waking him. Thankfully, they'd been so enthralled with the mountains in all directions and the rivers snaking along the roadsides that they hadn't even asked to watch a movie until dinnertime.

"Ever heard of the continental divide, kids?" Noel asked after spotting a sign for it. "We're going to be passing it soon."

Noel was behind the wheel again after Maddie had driven most of the afternoon. Charlotte didn't like driving when she didn't have to, and Jordan had neither gotten a license nor learned to drive.

"What's a continental divide?" Hazel was in the middle row and was squirmy enough to be unintentionally pushing her feet into the back of his seat.

"It's a ridge or highpoint running from way up north all the way down into South America." Using one hand to navigate the windy road, he made a V-shape with his other hand, his knuckles serving as the ridge. "Because it's so long, they call it the Great Divide. On one side, as drops of rain and melting snow accumulate, what doesn't sink into the ground becomes small streams that flow downhill into creeks, then into rivers, and eventually makes it to the Atlantic Ocean. Raindrops that fall on the other side of the Divide end up in the Pacific Ocean."

Even though all three beings in the car age five and under were on the cusp of major meltdowns, the twins were intrigued enough to ask a dozen questions, raising their voices over Liam's fussing. When Maddie gave him the go ahead, Noel pulled over along the Wolf Creek Pass at the Divide. Delaying their arrival a bit more wouldn't please Eleanor, who was at the cabin and anxious for their arrival, but not walking in with the kids in meltdown mode would be nice, too.

Eleanor and Charles had flown into Denver yesterday afternoon, then taken a charter flight to Pagosa. Even though the hours in the van had taxed everyone's patience at one point or another, Noel was glad they'd driven. The twins, and everyone else included, had seen things they'd never have seen otherwise.

As the van rolled onto the gravel lot that accessed a trail along the Divide, Liam's fussing crescendoed into angry wails. Maddie got out and made quick work of freeing Liam from his seat. With tear-stained cheeks and a pouty lip, he looked back at the van as if his confinement had been an unjust punishment.

"It's freezing out here," Maddie warned, soothing a hand over Liam's back. "Get your jackets on, you two."

Noel stepped out, taking a few seconds to appreciate the crisp, chilly air. High in elevation as they were, nearly eleven thousand feet, the temperature had dropped dramatically compared to when they'd last stepped outside.

While waiting for the twins to worm back into their shoes, Noel checked his phone and was surprised to find he had enough service here that several texts, missed calls, and a few new emails had popped up. Among the texts were four new ones from Eleanor, who, in light of their later-than-anticipated arrival, seemed certain they were dead despite the text update Noel sent earlier reminding her that they weren't making great time today.

Noel's jaw tensed as he skimmed her texts. They had an Eleanor-ness about them that grated his skin. This morning, when he'd called to say they were leaving Eads later than anticipated, she'd been brazen enough to ask in which room her son's ashes had passed the night. Noel figured it was better not to tell her they'd been left in the van. Instead, he'd shut her down, promising they had everything under control. As if he needed any more reminders that he wouldn't be here, stepping into this uncertain role with Maddie, had Landon not died.

"I don't see it," Hazel said after clambering out to take in the panoramic view. It looked different up here than it had most of the drive today with mountains hugging the road. Up here, the peaks looked gentler, more rounded, and there was an expansive, grassy field between the parking lot and the pines dotting the benign slopes all around. "I want to see where the water moves two different ways."

"I don't care about water," Benji said.

While Benji ran around pretending to be a plane, Noel led Hazel to the sign that talked about the Divide. Maddie and Charlotte hung with Liam, and Jordan headed with the dog into the field. Hazel seemed to get a better sense of what Noel had been talking about but soon decided her brother was having more fun.

As she ran after him, she called out for Noel to chase them, and the impromptu game that ensued dispelled enough energy that the kids' moods lifted tremendously. Liam laughed out loud several times as they took turns running with him in their arms. The twins quickly figured out he was kryptonite—whoever had him needed to run slower and were therefore the most easily tagged of the bunch.

Night was setting in heavily by the time they finished. On the walk back to the van, Hazel planted herself in front of Noel and raised her arms, asking him to carry her. When he lifted her, she leaned her head on his shoulder and pressed one palm against his cheek, a big yawn escaping. When they got to the van, she climbed to her seat without saying a word, and the spot where she'd touched his cheek felt alive and warm.

As they headed down the mountain toward Pagosa, the stray snowflakes they'd been spotting picked up, and soon it looked as if they were traveling through a snow globe.

"Is it going to snow enough to make a snowman?" Benji asked with a yawn. "I wanna make a snowman."

"Maybe," Maddie said. "There's a chance of snow here every day this week."

In the darkness, the headlights and gentle snowfall were mesmerizing, and for the second time all day, as Liam dozed, the rest of the group fell quiet, captivated by the dance of the snowflakes in the headlights.

After averaging a pace of just twenty miles an hour for the last several miles on the tight, windy roads nestled in thick woods north of town, Noel navigated down the long, private road that led to the cabin. He held his breath, hoping that, after a lengthy online search, the photos, virtual tour, and reviews held true, and he'd found a good place to spend the next five days.

Finally, they rounded a bend in the road, and the cabin came into view. "What do you know, we've made it."

The expansive cabin was built with traditionally notched white pine logs and peaked impressively at the center. It had a surplus of tall windows and a wrap-around front porch. The landscaping lights were on, sending a cascade of inviting yellow out across the gently sloped yard, and the porch lights and a few interior lamps glowed into the night.

"Wow." Jordan tsked. "I've never stepped foot in anything that pretty. Not even close."

"It certainly is beautiful," Maddie agreed.

Noel parked in the circular drive, and Ursa clambered to her feet as the twins squeezed around her in a race for the van door. When Charlotte announced with her usual flair that she was certain that this was exactly where they were all supposed to be, Noel couldn't disagree. Deep in his bones, he was feeling the same thing.

CHAPTER 34
MADDIE

The bright morning sun streamed in, warming Maddie's face and body. Tucked under a pile of soft bedding, she savored the realization that right at this moment, nothing needed to happen. No work, no school, no agenda. And judging by the silence pervading the house, it was safe to assume everyone was still asleep.

She could just make out her mother's soft, even breathing in the bed next to hers. The sound transported her back to when she couldn't sleep as a kid and found comfort in hearing it.

Maddie rolled onto her back and stretched as she looked around, appreciating the warm glow from the sunlight on the notched pine interior walls. Noel had chosen well. The cabin was gorgeous inside and out and, with five bedrooms and a spacious, open living area, it was big enough that everyone would have an opportunity to escape for a bit of solitude when needed.

Last night, the twins sounded like they were touring the Louvre while checking the place out. They were especially over the moon about the oversized antler chandelier in the dining room, the forest-animal decorated towels and sheets, and the ceramic bear toilet paper holder in the Jack-and-Jill bathroom that separated their room from Maddie's and her mom's.

Eleanor and Charles were footing the bill for this place and had therefore gotten dibs on the master bedroom with its private deck, luxury bathroom, and sunken tub surrounded by a wall of windows overlooking the remote woods. Given how they'd be leaving two nights before everyone else, Maddie hoped for an opportunity to try out the tub.

Awake enough to face the day, she tossed off her cozy covers. While it hardly seemed possible, she'd slept almost nine hours. She headed over to the wide window, the wood floors cool and inviting against her bare feet. Looking outside, she covered her mouth in delight. They were smack dab in an evergreen forest, its brilliant greens and browns dusted with fresh-fallen snow. A blanket of white powder covered much of the ground, hopefully enough to build a snowman.

A movement behind a copse of trees caught her eye, and Maddie gasped. Something big was out there, fifty or so feet away, walking among the pines. From her viewpoint, she was only able to see the back half of its body, a muscular, light brown one, with strong hind legs and a short, stubby tail. Given how she could only see half of it, it was hard to be sure, but it seemed a good deal larger than any deer she'd seen back home.

To her disappointment, the animal disappeared behind a thick pine. Maddie craned her neck, hoping for another glimpse. Thirty seconds passed, then a minute, and nothing. Finally, she saw movement again, but it didn't make sense.

Suddenly, she realized what she was seeing suspended in midair was a massive antler. The rest of the animal was still hidden behind the tree. No deer could have a set of antlers like that.

She dashed across her room, through the bathroom, and into the twins' room. "Benji, Hazel, wake up! You have to see this!" Any guilt over waking them was negated by the fact that waking up now would help them get into a routine here that didn't have them falling apart at any of a thousand unpredictable trivialities.

With the zero to sixty sleep-to-wake cycle that was a childhood superpower, Hazel popped up from the mound of covers she'd been buried in. "Is it a bear?" Her eyes grew big with excitement. On the ride here, they'd talked about the animals that inhabit the mountains around here, and black bear topped everyone's list of hopeful encounters, especially hers.

"No, but it's still really cool." When Benji didn't so much as stir, Maddie shook him awake before crossing to the side windows. Not only did they have the perfect view from here, the animal, an elk, was walking straight toward the cabin. Maddie held a finger to her lips as Hazel joined her. "We have to be quiet, or we'll scare him away."

Hazel's mouth gaped open. "He looks like Rudolf!"

Benji didn't need any further enticement. Hopping out of bed, he rushed over.

"It's an elk," Maddie said. "A big one. A boy."

The majestic creature was so big and powerful, Maddie was bowled over. His antlers had to reach four feet from tip to tip. "He's majestic, isn't he?"

"How do you know he's a boy?" Hazel whispered.

"Because of his antlers. Elk are in the deer family, and in the deer family, only males have antlers." Maddie knew this from the nature shows Landon had watched.

They hardly breathed as the big bull elk continued straight toward the house, stopping once he reached the edge of the porch. He sniffed the top rail, sending a shower of snow in their direction. Maddie wished she'd grabbed her phone but worried if she went for it now, he'd catch the movement through the glass and run off.

The elk was close enough that beads of moisture along the darker brown fur of his neck were visible. Maddie studied his long, sloping face, his rubbery nose, and the short, velvety hair surrounding his mouth and nose. Then there were his antlers and the way they projected up from the crown of his head between his ears.

Words like royal, magnificent, and surreal filled her head as goosebumps lit across her arms.

"Mom, can I go get Nana?" Benji whispered.

"Okay, but move slowly until you're out of sight."

The elk was moving casually along the side of the porch, pausing here and there for a sniff, and making Maddie wonder if the cabin owner left out food on occasion, but what kind of food would one leave out for an elk?

The floor creaked when Benji was halfway out of the room. The sharp sound must've been audible outside. The elk stopped walking and cocked his head in their direction, one of his antlers bumping against the closest porch column. Maddie stood frozen in place, certain he was looking right at her for the first time.

She was just barely aware of Benji coming back into the room, whispering but not really whispering in that way of kids. Then a louder-than-average woof filled the room as Ursa rushed in, beelining for the windows.

After a powerful snort that reverberated against the glass, the bull elk trotted into the woods in the same direction he'd come. Once he'd made it a good distance, he looked back at the house and snorted again.

"Oh, cool!" The exclamation hadn't come from Charlotte, not even close.

Maddie turned to find Benji dragging Noel into the room. She'd not been paying attention to the fact that her son had gone out the main door rather than slip through the bathroom.

Dressed in a pair of dark grey running pants and a white long-sleeve T-shirt, Noel looked fresh and awake like he'd been up awhile. Through the doorway, she spotted his open laptop on the living room coffee table.

While she likely had a serious case of bedhead.

"Can you believe it!" Benji yelled as Ursa continued to bark and growl, her front paws planted on the windowsill, and her tail wagging. If the baby had been asleep, he was awake now, and everyone else along with him.

"A bull elk with antlers like that is something to see, all right." Noel ruffled Benji's sleep-messy curls. "I took a walk a half hour ago, and I spotted a few females on the other side of the lake, though I didn't think we'd see any of them this close to the house."

Eleanor appeared in the doorway, her mouth puckering into a frown as her gaze landed on Maddie. Eleanor also looked to have been up for hours, her hair done, make-up on, and donning all the right high-dollar clothes for early May in Colorado. If Maddie's mother-in-law had ever been caught with bedhead and in an old night shirt, Maddie would eat slugs.

She focused on Noel because it was preferable to dealing with Eleanor. "Did you take Ursa with you, by chance?" It occurred to her that the big dog hadn't been in the room with her this morning even though it was where she'd been when everyone had gone to bed.

"Yeah. She was great. Your mom was in the family room earlier watching it snow, and Ursa was with her. I think your mom went back to sleep when I headed out with Ursa."

"Can we take her out again?" Hazel begged. "I want to walk in the snow."

"I wanna go too, but I wanna keep my pajamas on." Benji's tone pitched at the idea of getting out of his PJs first thing. It was never a promising sign when he woke up skirting meltdown mode.

"If you do, and your pajamas get wet, then you'll have to take them off when you come inside."

"I won't get them wet."

Right...but then again, this was vacation. Of sorts. "Okay. Give me a minute to get dressed, and we'll go out for a little bit. But no opening the front door until Ursa's leash is on. Not with elk so close to the cabin."

"I'll take them out, if you'd like," Noel offered. "You can join when you're ready. No rush." When Maddie was quick to agree, Noel looked back and forth between the twins. "How about you put on your boots and throw your coat over your pajamas? It's not that cold out there, and if your pajamas get wet, we'll toss them in the dryer."

Behind him, Eleanor was the picture of disapproval. Maddie wondered what was setting her off more, the twins going outside without changing first or the easy camaraderie between her and Noel.

Noel headed off to grab a hoodie, and Benji raced into the Jack-and-Jill bathroom. Leaving the door wide open, he started to pee. The sound carried into the room and sent Eleanor away with a frown.

Hazel began tugging out of her PJs. They were striped light and dark purple with a kitty face on the front, her favorite pair since Christmas. "I want to get dressed now and put these back on later."

After reminding Benji to wash his hands, Maddie pulled out the twins' thickest, wool-blend socks, then at the closet next to the front entry, Maddie helped them into their rubber boots, which would keep them dry but not warm. Ursa hovered nearby, hoping for another walk.

Eleanor was in the kitchen filling the coffee pot with tap water, but everyone else was in their rooms.

"I can help make breakfast in a bit," Maddie offered. "I'll

need to run by the store today, but I packed the cooler and tote bags with supplies for a breakfast of pancakes, chicken sausage, and eggs."

"Pancakes, pancakes, pancakes," Benji chanted in his monster voice as he shoved on his boots.

Eleanor shut off the water and swept a lock of hair from her forehead. "Once you're dressed."

It seemed impossible that three such benign words could carry so much weight. Even Benji stopped his pancake chant to glance at Maddie's nightshirt. Noel had just stepped out of his room and was headed their way. There was no way Eleanor's tone had escaped his notice, either, but Maddie refused to look his way in confirmation.

"Mommy always makes pancakes in her pajamas." Benji's tone carried enough "You seriously didn't know?" that Maddie felt vindicated.

Holding off on a response, she helped the twins into coats while Noel leashed Ursa. "You two, promise me you won't wander, not even a bit. Stay in Noel's sight at all times."

After agreeing, the twins headed down the steps, each using a hand to scrape the thin blankets of snow off the banisters on either side of the steps, making Maddie want to reach for her camera. Noel squeezed Maddie's arm before heading out with Ursa.

Once they were down the steps, Maddie shut the door and headed for the kitchen, opening overhead cabinets until she located the coffee mugs. Dehydrated from the trip, she pulled one out and filled it with water.

On the other side of the cabin, she could hear a shower running in the master bedroom, and Liam starting to fuss in one of the other bedrooms.

She was on the cusp of addressing the nightgown comment when Eleanor spoke. "I keep thinking how convenient it is, the way Noel's here to step into Landon's role. It's almost as if your little family is still intact."

Maddie choked on a mouthful of water. She set the mug onto the counter forcefully enough that it clanked against the granite. "Are you actually going there with this?"

Eleanor said nothing but stood straighter, squaring her frail shoulders.

How a woman who was so small could wield such dragon energy was beyond Maddie. "It's almost like you forgot a few things. Like how Noel is the twins' godfather, for one thing —a role Landon argued for back when my being around him still hurt like..." She couldn't finish that sentence. Not to Eleanor.

"Of course, I haven't forgotten. They were like brothers, those two boys. The things we did for Noel, too."

"I suspect Noel gave your son as much as he was given, in one way or another."

Eleanor raised one eyebrow high enough that it disappeared underneath her bangs. "I was only stating how convenient some of this must be for you."

"I heard you. It's what you're implying that's bothering me."

"If you feel the sting of truth, might I suggest you look deeper?" Eleanor's tone and look carried equal amounts of venom.

Maddie gestured briskly toward the wall behind which Liam's fussing was escalating. "Your son wasn't an angel, Eleanor. Not even close. If the two people behind that wall aren't proof enough, maybe the condom wrapper I found in his car is." She hadn't intended to tell Eleanor about this, but her mother-in-law poking at this wound proved too much of a trigger.

"I don't know a thing about condom wrappers in cars, but if that's true, I wonder if you've been asking yourself if your husband had needs you weren't fulfilling."

"Landon have needs I wasn't fulfilling?" Maddie's limbs burned with the rage flowing through them. "Maybe. Quite possibly. But let me assure you, that's a two-way street, Eleanor. Which is why—if you care to know—the day before Landon died, I was seeing a divorce lawyer."

The look on Eleanor's face was a mix of shock and revulsion.

"That call from the lawyer you must've spotted on my phone—she was calling back to see if I wanted to move forward." Maddie tried to catch the words tumbling from her mouth, but a dam had broken. "If Landon were alive, even if I didn't have a clue about the baby or him cheating on me, we'd be getting a divorce. And I would've chosen that *a million times* over what happened to him, but it doesn't change the fact that I was leaving him."

Eleanor pointed a finger in Maddie's direction like she was wielding a wand with which to curse her. "My son was a good man. I don't need you dishonoring his memory to my grandchildren!"

"I have no intention of doing that. Landon was a good father. He was a good son. He was a good friend to a lot of people. But *none of that* made him a good husband."

"Says the woman who got to stay home and raise her children." Angry red splotches dotted Eleanor's cheeks. "And if your marriage was so bad, why didn't he tell me?"

Heat raced down Maddie's limbs, warming her bare feet the same as if she were standing on heated tile. "The way he told you about the baby?" It was out before she could pull it back. Maddie could see the weight of it sinking in as Eleanor, flushing, looked down at the sink.

"He told me things," Jordan interjected from across the cabin, giving both Maddie and Eleanor a start. "Maddie isn't lying." She stood in the now-open doorway to her bedroom, holding Liam over her hip and patting his back. She was staring pointedly at Eleanor, and there was something in her tone that made Maddie do a double take even though she was too angry to process it. "He might've been the best husband he was capable of being, but sometimes people's best isn't good enough. You can trust me on that one."

Eleanor closed her eyes. "Forgive me for being a cynic, but we've hardly known you long enough for your words to have much credibility."

"Especially when they contradict yours, you mean?" Maddie spat, rising to Jordan's defense. In the five years she'd known her, Maddie had never had a confrontation with Eleanor this heated.

"Hey, Maddie…" It was Noel. He'd stepped inside again and was standing in the entryway. The front door was wide open behind him. With the baby fussing and the shower running, she'd not heard the door open, but there he was with Ursa, nonetheless. *How long has he been there? Had he heard the painful things Eleanor had implied?*

"Benji wants his gloves," he added, his voice as calm and steady as a member of a bomb squad. "The twins are out front, and I don't want to leave them long. Can you grab Benji's gloves for me?"

Maddie swallowed hard, a pile of words lodged in her throat.

Another door opened, and Charlotte walked out of their shared room. Had *everyone* been listening?

Charlotte, too, appeared considerably calmer than Maddie would expect if she'd overheard half of what had just played out in the kitchen. She crossed the room to stand beside her, closing a hand over her shoulder. "I'll get Benji's gloves, if you tell me where they are."

Maddie blinked, attempting to focus as her racing heart began to slow. "They should be in Benji's coat pockets. I made sure they were in there last night when I was hanging up his coat."

Just then, Benji's high, thin "Here they are" trailed in through the open door from out in the yard.

Noel looked pointedly at Charlotte. "I'll be back in a little bit, if you've got this."

Charlotte waved him off with a confident nod. "I'll put on a kettle of water for tea and hot chocolate for the kids." She patted Maddie on the arm. "Why don't you take some time to yourself and have a nice shower? I have a feeling it's going to be an eventful day."

CHAPTER 35

Maddie had just shut off the shower faucet when Jordan rapped at the Jack-and-Jill bathroom door —the one leading to Maddie's room. "I'm gonna need a few minutes."

"Yeah, sure. We'll hang here. Everybody is either outside or locked in their rooms, and I'm hoping to talk to you when we're alone."

Good thing Maddie had carried a change of clothes into the bathroom. She had no idea what Jordan wanted, but she didn't have the energy for one more thing. Her eyes would certainly be puffy for hours, and her voice would likely carry a nasal quality for just as long. Funny how when all that anger had begun to ebb, a mountain of grief had been waiting to be shed as well.

When the tears had started flowing, she'd curled up on the shower floor and sobbed hard enough that her ribs ached.

After a quick drying off, she slathered on some lotion, wrapped her hair in a towel, and yanked on a pair of yoga pants and a soft gray hoodie that clung like Velcro against her skin. She stepped out to find Jordan sprawled over the top of her bed. The baby was in the center, getting some belly time. His face lit up when he spotted her, and he hammered an empty single-serve juice bottle that had belonged to one of the twins against the quilt while grunting an "Oohhh!"

"Could you flip on the bathroom fan?" Jordan said. "You know, to muffle us."

"Jordan, if you're hoping to unload something heavy, I'm plum spent." Still, Maddie reached back in to do so. There was a reading chair by the window, and she took a seat on it. She tucked her feet cross-legged underneath her and draped a throw pillow over her stomach.

Jordan scooted to the edge of the bed, her back to her son. Given that it was a queen bed, and he was in the center and not mobile yet, this was probably fine, but Maddie would keep an eye on him regardless.

"You could say it's heavy, I guess, but after what just happened out there, my *not* telling you is worse than my telling you, I'm sure." Jordan's shoulders migrated toward her ears like she was bracing for a blow. "Though, I gotta say, I'm a bit terrified it'll change things."

Maddie's spine tightened reflexively. "How?"

"You and Noel…" Jordan gnawed at her lip. "You two had a serious thing for each other before you and Landon hooked up, huh?"

"Please don't tell me you slept with Noel, too." The words slipped out before she could pull them back.

"God, no. I wouldn't do that, and he's way too crazy about you anyway."

Maddie shook her head. Still in the center of the bed, the baby had realized he was no longer the center of his mom's attention and was attempting to turn himself in their direction, much like a lumbering seal on land.

After a quick glance at him, Jordan swept her hair into one hand and nervously swished it back and forth like a broom. "Even if Landon had never mentioned it, I'd have picked up on it anyway. You two are like magnets trying really hard not to be magnets."

A dozen excuses raced to the surface, but Maddie swallowed them down. "Jordan, where are you going with this? And what did Landon tell you anyway?"

"What he should've told you years ago." Jordan looked down at the floor then back up. "Back when you first started working at the restaurant, you wrote Noel a letter and gave it to Landon to give to him."

"Are you telling me Landon didn't give it to him?" Even as she said it, she knew this wasn't true.

"He gave Noel a letter." Jordan looked like she was about to jump off the diving board. "Just not the one you wrote. I don't know exactly what it said. You'll have to ask Noel, but my understanding is that it was a 'keep moving, I'm not interested' kind of letter."

Jordan expected her to believe Landon had forged a different letter? No way. Landon had been a lot of things, but conniving wasn't one of them.

The baby was fussing enough that Jordan leaned over and helped him face their direction, then she tapped the juice box in hopes of returning his attention to it. Instead, he spotted Maddie and reached out for her, but Maddie wasn't biting. Not right now.

"If there's proof in any of this, it's in the way Noel looks at you," Jordan added. "Someone who looks at you like he does could never have ignored a love letter from you."

"That doesn't make any sense. Why would Landon do that?" An exasperated plea had crept into her tone. "He could've cared less about me back then, and he and Noel were like brothers."

"He didn't do it. Not really. Not intentionally." Jordan shook her head, her expression reflecting the intensity of emotions inside her. "You know what they say, 'A butterfly flaps its wings...' You gave him a letter. He dropped it, and someone else saw it and intervened. When Landon got it back and passed it on, he genuinely didn't know it wasn't the one you'd written."

Maddie blinked eyes that might as well be crusted with sand from all the crying in the shower. Someone else saw it and intervened. Who? Nausea flooded in. Only one person had ever hated her enough to alter a letter she'd written. All the looks over the years, the pointed words. "Eleanor?" It came out in a whisper.

Jordan slumped forward, locking her hands on her knees. "Yeah."

"*Why?*"

"Because there's something about her that's broken. Because she has an incessant need to win, and in her world, to win, other people need to lose. She'd worked her way into restaurant ownership, and for whatever reason, she felt threatened that you'd do the same."

Maddie pulled the towel off her head, and thick, damp curls spilled onto her shoulders. From outside the room, muffled by the bathroom fan, she heard the front door opening and the kids, dog, and Noel stomping their feet dry and laughing.

The realization sank deeper, and Maddie suspected she was about to be sick. This. Wasn't. Happening. But the truth of it shimmered like rays of the sun on a pond. In Eleanor's mind, Noel was hers to claim. *"They were like brothers, those two boys. The things we did for Noel, too."* This morning wasn't the first time Maddie had heard her say that. She thought back to the early days working at the Row House. Everyone had been warm and friendly and open to Maddie's ideas, especially Charles. Everyone except Eleanor. Nothing Maddie had done had pleased that woman. Nothing then, and nothing since.

Dropping the towel on the floor, Maddie stood on legs that felt like rubber. She crossed the room and opened the door to exclamations of the twins, eager as they were to tell her about their trip outside. Noel was lining up their boots on the side of the rug nearest the vent, and his back was to her. Her mom was in the kitchen, wiping down the counter. Charles was on the couch, reading on his iPad. Eleanor was sitting in one of two reading chairs nearest the bay window, staring into the snow-covered woods, her hands folded in her lap, looking small and frail and not at all like someone who'd unleashed a chain of dominos no one could've anticipated where they'd fall.

The world had just tilted on its axis, and no one seemed to have noticed.

The kids were raising their voices, attempting to outtalk one another, but Maddie held out a hand as she passed by. She needed a minute, several most likely. And she needed to look Eleanor in the eye.

Jordan hung, Liam fussing in her arms. The twins ran over and started tickling the baby's feet, turning his fusses into giggles in a millisecond.

Maddie stopped in front of Eleanor's chair. For a string of heartbeats, Eleanor continued to stare into the woods, but then she met Maddie's gaze and held it for a breath or two, equal parts guilt and defiance lining her face. Maddie realized with a start that her mother-in-law's hands were visibly shaking as if she'd guessed what Jordan had been doing in Maddie's room.

"My letter to Noel... *Why?*"

Eleanor smoothed one hand back and forth over the other, her chunky diamond and gold rings getting in the way, as Charles looked up from his e-reader over the tops of his glasses.

"Why... I've had a long time to think about that, and I've come up with a dozen different reasons." She shrugged her shoulders almost imperceptibly. "The only one that sticks is that I never would've hired you. Cruel as it sounds, it's the truth. I wouldn't have cared how promising you were. Forget Noel. Forget Landon even. Forgetting how I would've chosen someone quite different in their lives, the truth of it is, I especially didn't want you in my restaurant."

Charles leaned forward on the couch. "*Your* restaurant?" For two simple words, they effectively carried the weight of a marriage that had been dysfunctional for years. "And what are you two talking about?"

Eleanor pursed her lips. "This," she said, pulling out a piece of paper from the front pocket of her sleeveless vest. "When I decided to bring it along, I told myself it was to burn it here in my son's final resting place. To finally be done with it. But I think somehow I knew this was coming. Well before I saw the look on that girl's face a half hour ago."

Maddie blinked, then blinked again. She might as well be standing on a spinning top, trying to make sense of the world as it flashed by.

When Eleanor stretched out the letter in her direction, rings gleaming, Maddie took the single sheet of folded paper and sank to the floor. She didn't even have the strength to take a few steps away from the woman who'd so facetiously twisted her fate—*all* their fates.

The living room filled with the rest of their party. As soon as they spotted their mom sitting on the floor, the twins ran over, giggling and climbing on Maddie's back like little chimpanzees, thoroughly wet from playing in the snow. Charlotte joined Charles on the couch, while Noel knelt next to her, his expression layered with concern, and his cheeks rosy from the cold.

Maddie held his gaze for only a second before turning her attention back to the letter. She remembered the stationery exactly. She'd picked it from a stash Charlotte had given her when she and Saanvi moved into an apartment together after pastry school. For something written six years ago, its folds were still crisp and pristine. She remembered the deep lavender color of the pen. She remembered the words without needing to read them.

Noel closed a hand over Benji's shoulder to get his attention. "Hey, you two, how about we get those clothes off and give your mom a minute?"

"It's okay." Maddie no longer needed a minute, but Noel did. A butterfly flapped its wings, and a budding relationship didn't come to pass. Twins came into the world who otherwise would never have been. A vibrant and out-of-control life ended prematurely. A child was born who tied them all together. "I've got the kids," she said, offering the letter his way, holding it high enough to keep it from getting smashed by their antics. "This is for you. It's a bit late, but better late than never." She leaned over and pressed a light kiss against his temple as if doing so might relieve some iota of the pain about to thunder his way.

He took it and shook his head, looking from her to Eleanor to the folded letter.

Eleanor's words were the same ones Maddie would've chosen. "It'll make sense when you read it." After a pause, Eleanor added, "Everything except for the why, I expect. Even doing my best to explain it, I'll come up short. I'm hoping instead you'll accept an apology. I've never been good at giving them, but I can see clearly that one is owed."

Noel took the letter and stood up, but not before Maddie caught the glimpse of understanding as he opened it and skimmed the first line. It was there in his expression, understanding blending with the weight of it all.

Maddie wrapped an arm around Hazel's waist and sunk the fingers of her other hand into Benji's curls. The dominos were falling again, and God only knew where they'd lead.

CHAPTER 36

NOEL

oel resisted a primal urge to topple the rough-strewn cedar coffee table at his side and smash a few of the nearest woodsy trinkets against the wall. For years, he'd given Eleanor the benefit of the doubt on being a driven but decent person, even when evidence stacked up to the contrary. But never in a million years would he have believed she'd do this.

He skimmed Maddie's letter twice. Later, when the shock wore off, he'd read it again. Not only was it beautiful, but it also mirrored everything he'd felt at the time she'd written it.

He walked over to the wall of windows a few feet from Eleanor and stared outside, a numb disbelief weighing down limbs still tingling with unspent rage. Underneath that was a stomach-curdling nausea. Had it not been for his own pride, Noel could've reconciled this years ago and saved Maddie a boatload of pain. As much as he hated Eleanor for keeping the two of them apart, he blamed himself and his stupid ego for not fixing this sooner. How many times after Landon handed him that letter had he wanted to call her or fly back to St. Louis to see Maddie face to face?

When Landon had shown up at his apartment that day,

Noel had been on the phone with the airline for nearly an hour, trying to delay his series of tickets to Spain departing later that day in hopes of seeing Maddie before he left. They were meant for each other. He'd believed it then, just like he'd believed it ever since.

But like an idiot, he'd tucked tail and ran.

After extracting herself from the twins' bear hugs, Maddie joined him at the window and closed a hand over his bicep. Locking his arm around her back, he pulled her close. She'd been crying earlier, but there was a brightness to her gaze despite all she'd been handed this morning. "Maddie, I had no idea…"

"It's okay. Let me get the kids into something dry and get them settled. We'll talk." She turned toward Eleanor, and her back arched almost imperceptibly. "And so will we. I know you know it, but this changes everything. It's why you never came forward until you had to."

Eleanor shifted in her chair but kept silent, wearing her dignity like a shawl.

Now that the twins had stopped wrestling, Hazel had picked up on the energy in the room. "What are you going to talk about, Mommy?"

"Big people things." After giving Noel's hand a squeeze, Maddie herded her kids off to get changed. Most likely not wanting to face Eleanor's wrath, Jordan trailed after her.

Once the bedroom door closed behind them, Charlotte was the first to speak. "I can't believe I never put this together. I was so interested in blaming Landon I was blinded by my prejudice against him."

The righteous anger that always seemed to be underneath Eleanor's surface flared. She sat forward, gripping the tops of the armrests, glaring at Charlotte. "My son was a good boy. His whole life, he had people like you judging him, but if he was anything, he was always well intentioned."

Charlotte made a sound deep in her throat. "Every bone

in my body wants to tell you where to go for doing this to my daughter, but that honor belongs to Maddie when she's good and ready. Noel, too."

For the first time since this bombshell dropped, the room fell quiet. Charles stood up and headed for the kitchen, where he began rummaging through the fridge. "You've done it this time, Eleanor."

Eleanor didn't breathe a word in reply. She stared out the window, her hands folded on top of her lap, looking weak and shrunken compared to the Eleanor of such a short time ago when Landon was still alive. She could be in no doubt that this news had the potential to excommunicate her from her grandchildren.

"Answer me this, Eleanor, and give me the truth." Noel refolded the letter and slipped it into his pocket. His tone barely hinted at the mountain of anger rumbling inside him. "Did Landon know what the letter said when he handed it to me?"

She was quiet for so long that Noel wondered if she would respond. "No. He didn't. He came to me later, after you read it." Her tone was more pleading than he'd ever heard it. "He'd realized he'd been handed a love letter but delivered another."

He dragged his hands through his hair. "Why, Eleanor? *Why?*"

"The best that I can figure, it was for the reason I told Maddie. I wanted her out of my restaurant enough that I felt entitled to play cupid. Maybe I hoped she would tuck tail and leave."

From the kitchen, Charles smacked a cabinet door closed. "Playing cupid is getting people together. What you did… It's…it's *sickening.*"

Eleanor straightened in her chair. "I lost my son that day, Charles. Not the way we lost him in February, but I lost him all the same, and I've paid for it every day since. He barely came to the house for months. He'd hardly return my calls. He wouldn't even look me in the eye most days when we saw each other at the restaurant. No doubt, he dated Maddie just to spite me."

"Enough with that talk!" Noel's tone was harsh enough that Eleanor's eyes widened. "What just played out here a few minutes ago—that was a confession, not an apology. If you want those kids in your life—*all three of them*—I suggest you figure out how to make one, foreign as that might be."

He took off without waiting for a reply. After shoving into his wet boots, he headed out without a jacket. Ursa hopped up from where she'd been camped out at the back windows and trotted toward him, but Noel shook his head. "Not this time."

He had no destination other than to get a bit of breathing space. He walked and walked, snow crunching under his feet. For a mile or two, he kept a brisk enough pace to feel a continuous burn in his lungs in the thin mountain air.

Abruptly, he stopped in his tracks and addressed his best friend's ghost. "Why didn't you tell me when you figured it out? Was it because you were protecting your mom or because you wanted Maddie for yourself?"

He wanted more in response than the quiet morning greeting him, but seconds passed into minutes, and the mountainside all around remained exceptionally silent. He walked on, weaving a path through the evergreens, the snow crunching under his boots. Without a coat, the mountain air was cold enough to blanket him in a sterile numbness.

Landon's hooking up with Maddie had been more than just a passive-aggressive response to a mom whose orbit he was so inextricably caught in, Noel realized. His buddy had been the kid who'd been torn to pieces about an injured rabbit they'd found near their fort and tried but failed to save. Landon would've been devastated by his mom's deceit, yet outing her would've been damn near impossible for him, given the hold she'd had on him, back then especially.

"You should've told me. By God, you should've told me."

It was a memory of him and Landon near here the summer before their junior year in college that made Noel stop in his tracks. The cabin skirted the edge of the Weminuche Wilderness. He and Landon had road tripped to the area twice while in college, once to ski, the second time to mountain bike. They'd been biking somewhere near here, tearing down uneven slopes. Adrenaline had been surging wildly through Noel's veins even before Landon hit a rock hard enough to flip over his handlebars and go flying several feet. He'd done some sort of duck and roll and came out of it with a handful of scrapes and bruises and a grin that spread from one ear to the other.

That time, anyway.

Noel raised his fists, screaming up into the rich blue skies above. When one scream wasn't enough, he screamed again and again until his throat burned like fire. When there was nothing left, he dropped to his knees, the snow soaking through his jeans. Had there ever been a version of Landon's life that left him alive after thirty-two?

When the anger began to recede, Noel took his first real look around. The only sounds were the soft wind cutting through the trees and the chittering of a bird in the brush nearby. He closed his eyes, listening and breathing in the chilly air as an unexpected peace settled over him.

Finally, he got up and started back in the direction he'd come. He was lucky he'd left tracks in the snow because he hadn't been paying attention to where he was headed. Now that he was drained of most of his anger, he found himself in just as much of a hurry to get back as he'd been to leave. He wanted to take Maddie in his arms and never let her go.

Nothing was ever going to be the same again.

Less than an hour earlier, he and the kids had been

knocking snow off pine branches and laughing as Ursa chomped down on the snowballs they threw for her. The moment had been as close to perfect as moments came, despite the nagging reminder at the back of Noel's mind that he was an interloper in their lives—their father's best friend, stepping in to take on the role of caregiver in the space of a massive void in their lives.

This new knowledge freed him from that line of thinking. There were no interlopers here. There was only love and circumstance. An unpredictable string of circumstances, actually. Ones that led to the twins' creation, and Liam's too.

But now, it was his and Maddie's turn, and Noel didn't want to waste another minute of it.

CHAPTER 37
MADDIE

Maddie helped the twins navigate their first but surely not last negotiation with the baby over which toys he was allowed to hold—and undoubtedly chuck to the floor—while waiting for Noel to return from his foray into the woods. Charlotte and Jordan were shooting occasional glances her way like she was a grenade without its pin. Wisely so, Eleanor had retreated to her room, and Charles had followed.

When Noel finally stepped inside, that look of sickened shock was gone, and his cheeks had a wild glow about them. Without stopping to kick out of his soaked boots, he strode across the floor and took Maddie into his arms despite protests from Liam, who was on her hip and pouting at having Benji's ATV taken from him.

Locking an arm around her and cupping the other hand along her chin, Noel pressed his forehead against hers. "I love you, Maddie," he whispered in her ear just low enough that the arguing twins wouldn't hear.

Maddie closed her free hand at the side of his head, her fingers getting lost in his thick hair. How could it feel as if it had been both an eternity and a single day since they'd embraced like this?

When the baby fussed at being the cream in their cookie, Charlotte extracted him from Maddie's arms. "I've got him. Take your time. God knows you deserve it."

Maddie stepped in closer and had just long enough to appreciate the rhythm created by the rise and fall of their lungs pressing against one another before life eventually pushed in—Benji had decided that if his ATV was too important for Liam to hold, his sister shouldn't hold it, either. When their calls for assistance weren't met, the kids eventually noticed what was happening above their game on the floor.

"Big people hugging is yucky," Benji said, making a face while Hazel eyed them pensively.

Maddie didn't concur. "I think it's beautiful." To Noel, she added with a small smile that pulled into a big one, "What you said just now, right back at you."

⸻

Given that the day continued to unfold at the same wild pace of the runoff from the melting snow that had been flowing down the bulging mountain streams and rivers on the drive in, it wasn't until nightfall that Maddie and Noel had an extended stretch of time to themselves. The sunlit hours had been too full of the needs of children and babies, grocery shopping, snow play, and the eventual making of an uneasy truce with Eleanor.

Suspecting the twins would fight sleep, Maddie sat next to each of them on their twin beds in turn, patting their backs as they settled down. Last awake was Hazel. As soon as her breathing was relaxed and steady, Maddie snuck out the twins' main door to the interior of the cabin. The living room and kitchen were empty and lit by a single lamp, and the dwindling fire still glowed in the fireplace.

Spying the light flowing from underneath her bedroom door, Maddie stepped inside to find her mom in bed reading by the lamplight.

"They're asleep?" Charlotte peered over the top of her reading glasses, appraising her.

"Yeah, like little bear cubs. Where is everybody?"

"Medusa went to bed, and Mini-me followed her. After the baby fell asleep, Jordan confiscated Noel's laptop and dashed off to her room. Seems like something about today lit a fire under her. As for Noel, who I'm guessing is the crux of your 'everybody,' he stepped outside with Ursa about ten minutes ago as I was headed in here."

Maddie smiled in response to her mother's accompanying look even as she headed into the bathroom for a quick freshening up. Thankfully, her eyes no longer resembled used tea bags as they had this morning.

"How are you feeling about all this? Considering?" Charlotte rested her book on her lap atop the covers when Maddie rejoined her. It had been checked out from the library and was on how to read auras—go figure.

"Weirdly, better than you might guess."

"You never were one to hold a grudge for long. Remember third grade when Lenora stole your swimsuit, and her mom found it and made her give it back? You still invited her to your birthday sleepover a few weeks later."

Maddie sank onto the foot of her mom's bed. "A stolen swimsuit in third grade is an entirely different level of treachery than what Eleanor's done. Real forgiveness won't come so easily. But if I could go back and change things, I wouldn't. Obviously. To have my kids, everything needed to happen exactly as it happened. And I did love Landon, Mom. In a different way than how I feel about Noel. They weren't wasted years."

Charlotte settled back against her pillow. "For certain."

"You wanna know what? All afternoon, this freedom has been filling me. Eleanor will *never* have any sort of hold over me again. Until this morning, I had no clue how big her hold on me was. Even when I was telling her no and resisting her, she was still there in my mind, taking up so much space."

Charlotte hmphed softly. "I bet that's freeing." She had a far-off look that made Maddie think of her mom's non-existent relationship with Maddie's grandparents, strait-laced snowbirds who disapproved of their whimsical daughter and who'd moved to Florida years ago and never looked back.

"It is."

"What about the kids' relationship with her? Have you thought about it?"

Maddie shrugged. "I'm going to let the anger settle before I make any decisions, but whatever happens, it'll be on my terms. As much as she loved her son, she's never had much influence over them, and she'll have even less now."

Charlotte was quiet for several seconds before nodding appreciatively. "If I say so myself, I know how to turn out a pretty stand-up kid."

"I love you, Mom." Maddie leaned over to hug her before standing up. "Hey, before I go, mind if I open both bathroom doors so the twins can find you if they wake up? After their day, I'm doubtful they will, but just in case."

"Of course. I won't wait up for you, either, but don't forget to have some fun as you step into this, will you? You've earned it. You both have."

"Amen to that."

The main room was still empty when Maddie headed out. Everyone's boots were lined up near the front door on two long, thick rugs that were chilly and wet under Maddie's bare feet from the clumps of snow that had melted onto them. Maddie slipped into her boots and grabbed her coat from the closet. She stepped outside and headed down the porch steps, savoring the cold, mountain air in her nostrils and against her cheeks.

Noel was nowhere in sight. After heading deeper into the yard, she gazed up at the cloudless, star-studded sky. It was something to appreciate, being outside in the mountains on a quiet spring night. Blue-white moonlight poured over the yard, bright enough to create shadows from the trees on the snow.

She'd been standing outside long enough that the cold air was beginning to seep through her coat and pants when she heard a crunching in the snow a few dozen feet away behind a dense stand of evergreens. "Noel?"

"Yeah, it's me." Ursa emerged from behind the trees first, with Noel trailing behind on the other end of the leash.

"For a second there I was worried the elk was back." After another step or two, Maddie paused mid-step. *This is it—the first day of the rest of your life. No small talk allowed.*

She burst into a run, her wet boots clunking loudly as they smacked against the ground. Ursa woofed as Maddie reached them. She locked her hands around Noel's neck and jumped, hoisting her legs around his hips as his hands locked around her thighs. She pressed her lips against his with the same intensity as if he were water and she'd been wandering around the desert.

He smelled like the fire he'd been tending in the fireplace, and he tasted of the smores they'd enjoyed in front of it earlier tonight. She could taste the sugar and chocolate on his lips and tongue and appreciated his late-evening stubble against her fingers.

She was craving more when he pulled away and leaned his forehead against hers. "Maddie, I've loved you every day since the night we met. Even when I wasn't supposed to."

Tears stung her lids. "Me, too." The broken pieces of

herself were mending together, halves becoming whole. Those invisible forces her mom was always talking about, the ones ruling human nature, Maddie had no doubt this was the largest of them. It welled up inside her, big and beautiful. "Me, too. Me, too."

While Ursa sniffed the ground, she kissed him a second time, savoring the wetness of his tongue, the soft but solid pressure of his lips, the way their mouths moved around one another. Finally, she pulled away. She could've planned what she wanted to say to him for a million years, but it took being here in his arms to know it with this certainty. "Noel, there's something about this that I need you to understand."

"Anything."

"This whole mess, it's as much my fault as it was Landon's for not outing her when he figured it out."

"How so?"

"I was so ready to believe I wasn't enough for you that I never questioned anything."

"Oh, Maddie—"

"I need to say this," Maddie said as she slid out of Noel's arms and onto solid ground. "Landon promised me that he gave you the letter and that you read it in front of him. And I let that be my answer. My mom made this brave choice to raise me alone when she was just twenty and had next to nothing, and I'm *so* thankful for that. But growing up without a dad... A part of me was so ready to believe that I wasn't good enough to have that—to have you."

Noel shook his head. "It was my fault, Maddie. Everything inside me screamed not to take no for an answer, at least not unless we were face to face. But I left on that plane, and the rest of it—you getting pregnant—happened so fast, I was just in shock."

"It did happen fast. So fast. But, Noel, I hope you know that all of this, it was meant to happen this way."

"I've been thinking about that, too.

"Not only because of the kids. Because of me. I wasn't ready yet. I wasn't ready for you six years ago, no matter how much I wanted you. I needed the experience of having Landon as a husband. I needed to fail and dig deep and look within. I needed to make peace with my scars. All of them." She brushed her lips against his. "And let all the rest go. Does that make sense?"

"Yeah, it does." He brushed his lips over her forehead, along her brow, and down her temple before finding her lips again. "I'd have waited longer if you needed it. The way I love you, the way we fit, there could never be anyone else."

"The one promise I can make you is that you don't have to wait for me anymore. You'll never have to wait for me again."

Ursa, who'd walked to the far reach of her leash, barked several times, staring off into the darkness, ears pricked forward. Ten or fifteen feet ahead, a few loud snorts filled the air, followed by the sound of hooves thundering away.

Noel cocked an eyebrow. "I guess we had company."

"I'm putting it to the time of year and location, but mom swears all the elk sightings today are fortuitous," Maddie said, giggling.

"Oh yeah? How so?" he asked, brushing back a lock of her hair.

"I don't know. I stopped listening at fortuitous."

He chuckled. "I probably would've, too."

She offered out a hand, palm facing up. "Care to join me?"

"Where?" he asked, taking it anyway.

She cocked an eyebrow and started leading them back toward the cabin. "Your room."

He stayed in place, squeezing her hand. "You sure you're ready for that? Here?"

"It's the first day of the rest of our lives. And the one thing I know with absolute certainty is that I don't want to miss another one not having made love to you."

Noel stepped in and kissed her again in a way that was slow and unhurried and lit her on fire. "My sentiments exactly."

CHAPTER 38

After breakfast, Maddie cleared the big dining table between the open kitchen and living room and pulled out the handmade paper and natural watercolor markers she'd ordered for Landon's ceremony. Back home, she'd used the thick paper to print a few pictures of the kids and Landon. Since this wasn't a gravesite, the only items being left behind today would be fresh cut flowers from the grocery store, those pictures, and any letters and drawings that any members of their party were compelled to make this morning.

After getting the twins settled at the table with the markers between them, she started to step away for a quick shower.

"But can't you stay?" Benji muttered. "What if I don't do it right?"

She pressed a kiss onto the top of his head. "This is your picture for your father. There's no wrong way to do it, so long as what you make comes from the heart."

When she returned fifteen minutes later, everyone except for Charles, who was over at the couch reading on his e-reader, was at the table working on something for

Landon. Jordan was helping an unusually contented Liam hold a marker while redirecting his hand to the paper rather than his mouth, which was making him giggle. Their paper was dotted with a series of squiggle marks, but Jordan seemed pleased with it. Charlotte was copying her favorite passage of Kahlil Gibran's *The Prophet* onto hers, an act which touched Maddie immensely. Charlotte wasn't one to share her love of the book and its poems with just anyone. Likely, what had come to pass yesterday played into things.

Noel had a pencil and was writing rather fiercely, his expression set in stone and a few stray tear trailing down his cheeks. Eleanor was sitting in the chair next to Benji, watching her grandson attentively, which raised Maddie's hackles until it became clear all she was doing was guiding him with his spelling upon request.

"How do you spell dog?" Benji had a solid grasp of the alphabet but had yet to pick up on phonetics the way his sister had. He'd drawn a grouping of stick figures, one off to the side and floating higher on the page. Alongside it was a four-legged stick figure that Maddie presumed was the dog in question.

After adding the letters to his paper that Eleanor dictated, Benji dropped his marker and shoved his paper aside. "I hope daddy has a dog in heaven."

"Like Ursa? Or maybe a cat like Leo," Hazel interjected, looking up from her drawing. "Leo was daddy's cat most."

By the way his eyes widened, Benji was clearly alarmed by his sister's comment. "This is a different dog. One that's already in heaven."

When Maddie spotted the oversized butterfly Hazel had drawn flying over a field of flowers, she met Jordan's gaze and smiled, certain they were thinking the same thing. A butterfly flaps its wings…

"Mommy, aren't you going to leave something for

daddy?" Hazel had gotten a line of green marker on her face that ran the length of her jawbone.

Knowing her daughter was right, Maddie sank into the open chair next to her mom. She picked up a lavender colored marker and removed the cap, but her hand froze above the paper. She had no idea what to leave for Landon. She'd been so busy with Jordan and the baby in the house, preparing for the trip, and being present for her kids, she hadn't given any thought to her own final goodbye to the man who'd fathered her kids and with whom she'd spent six years of her life.

She sat still for several minutes, popping the marker's cap off and on again, realizing this was more complicated than she'd made it sound to Benji.

Charlotte finished copying the poem and closed her book. Whether Noel ran out of paper or words first, Maddie wasn't sure, but finally he put the pencil down and folded his letter several times over before slipping it into his pocket.

Tired of the activity, Liam tossed his marker several feet across the floor and grunted, making Jordan huff about the work he caused. Ursa lumbered onto all fours to give the marker a sniff before losing interest and settling down again, this time on the couch, while Liam fought like a linebacker to get closer to his half-brother who was two chairs down and starting to play with the markers rather than write with them.

Finally, Maddie knew just what to say. She wrote so that it filled the page:

It's
Bigger
Than
Us

Leaving the paper on the table, she stood up and, seeing that Jordan was nearing her limit with Liam's neediness, offered out her arms his direction. Liam gave her a big, slobbery grin, revealing the tooth that had broken through this morning. Taking him, Maddie pressed a kiss against his forehead, not in the least bit worried who saw her do it.

An hour later, after snacks for the kids and a bit of belly time for Liam, they all dressed in their warmest clothes and piled into both vehicles for the short drive to the trail leading to the spot where the ceremony would take place. All of them, even Ursa, made up a considerably more somber group than they'd been while playing in the snow yesterday.

Benji grasped Maddie's hand and held it the whole way through the woods, not even pausing to shovel snow into his mouth when she wasn't looking. An early morning snow had dumped another inch or two of white powder onto the ground and trees, but the sun was out again, and it was starting to melt in places where the sun shone on it.

"When your dad and I were Jordan's age, we skied up there on those slopes," Noel said, nodding toward the mountain peaks rising above the evergreens. "Biked them in summer, too. There are lifts around the other side of the mountain, but where we're going, you don't need a lift."

"Did he wear a helmet?" Hazel's soft words were nearly swallowed up by the crunching of snow underfoot.

Noel reached for her hand and squeezed it. "Yeah, he almost always did back then."

After that, it fell quiet again.

Just as Benji was losing steam, Noel asked if they could hear the rushing water. Maddie stopped walking to listen, and sure enough, she could hear a softly rushing stream or river. "We're almost there," he added. "There's a little valley ahead. It butts up against the mountain. Your dad thought it was the most beautiful place he'd ever seen."

As Noel promised, the trail led around a corner and opened to a remarkable view of a valley tucked against the gently sloping mountainside with a river cutting in between them. A handful of snow-covered picnic tables graced the empty valley.

Eleanor walked over to the closest one, brushed off the bench, and took a seat as if she didn't have the strength for another step. She looked around, taking in the view and brushing tears from her cheeks. Charles followed her over but kept standing, the urn clamped awkwardly in his arms.

Noel had been right to encourage this place for Landon's ashes. From St. Louis, it was anything but a quick trek here, yet for the rest of her kids' lives, they could make the occasional pilgrimage here and connect with this beautiful place their father had loved.

She and Benji crossed over to the bank of the river to find that the sun had melted enough of the snow that dozens of smooth rocks jutted above it. Benji grabbed one that was dark and oblong and lodged it into the ground next to another, the wet ground instantly creating wet patches on the knees of his snowpants.

"Hey, how about we wait a bit to play?"

"I'm making a rock pile so we can 'member this place."

Hazel joined in without pause. After checking with Maddie to see if she was in agreement that Ursa could be trusted off-leash in this remote area, Noel started helping, too. "Great idea. They call that a cairn." Maddie kept an eye on the dog until it was clear she had no interest in walking more than a handful of feet away, then she passed off the backpack of supplies to her mom and began helping as well. Ursa lapped up some water from the edge of the swollen river and sniffed random rocks and mounds of green that pushed up above the snow. After a while, she stretched out on the snowiest section where the bank met the field, thumping her tail as she watched them work.

Before long, hands stinging from the cold rocks, they'd created a rounded pyramid of smooth river rock that was a couple feet wide, and the snowy beach was dotted with their footprints. Soon, everyone in the party had added rocks to the pile. Hazel even held one up for Liam, who grinned and shook it before it slipped from his grasp, hitting the pile, and rolling off. He grunted after it, but Hazel told him no in a gentle tone that was becoming her big-sister voice before finding a spot for it on the mound. "When he's bigger, we can tell him he helped."

Maddie blinked back a few tears at this show of unity. After taking the backpack from her mom, she pulled out the twine and helped the twins make a cross of two sturdy sticks they'd found near the cabin yesterday. Once the cross was stabilized in the ground, everyone added their letters and pictures, securing them with smaller rocks on top of the mound.

When they were finished, Maddie noticed the baby reaching for her and took him into her arms. After pressing the flat of one small hand against her cheek the same as Hazel had done when she was little, he settled into a space of contentment and watched the commotion.

Before Landon's ashes were scattered, Eleanor read from a prayer book that she'd brought along and followed the prayer with a speech that was short and unscripted and moved Maddie deeply. "Landon was my only son and a good one. I know there are times that he could've done better, the same way his father and I could've done better by him." She looked around the group, holding Maddie's gaze longest. "The things I'd do over if I could are longer than a freight train. I console myself every day that he'll live in our memories, *all* our memories." She steadied herself against her husband, drawing Maddie's attention to how she'd aged these last few months.

"He'd like that we're here together, all of us," Maddie said. Maybe it was temporary, but her anger at her mother-in-law had diminished considerably in just over twenty-four hours. "Just like he'd be happy to know we're doing this here in this remarkable place."

With Charles's guidance, Eleanor and the twins helped empty the urn around the base of the rockpile.

"What happens to daddy's ashes?" Hazel asked. "Will they turn into rocks?"

"No," Maddie said, "but they'll become part of the earth all the same. Some of the ashes will work their way into the mud when the snow melts. The rest will be scattered by the wind and rain."

Taking in the pristine, rambling beauty of the river and the tall evergreens stretching up the mountainside, Maddie smiled. The hot anger toward Landon that had been nestled inside her these last few months had melted away, and in its place was a forgiveness lighter than any she'd imagined. "I'll always remember how one day, when you kids were three years old, we were walking home from the grocery store, and it started to rain. When you were both on the cusp of falling apart, he picked you up, one in each arm, and made a game out of it by pretending to be knights going on a monster hunt. After that, for nearly a year, it was next to impossible to stop you two from running outside whenever it rained."

Jordan swiped at the tears running down her cheeks. She knelt in front of the twins, taking their hands in hers. Kneeling next to them, she could easily be mistaken for a cousin or older sibling. "Your dad loved you so much. My whole life, I never saw anyone light up the way he did when he talked about you two. I know I'm not great at it, but that love he had for you made me want to be a mom to Liam. I'll never forget that about him."

Benji dragged his arm under his nose, making a mess of his coat sleeve. "I liked when we played in the snow even more than in the rain."

"Me, too," Hazel agreed. "And in the pool. And in the blanket forts." Hazel burrowed her head against Maddie's hip. Shifting the baby to the other side, Maddie hugged her close, touched by how the twins understood without being told that they were honoring their father with their words.

"He was the best of friends when I really needed one," Noel said. "I remember how in middle school, he talked me into doing a comedy skit for a talent show. When I froze up and couldn't remember one of my lines, Landon took the attention off it by doing a running jump off the stage even though it got him a trip to the principal."

Everyone laughed again, this time harder. "I always thought he was just being a ham," Eleanor added, wiping fresh tears from her eyes.

Once the string of memories was shared, and it was time to head back along the trail, Maddie was willing to bet she wasn't the only one feeling a completion that had been a long time coming.

CHAPTER 39

ELEANOR

At the edge of the woods, Eleanor's feet refused to carry her another step. She waved everyone on and would've waved Charles along, too, but he was stuck to her side like a faithful bulldog. *He's lost his only son, too,* came a kinder voice inside her than she was used to hearing.

Maddie hesitated, her expression void of the accusation it had harbored yesterday, but Eleanor waved her on a second time. "Go on. Please. It's a well-marked trail, and we won't be far behind. I could use another few minutes to take this in. We'll meet you back at the cabin."

After the group headed on, and Hazel yelled back that she'd make deep tracks with her boots so they could find their way, Eleanor returned to the picnic table where she'd sat earlier. She sank down, her strength giving out far enough above the bench that she collapsed with a plop that reverberated along her tailbone.

Charles joined her, and this time, rather than standing, he took a seat alongside her, his stubby fingers locking over his knees after he set their son's empty urn on the table. For the longest time, neither of them said a word. Eleanor watched the golden afternoon sun shining on the mountain and making yellow-gold ripples on the river out past the insignificant mound that would serve as her son's final resting place.

Never in her life had she felt so empty, so void of herself, as if she was nothing more than an eggshell that had been hollowed out for decorating. All the anger and blame she'd been harboring had seeped out.

It was easier to be angry, she realized after a minute or two of contemplation. This emptiness was far harder to endure than the sharpest need for vindication, but Eleanor suspected her body was pocked with holes now. It seemed impossible that she could ever fill up with anger again.

Like it or not, the path forward for her was one of remorse and humility, both things she'd never learned how to express, and everyone knew how difficult it was to teach an old dog new tricks. Eleanor was a born driver; her whole life, she'd been the one to make things happen, and now she was at the mercy of others. It was not going to be easy.

"We lost him, our boy. I never expected that. Not our boy." Even to her, the words sounded hollow and insignificant.

Charles swiped a knuckle under his nose and sniffed. "I was thinking earlier about how I can't remember the last thing I said to him. I think maybe it had something to do with the produce delivery being short a bushel of tomatoes. If we talked again that morning, I don't remember. It's not what I'd have picked to say if I knew I wasn't going to get another chance, that's for sure."

It was a foreign movement, but Eleanor deliberately closed her hand over his. Charles had long ago accepted that Eleanor didn't enjoy unplanned touch and had stopped reaching out to her. He'd also never been one to wear gloves even in the coldest of weather, and his hand was cold. The skin on top was both hairier and drier than she remembered, too.

While he had every right to reject her, he turned his hand over and locked fingers with her. His palm was more welcoming, and there was a small callous at the base of his pointer finger that had been there when they first started dating. Something about this was unexpectedly comforting.

"I remember mine," she replied. "That afternoon as he was driving out for that ride, I argued with him about coming over for a late lunch that Sunday. Not argued but pushed. There was a birthday party or something or other the twins were supposed to attend, but it had been close to a month since we'd had everybody over, and I remember making a point that Hazel and Benji were growing up too quickly." After pausing to take a steadying breath, she added, "I remember his answer, too."

"Oh, yeah?"

"He said, 'Not *too* quickly. Just quick enough.' He was good at that, wasn't he? Accepting things for what they were."

"Yeah, he was. People, too." After a muted humph, he added, "Liam's proof enough of that."

"I can't help but think how we failed him—our Landon." She paused to close her eyes. "No, not we. How *I* failed him."

Charles gave her hand a squeeze. "You didn't fail him. You were there for everything. The tooth fairy visits, the school parties, the doctor appointments. The middle of the night 'I can't get back to sleep' nightmares. You were always there, Eleanor. So much so, you had a hard time letting go."

"I could've done better though—or differently, at least. I could've done differently."

Charles was quiet for so long Eleanor didn't think he was going to answer. "I think, Eleanor," he said finally, "that if Landon were here, he'd tell you what matters is that you do differently now."

She wanted to say that she would, for Landon's sake, and

she intended to, but the words wouldn't come. Instead, all she could do was give Charles's hand a squeeze in return, and she hoped, for the moment, that it was enough.

CHAPTER 40

JORDAN

The noises of the twins as they clomped about downstairs drifted upward, and Liam began to stir in his sleep, drawn as he was to his half-siblings. What had woken them so early, Jordan didn't know, but since moving in here, she'd figured out it wasn't just Liam who fought sleep. At five, the twins weren't as demanding, but they could wear Maddie out just the same way Liam did her. Motherhood, it seemed, was an equalizer when it came to yanking women down a few rungs in terms of self-care.

Maybe that was the price you had to pay for the good parts: the infectious laughter, the bottomless snuggles, the experience of a tiny-but-perfect hand in yours. More and more, Jordan was thinking of it as a win-win instead of a win-lose. Her therapist had helped with this, Jordan was certain, but she liked to think she'd have gotten here on her own.

Sitting at the east-facing window seat in a room she'd been sleeping in for a solid month now—not including the trip to Colorado—Jordan traced a fingertip over the cool glass pane next to her. She'd seen enough sunsets over the years that they blended, but she couldn't remember paying attention to a sunrise before. Ever. Since coming here, she'd caught three of them. The first had been while sitting in this exact spot while attempting to sway Liam back to sleep without a rocker after a restless second night up here. As the big orb edged higher on the horizon, its brilliant rays shining on the dirty, split pane window, she'd become transfixed by the silent wonder of it.

This morning, while slipping in and out of a doze, she'd crawled out of bed for the sole purpose of catching it. Just as it peeked over the horizon, it didn't hurt a bit to stare directly at it. The higher it got, her eyes burned from the brightness, but she lowered her lids to a fine squint and watched anyway. When it had nearly crested—a flaming globe about to pop over the horizon—Jordan held her breath until a thick line of sky was visible underneath the piercing red-orange ball. Something about the experience was like catching a whisper she'd never been able to hear before. Something about it made her want to give a *Lion King* worthy salute to the day… or at the very least whisper "Hallelujah."

Maybe, she realized, the miracle in all this was that something had opened inside her, gracing her with the wherewithal to catch something she would've missed before.

When the moment passed, Jordan tiptoed over to the Pack and Play where Liam was still dozing. She stood over him, her bare toes curling into the rug, and watched him the same way she'd been watching the sun. Those first several months of motherhood, her world had been so gray, she hadn't experienced that whisper of awe toward him that swept over her at times now. The smooth, flawless skin that darkened to beet red when he was upset and howling over something, the soft noises he made in his sleep, the flexing of those tiny but pudgy fingers while searching for something to grip.

She wondered if her mom had ever experienced a similar

hallelujah moment looking at her when she was a baby. Who was she kidding? Probably not.

By the time Liam was fully awake, and Jordan had made it downstairs with him in her arms, Maddie was out of the shower and fixing the kids' breakfast, her wet hair tied up in a towel. Spotting the twins at the island, Liam gorilla grunted and attempted to lurch from her arms. That grin of his, it really was ear to ear around those kids. Knowing it was a losing battle to fight him, Jordan let him stand on the edge of the counter facing them and supported him as he bounced up and down, making the twins giggle and coo at him.

"Talk about apples and trees," Maddie said with a smile, and Jordan knew right what she was talking about. She was wondering if Maddie had spotted her late-night email just as she spoke. "So, I got your email."

"Oh yeah?" Jordan's cheeks grew hot at the thought of having the conversation that had been playing out in her head ever since their Colorado trip. Before giving birth to Liam, she'd have slept on that bench all night after Ethan and Ainsley kicked her out rather than ask to stay here. *Maybe so, but it was your giving birth to Liam that put you on that bench in the first place.* But whether asking for help was her MO, Jordan needed to get over it.

Besides, Maddie had read her email and was still smiling —that was something, wasn't it?

Maddie was making the kids peanut butter and banana toast and sucked at a stray dab of peanut butter on one knuckle. "I think it's a great idea, going back to school. I didn't have a ton of time before hopping in the shower, but I clicked on a few of the links you sent. Seems like there're some substantial scholarships out there for single moms. And architecture? That's awesome."

"Yeah, it was staying in that vaulted cabin that got me thinking about it. And math has always been pretty easy for me. I hear that has a lot to do with making it through the degree."

"I bet."

Jordan swallowed. The next part wasn't so easy. The part about not having anywhere to go until school started in August—assuming she got in and landed the necessary scholarships and financial aid packages, that was. She was still working out how to ask how long she could stay without wearing out her welcome when Maddie went there on her own.

"Jordan, you might as well be a deer in headlights. As far as I'm concerned, Charlotte's offer stands. You have a place to stay while you get back on your feet."

"I appreciate that, but the thing is, even if I score one of those on-campus housing units for single mothers, that's still three months from now. And if I don't, well, if my history says anything, it's that I haven't yet figured out how to be on my feet yet."

Maddie's answering smile was nothing but kind. "I can't say I've known many twenty-one-year-olds who have been, me included."

"You're really sure? Now that Noel's in the picture, I guess I wanted to make sure things hadn't changed."

"You living here has nothing to do with Noel. And despite our feelings for one another, he and I are still on the ground floor of dating." Maddie waggled a finger toward the twins who were too busy cooing over Liam to hear what they were talking about. "It's a bit like driving with the emergency brake on, but we're keeping it slow."

Jordan blinked back unexpected tears as the twins attempted to outcompete one another with silly faces, and Liam belly laughed. It was too good to be true. No more losing sleep over making sure there was a roof over Liam's head, and no more dreading having to tuck tail and go home to her mother. "I won't make you regret it. I promise you that."

"I know. Just like my mom knew before she extended you the offer. Besides, who'd deny these three goobers quantity and quality time like this in their formative years?"

When Maddie stepped close to slide plates in front of the twins, Jordan surprised herself by locking Maddie in a hug. There was so much she wanted to say, words of thanks, words of affection, but she'd grown up without expressing or receiving them, and her throat locked up entirely.

"It's all good." Maddie patted her back as Jordan's shoulders shook with the release of silent tears.

"Why are you hugging?" Hazel asked abruptly. "Did something happen?"

"Big people hug each other, too," Maddie said. "And a lot of things have happened, but all of them are good."

A few hours later, Jordan's phone buzzed with a text she wasn't expecting. It was Ainsley, who hadn't blown up her phone in weeks.

HEY WHERE U BEEN, GIRL? WE'RE MISSING YOU. WANNA HANG TODAY?

Jordan processed this unexpected invitation for the better part of an hour before replying. They'd been apart a little less than two months now, but it seemed longer. Ethan and Ainsley had thrown her and Liam out after weeks and months of tension, but they'd been her best—and only—friends for a long time. They'd been in the room when Liam was born, but it was Liam's arrival that changed things, that drove them apart, and Lord knew, Jordan had spent too much time resenting him for it.

It was this thought that helped Jordan come up with an answer.

BEEN MISSING U TOO AND THANKS, BUT NAH, I'M GOOD.

And, after climbing a long way to get here, Jordan realized she was.

CHAPTER 41

MADDIE

Like in the case of the tortoise and the hare, sometimes life moved along at a relaxed and steady pace, and at others, in leaps and bounds. Maddie credited a stop at a roadside bakery on the drive home from Colorado to the idea that led to her and Noel signing a joint contract on a commercial property a few months later. "I wish they sold treats for dogs here like the ones you make," Hazel had said after being told that a cupcake for Ursa wasn't a good idea. "The ones that are good for her."

It wasn't the first time the idea had occurred to Maddie to open her own bakeshop catering to both people and dogs— one featuring only natural food coloring and flavors—but it was the first time she was empowered enough to act on it.

On closing day, Maddie planned a picnic and invited the whole gang in celebration, including Saanvi, who drove down from Chicago for the event, and Charles and Eleanor. Maddie's mother-in-law had accepted the boundaries she'd laid out since their Colorado trip with surprising humility, and Maddie had decided to include her in good faith today. No doubt, forgiveness came easier with the awareness that, had it not been for Eleanor's actions, Maddie's children wouldn't be here. Eleanor had also lost the one person she'd have gone to the ends of the earth to protect. Maddie had found it in her heart to trust that life had served Eleanor the lessons she most needed to learn—Maddie, too, for that matter.

The building Maddie and Noel had landed on after touring dozens of possibilities was built in the mid-1940s and was red brick like so many others in the city. Just five blocks from Charlotte's house, it had been divided decades ago, one half leased to a car repair shop that closed a few years back, and the other to a former carpet store that folded and then became a coffee shop around the turn of the century.

The coffee shop had been on the verge of folding, too, but was changing hands and would reopen in less than a month under new management. Maddie was thankful to have a tenant for the other half of the building from the onset. She didn't need the full space, and the rent received for the other half would nearly cover the mortgage. Noel had officially left LightSource to venture into the world of independent contract engineering, and he liked the idea of working remotely in a cozy coffee shop next door to Maddie some days.

Saanvi had been the first to arrive. She'd been checking out the exterior of the building when Maddie and Noel got here after signing the closing paperwork. Maddie had FaceTimed her from here when she'd decided that this place was the one, and Saanvi was even more enamored of it today in person.

Because Saanvi couldn't yet be in the same room as Eleanor without glowering, when Eleanor and Charles pulled up, she'd headed next door to help Charlotte with the twins and Liam, and now it was their turn to look things over.

Eleanor perused the empty service station, heels tapping on concrete as she walked. Her arms were folded, and her chin was tilted upward just enough to make it clear that no matter how hard she tried, Eleanor would always be Eleanor. She'd regained a few pounds since their trip and didn't look quite as frail. That probably helped. "There's potential here, I'll give you that."

"Quite a lot of potential," Noel agreed, winking at Maddie.

Maddie bit back a laugh. Eleanor had really been trying the last couple months. Last week, on her and Charles's evening to babysit the twins—Maddie and Noel's weekly date night—Eleanor had actually fingerpainted with the kids.

On top of this, Maddie recognized that her mother-in-law knew what it took to be a successful entrepreneur in the restaurant business. She had first-hand knowledge and industry connections that would prove helpful as Maddie got closer to opening, but one thing Maddie wouldn't be doing was accepting her in-laws' offer to invest in the venture.

While this half of the building had been empty for more than a year, a faint smell of grease lingered from the oil stains on the concrete floors, but Maddie's renovation plans included a complete remodel. With its all-brick exterior, its location, and exposed-brick interior wall, the building was worth whatever renovations were needed.

Maddie was using most of the money from her house sale in this venture, and Noel had more than matched her investment. As Landon had hinted more than once, Noel had earned a good living as an engineer the last five years, but he'd also grown those earnings through investments.

"These service bay doors, will you convert them to glass windows?" Eleanor nodded toward the three floor-to-ceiling sliding doors.

"Two will be all glass. The one in the center will become the main entrance."

Eleanor nodded appreciatively as she brushed her fingers over the exposed interior brick wall on the side of the building. "A large, middle entrance will be nicer than the small one at the side, no question. And surely, you'll add a door along the wall between the two businesses? I suspect you'll share a sizable portion of customers."

"Yep, we're putting a glass door there, too."

Charles murmured approvingly as he trailed behind Eleanor. "Location's good, seems to be decent street traffic, and there's a nice selection of businesses nearby. I think you've got a good shot of making this work."

"We think so," Maddie and Noel agreed at the same time.

"Catering to dogs, though," Eleanor said with a similar incredulity as if the business would be smack dab in the center of a lake. "How will you pass inspection if you let dogs in here?"

"Maddie's catering to dog owners, not to dogs—and to anyone in the mood for a great cupcake, regardless of whether they'd like a matching one for their pup."

"And as with any food service establishment, dogs will have to stick to the patio," Maddie added. "Which is why we're adding a full-service walk-up window so people can stop by with their dogs in tow."

Eleanor smoothed her faultless hair further into submission. "Like I said, there's potential here. Though I suspect it's fifty-fifty whether it'll turn into something that's all the rave or be a bust." As if remembering her commitment to civility, she added, "Though that's typically the case in food service."

Maddie shrugged. "I suspect my old instructors would agree, but that's life for you. You never know until you do."

After their tour, they headed next door. When they walked in, Liam was at a booth, attempting to pull up. Now that he was crawling, he was difficult to keep still. When he spotted Maddie, his face lit up, and he grunted like he was proud of himself.

The twins were splayed out on the middle of the floor,

playing with a jumbo-sized tic-tac-toe board. Hazel looked up in earnest. "Mommy, is this ours?"

"The game?" Maddie asked, swooping Liam into her arms to plant a kiss on his cheek.

"Yeah," Benji added, "We want to bring it home, but Nana says we can't."

"Nana's right. We own the building, but everything in here will be bought by the new owner of the coffee shop." It had been worked out in the closing deal on the building that if the coffee shop transfer of ownership were to fall through, all the contents would be theirs by default, but that wasn't Maddie's hope. She loved the idea of a coffee shop next door to The Cup and Pup Cake Stop and didn't want to put any energy into it not going through.

"But it's ours now, isn't it? Ours and Noel's?" The kids had dropped the "uncle" in Uncle Noel at Maddie's request. Life was complicated enough without all the parents at school assuming Noel was Maddie's brother.

"We bought the building with the goal of starting up the bakery next door. We don't need this space, so someone is going to rent it from us. In the meantime, we're free to hang out here whenever we'd like to."

"It's a perfect space, isn't it?" Saanvi asked, her dark eyes settling on Eleanor.

Eleanor brushed the tip of her pointer finger over her throat. "Maddie chose well." After a slight delay, she added, "Noel, too."

"That was all Maddie." A smile parted Noel's lips as his gaze locked with hers.

Maddie's cheeks warmed pleasantly. It was something she was still getting used to—the easy camaraderie she shared with a fully functional partner who not only had her back but who had her best interest in mind.

Eleanor reached a tentative hand toward Liam. "May I?"

"Sure." Maddie handed him over even though he tried squirming his way back.

"Will Jordan be joining us for the picnic?" Charles asked.

"She's going to try. Her summer classes are in full swing."

Aware that it had the potential to be a double-edged sword, Jordan had accepted Eleanor and Charles's offer of financial support to help get her through college without acquiring debt, and without a reason not to, she'd kickstarted matters by enrolling in a few classes this summer.

Eleanor insisted there were no strings attached. She and Charles wanted her son's youngest child's mother to have access to a college education. Nothing more. Maddie knew they could afford it and figured Jordan was proving she could stand her ground, should the need arise.

"It's nice out. How about we eat at one of the tables outside?" Charlotte said over her shoulder after getting up to rummage through the picnic basket.

Everyone agreed, and in a matter of minutes, the table was set, the twins had finished another game of tic-tac-toe, and everyone was filing outside for a meal of homestyle fried chicken, potato salad, cornbread, and all the fixings. Maddie was trailing out behind the twins when she felt a hand on her back.

"Got a minute?" Noel asked. "There's something I'd like to show you next door."

"Yeah, sure." She followed him over but waited until the door fully shut to say anything else. "Let me guess, you're wanting to place dibs on who manages to be civil longest, Eleanor or Saanvi?"

"My money's on Saanvi losing her cool first. That side eye of hers, I swear," he said with a laugh. "Seriously though, there's something I was going to give you out there, but I decided I'd rather give it to you alone in here."

"Oh, yeah? What?"

Noel headed to the service counter where he'd left his

backpack earlier. "Don't get any ideas." He grinned as he unzipped the pack. "It's just something I found that I figured you'd appreciate." After reaching inside, he pulled out a butcher-paper wrapped present that could only be a book.

Taking it, Maddie brushed her lips against his. "I wish I had something for you to commemorate this, too."

"Just being with you is my something."

"Damn, you're sweet, you know that? Open it now?"

He nodded. "Yeah, now."

Maddie wedged one fingertip underneath the taped sides and worked open the thick paper. *Baking with Julia*. "Noel, I love it! You remembered that was my show." She was eager to flip through the pages, but she first needed to take off a silk ribbon tied around the book. "You know me so well. You always have."

"Well, the image of a middle-school aged Maddie finding her way through adolescence thanks to the escape and inspiration she got watching that show wasn't something I'd forget."

Holding the book out of the way, she hugged him tightly. "When the remodel is finished, I'll put it here on a shelf behind the counter. Maybe we even decorate a little to match —a cookbook theme or something."

Noel stepped back half a foot. "Maddie, open it."

She swallowed, realizing she'd missed something. His breathing was a touch shallow, and color lit his cheeks. Noel was nervous—or excited. Her own heart racing, she slipped off the ribbon. Inside, a bookmark was wedged into one of the center pages. Opening it there, Maddie found a delicate diamond ring tucked snuggly against the spine, white gold with a single diamond—exactly what Maddie would've chosen for herself. When she looked up, Noel had dropped to one knee.

"Oh my God—yes. A thousand times over, yes."

Laughing, he shook his head and locked his hands over her hips. "You should probably let me ask first."

She fanned her face as adrenaline coursed through her. "Okay, but for the record, it's not going to change my answer."

"That's good because I've never been great with words. I had a whole paragraph or two memorized, but I'm drawing a blank."

"I know your heart. I don't need your words."

"Maybe so, but I need to say this. I know we agreed to take it slow, and we can take as much time as you need. But these last few weeks, all I could think of was that I'm committing to a property loan with you when what I really want to commit to is a life. A tornado could tear this place apart, or competition could open down the block, and you're so damn resilient, you'll roll up your sleeves and figure it out, but Maddie, every day for the rest of my life, I want to live committed to you, and I don't intend to let anything —*anything*—come between us again."

"Nothing will—we won't let it." She brushed away the tears sliding down her cheeks, and as she did, she spotted Saanvi on the other side of the glass door taking pictures with her phone, her mouth gaping open in delight. Laughing, Maddie waved her off. "Two minutes please."

"The ring…slide the ring on, then I'll go!" she said, her voice muffled through the glass.

Maddie turned back to Noel. "You told her, I take it?"

"Your mom must have."

"My mom knew? I can't believe she didn't accidentally give it away."

Still on one knee, Noel took the ring and slipped the book onto the counter. "Damn cameras. What do I do now? Ask again?"

Maddie offered out her hand, fingers slightly splayed.

"No need. I'll marry you, Noel Warren, so long as you're okay with all that I come with."

"All you come with?" He raised an eyebrow. "Like how you sort laundry differently than me, or perhaps the lack of animal products in your mom's fridge?"

Laughing, Maddie waggled her finger, and he slipped it on. When it fit perfectly, she pulled on his arm until he got to his feet, then drew close for a kiss. When the kiss ended, she glanced over to find that they had privacy once again. "I more meant the Saanvis, Charlottes, Jordans, and Eleanors in my life. Mostly though, I mean those three kids outside. If they aren't a deterrence, we can talk about laundry and the contents of Charlotte's fridge all you'd like."

"I love those kids." His smile fell and his expression grew serious. "All three of them. And I promise to help keep their memories of their father alive, too."

"I know you will. My mom was right. I knew everything important there is to know about you right from that first night we met. Mostly that doesn't happen for people, but it did for us."

"It did, didn't it? And all the nights since, they've been leading us here."

As he rested his forehead against hers, Maddie laughed at the realization that he was right. A thousand separate, seemingly drifting roads had led them exactly where they wanted to be.

ACKNOWLEDGMENTS

I've been writing long enough to understand that some stories develop quickly, and others take their sweet time. I completed the first draft of this novel nearly two decades ago. I was a novice writer and knew nothing about the publishing industry. When my manuscript queries were met without success, I put the story aside and moved on to another one. While it wasn't my only manuscript tucked away in a drawer, it was the only one that nagged at me, breathing over my shoulder as I grew as a writer. A decade later, when I was knee-deep in a string of publishing contracts for the Rescue Me series, I decided that a watered-down version of the book was better than nothing and wove its basic premise into a romance set at the High Grove Animal Shelter in *Love at First Bark*.

While *Bigger Than Us* is—among other things—a love story, it isn't a lighthearted romance. The version of it that appeared in *Love at First Bark* required more developmental editing than anything I've written before or since. I figured my editor hated it, but when edits were finished, she proposed I tell the story again as it was meant to be told and free of the constraints of romantic fiction. There were other contracted manuscripts to finish first, but eventually, I rolled up my sleeves and listened to these characters, drafting the story anew as they wanted to tell it.

Given *Bigger Than Us's* indirect path to publication, I suspect there are more people to acknowledge than I'll remember to list here. Thank you, Deb Werksman, my editor through nine manuscripts, for encouraging me to get out of the way and let Landon be Landon. Amanda Heger, a dear friend and talented author, your keen insight has been invaluable more than once. Jess Watterson, my agent at Sandra Dijkstra Literary Agency, thank you for championing this story through two sharply different narrations. Critique partners Carol Coventry, Susan Steggall, and Cynthia Bogard, I appreciate your varied feedback that helped strengthen the story through your unique perspectives. Much gratitude to Theresa Murgola, an astute copy editor and one of my go-to beta readers. Sandy Thal, thank you for loving this story first and for loving it still, all these years later. Thank you to Jennifer Jakes and Kim Killion at Killion Publishing for your support throughout this process.

Thanks to my family—my kids especially. You two were babies when this story first lit my imagination. Over the years, you've come to know the characters so well, you don't even need reminders as to which story I'm referring to when I'm discussing them. Don't worry—I promise to talk your ears off about my next project, too.

Finally, thank you, dear readers, whether you've been with me through several stories or are joining new. In this story of loss, hope, forgiveness, and learning to trust yourself, it's my hope that you've found something to carry with you.

ABOUT THE AUTHOR

Debbie is the celebrated author of ten contemporary romance and women's fiction novels that touch the heart. Her books have received numerous accolades including a starred review from Publishers Weekly, an Amazon editor's pick for best romance, and a HOLT Medallion award.

She lives in Saint Louis with her family, a thoroughly spoiled rescue dog, and two quirky cats who ought to be named Pete and Repeat. When she isn't writing (or reading), you can find her hiking in the Missouri woods, working in her garden, or savoring time with family and friends.

Bonus content at authordebbieburns.com

facebook.com/authordebbieburns

instagram.com/_debbieburns

bookbub.com/profile/debbie-burns

READING GROUP GUIDE
for
Bigger Than Us

1. Given the state of her marriage, Maddie struggles to find words to honor Landon at his Celebration of Life. As the novel progresses, truths come to light that complicate things further, yet she ultimately finds forgiveness for him. What are the biggest reasons affecting this change?

2. In conversation with Saanvi the morning after Landon's Celebration of Life, Maddie mentions that her upbringing likely caused her to miss certain warning signs early in her relationship with Landon. How was Landon similar to Charlotte when she was a young mom? How was he different?

3. A largely unexplored topic for Maddie is her paternal DNA. Given the novel's events, do you believe that she may have a change of heart and want to take a DNA test in hopes of connecting with her father?

4. Similarly, Maddie acknowledges throughout the novel that her desire for structure and predictably are a result of her unstructured youth with whimsical Charlotte. Later, she acknowledges unaddressed wounds from growing up without a father. Do you believe these have shaped her equally? By the novel's end, has she reached resolution with either/both? Why or why not?

5. Rather than wait until her children reach adulthood, Maddie opts to pursue a relationship with the twins' half sibling. How might their lives be different because of this? Do you agree with Maddie's decision?

6. At the novel's end, Maddie believes Eleanor has been humbled sufficiently enough by life events that she decides to move forward with her in continued relationship, albeit cautiously. Do you agree with this decision? Why or why not?

7. How might this story be different had Landon lived and Maddie pursued divorce? Do you believe she and Noel would have eventually gotten together without Jordan coming forward about Eleanor's foul play? Do you believe Maddie would've reached the same state of healing and forgiveness?

8. Do you think life for Maddie will settle down, or will she continue to face challenges? If so, which might be her biggest ones?